THE AUTHOR'S GUIDE TO MURDER

THE AUTHOR'S GUIDE TO MURDER

A Novel

Beatriz Williams, Lauren Willig, and Karen White

WILLIAM MORROW
An Imprint of HarperCollinsPublishers

THE AUTHOR'S GUIDE TO MURDER. Copyright © 2024 by Beatriz Williams, Lauren Willig, and Harley House Books, LLC. All rights reserved. Printed in the United States of America. No part of this book may be used or reproduced in any manner whatsoever without written permission except in the case of brief quotations embodied in critical articles and reviews. For information, address HarperCollins Publishers, 195 Broadway, New York, NY 10007.

HarperCollins books may be purchased for educational, business, or sales promotional use. For information, please email the Special Markets Department at SPsales@harpercollins.com.

FIRST EDITION

Designed by Michele Cameron

Library of Congress Cataloging-in-Publication Data has been applied for.

ISBN 978-0-06-325986-7

24 25 26 27 28 LBC 5 4 3 2 1

To the people of Scotland—we're sorry.
And thanks for the plaid.

THE AUTHOR'S GUIDE TO MURDER

PROLOGUE

KINLOCH CASTLE
10 DECEMBER 2022
A murder is reported . . .

DETECTIVE CHIEF INSPECTOR Euan Macintosh had never seen a crime scene like this one before.

Torches guttered in iron holders along the walls of the octagonal chamber, illuminating the body of a man, dressed in little more than strategic strips of black leather, sprawled face down in a puddle of something that gleamed pale and sticky. The sickly sweet scent made Euan feel like retching—or that could just be the sheer amount of punch he'd consumed at the Kinloch ceilidh last night. Did it count as last night if one hadn't been to bed yet?

Erotic tapestries lined the walls: Europa, pursued by a bull; Leda, in the process of being ravished by a swan. The torchlight glinted off bare breasts, reaching arms, arched necks, and the bare buttocks of the man splayed on the floor.

A pseudomedieval chalice, enormous, inlaid with rough-cut jewels, lay where it must have fallen from the man's outstretched hand, spilling its honeyed contents.

A stag's head lolled on the flagstones next to the body, lopsided due to the loss of a branch of antlers on the left.

The inspector didn't need to ask what had happened to the

missing antler. It was protruding from the back of the man lying on the floor, into which it had been shoved with considerable force.

No chance of natural death here. Euan repressed the urge to curse. His first murder since returning to Kinloch and it couldn't be a simple brawl at the pub gone terribly wrong.

A sheep bleated, nosing at the puddle spreading out around the corpse.

A stern-faced man in a kilt tugged the sheep away. "Dinna ye be drinking that, Beatrice. Ye don't know where it's been."

Calum MacDougal. Gillie. General factotum at Castle Kinloch. Employed by the man who now lay face down in a pool of mead wearing what looked like a woman's dominatrix costume.

Euan gestured at the body. "I take it that's—"

"The novelist. Aye."

American. Had written a book Euan hadn't bothered to read because it sounded like poncey nonsense. Rented out the castle for writers' retreats at Castle Kinloch. Euan had never met the man but he'd seen his face on the posters the man had plastered across the island.

He didn't look like his poster now.

"I've rung the medical examiner," said Calum expressionlessly.

Euan felt bile rise in his throat—and not just because of the scene before him. Euan had seen all sorts of brutality during his time with the Met in London. Gun violence, knife violence, brass-knuckled violence. But those had been simple crimes compared to this. And there, the suspects weren't people he'd known from a boy.

"You found the body?" Euan asked brusquely.

"That'd be me nan." Calum looked sideways at Euan. "Or would ye be needin' her full name for the record, Chief Inspector?"

"Where is Mrs. MacDougal?" Euan asked. "I'll need to speak to her. For the record."

"At the castle. I sent her back to get warm. She was fair fashed as ye may imagine."

Euan followed Calum through a tunnel that led from the free-standing tower—a landmark on Kinloch, the Obelisk—to the castle itself, where Morag MacDougal stood like a wraith in the Great Hall, her white face and white hair standing out starkly against the black of her dress, making her look like a black-and-white photo of herself.

Euan had known Morag since he was a boy. She'd rapped his knuckles with one hand and fed him scones with the other. And now he had to question her about a murder. It felt like an impertinence.

Calum made a clucking noise and wrapped his grandmother in a Kinloch plaid. "Ye'll catch yer death."

"Death," she echoed. The keys hanging from the gold chain at her waist clanged like the tolling of a bell. "Death has come to Kinloch. . . . It's a reckoning. A reckoning, I tell ye. . . ."

"Can you tell me who else was in the castle?" Euan asked hastily. Morag MacDougal in her prophetic mood was a bit much before breakfast.

Behind him, Beatrice the sheep bleated plaintively. Euan swatted her away before she could nose under his kilt.

In the distance, he could hear the sound of a siren: PC McMorris coming up from the village, bringing the medical examiner with her, and thank goodness for that. Euan wished he were wearing something more official and not the dress kilt and blazer he'd worn to the ceilidh the night before. Would it be sexist to send PC McMorris back to fetch him some trousers?

Before he could act on that thought, a commotion arose from above.

"We need to take a selfie!" an American voice trilled.

What the—

"Shove up, you're blocking the way." Three women tumbled down the stairs, shoving and elbowing one another, all talking at once. They came to an abrupt halt just shy of the landing, staring at Euan.

They all wore plaid, but in nothing resembling any tartan Euan had ever seen on Kinloch. Their jarring plaids were enough to give anyone a headache, much less a man who had been called out before he'd had a chance to go to bed and was still feeling the effects of the fabled Kinloch punch.

One of them appeared to be wearing nothing at all underneath her plaid dressing gown.

He'd seen her at the ceilidh. Dancing. In skintight plaid.

Euan turned to Calum.

"What the devil are they doing here?"

Calum looked at him apologetically. "These'll be the Amerrrrr-icans. The authors. Staying at the castle for the retreat."

This was all the morning needed.

Americans. Why did it always have to be Americans?

PART I

CHAPTER ONE

Cassie

Excerpt from police interview with Mrs. Cassandra Parsons Pringle conducted by Detective Chief Inspector Macintosh, 10 December 2022

DCI: Let's return to the nature of your relationship to Miss Endicott and Miss—er—Miss de Noir. You claim to be writing a book together?

PRINGLE: Yes, that's right. I know it sounds a little unusual, but—

DCI: It sounds mad, Mrs. Pringle. Frankly.

PRINGLE: Well, it's not! We have a contract and everything. From a reputable publishing house. G.P. Morrow? You can call up our editor, Rachelle Cohen—*ring her up*, as you say here across the pond—and she'll explain everything.

DCI: All right. Why, then?

PRINGLE: I beg your pardon?

DCI: Why write a book together? Set on Kinloch, of all places.

PRINGLE: [*laughter*] Oh, you know the old story! Three writers walk into a bar—

DCI: May I remind you that a man has been found *dead*, Mrs. Pringle. Levity is hardly appropriate.

PRINGLE: I'm so sorry. It's not a joke. It really *is* how we met. The three of us were at a convention together a year or so ago— Bouchercon? In Las Vegas? We stayed at—

DCI: I beg your pardon. A *voucher* convention?

PRINGLE: [*laughter*] Not voucher, *Boucher*. Crime fiction? Anthony Boucher? He was a mystery writer, one of the greats. Haven't you read him?

DCI: No.

PRINGLE: Oh, you're in for a treat. I'm surprised you're not familiar with his work, as a detective chief inspector and everything. You know, I think I have one of his novels in my handbag here. *Nine Times Nine.* I'd be happy to let you—

DCI: Put your handbag away, Mrs. Pringle. This is a police interview.

PRINGLE: [*laughter*] Oh, right. Sorry. Anyway, the convention's named after him. It's the biggest thing ever. Thousands of people. Writers, fans, agents, editors. *Everybody* goes. As a mystery writer myself, I can't miss it.

DCI: Yes. Tell me about your writing, Mrs. Pringle.

PRINGLE: Oh, gosh. Where do I start? I have three different series running at the moment, each under a different pen name. Right now I'm working on the ninth book in my Haunted Farmers' Market series—that's set in a little town in rural North Carolina, where I grew up, lots of banjo and artisan cheeses— and the third book in my new Moggies, Mocha, and Murder series, which features a crime-solving cat who lives in a coffee cooperative outside of Seattle—

DCI: A *cat* who solves crimes?

PRINGLE: My readers just adore her. She's part Maine coon. You know the breed? Or is it too American for you? Big and fluffy, with a real nose for clues. Oh, and I'm just plotting out the twelfth Little Bake Shop mystery. That's my personal favorite. I love to bake. Do you like to bake, Detective Chief Inspector? You look as if you could use a scone or two, if you don't mind my saying so.

[*brief silence*]

DCI: So you've written a great many books, Mrs. Pringle. Why take the trouble of writing one with two other women?

PRINGLE: Why, for the fun of it! Writing is so much more fun when you do it with your best friends.

DCI: Best friends? That's how you characterize the relationship among the three of you?

PRINGLE: Oh, yes. Very much so. We're like long-lost sisters. We bonded *instantly*. It was the third day of the conference. We were all a little burned out. You know how it is. I was sitting at the bar, nursing an Irish coffee, my usual, and I happened to notice this glamorous woman two stools down, nursing a double bourbon. That was Kat, of course. Then Emma marched up and ordered something called a French 75, and I just *had* to ask her what was in it—I've had this idea for a series of murders at one of those champagne cellars in France, I mean just *think* of all the fun research—and we all got to talking and realized we were just *meant to be friends*. I think we talked all night. We missed the big dinner and the awards presentation—none of us was nominated, sadly; that's one of the reasons we were drowning our sorrows—and at some point, I don't remember when, one of us was talking about how lousy it was to go on book tour alone, you know, nobody to talk to except all those medical device salesmen trying to hit on you at the hotel bar. We said to each other, wouldn't it be *so much more fun* to tour together? And *I* said—at least I *think* it was me, I'm afraid we'd all had a little too much to drink at that point—I said, well, we should write a book *together*! And then our publisher would pay for our girls' trip— I mean, book tour. And our bar bill.

DCI: That's it? For the free drinks?

PRINGLE: Well, and the money, of course. But mostly so we could have an excuse to get together again. So we ran into my editor the next day—Rachelle was there at the convention with us—and said we had this brilliant idea to write a novel together. She laughed us off at first, naturally. I mean, what a crazy idea, right? But then we came back a month later with a real book proposal. It's called *Fifty Shades of Plaid*—

DCI: *Fifty Shades of* Plaid?

PRINGLE: [*laughter*] Isn't it brilliant? Back when Emma was doing the research for *The Unsinkable Prunella Schuyler*— that's her latest novel—she came across the story of the unsolved murder of the laird of Kinloch Island. I'm sure you've heard of it?

DCI: [*pause*] Refresh my memory, if you will.

PRINGLE: Why, Naughty Ned, of course. The orgy master himself. Poisoned during a house party in the autumn of 1900. It was just perfect for us—a sexually charged historical murder mystery. Best of all, it's set in Scotland!

DCI: Best of all? Why do you say that?

PRINGLE: Because we all love Scotland so much! We're huge *Outlander* fans. Have you read *Outlander*?

DCI: No.

PRINGLE: Watched the series on television? Telly, as you call it?

DCI: No.

PRINGLE: Och, aye! [*laughter*] That's my Scottish accent. Pretty good, isn't it? Listen to this. [*sound of clearing throat*] You've got to crrrross the bridge to get to Ballykissangel! What do you think?

[*brief silence*]

DCI: I'm afraid that's Irish.

TUESDAY, DECEMBER 6
Three days before the murder . . .

A T FIRST, CASSIE thought the narrow, placid face that poked into view over the back seat of the Land Rover, right between Kat and Emma, belonged to some kind of stuffed animal. A Scottish prop, to delight Kinloch's guests as they drove from the ferry to the castle.

Then the mouth opened and took the end of Emma's ponytail between its teeth.

Cassie turned forward and stared out the windshield to the road unraveling among the shadows ahead. "Um, Mr. MacDougal? Did you know there's a sheep in the back of your vehicle?"

The driver grunted. "Och, aye. That would be Beatrice."

"She's eating Miss Endicott's hair."

A noise of dismay came from the back seat. "Oh my God. It's a *sheep!*"

"Well, that explains the smell," said Kat.

MacDougal glanced in the rearview mirror. Cassie could have sworn she spotted a twitch at the corner of his mouth, but she couldn't be sure. The air was dark and the mouth was Scottish. It was nearly three o'clock, and the sun had begun to set. At least,

Cassie assumed it was setting, somewhere behind that layer of charcoal December cloud.

"Och, she's only giving ye a wee trim, Miss Endicott," Mac-Dougal said. "Being as yer hair's the color of her dinner. Here we are."

The Land Rover heeled to the right in a spray of gravel.

"Here we *are*?" said Kat. "Are you *kidding*? There's nothing *here*! Except this damn sheep."

"Stop it!" said Emma. "That's my *hair*, you beast!"

MacDougal made a growling noise from somewhere inside his esophagus and tightened his hands around the steering wheel. Cassie squinted through the gloom. Was she seeing things, or did a light flicker somewhere in the middle of all those shadows? She glanced down at the phone clutched in her hand. No messages, not a single alert. Maybe the signal was spotty? A small island in the Inner Hebrides, you couldn't get more remote than that.

My God, she'd made a terrible mistake, hadn't she? Traveling so far. What was she *thinking*?

The Land Rover bounced from rut to rut. Another light popped out, like a distant star. A large, hulking shape emerged against the lead horizon.

"There it is!" she cried. "Look, it's the castle! At least, I think it is."

"I don't see anything," said Kat.

"I *can't* see anything," said Emma. "This *animal* won't leave me alone."

MacDougal slammed the brakes. The Land Rover jolted to a stop. From the pocket of his coat he drew a cell phone and tapped furiously on the screen.

"What's the matter?" Cassie asked.

"Bluidy autocorrect," he muttered. "Now, then."

The dark shape on the horizon blazed into light, revealing every last battlement and turret of the medieval castle that towered before them. MacDougal made a satisfied grunt, put the phone back in his pocket, and hopped from the Land Rover. Cassie opened her door and climbed out to stand on the gravel, mouth hung open. She heard the other doors open and smack shut behind her, the indignant *baa* of the sheep as its dinner was snatched from its jaws. The castle glowed before her like a dream. Like when she and Chip took the kids to Disney World.

"Oh my!" Cassie breathed out.

"No way, is that a *moat*?" said Kat.

Emma snorted. "Kids, it's a fake, remember? *I* grew up in a house older than this one. Look at that stupid portcullis. Did you ever see anything less authentic in your *life*?"

"Oh, give it a rest for once," said Kat. She rummaged in her handbag and pulled out a phone. "All right. Smiles, everyone. Group selfie at the castle."

"Do we have to?" said Emma. "Social media is so demeaning."

"Wow. Can you say privilege?" said Kat.

Cassie glanced back at MacDougal, who tenderly lifted the sheep from the back of the Land Rover and set her on her little hooves so he could reach the suitcases. She prayed Beatrice was house-trained. House-trained! Another pang of longing pierced her gut. She'd left home in the middle of potty training Dash, her youngest. Would Chip remember to keep an eye on him? Know to look out for when Dash bent his wee knees and—well, started to wee? She looked reflexively at the screen of her phone. One bar, that was all. One stunted little signal bar and no alerts. Just the cover of her next book glowing in her palm—a fluffy tortoise cat curled around a coffee roasting machine. And the time, 3:02 P.M.

Kat called out, exasperated. "Cassie, what's the problem? Come on, cuddle up. We're besties, remember?"

Cassie stuck her phone back in her coat pocket and turned to join Emma and Kat, backs to the castle. She put her arm around Emma's stiff waist and stuck a delighted expression on her face.

"Everyone say *prosecco*," said Kat.

"I can't believe I'm doing this," said Emma. "I don't even like prosecco. Only secretaries drink that crap."

"Shut up and smile at the damn camera, okay?"

Kat stretched out her arm and lifted the camera to various angles, trying to get the castle in frame behind them. Cassie stared at the screen and wished her hair were a little less frizzy in the Scottish damp. Kat's sharp fingernails dug into the small of her back.

Kat barked in her ear. "Cassie? Yoo-hoo? The lens is on the left."

"Oh, sorry," said Cassie.

"Just take the damn picture," Emma said, through a clenched grin.

The flash went off. Kat pulled away. "I swear to God," she said, "I'm going to murder you both."

INSIDE THE HALL, a skeleton glared at them from the bottom of the grand staircase.

On closer inspection, it was a woman—tall and cadaverous, white hair pulled back in an icy knot at the back of her head. You could tell she was alive because her eyes were blue. Also, she stepped forward and held out a bony hand in Cassie's direction.

"Welllllcome to Kinloch," she burred. "How was yer journey?"

"Oh, just wonderful!" Cassie said. She clasped the woman's hand and found it warmer than she'd expected, hardened with calluses. "The ferry crossing was—well, it was—"

"Dramatic," said Emma.

"Nauseating," said Kat.

The woman looked past Cassie's shoulder to the doorway, where MacDougal staggered in under the weight of a suitcase resembling a steamer trunk. Her face softened. "I see you've met our Calum," she said fondly.

The suitcase thumped on the flagstones. MacDougal straightened and flexed his arm. He certainly was a *strapping* fellow, Cassie had to admit. When they'd staggered off the ferry, exhausted and bilious—well, except Emma, who'd spent her summers sailing off the coast of Maine and regarded Cassie's green face with an eyebrow of amused contempt—Calum MacDougal had appeared out of the mist like an extra from *Braveheart*, broad of shoulder, sturdy of leg, bright of kilt, red hair curling under his Scotch bonnet.

Well, well, purred Kat, shedding her *mal de mer* in an instant. *I wonder what he's got in* his *sporran.*

He'd escorted them to an ancient safari-green Land Rover, painted on each side with the silhouette of a Rapunzel tower and the words *Follow Me to Castle Kinloch!*, then retrieved their suitcases and tossed them in the back (the *boot*, Cassie reminded herself) with as much effort as—as—well, as her husband, Chip, might shoulder a two-by-four on one of his renovation projects.

So entranced were Emma and Kat as Calum had hustled them into the back seat, they'd apparently failed to register the presence of a full-grown ewe staring inquisitively between them.

Well, who could blame them? Neither woman had six kids and a husband back home in North Carolina, a mortgage and a Costco membership and a twelve-year-old gas-guzzling Yukon that needed new tires. Emma and Kat could ogle Kinloch's answer to Jamie Fraser all they wanted.

They were certainly ogling now, as Calum MacDougal turned on his heel and stalked back out of the hall to retrieve the remaining luggage from the Land Rover. You could practically slice the current of sexual interest with a—a—oh, what did they call those little Scottish daggers, the ones Scotsmen tucked in their belts? Emma would know.

A dirk, that was it.

Cassie glanced over her shoulder. The white-haired woman frowned ferociously at Kat's backside, which was covered by a layer of skintight black leather like an oil slick that poured down her legs and disappeared into a pair of black stiletto boots, stamped with silver studs along the seams. How on earth had Kat walked across the drawbridge, under the portcullis, and through the courtyard without losing both heels inside the cracks between the flagstones? It was a feat beyond Cassie's imagination.

And speaking of dirks, it looked like Kat was about to find one planted right between her shoulders, if that Kinloch woman's face was any clue.

The nervous laugh rose in Cassie's throat like it always did—instinctive, unstoppable. She heard herself giggle and smothered it with words. "My goodness, Kat! What have you got inside that suitcase of yours? It's big enough to hold a dead body."

Emma snorted out a laugh. Next to her, Kat swiveled around and stared at Cassie. Her red mouth thinned to a slit.

"Looks like you hit a nerve there, Cassie," said Emma.

Cassie opened her mouth to apologize, but before she could gather the words, Calum MacDougal stomped back into the hall and set the remaining luggage next to Kat's trunk. Behind him, Beatrice poked an inquisitive face around the doorway. "Will that be all, lasses?" Calum grunted.

Kat put one hand on her hip. "You tell me."

Cassie leaned to Emma and whispered, "Do we tip?"

"I only tip in restaurants," said Emma. "Ten percent, max."

The white-haired woman said briskly, "All right, then, Calum, me lad. We'll be needing ye to take these bags to the ladies' rooms."

MacDougal cracked a smile at one corner of his mouth. He snapped a salute and bent to grasp the handle of Kat's trunk.

"Stop!" exclaimed Cassie, staring at her quilted blue floral Vera Bradley bag next to Emma's worn black wheelie and Kat's gigantic steamer trunk. She snapped her fingers. "I have an idea!"

Kat rolled her eyes. "Of course you do."

"Let's take a photo of the three suitcases and ask *Which Author?* You know, which one of us owns which suitcase?"

"*That*," said Emma, "is the dumbest social media gimmick I ever heard. Besides, it's kind of obvious, right?"

Cassie pulled out her phone. "It's just for fun. And it'll only take a second, I promise."

Behind them, the woman cleared her throat.

"Ye'll be wanting these," she said, holding out three dark green folders, embossed with the same Rapunzel tower logo as the Land Rover, above the words "Welcome to Castle Kinloch" in loopy gold letters.

Cassie slid her phone back in her pocket and reached for a folder. "Ooh, what's this?"

"That'll be the itinerary for yer stay. Map of the castle, mealtimes, suggested dress, spa menu—"

Kat snatched her folder. "There's a spa?"

"Open on Thursday," said the woman. "I've already taken the liberty of scheduling yer appointments. Ye'll want to look yer best for the ceilidh on Friday—"

"A ceilidh!" exclaimed Emma. "You mean a real one? A genuine, authentic *ceilidh*? Is it here at the castle?"

"Why, it'll be in the village, of course. The village hall, that's where we've had them since—well, since we've been having them."

Kat looked up from her open folder. "What the hell is this? A sheep's milk facial? Peat body wrap?"

"We use only the finest orrrganic ingrrrrredients, grown here on the castle grounds."

"Oh, yes! I've heard so much about your gardens," said Cassie. "I hope you'll show them to me tomorrow. Legend has it there's an ancient poison garden. Is that true?"

The woman turned a hard stare on her. "It's December. There'll be nothing growing in the beds, ye understand."

Cassie smiled warmly. "All the same, Mrs. . . . I'm sorry, I didn't catch your name?"

"Morrrag MacDougal," the woman said. "Mistress of Castle Kinloch."

"Mistress? What does that mean, exactly?"

"It means I oversee everything to do with the running of the castle, Mrs. Pringle."

"So, like a housekeeper," said Kat.

Morag turned to Kat with a look of death.

"What an exciting job!" Cassie burbled. "Do you get to oversee the kitchens?"

There was a long, heavy pause before Morag swiveled back to Cassie. "The kitchens fall under my purrrview," she said, rolling the "r" in *purview* to its maximum possible extent.

"Ooh, lucky you! I'd love to have a look! If you don't mind, of course."

"Actually," said Emma, "we'd like to have a look at everything. If you don't mind. We're fascinated by the castle's history, as a matter of fact. Such as it is."

"Ye'll find a leaflet in yer folder regarding the history of Kinloch, Miss Endicott," said Morag. "In the meantime, ye'll be wanting to change for the laird's dinner—"

"The laird's dinner? Does that mean the great man himself will make an appearance?" said Emma.

Morag lifted both eyebrows. "The grrrreat man?"

"Brett Saffron Presley, I mean. He bought the lairdship fair and square, right? Along with the castle and its contents."

"Mr. Presley," said Morag, pronouncing the words like drops of acid, "does not grrrace the table when guests are prrresent. That's made plain on yer reservation confirmation. On the back side, if ye please," she added, as Cassie reached in her handbag and yanked out the packet of travel forms.

Cassie turned over the last paper and discovered a paragraph in tiny print next to an asterisk at the bottom. *Brett Saffron Presley Writing Retreats™ do not include Brett Saffron Presley. Maximum of five guests per retreat. All fees to be paid in advance.*

"Then why do you—"

"They'll be piping ye down at six sharp," said Morag. "And ye'd best mind the time. The dinner is a formal affair and strrragglers will not be admitted."

"I have just the outfit in mind," murmured Kat.

"Before ye make yer selection, Miss de Noir, I'll be referrring ye to the leaflet entitled *Suggested Dress for Mealtimes and Special Events.* Page four. Now, come along, then. We'll show ye to yer rooms. Calum? Leave that poor sheep outside where it belongs. She can't follow ye everywhere."

From the doorway, Beatrice made a defeated bleat. Morag turned and started up the staircase.

Cassie leaned toward Emma. "How does she know our names?"

Emma shrugged. "She's a housekeeper. She's supposed to know this stuff."

"Oh, Mrs. MacDougal!" Cassie called out.

Their hostess stopped and turned. "Morag will do," she said quietly.

"Oh! I'm sorry. It's just that—I'm looking through these leaflets—these wonderful leaflets, you've taken such trouble—it's just that I don't see anything about the Wi-Fi? Do you have Wi-Fi? I mean, I hate to be such a boring *American*, it's not like I'm addicted to TikTok or anything, it's just that I have six kids back home and I need to stay connected, you know? In case there's an emergency?"

"Six children!" exclaimed Morag.

"I apologize on her behalf," said Kat. "She was out sick when they explained birth control in health class."

"My aunt had a dozen kids," said Emma. "Of course, she lived on a commune."

Morag looked from Kat to Emma and back to Cassie. For the

first time, her blue eyes softened. "Och," she said. "With frrriends like these."

Cassie forced a bright smile. "Oh, we just like to tease each other! Tease, tease, tease, that's how we celebrate our friendship!"

"In any case, ye'll find a network called EweOnline on yer phone. I'm told it's not so quick, but it should suffice."

"EweOnline," Cassie repeated. "What's the password?"

Morag turned and resumed her climb. "There is no password."

Behind them, Calum thumped up the steps with the luggage. The staircase was made of oak and the clatter of their shoes echoed from the walls, as if a herd of cattle was making its way through the Great Hall. At the first landing Cassie stopped and stared out the enormous window that overlooked the twilit gardens below. In the distance, about a hundred yards away, the castle lights reflected against the stones of a single tower that reached from the turf to poke at the low-slung clouds.

A shiver made its way down Cassie's spine. "There it is," she murmured.

Emma came up next to her and snickered. "Insert your own phallus joke, right?"

"Yeah, well, it's all fun and games until someone gets hurt," said Kat.

Something about the tone of her voice made Cassie turn. Kat had one of those sharp, fine-edged faces that narrowed to a point at her chin. Long swoops of kohl outlined her large brown eyes, fringed by lashes so thick Cassie wondered if they were real or fake. She'd touched up her scarlet lipstick in the Land Rover, although an untimely bump had caused a smudge at one corner. But underneath all that glamor, in the blue glow of twilight, Kat's face had a doe-eyed, almost fragile quality. She gazed past Cassie's ear at the tower standing all by itself across the garden, while Emma continued up the stairs after Morag.

"I'll bet there's a terrific view from the top," Cassie ventured, with as much cheer as she could muster.

A voice called down from the stairs above. "There'll be nae climbing up the Obelisk! Strictly off-limits to the hotel guests, by order of himself."

Kat snorted. "Likes his privacy, does he?"

Cassie looked up, where Morag's face floated ghostlike over the banister, staring down at them. "Bad things happen thairrrr," she murmured, and resumed her climb.

Just before Cassie turned after the others, she glimpsed Calum MacDougal, standing stock-still in the middle of the staircase below. He carried the trunk over one shoulder, the wheelie in one hand and Cassie's trusty Vera Bradley bag tucked under his arm, and he was staring upward at the space Morag had just vacated as if he'd seen a ghost.

CHAPTER TWO

Emma

Excerpt from police interview with Miss Emerson (Emma) Endicott, 10 December 2022

DCI: [*sound of shuffling paper*] Just to verify, Miss Endicott . . .

ENDICOTT: That's *Ms*. And two "t"s at the end of Endicott. [*pause*] Like the Boston Endicotts.

DCI: I don't know who that is, *Ms*. Endicott with two "t"s. Now, according to my notes, you along with Mrs. Pringle and Ms. de Noir are best friends who decided to write a book together. . . . [*sound of paper shuffling*] Let's see . . . yes. So you could get a publisher to send you on a girls' trip.

ENDICOTT: And get our bar bill paid for, too. Yes. That's the gist of it. Because we really are close. We're the best friends we never knew we wanted. We complement each other.

DCI: Right. As Mrs. Pringle pointed out. But you're all successful writers on your own. It's unclear what you hoped to achieve by joining forces.

ENDICOTT: Well, we all have our own areas of expertise we bring to a collaborative novel. For instance, I'm the expert on all historical detail. I'm known for my ability to burrow through volumes and volumes of dusty texts to find that one tiny bit of information to make a story more authentic. Did you know that the whole rise of men wearing powdered wigs in the seventeenth century was all because of the prevalence of syphilis? It . . .

DCI: Ms. Endicott, as fascinating as that might be, may I remind you that we are in the midst of a murder investigation?

ENDICOTT: Of course. I just wanted to make sure you understood that we aren't, or at least *I'm* not, an ignorant American. I've written over thirty books, all about important women who have been written out of history because they weren't deemed important enough. Perhaps you're familiar with my latest work of biographical fiction, *The Unsinkable Prunella Schuyler*? She's a distant relation of mine. She survived the sinking of the *Lusitania*. Prunella was actually a guest here at the castle in 1900, for a grouse hunt and house party. The same house party where Sir Edward Kinloch was murdered, actually. Lady Edwina Kinloch, known locally as Lady Ned, as I'm sure you know since she was much beloved by the people on the island, was a particular friend of hers, actually. I . . .

DCI: [*sound of restless shifting in seat*] No, I'm not familiar. With the *Lusitania*, yes, but not with Brunhilda Whatever.

ENDICOTT: Her name is Prunella. . . .

DCI: I don't see the relevance, Miss Endicott. So, to continue. What about your two best friends? Tell me more about them and what they bring to this collaboration.

ENDICOTT: Well, Kat knows all about sex—she literally has an advanced degree in it. She brings the erotic sizzle. Something I really don't have the time to delve into because I'm much more serious about the history and the writing.

DCI: I see. And what about Mrs. Pringle? What does she add to the group efforts?

ENDICOTT: Cassie? Well, she knows all about murder—you know, how to kill someone and get away with it. [*pause*] I mean, not in real life.

DCI: Of course not. So you're aware of the history of Kinloch Castle, then?

ENDICOTT: We wouldn't be here if we weren't. I already knew a lot about it because of my research on Prunella Schuyler, so I had to fill in the other two. Let's just say that historical detail isn't their forte. Anyway, we know the tower was rebuilt from the remains of the original fourteenth-century tower house built by Kenneth MacKinloch. The rest of the so-called castle only dates back to the Edwardian period, despite the Disney-like additions of crenellations and arrow slits on the north tower. And the laird at the time, Sir Edward Kinloch—otherwise known as Naughty Ned—was well known for his debauchery and his collection of sex toys. I also know that he was murdered in 1900 during a house party, and his murder was never solved. You see, I *do* know my history.

DCI: Apparently. Is there anything else you think I should know?

ENDICOTT: [*pause*] Yes. About Cassie. Not that I think you'll be using it in this investigation, but I think it should be mentioned in the quest for full disclosure.

DCI: I see. And what would that be?

ENDICOTT: She is completely ignorant about the history and significance of the Scottish tartan. The only thing she really knows about the subject is that Lands' End is a great source for all things plaid.

Three days before the murder . . .

Y OU CANNOT *POSSIBLY* be serious about wearing that," Emma
said, taking in the practically sheer fishnet bodysuit with
three strategically placed triangular patches of black satin to
prevent Kat's outfit from crossing the line from provocative to
obscene.

"Don't you like my boots?" Kat lifted one of her long slim legs
encased in black patent leather thigh-high stilettos then continued her descent into the Great Hall. Emma could almost feel the
paint cracking over the eyeballs in the male portraits hanging on
the walls around them, and some of the women, too.

"We're all supposed to be wearing plaid!" Cassie reached into
her large, quilted tote and pulled out a cluster of fabric swatches.
"We all chose our own tartans, remember? Based on the clans
they represented. Where's your plaid, Kat?"

Kat continued to walk toward Calum, who stood by the giant
stone hearth in the Great Hall and held a tray of drinks. "I could
show you," she said, plucking up a glass with aubergine-tipped
fingers. "But then I'd have to strip." She winked slowly at Calum
before licking her lower lip.

Emma looked down at the Gordon plaid skirt she'd pulled
from the back of her mother's closet. Her mother had worn it fifty
years prior when she'd attended the Chapin School in the days
when there was still money to pay for private school education.
Frugalness and blue blood ran in tandem through the veins of
the Endicott family. Outworn school uniforms remained in the
closets of the century-and-a-half-old drafty pile of bricks they
called home alongside a collection of wigs worn by long-dead ancestors and a drawer full of carefully folded used wrapping paper

and other family detritus from the last century. The Endicotts' frugality skated precariously close to tightfistedness, a source of pride for Emma's mother, who embraced her thriftiness if only to avoid the uglier words of destitute and insolvent.

"Call me what you want," Emma said, slinging her ponytail over her shoulder, "but at least I'm a team player." She took one of the glasses from Calum and gave him her biggest smile. Not every good-looking man liked the overblown sexpot like Kat. Some actually preferred the girl-next-door type. Which Emma was. Sort of. If one could overlook the whole Atlantic Ocean thing. To show just how sporting she was, she lifted her glass and swallowed it down in one shot before grabbing two more.

"By the way," Emma said, approaching Cassie with a drink for each of them. "Those tartans you gave us were wrong. You chose patterns from the southern border clans, none of which one would technically see here in the Inner Hebrides."

"You could have said something at the time, you know," Cassie said, sounding hurt, which immediately made Emma feel awful. Ever since childhood, being the fourth girl with ill-fitting hand-me-downs in a neighborhood full of houses with shiny new roofs and even shinier new cars, she'd fallen into the habit of showing off her intellectual superiority to compete in that sort of environment. And win. Not that she just assumed she was always the smartest person in the room, but she usually was. But she hadn't meant to hurt Cassie's feelings. That would be a lot like kicking a puppy. And Emma loved animals, especially dogs. And horses. Maybe even sheep, but from a distance.

"I'm sorry," Emma said truthfully. "At the time, it didn't seem important."

"And it's still not," Kat said as she strutted back toward Calum for another drink. She paused midstride in front of a large, framed poster hanging on the stone wall next to a full-size human skeleton, which was most likely the reason none of them had noticed the large frame before. Cassie and Emma joined Kat in front of the poster, each of them wearing expressions from wry amusement (Kat) to distaste mixed with guilt for the initial reaction of distaste (Cassie) to plain incredulity (Emma).

A highly photoshopped picture of a man with a chiseled jaw, not-quite-perfect nose, and deep, penetrating blue eyes—possibly kohl-lined—beneath dark arched eyebrows stared challengingly out of the frame. Despite the obviously contemporary clothing, he wore a Vandyke beard with a thin mustache, his thick and wavy dark hair backcombed from a smooth, probably Botoxed forehead. He was looking slightly off center from the photographer, his head resting gently on a well-manicured hand in an esoteric pose meant to look as if the subject might be contemplating the meaning of life or, more likely, already knew what that was. Above his well-coifed head were the inspirational words, "Wake Up. It's Kill It O'Clock."

"What the f—" Kat began.

"Fudge," Cassie quickly interjected as both she and Emma moved to stand beside Kat to examine the poster. "Isn't that . . . ?"

"Brett Saffron Presley," announced a deep voice in a cultured English accent from behind them. "Internationally bestselling author, spokesperson for the famous Presley How-to-Write-a-Novel software, in-demand speaker, and—most importantly for the three of you—the brains behind the globally lauded writers' retreats here at Kinloch."

The three women turned to find a man in his late thirties with dark blond hair, pale green eyes, and a broad smile that seemed to be fighting a smirk. He was tall and well-built, but more in a lacrosse-player way than the rugby-player physique of Calum-in-the-kilt. A gray-and-white shaggy sheepdog sat obediently by his side, its thick tail whacking against the man's trouser-clad leg, its long pink tongue lolling as it grinned at Emma and her cowriters.

The man assessed the three women with a cursory glance, his eyes lingering on Emma just a second longer, making her wonder if she had toothpaste on her face. "Allow me to introduce myself. My name is Archie—short for Archibald—but I'll answer to both. I am the estate manager here at Kinloch and available to you for anything you might require during your week here on the island. And this," he said, leaning down to give a few scratches behind one floppy ear before placing a firm pat on the dog's furry side, "is Loren. She's the best sheepherder I've ever had, and my constant companion. If you can't find me, look for Loren because I won't be too far away."

He shook hands with each woman as they introduced themselves, Emma clinging to his hand just a moment longer to get a better look at him. "Are you English? I don't detect a Scottish accent."

"Och, aye," he said with an exaggerated burr. "I'm full Scottish, at least according to my mother and father." He dropped the accent with a smile. "I went to school in England."

"That makes sense, then," Emma said, dropping his hand. She made the mistake of looking at Kat, who mouthed the word "gay." Emma resisted rolling her eyes. Typical Kat. Just because Archie wasn't bulging with thews like a Karyn Black hero didn't mean he was gay. Emma knew plenty of men who wore pink Brooks Brothers shirts and dated women. But now that Kat had said it, Emma couldn't unthink it. Besides, Kat was a verified sex expert so she'd know. But Emma would be lying to herself if she didn't admit to being disappointed.

The large double doors adjacent to the fireplace, with giant lions' heads carved on them, opened inward, revealing Calum holding a bagpipe. Emma looked at the fireplace where he'd just been, holding the tray of drinks, thinking he must have a twin. Apparently, he was simply very agile. And quick.

"Shall we?" Archie held out his hand to indicate to the women that they should precede him into the dining room. "Please follow Calum as he pipes in the haggis carried by Morag and we follow them around the table before we find our seats. Your place cards are already on the table."

Kat was refocused on the wall poster until Emma tugged on her arm. "Come on, Kat. I'm starving. Nothing to see here,"

"Male author," Kat said as she coughed into her hand. "I mean, who would even admit to knowing that stupid quote, much less agreeing to have it printed on a poster with your face on it?"

"No kidding," said Emma, following Archie into the dining room. "If you look up 'insufferable male author' in the dictionary, you'll find that picture."

"Girls," Cassie whispered from behind. "Be nice."

Calum proved himself a more-than-proficient piper. Emma wasn't the only one noticing how Kat watched Calum's handling of the mouthpiece as Cassie, who was next to Kat, gave her a sharp poke in the ribs, making her yelp.

After they were all seated, Calum excused himself and Morag cut open the haggis and began serving it to the diners. Kat immediately pushed hers away. "I think I'm going to pass on this. Isn't it just sheep guts and organs stuffed into their stomach sac?"

Embarrassed on Kat's behalf for making them all look like rude Americans, Emma stood and began to recite from memory with her best approximation of a Scottish accent:

"Fair fa' your honest, sonsie face,
Great chieftain o' the puddin-race!
Aboon them a' ye tak your place,
Painch, tripe, or thairm:
Weel are ye wordy o' a grace
As lang's my airm."

After a stunned silence, Emma said meekly, "That's from Robert Burns's 'Address to a Haggis.' He loved the dish enough to write a poem about it." She looked around the table to find Cassie giving her a pitiful smile and both Kat and Morag rolling their eyes. She sat down quickly and was about to pick up her fork when the sound of hearty clapping came from the end of the table where Archie sat.

"Well, done, Emma. I dare say that not many of our visitors know that. Even your Scottish accent was good—and definitely better than mine."

"Thank you," Emma said, looking down as she felt her cheeks flame. She wasn't used to getting compliments. Her mother had always told her that they were the cheapest sort of flattery so she'd never sought them, either. But that didn't mean that she didn't appreciate Archie's words.

Emma took a bite of haggis to be polite, then glanced around the room to keep her mind off of what she was eating, her gaze settling on a full-length portrait in a gilded frame hung over the sideboard. The subject was a beautiful young woman wearing a high-necked white lace pin-tucked blouse with a dark, narrow fitted skirt. Her hair was done in a simple style, and she clutched a bouquet of flowers in one hand. There was something about her eyes that seemed somehow familiar.

She quickly swallowed. "That's the Boldini portrait of Lady Ned! I've only seen pictures of it in books—could that be the original?"

"It is indeed," Archie said. "It was on loan to the National Gallery, but now it's back here at Kinloch where it belongs."

"How exciting for us," Cassie said. "And what a beautiful woman. Although I think there's something in her eyes. Like she knows a secret or something. Don't you think, Emma?"

Before Emma could answer, the door to the kitchen opened

and Morag reappeared with more serving dishes, followed closely behind by Calum, his kilt now replaced by the uniform of an Edwardian servant complete with tight black trousers, starched white shirt with bow tie, and a closely fitted tuxedo jacket that snuggly gripped his bulging back and shoulder muscles.

To keep herself from staring, Emma looked around at her tablemates and spotted Cassie digging her phone out of her ever-present tote bag and looking at the screen. Her face went from hopeful to worried disappointment.

"Still no texts or calls from home?" Emma asked.

Cassie shook her head. "No. And I know Chip has it all covered, and he's a great father, but it's not the same, you know? Especially trying to corral six children while potty training the youngest. Not to mention . . ." She stopped, gave a shallow smile. "He didn't even want me to come. We've . . ." Realizing everyone was now focused on her, she dropped her phone back into her tote and gave a nervous laugh, a sound that never failed to grate on Emma's nerves. "It doesn't matter. I'll just call them later. I need to figure out the time difference, which I always find so confusing."

Kat dropped her fork onto her plate with a clatter. "Every time I hear you talk about your kids, it makes me want another cigarette." She reached inside the low-cut neckline of her outfit and pulled one out along with a small lighter. "Is there an ashtray or can I just use my bread plate?"

With a quick movement, Morag snatched the cigarette out of Kat's hand, crumpling it into her bony fist. "There'll be no smoking in the castle, lassie. Are ye daft?" She scowled at Kat. "Ye've no more sense than a wee babe."

Feeling uncomfortable with any sort of conflict, Emma quickly changed the subject. Focusing on Archie, she said, "I understand there's a rather impressive Edwardian sex toys museum that Mr. Presley has thoughtfully curated. As an avid historian, I was hoping to have the chance to see it." She'd normally be embarrassed to be broaching such a topic in mixed company, but this safely fit into the category of research.

Archie's face hardened. "The museum isn't quite open for visitors yet. Mr. Presley is still adding to his . . . collection."

"That's a shame," Kat said, sounding like she meant it. Because she probably did. "We understand that it's Mr. Presley's policy not to join his guests so we're not expecting to see him, but is he in residence right now? Some of us might want to get a glimpse of the legend. So we can talk about it on social media."

"He is currently in residence. But you won't be seeing him." Archie's expression made it clear that he didn't believe it to be too much of a loss. "He's in seclusion right now working on his next book. He is not to be disturbed."

"Must be nice to be a male author," Kat said under her breath.

Choosing not to acknowledge her comment, Archie said, "But I'm sure you'll find that Kinloch has more than enough to occupy your time here."

"Like lots of men in kilts?" Kat said. "I've always wondered what—"

Kat's question was abruptly cut off by Emma sending a swift kick to Kat's boot-clad shin that probably hurt her toe more than Kat's leg. "We're actually more interested in the castle and its history than Mr. Presley, although as you can tell, we're all a little bit in awe of Mr. Presley." Emma grinned broadly. "We're his biggest fans."

"Oh, yes. We certainly are," Cassie agreed, nodding vigorously. "Since his very first book. I don't usually read books written by men, but I picked one up because I'd heard about his mentoring programs to help unpublished authors including scholarships to conferences. I remember thinking I should support an author who so willingly helps others and let's just say I became a lifelong fan after reading that one book. Still am."

Cassie sent Emma a pointed look, like a relay racer getting ready to hand over the baton. "Yes. Same," Emma said. "His philanthropy was the whole idea behind acquiring Kinloch and creating these writing retreats. We're all multipublished so we didn't qualify for one of his scholarships, but I know he's helped a lot of writers. Hopefully one day we'll be as successful as he is and can use his example of generosity. Right, Kat?" Emma looked at Kat, who appeared to be a bit green around the mouth. Except her haggis still sat on her plate, untouched. "Right, Kat?" Emma repeated.

Kat seemed to shake herself out of her stupor. "Oh, yes. Right. Mr. Presley is known for his generosity. As well as being a great writer." She finished her glass of wine in one long gulp. "I mean, from what I've read, Kinloch was falling down before he acquired it, and then he restored it and the village has come back to life again. I'm sure that's all wonderful for the people of Kinloch."

"You'll have to ask them, I suppose," Archie said with a tight-lipped smile.

"But what we'd really love to hear more about is the history of the Kinlochs." Emma leaned forward conspiratorially. "You see, we're actually here to write a book together. About what happened to Naughty Ned, the lecherous Edwardian Kinloch laird, and his rumored sex parties."

"And his unsolved murder," Kat added, a little too gleefully. "So when we told our editor, Rachelle, that we wanted to write a book together—instant besties!—she instantly thought of Kinloch. Between the history and Mr. Presley's retreats, it was a no-brainer that we all come here to research and write. I know there has to be a lot of dirt about the Kinlochs that has yet to be dug up, and we think we're the right people to do it. And we mean to uncover *everything*." She leaned back in her chair with a sultry smile.

Archie pushed away his untouched plate of sticky toffee pudding. "Very admirable, ladies. But you're certainly not the first group who's come to Kinloch in a futile attempt to solve the mystery. I'm afraid you're destined to come to the same conclusion as I have, that some crimes aren't meant to be solved." He slid back his chair then stood. "If you will excuse me. I have duties to which I must attend." With a stiff bow, he walked quickly out of the room through the swinging kitchen door, the faithful Loren trotting by his side, the sound of his heels landing hard against the stone floor punctuating his departure.

Finding themselves alone in the room, the three women stood. Emma faced Kat. "You were laying it on a bit thick, don't you think? And way to go offending the one guy who probably has the most information to share with us."

Kat turned on her. "At least give me some credit for not spilling the beans about BSP's *generosity*. Because I really, *really* wanted to mention the fact that only young, attractive women writers ever win his scholarships. Or that they're only worth about five hundred bucks and that he only gives out one per year. And then he charges a small fortune to attend his retreats where he doesn't even appear." She crossed her arms over her chest. "You're welcome, by the way. Somebody has to ask the hard questions. We only have a week, remember?"

Cassie came to stand between them. "Come on, girls. We're supposed to be BFFs. Let's not ruin it on our first day." A successive number of beeps came from inside her tote. Pulling out her phone, she looked at the screen and yelped with excitement. "I've got to go—I've got a lot of missed calls and messages that I need to take care of."

"You can't go now," Kat said with an aggrieved voice. "We have to work. This is a collaboration, remember? We're supposed to be working together."

"I know, I know. But don't worry. I promise I'll make this quick and won't hold us up. Promise."

They all turned to the slowly opening double doors. With a collective held breath, they waited until both doors were fully ajar, revealing a somber Calum, still wearing his Edwardian servant's attire. "Ladies," he said as he stepped back to allow them to exit.

Emma was the last to leave, glancing back to find Calum watching, his cool and calculating eyes following them as they passed the poster of Brett Saffron Presley, each feeling compelled to give it a cursory glance before heading up the grand stairs. When Emma reached the landing, she turned to see Calum still watching, assessing. Emma quickened her steps, running the rest of the way to the top until she could no longer be seen from below.

CHAPTER THREE

Kat

EXCERPT FROM POLICE INTERVIEW WITH MS. KATJA DE NOIR,
10 DECEMBER 2022

DCI: The deceased was discovered wearing a corset composed of leather and crimson lace, fishnet stockings, stiletto heels, and a dog collar.

DE NOIR: Each to their own.

DCI: Don't you mean *your* own, Miss de Noir? These items of clothing were purchased with your credit card at a specialty shop in Brooklyn, New York.

DE NOIR: If that's what the credit card receipt says, it must be true.

DCI: Why was the deceased in your clothes?

DE NOIR: How should I know? So he went into my drawers. He wouldn't be the first.

DCI: Are you suggesting your personal belongings are searched on a regular basis?

DE NOIR: When I say drawers, I don't mean furniture. You know, *drawers*? Like underwear.

DCI: We call them pants. I understand you once worked as— I believe the technical term is—a dominatrix?

DE NOIR: If you'd like a demonstration, you'll need to book an appointment.

DCI: [*prolonged silence*]

DE NOIR: Look, grad school doesn't come cheap. It was more educational than waiting tables. You'd be amazed by what I can do with a whip and a can of whipped cream.

DCI: I think I can forgo the pleasure—but it seems the deceased felt otherwise.

DE NOIR: And you came up with that how? I wasn't in those clothes. He was. Do you need me to interpret that for you, or can you connect the dots for yourself?

DCI: What exactly *was* your graduate degree in, Miss de Noir?

DE NOIR: If you must know I have an MFA—that's a master's of fine arts to you—from the Iowa Writers' Workshop and a master's in clinical psychology from NYU. Do you have anything you'd like to share, Detective Chief Inspector? If you'd just like to lie down on the couch over there . . .

DCI: And was your, ahem, career as a dominatrix part of the, er, therapeutic regime?

DE NOIR: What? Are you going to try to make out that Mister Fancy-Pants was an obsessed client and I killed him? I mean, that would make an excellent book—but not one of my books.

TUESDAY, DECEMBER 6
Three days before the murder . . .

N O ONE FOR a nightcap, then? No bonding over a wee dram of Laphroaig?"

Kat simpered at herself in the mirror of her bedroom. She was, surprise, surprise, speaking only to herself. Kat twisted so that she could admire her silhouette in her mesh bodysuit. Wasted, utterly wasted on this lot. It jarred oddly with all the plaid behind her. Plaid hanging from the rails of the big, boxy canopy bed. Plaid upholstery on the easy chairs in front of the fireplace. There was even a pair of complimentary plaid slippers peeking coyly out from under the edge of the bed. It was like a J.Crew wet dream. Her half sisters would love it.

Kat grimaced. Her half sisters would also love Emma and Cassie. More to the point, Emma and Cassie would love her half sisters. They could play tennis and go shopping together at J.McLaughlin.

"Three authors walk into a bar . . . Besties at first sight. The sisters I never had. Vomit."

They couldn't even keep up the pretense for one night. This was going to work how? Kat should have known better than to let herself get looped into this lunacy. Sisterhood in action! Three best friends write a book together! Shore up your flagging sales by pooling your readership and expanding your genre boundaries!

Okay, maybe they weren't putting that last bit in the press release.

After a spectacular first book, Kat's sales had been gently sinking for years. Cassie had a devoted following spread out over dozens of books that sold for peanuts. Everyone agreed Emma's research was brilliant and her prose was equally brilliant—if you were trying to use it to fall asleep. It just so happened they all had the same editor, the brilliant and well-shod Rachelle, known for her sharp edits and equally sharp stiletto heels. Why not join forces? Rachelle had suggested. Emma's research smarts, Cassie's heart, Kat's verve. Or maybe she'd said nerve. Either way, it was a surefire winner.

If they didn't kill one another first.

She'd thought she could do it, she really had. Just lie back and think of England. Er, Scotland. Sure, Cassie wrote the most vomitous nicey-nice tripe and Emma couldn't get out of bed without first footnoting it and checking her references in triplicate, but, whatever. It was just one week.

But now that they were here . . . Kat just didn't see how this was going to work. There was Cassie, running off to phone home like an attenuated E.T. And Emma—the woman couldn't lie to save her life. She couldn't even mildly dissemble.

They were doomed. Doomed.

Kat prowled restlessly around her aerie. The Tower Room, Morag had croaked at her, laying on the gloom with a heavy hand. "Try not to be nervous," Morag had warned with a smirk, only it had come out as "nairrrrrrrrvus," with about ten times the daily recommended quantity of "r"s.

Did she look like someone who was prone to nerves?

Full of nerve, yes. Oh, the nerve of her, as teachers on three continents had been wont to write in her report cards. Nervous, no. Kat wrote about shape-shifting demons and vampires for a living. Her first book had been an existential examination of the boundary lines of good and evil, of repression and desire, that just happened to also have a rollicking good plot, thank you very much. Also a superhot immortal demon hero. An erotic *Night Circus*, they'd called it. A literary *Discovery of Witches*. *Labyrinth* for grown-ups without the dancing muppets and the '80s blue eyeshadow. A midnight kingdom of blurred boundaries, shifting morals, and infinite peril.

No, she wasn't nairrrrvous, even if the moonlight cast strange silver shadows across the floor and the casement windows creaked in the wind as though a hand were shaking them, trying to find a way in. A draft slid across the back of Kat's neck, like an icy finger caressing the nape of her neck, a demon lover come to call. . . .

Ha. She'd given up on demon lovers along with unicorns.

Kat flopped down on the great canopy bed. The underside of the canopy was embroidered with the Kinloch coat of arms. Kat had no doubt Emma would tell her it was an unconvincing modern reproduction, but she had to admit the effect was good. There had been a time in her life—somewhere between Okinawa and Fort Bliss—when she would have thrilled to the romance of it. As she moved with her father from base to base, the medieval Scotland of her Karyn Black romance novels had felt much more real and permanent than the back seat of the school bus or yet another beige room in a beige apartment.

She hadn't read one of those in years. In her grad school years, it had all been Foucault and Derrida and a bit of Angela Carter for light reading. But now Kat found herself thinking nostalgically of those old bodice rippers, with the alpha male Scottish laird and the unnaturally plucky heroine who would bring him to his knees (often quite literally). *A Laird in Winter. Sweet Savage Laird. The Laird and the Lamb.* In those books, when the hero was a jerk, it was because he was suffering from Deep Personal Torment and qualms of conscience—not just because he was a jerk.

Sometimes there was no backstory. Sometimes a jerk was just a jerk. Like the asshole on the poster in the lobby.

Kill it o'clock? Please.

The worst of it was, his first book had been *good.* Not just "I'll read this because the *New York Times Book Review* says I should" good, but actually good. His characters—they were real, they were flawed. They felt and bled and did stupid things, not because they were stupid, but because that's what people do. They make mistakes and they double down and they get mired in predicaments they never intended, but can't figure out how to get out of.

Like a castle in Scotland in winter with no Wi-Fi, accompanied by Prep School Pollyanna and Redneck Martha Stewart.

Was it too late to catch the next flight out of here? Oh, wait. They didn't even have flights here. Just the ferry, which, apparently, only operated on odd Tuesdays when the ferryman felt like it.

Like the setup for an Agatha Christie novel. Only, if Morag were to be believed, with more ghosts and ghoulies and things that go bump in the night.

"No one's actually *seen* the White Lady," Morag had said meaningfully. "It's just the nairrrrrvous that say they can hear her moaning. There's some as belong at the castle and there's some as dinna. An' if ye dinna . . ."

Kat flopped over onto her side. Cliché, cliché, cliché. She was surrounded by clichés.

The move brought her nose to nose with the pamphlet on the bedside table. Oh Lord, not Brett Saffron Presley's *Just Do It! Anyone Can Write—But Not Like Me Because I'm Da Man.*

It wasn't. But it was almost as bad. One of those shiny self-pubbed jobbies with a dramatic picture of the roofline of the castle illuminated in shades of orange and black. *The Curse of Castle Kinloch* blared the cover, in lurid red letters.

Subtle.

Kat flipped idly through, looking for Morag's White Lady. Even by the standards of local ghost stories, it all felt a bit thin. Had the author gotten all her ideas from Karyn Black novels? There was the Norman conqueror who found his heart conquered by a local beauty (yep, pure *Laird and the Lamb* there), but in this version she murdered him (or, as Morag would undoubtedly say, murdairrrrrred him) as he slept the sotted sleep of the deflowerer (direct quote). Confused murdered Norman knight could be seen wandering the battlements, scratching his balls. (The book didn't say that.)

The battlements of the castle that, according to Emma, hadn't even been here till the mid-nineteenth century. Right. Nice one, ghost story author.

The island was taken over by a branch of the Kinlochs of Fife— whoever they were. Did they also have a pipe and a drum and fiddlers three? Was a fife called a fife because it came from Fife? Kat resolved not to ask Emma.

But here—Kat sat up straighter—here was the good bit. The castle crumbled into ruin. Something to do with Cromwell, whatever. The family line died out. And some good-for-nothing Englishman who'd made a fortune in—wait, what did that say?

Ah, condiments.

Whoever had the pamphlet printed had used an ornate, pseudo-Gothic font and really cheap ink, and the combination made the prose tough going. For a moment, Kat had harbored the joyous hope that the fortunes of the present Kinloch family had risen—ahem—through the sale of early Victorian prophylactics. But, no. The family fortunes were founded on a particular brand of Gentleman's Relish, which had been so relishalicious that the family had been able to sell the concern for a whopping great sum, buy a Scottish island, construct their own faux baronial castle, and go on to live the life of Lairds of the Manor.

Unfortunately for the populace at large, the son of the Relish King, one Edward Kinloch, had ideas about what it meant to be laird, with particular attention to such lairdly duties as the droit du seigneur, in which, the author of the pamphlet helpfully explained, the landowner deflowers the local village girls on their wedding night.

Not content with droiting his seigneur, Edward, aka Naughty

Ned, had turned to more inventive pleasures, turning the remains of the old medieval tower into an orgy pit. Because Ned liked to tart up his excesses with a sparkly coat of mysticism, it was known as the Obelisk, even though it was about as akin to an actual obelisk as Elizabeth Taylor was to Cleopatra.

The writer of the pamphlet dwelt lovingly on Ned's shenanigans, on the psychedelic mead he brewed specially, on the louche and aristocratic friends he invited for fantastical orgies, and his vast and inventive collection of Edwardian sex toys. It was, Kat thought, all pretty tame stuff once you dropped the over-the-top prose. Ned was nothing more than a randy Edwardian frat boy and no matter how you dressed it all up in costumes and fancy scenery and just a hint of the occult, rape was still rape.

He'd been nothing more than a bully who'd picked on women who didn't have the resources to fight back. And he'd brought his friends. He'd tossed those girls to them like gifts.

Kat's hands were curled like claws around the book, her dark-painted nails digging into the shiny laminate of the cover.

She took a deep breath, and then another. She wasn't those village girls. She was a modern woman. With very, very sharp nails. And stiletto heels. And a whip.

But that didn't mean that jerks like Ned didn't exist. Or that they didn't still exercise their own raw power, even if it was no longer dressed up in cravats and riding crops. Or that they couldn't destroy a life.

Kat forced herself to focus on the page in front of her. The picture was of one of Ned's orgies in the Obelisk. A fire blazed in a brazier in the middle of the room. The girl was being brought forward, robed in something long and diaphanous, a flower crown on her unbound hair. The men, in various states of inebriation, leered—but they pulled back at the same time.

Ned stood in the middle, holding a long staff in one hand, the firelight casting strange shadows across his face.

Whoever had done the woodcut prints had caught . . . something. Something raw and menacing and darkly sexy.

The prose was crap. The story was crap. But those woodcuts . . .

In the research briefing Emma had sent around, Ned was just another Edwardian playboy like his buddy, Edward, Prince of Wales, out for cheap thrills, a petty bully who got his kicks out of coercing the unwilling.

The man in the woodcuts . . . There was something else going on there. He seemed half-amazed, half-terrified by the forces he was attempting to command, Faust seduced and double-crossed, fallen prey to his own fantasies, pleasure mingled with terror.

And the woman—she wasn't the innocent lamb to the slaughter of the text. They were falling back from her, those drunk men, aroused and afraid at the same time. What was she? Who was she?

Kat's laptop lid was up before she'd even realized she'd crossed the room. She could half consciously hear the click of the keys as her thoughts clattered onto the screen. The village girl—not a victim, not an innocent patsy, but the repository of ancient power. The seventh daughter of a seventh daughter. Unaware of her own powers. Feeling the stirring of forces only she could control—if she could master them in time.

And Ned—what if this wasn't just a more entertaining way to pass the time than a game of cards? What if he'd gotten mixed up with the occult while at Oxford—or Cambridge—or wherever he'd gone, Emma would know. Maybe it had started with good intentions. Maybe he'd wanted to bring prosperity back to the blighted island. All it took was one sacred ceremony, something vaguely Wicker Man, just a bit of sexual excess to bring the crops on, everyone has fun, the fields flourish, all good, but it hadn't turned out that way, and the forces he'd raised demanded more and more and the darker pleasures called to him, trapping him, and only

Village Girl—damn, she had to give her a name, something—could defeat him, but first she'd have to fight her feelings for him, for the man who was still in there somewhere—or was he?

Kat sat back hard in her seat, drained and exhilarated, her cheeks flushed, her breath coming fast. There was nothing like the rush of writing down ideas for a new book, when it was still as pure and perfect as the first snow of winter before kids trod it to slush and dogs peed in it.

She hadn't been this excited about a story—hadn't seen a story so clearly—in years.

Slowly, reality returned, along with the cold chill from the casement window, which was doing things to the back of her neck again. This was not the book they were here to write. This was not a book Cassie and Emma would ever let her write. Emma would protest that wasn't what happened. Cassie would want to cutesy it up and tie up the ending in a neat bow, with everything solved and resolved. The proposal they had sent Rachelle had been true crime turned fiction, a historical murder mystery re-creating what had actually happened: not a battle of mythical forces. Even if the battle of mythical forces would make a much better book.

The sense of loss made Kat feel sick, physically sick.

Dammit, there was so much potential here and, like Kat's bodysuit, it was just wasted on present company.

What if she struck out on her own? Through the wavy glass of the casement, Kat could see the Obelisk on the hill, calling to her. Cassie and Emma couldn't do what she could do with the material; they didn't even want to, or else they'd be out there, prowling the grounds, making use of every minute they had. Emma was going to turn this into dry as dust bio-fic. She could probably make an orgy sound like a laundry list, so many bodices ripped per reveler. As for Cassie, she'd tart it up into adorable village antics with the little old ladies of the village coming up with a corny scheme to poison Naughty Ned with his own Gentleman's Relish, and probably a half-dozen comic relief subplots, and a gentle romance thrown in just for ballast.

Whereas in Kat's hands . . . A darkly erotic struggle. Ancient gods. Hidden powers. Lust and ritual and vengeance.

What if this was *the* book? The book she'd been waiting for? That first book—it had been like a fever. She'd poured all her hopes and fears and fantasies into it, with no idea that she was breaking genre lines or that, by rights, it didn't fit into any part of the market. She hadn't realized that its success meant that they'd want her to write it again and again and again. It was her brand, they'd told her, and with each sequel the covers had become kitschier and the plots more contrived and the sales smaller and she'd become smaller and smaller with it, a caricature of herself.

But now—she felt the old spark again. The magic. This was *the* book, she could tell. It was hers. It was calling to her.

Kat was already wearing black. She always wore black. All that was needed was to yank on a pair of black ankle boots and throw a black wrap on over her jumpsuit. The dark corridors of the castle welcomed her, as a long-lost lost daughter. Her feet danced nimbly over the uneven stone stairs, along the carpeted corridors. The great front door gave her a moment of pause, but the key was in the lock. Kat felt a wave of triumph as the door swung open, silently, as though it were beckoning her through.

Gravel crunched beneath her feet, then the wet squelch of grass. A formal garden lay between the castle and the Obelisk, boxwood hedges forming arcane patterns, statuary silvered by moonlight. A nymph presided over a bare fountain. Kat made her way by touch through the rows of shrubbery. Some idiot—and she knew exactly which—had installed Disney World lighting, making the Obelisk glow in the night, dimming the power of the moonlight.

Trust Mr. Kill It O'Clock not to recognize actual atmosphere when it was handed to him on a platter. There ought to have been torches flaring on either side of the door, casting flickering red light across the arrow slits. Instead, the tower was lit like Cinderella's castle on a Saturday night. All they needed was a bunch of hooded men in their orgy outfits singing "It's a Small World After All."

No. Kat shoved a jagged chunk of hair back behind her ear. She wasn't going to let Jerk Face ruin this for her. He wasn't going to ruin anything else for her ever again.

Just-Call-Me-Archie hadn't lied. The great man himself, Mr. Kill It O'Clock, was hard at work, or whatever it was he did. Through an artistically placed faux arrow slit, Kat could see the glow of his computer screen, the furious modernity of it at odds with the worn tapestries hanging on the walls.

Of course, he'd have a Mac in a medieval tower. Kat focused on the details to try to blot out the crawling feeling his physical presence gave her. It had been easier seeing his poster. He'd looked so douchey, so airbrushed and ridiculous, that it had been easy to forget how compelling he could be in person, with his hair mussed and glasses on for use rather than show. That was something the posters didn't show: the charisma. The pretense of harmlessness. He looked like a guy you could trust. *A guy you could trust to look out for himself*, Kat reminded herself.

Whatever he was working on, he was hunched over the keyboard with great focus. Kat was surprised by his dedication—rumor had it that his last book had been ghostwritten. She scrambled for a foothold, her fingers grasping the sill, trying to pull herself up far enough to see better.

That wasn't a Word file. That was . . . Goodreads?

As Kat grappled with the stone face of the tower, one of her dangling feet kicked something. She wasn't sure what it was—loose masonry?—but it sounded like the cannon at West Point on the Fourth of July.

Presley turned.

Kat dropped. Driven by sheer, atavistic panic, she veered left, running away from the tower, away from the view of that arrow slit, heading for the safety of the shrubbery. Women had run here before, pursued by men who meant to hurt them, men with the power to do anything they liked, and no law to hold them.

She craned her neck behind her, just to make sure no one was emerging from the Obelisk, no one was in pursuit, and immediately slammed into someone coming from the other side, someone large and solid who grabbed her by her upper arms as though she were as light as the mesh of her jumpsuit.

Kat struggled, kicking and bucking, and heard a very satisfying Scottish "oooph" as the hands holding her opened, leaving her sprawling inelegantly on the turf.

"Ye didna ha' to go and do that," gasped the man-mountain in front of her, clutching his sporran.

Kat blinked a few times, feeling the world snapping back into focus. No drunk revelers behind her ready to ravish her. No one about to sacrifice her in arcane rites. "You grabbed me."

"Ye ran into me." Slowly, carefully, Calum straightened, holding out a hand to her. "What are ye doing out at this time of night?"

Kat felt his broad, calloused palm close over hers. This was not a hand that spent its time poking at keyboards. This was a hand accustomed to hard, physical labor. The old toolbelt fantasy. Kat had never really felt it—she was more a seduced-by-Mephistopheles sort of girl—but Mephistopheles hadn't worked well for her. Maybe it was time to try something more . . . earthy.

Kat swayed toward him. "I could ask the same of you. Are you looking for your lover?"

"No. My sheep." There had been a reason all those romances of her childhood featured Scots. Even "mah sheep" sounded sexy in that accent. Perhaps it was the incomprehensibility that was part of the charm, the gender gap turned language gap. Can't understand 'em, have to have 'em.

"So what you're saying is . . ." Kat ran a finger up the thick linen of his shirt. "You're searching for something warm and woolly."

"Ye could say that." Politely but firmly, Calum removed her hand from his person. It might have been her imagination, but Kat thought he held it a moment longer than necessary as he said, in his deep Scottish voice, "I'll see ye back to the castle."

He didn't have the polished and plucked manscaped looks of a Jerk Face; his face was as craggy as the hills behind them, with the same wild charm. "What if I'm not ready to go in yet? You know what they say. The night is young."

"The night might be young," said Calum, and Kat could have sworn she saw the flicker of something resembling a smile, "but I'm not. Some of us have to be up with the coos."

Given the man had a sheep, Kat suspected the cows weren't just a metaphor. "I never said you had to stay with me," she said huskily.

Calum didn't take the bait. He stood, looking down at her. "A word of advice."

Kat looked up at him from under her fake eyelashes. "Go wild. Don't just confine yourself to a word. Make it a whole . . . sentence."

He did. "Ye dinna want to go walking the grounds by night."

That wasn't a sentence she wanted to hear. Kat tapped a finger lightly against his rock of a chest. "I'm not afraid of things that go bump in the night."

Behind Calum, the Obelisk glowed like a beacon. "Ye should be."

CHAPTER FOUR

Cassie

Excerpt from police interview with Mrs. Cassandra Parsons Pringle, 10 December 2022

DCI: [*thwack of thick stack of paper*] Mrs. Pringle, I have here the complete list of queries from your internet search history over the past two years.

PRINGLE: Oh my.

DCI: Fairly extensive, as you see. [*sound of shuffling papers*] Some rather mundane—can you tame a squirrel, how do you pronounce "acai," what is TikTok—and some rather more extraordinary. How much blood comes out when an eyeball is stabbed. How many peach pits to extract a lethal dose of cyanide. How do I access the dark web. Can the FBI subpoena my internet search history. [*brief pause*] I assume you discovered the answer to that question is yes?

PRINGLE: [*laughter*] I guess I should have cleared my search history?

DCI: How long does it take to suffocate a 270-pound man with asthma. Symptoms of polonium poisoning. And my personal favorite—force exerted on human cranium by a hundred gallons of buttercream frosting dropped fifty feet.

PRINGLE: Look, Detective Chief Inspector. I'm a mystery writer. Surely you understand that I kill people for a *living*? [*laughter*] I mean, not in real life, of course! In my books. I'm always looking for new ways to commit murder. My readers expect fresh ideas. Originality. They want to be surprised.

DCI: How to eliminate blood residue from linoleum?

PRINGLE: [*laughter*] Well, you've got to get away with it afterward, you know. Or else what's the point?

DCI: Indeed. [*sound of shuffling papers*] What about this, Mrs. Pringle? Last March, it seems you took a particular interest in methods available for chemical combustion using common household materials.

PRINGLE: Oh, that wasn't for my *books*. That was my son's science fair project. He won first place!

DCI: [*brief pause*] Congratulations.

PRINGLE: Of course, there was just a *teeny* bit of damage to the school gymnasium, but luckily my husband is both a volunteer firefighter *and* a house builder, so it all worked out in the end.

DCI: Your husband?

PRINGLE: Chip. Yes. He's wonderful. So supportive of my career. So handy around the house. And the kids! We're just very, very, very happy. Very happy together. So very, incredibly happy right now.

DCI: Hmm. Yes. [*sound of shuffling papers*] So you wouldn't be thinking of poisoning him, then?

PRINGLE: Chip? Poison *Chip*? Oh my goodness, no. No, no. The father of my children? All six of them? [*laughter*] *Whatever* gave you that idea?

DCI: Because you seem to have conducted extensive research on a wide range of poisons, Mrs. Pringle, and how they can be baked into irresistibly delicious treats.

PRINGLE: [*laughter*] Well, naturally. That's my favorite plot device. I assume you've read my Little Bake Shop series?

DCI: I'm afraid I haven't had the pleasure.

PRINGLE: What? Not even *The Cupcake That Sat by Itself*?

DCI: [*brief pause*] What exactly *is* a cupcake, Mrs. Pringle?

WEDNESDAY, DECEMBER 7
Two days before the murder . . .

A SHARP KNOCK rattled Cassie's bedroom door, just as she closed her laptop in frustration.

Yesterday evening had summoned a flood of emails into her inbox. She'd replied to one editor suggesting some minor tweaks to the latest Little Bake Shop cover (*Maybe the blood-red frosting on the wedding cake is just a bit overbaked? Ha ha! No pun intended!*), emailed another editor about the sample clips of audiobook narrators for the upcoming Moggies, Mocha, and Murder novel (*The second one really nails Agatha's knowing meow, don't you think?*), and begged her agent to ask for a deadline extension on the next Farmers' Market mystery (*Och aye, we're just up to our necks in research right now, ha ha! And I've never asked for extra time before, remember*).

None of these emails had gone through yet.

And not a single word had arrived from her husband.

"Who is it?" she called out, more brusquely than she intended.

The knob rattled. Kat's voice muffled through the thick wood. "It's *me*, who do you think? Could you open this damn thing?"

Cassie sighed and rose from the antique wooden chair—at least it *looked* antique, kind of Chippendale-ish, burgundy damask seat, Emma would know for certain—to unlock the door. Kat stalked in, wearing her everyday black leather pants and stiletto ankle boots, teamed with a shiny black vinyl bustier. She'd gathered her hair in a messy bun high on her head, and her black eyeliner was a little shaky.

"What, aren't you dressed yet?" she snarled at Cassie.

Cassie gathered together the edges of her dressing gown. "It's only seven o'clock."

"Well, for those of us who couldn't sleep last night, it's pretty damn late."

"I didn't sleep, either. Not much, anyway."

Kat glanced at the laptop on Cassie's desk. Cassie couldn't be sure, but her eyes might have softened, ever so slightly. "No word from home?" she asked.

"Not since dinnertime yesterday. Do you think maybe they turn off the Wi-Fi at night?"

"That's the stupidest thing I've ever heard. What, to save electricity?"

Cassie picked up her phone from the bedside table and saw a news alert from the *New York Times*, something about a congressional hearing for a politician she'd never heard of. Nothing else, not a single text. Of course, it was still the middle of the night in North Carolina. She should be glad! No news was good news, right?

"I know you don't like me, Kat," she said softly, still staring at the screen, which showed one tiny bar of cell coverage, "but you don't need to be so mean."

Kat crossed her arms beneath the thick underwire of the bustier, shoving her breasts chinward. "Look, I'm sorry. I don't *not* like you. Honest. It's just that I don't . . . you know . . . *like* you."

"That doesn't make any sense."

"Well, I'm undercaffeinated, too. So sue me."

"Don't they have coffee in the kitchen?"

Kat made a face. "Just that instant Nescafé crap."

"Oh dear." Cassie forced some sympathy into her voice.

"Like they're trying to poison us or something. You'd think—" Kat caught herself, like she was about to make some conversation and remembered just in time how much she loathed everything about Cassie.

Especially her conversation.

I don't not *like you. It's just that I don't* like *you.*

Well, what could you say to that? They weren't exactly peas in a pod, were they? Cassie put a self-conscious hand on her frizzy hair, mostly confined within the twists of a plaid scrunchie. On her feet, she wore a pair of plaid sherpa-lined slippers she'd found on clearance at Lands' End.

Kat would probably rather slit her own throat than wear a pair of plaid Lands' End slippers.

"Anyway," said Kat. "Last night, while I was trying to get my brain to sleep, I couldn't help thinking that to get this thing started, we really, *really* need to find that *supposed* secret tunnel"—she lifted her hands and made quote marks around *secret tunnel*—"that *supposedly* leads to the tower. That way we could snoop on our boy BSP without anyone noticing."

"I found the castle floor plans online and downloaded them to my computer," said Cassie, "but I don't remember seeing anything that looked like a secret tunnel."

"Well, open your laptop and let's have a look."

Cassie looked to the floor. "They're still on my desktop computer at home. I meant to print them out and bring them along, but—well, I was so busy finishing up the laundry and the school lunches and cooking up all the casseroles and putting them in the color-coded containers—"

"All right, all right. So we'll just find a set of floor plans here. They must have them lying around. The Historical Society in the village, I'll bet."

"I agree. But I just don't know how we go about hunting around for the castle floor plans without arousing everyone's suspicion."

"Easy," said Kat. "We lie."

"Lie?"

"That's right. We go into the village and tell everyone we're looking for decent coffee—"

"I'd rather have tea."

"Oh, for Pete's sake. Of course you would. So tell them you're looking for—I don't know—an internet café. So you can catch up with the rug rats back home."

"What about Emma?"

"You snooze, you lose." Kat pivoted on a stiletto and started for the door. "Anyway, meet me downstairs in five minutes. I can't wait any longer."

"I'll be ready," said Cassie.

Kat swung the door open to reveal Emma, hand poised in the knock position.

"Holy crap!" Kat snapped. "What in the hell are you doing here?"

Emma looked from Kat to Cassie and back again. "What are *you* doing here?"

"Conspiring against you, obviously."

Cassie caught a glimpse of Emma's wan face over Kat's shoulder. Underneath her eyes, a pair of purple shadows gave her a bruised, fragile air. Like Kat, she was fully dressed, although Emma wore a frayed Barbour jacket over wide-wale corduroys the color of rust and a pair of green Hunter wellies.

"Is everything all right, Emma?" Cassie asked anxiously. "Has something happened?"

"I couldn't sleep," Emma said. "Is anyone up for a walk into the village?"

OUTSIDE, CASSIE DREW the damp, chilly air into her lungs. Everything smelled of wet rocks and wet grass and wet sheep, with just a hint of the sea underneath. "Ah, Scotland!" she sang out. "Isn't it just like—well, Scotland?"

"I was about to say it's like Maine." Emma breathed deep next to her. "Maine in August. Oh, look. Isn't that the dog?"

"What dog?" said Kat.

Emma pointed to the floppy-eared sheepdog, loping across the short brown grass toward them. "That one. Archie's dog. You know what he said. If you can't find him, look for Loren?"

"Or if you see Loren—" Cassie began.

"There he is!" exclaimed Emma. "Crossing that fence over there."

"What do we do?" said Cassie.

"Just wave," Kat said. "Wave and hurry on, before he catches up."

"But that would be rude."

"Look, *you're* the one who hates lying," said Kat.

"Me, too," said Emma. "I'm a terrible liar."

Kat threw up her hands. "The two of you write fiction, remember? *Fiction!*"

"I agree with Cassie," Emma said. "It would be rude to keep walking without saying hello. It would be . . . *suspicious.*"

Loren reached them, tongue lolling. Cassie bent to offer her fingers. The dog's wet nose bumped her knuckles and Cassie felt an ache between her ribs. She'd left Sally, her four-year-old Havanese, at home with Chip and the kids. Had they remembered to feed her in the special bowl? Had Chip let her sleep on the bed?

There was no telling. Chip hadn't texted since yesterday morning.

"I don't think we have a choice," said Kat.

Archie came striding toward them, one hand raised. He wore one of those flat woolen caps low on his brow and a pair of dirty wellies identical to Emma's, like he'd just stepped off the set of *Midsomer Murders*. His smile broadened between his ruddy cheeks. "You're up early, ladies! Enjoying the country air, are you?"

"We're headed down to the village," Emma said.

"That's right," Kat said swiftly. "I'm looking for coffee, Cassie needs a decent internet connection, and Emma . . . um . . . Emma wants to . . ."

"Emma wants to visit the Historical Society in the village," Cassie put in. Her cheeks went up in flame; she hoped Archie didn't notice.

Thank goodness he'd turned to Emma.

"But I'm afraid the Historical Society's only open on alternate Thursdays," he told her.

Emma didn't miss a beat. "Actually, I was hoping I could convince the director to open it for us. Since we're so pressed for time and everything."

Cassie beamed at her, not that she noticed.

Archie lifted his hand to adjust the brim of his cap. "Weeelll," he said, an unexpectedly Scottish noise, looking off in the general direction of the village, "that'd be Bruce, and I expect you'd find him down the pub at this hour, having a wee breakfast."

"Ooh, there's a pub?" Emma said eagerly. "How old?"

"Old enough." Archie winked at Cassie. "Moreover, I do believe it's got an internet connection."

"You CALL THIS a village?" Kat said. "It's literally three buildings."

"Not *literally* three buildings," Cassie said. "There are at least ten, by my count."

"Houses don't count. I need civilization. I need Starbucks."

"Starbucks? You've got to be kidding me," said Emma. "We're in Scotland. You can drink your fancy mocha matcha macchiato whatevers back home."

Cassie stared down the row of buildings. Kat did have a point—there wasn't much to the village, though the stone cottages were certainly picturesque. Almost *too* picturesque, she thought. Like somebody's idea of what a tiny Scottish hamlet should look like. She spotted a painted sign hanging near one of the doorways, depicting a saturnine man who held a small, frightened sheep in his arms.

"Look, this must be the pub," she said. "The Laird and the Lamb, I think."

Kat pressed a hand against her chest. "It can't be," she murmured.

"All right, girls." Cassie rummaged into her tote bag and produced her phone. "Picture time!"

Emma groaned. "Do we have to?"

"Yes, we have to. It's an adorable shot! With that authentic pub sign in the background? Come on, what could be cuter?"

"I don't do cute," grumbled Kat, but she stepped obediently into frame behind Cassie and aimed a seductive smile at the camera. Emma stuck her head toward Cassie's other shoulder and bared her teeth.

Just as Cassie found the right angle and pressed the red circle, the door behind them swung open and a man strode out of the pub.

They spun around in unison. He was tall and square-jawed, and his cheeks were still pink from the warmth of the pub. A worn macintosh stretched across his thick shoulders; a paper bag dangled from one hand.

Like Chip, Cassie thought. For an instant, she experienced a visceral surge of joy.

At the sight of their three inquisitive American faces, the man's eyebrows shot up.

"Rawr," said Kat.

"Don't you ever give it a rest?" hissed Emma.

With a couple of fingers, he touched his flatcap—exactly like the one Archie had been wearing—and muttered a few words before hurrying on. Cassie grabbed the door just before it banged shut behind him.

"Good morning to you, too!" Kat called, over her shoulder, and then—in her outdoor voice, just as they crossed the threshold—"*Asshole.*"

Everyone looked up. The air fell silent.

Cassie glanced around the interior—warm wooden beams, bar along one side, darts on the wall, faint odor of stale beer and fried food. A pair of men hunched over their plates at a table in the corner; a few more diners scattered around the other tables, another one at the bar. A red-haired woman sat by herself with a thick novel and a pint of dark ale.

Cassie had the feeling Kat was going to be disappointed in the latte service.

Emma cleared her throat. "We're looking for a man named Bruce," she announced.

Three hands went up, including those of both men at the corner table.

"Bruce the director of the Historical Society," Emma said.

The hands went down, the shoulders shrugged, the faces returned to breakfast. From the bar came a woman's cheerful voice, just a hint of a brogue. "I'm afraid he's already been and gone, dearies. But ye're welcome to stay and have a bite to eat for yer trouble. Jamie, love, be a dear and move yer bluidy carcass to one side."

The man at the bar stood and grinned. "Anything you say,

Fiona." He moved his plate and his coffee cup down two places to the right.

Fiona was tall and curvy, wearing snug jeans and a plain apron and an air of jaunty competence. Her curling gold hair was streaked with ginger and pulled back in a ponytail from her fresh, round face. Cassie wanted to bake her a muffin and ask her how she kept her hair from frizzing in this damp. Instead she set her tote bag on the counter and thanked the man who'd made room.

"It's no trouble." He wiped his hand on a napkin and stuck it out. "Jamie MacDougal, the veterinarian of Kinloch."

"My goodness, is everyone on this island named MacDougal?" Cassie exclaimed, shaking his hand.

"Incest alert," muttered Kat.

Cassie kicked her foot underneath the bar. "I'm Cassie Pringle. My best friends, Kat and Emma." She waved her hand at them and settled on the wooden stool.

Jamie made a salute down the bar. "You'll be the Americans staying at the castle, then?"

"How'd you guess?" Cassie said, in her deepest southern accent.

Jamie's mouth twitched. "Welcome to Kinloch, then. Fiona, why don't you bring these lassies the full Scottish, aye? And don't skimp on the black pudding."

"Och, I wouldna dare," Fiona said, grinning. She turned for the kitchen.

Kat waved her arm. "Wait! Before you go! I'll have a venti triple vanilla latte with a drizzle of caramel, extra sugar, extra foam."

Fiona's eyebrows went up. She set one hand on her hip, dangling the dishrag, and took in Kat's eyeliner, the thick black satin choker around her pale neck. The bustier, which was just visible underneath the coat Kat had left unbuttoned. Cassie felt herself blushing, even though it wasn't her own skin on display.

"So that'll be a coffee with milk, aye?" Fiona chirped.

• • •

"You have to understand," said Jamie, "the people here are very sensitive about the history of the island. Naughty Ned, he's not just a panto villain to us. What he did to the families here—him and his depraved London friends—the poor lasses—" He shook his head and turned to his coffee cup. "It was a reign of terror, that's what it was. Poor Lady Ned did her best to help, that's certain. An angel of mercy. But there's no keeping a demon like that from what he wanted. When he was murdered, why, Kinloch rejoiced, though you won't hear such things in the official histories."

"So how do you know about it?" Emma asked. "I mean, if I'm not mistaken, that accent of yours isn't Scottish. Midlands, if I had to take a guess. Yorkshire?"

He smiled and shrugged. "You pick up stories, living here."

Next to Cassie, Kat tucked into her breakfast with gusto. Cassie touched the black pudding with her fork. "I'm sure it was awful. Terrible. But that's why we're here. We want to bring his crimes to light. Give the—uh—the poor lasses he injured some justice."

"You'll not find much. The women themselves are all dead, of course. And most of the records were destroyed, if they ever existed."

"But surely there are archives somewhere, right?" said Emma.

"I don't doubt there are. But sometimes the truth doesn't lie in the archives or the newspaper articles, Miss Endicott. The legacy of Ned's wickedness lives on in the stories of the survivors, passed down from mother to daughter. And you won't find many who will give up their secrets to strangers."

"But the building of the Obelisk, for example—"

"I'm afraid most people would like to forget the Obelisk even exists," said Jamie, in a chillier voice.

Kat lifted a colorful trifold brochure from the pile stacked at the bar's edge and dangled it from her purple-tipped fingers. *Coming Soon!* it announced. *Enter the Erotic World of Naughty*

Ned with the Kinloch Experience. "Really? Because I kind of got the impression that Kinloch *revels* in all this history. Naughty Ned and his naughty ways."

"Och, that's your American Presley fellow," said Jamie. "I don't deny Kinloch needs the tourists, more's the pity. People left in droves during Ned's time. Then the war came and killed the few lads who'd remained. For years—decades—Kinloch lay fallow. But this idea of turning Kinloch's terrible past into some kind of voyeuristic amusement park . . ." He shook his head. "I'd say not everyone's happy to have old wounds opened."

Cassie set her knife and fork on the edge of her plate and turned to Jamie. He had a pleasant, pink-cheeked face—ears sticking out, light brown hair in a curly mess atop his head, good nature beaming from his hazel eyes. Your friendly neighborhood veterinarian, kind to animals and people alike. But she thought she also caught a shade of wariness in those eyes.

He stared a little too long at each of them, a little too bright.

Fiona walked by with a pot of coffee. Kat stuck out her cup for a refill, then Emma. Emma added a drizzle of cream and stirred in slow circles.

"So," she said slowly, "if we want to know more about the real Kinloch and its history, who should we talk to?"

Jamie rose from his stool and pulled a ten-pound note from his wallet, which he laid on the bar with a nod in Fiona's direction. He picked up his cap—the same darned cap every man in the village seemed to be wearing, Cassie thought; maybe they'd bought a whole box of them on the mainland and shipped them over on the ferry.

Smiling, he fixed the cap on his head and gazed at Emma. "If you really want truth instead of titillation," he said, "I'd say Archie's your man."

CHAPTER FIVE

Emma

Excerpt from police interview with Miss Emerson (Emma) Endicott, 10 December 2022

DCI: [*sound of chair legs scraping floor*] So, Ms. Endicott, I'm curious about something. For someone such as yourself who is so keen on historical accuracy, why Castle Kinloch? There are far older castles in all of Scotland with unsolved murders lurking around every loch. Castles with their historical bits still intact.

ENDICOTT: Well, there's the writers' retreat that gave Kinloch the edge when we were deciding. There were several in the running.

DCI: Would you happen to have that list handy?

ENDICOTT: Um, er, not here. [*pause*] You should ask Cassie. She was the one who arranged everything so she probably knows.

DCI: Yes. That would be Mrs. Pringle. [*sound of shuffling papers*] The one who, and I quote, "She knows all about murder—you know, how to kill someone and get away with it." Is that correct?

ENDICOTT: In her books, I meant. [*sound of chair creaking*] Could you add that in, please? Accuracy is always important.

DCI: [*heavy sigh*] What else does Mrs. Pringle add to your collaboration?

ENDICOTT: She's from the American South so she's really good at making sure that two people in a romantic relationship in our novel aren't too closely related. For American audiences, at least. Consanguinity was a mainstay throughout European royal families for centuries. And we all know about the Hapsburg jaw. That was the direct result . . .

DCI: Consanguinity?

ENDICOTT: Marrying a biological relative. For instance, with everyone named MacDougal here, my guess is there would have been . . .

DCI: Please stop.

ENDICOTT: I'm sorry. Are you related to . . .

DCI: No. But I have the start of a megrim from your . . .

ENDICOTT: You're a Macintosh, right? Nothing to do with the apple although a lot of people assume because of the name it originated in Scotland and not in Canada back in 1811. . . .

DCI: [*audible gritting of teeth*] Ms. Endicott, you attended Bowdoin College, correct?

ENDICOTT: [*pause*] Yes. And the correct pronunciation is BOH-don.

DCI: Thank you for that. [*sighs*] As a recipient of the Endicott scholarship for lacrosse. Any relationship to you?

ENDICOTT: Same family. [*small cough*] Different line.

DCI: You studied creative writing, graduating with stellar marks despite playing women's lacrosse all four years, including team captain for your final two.

ENDICOTT: Is that a question or a statement? I make a living being specific with details, so I need clarification. I find your method of interrogation confusing.

DCI: [*heavy sigh accompanied by agitated paper shuffling*]
Are any of my aforementioned statements incorrect?

ENDICOTT: No.

DCI: For additional funds, you also spent weekends as the lead
singer with a cover band you formed, the Brontës. [*long silence*]
Yes, Ms. Endicott, that is a question.

ENDICOTT: Yes. We were in demand for summer weddings
because of our sensitive remastering of Loreena McKennitt and
the Decemberists, minus the historical reenactments—although
if it had been up to me . . .

DCI: Did you know the deceased, Mr. Presley, at Bowdoin? You
both attended at the same time.

ENDICOTT: [*sound of rustling corduroy and creaking chair
seat*] Yes. [*clearing of throat*] I believe he may have been in a
few of my writing classes.

DCI: That's all? Just a casual acquaintance?

ENDICOTT: From what I remember. [*high-pitched chuckle*]
That was a long time ago. You know how that is.

DCI: Actually, Ms. Endicott, I don't. I remember everything.

WEDNESDAY, DECEMBER 7
Two days before the murder . . .

AFTER THREE MORE insufferable selfies orchestrated by
Cassie on the way back to the castle (each posed with a
different sheep), Emma sloshed on ahead with her Hunter boots,
easily overtaking Kat in her hooker footwear and Cassie, who was
too polite to leave Kat behind.

Emma's boots were at least fifteen years old, and true to the brand, the lining had held through all that time. Until now. A Scottish winter apparently was their Waterloo, and the lining had finally given way to a hole from which her big toe could protrude. It was currently cutting into her skin, propelling her to move quickly. Just in case anybody asked why she wasn't walking with her two "besties." She'd rather choke on haggis.

To keep her mind off the pain, she began singing out loud, uncaring who might hear. Music had always been the one thing that remained a constant source of needed distraction throughout her life. As a child huddled under a mound of blankets in her freezing bedroom during a Massachusetts January because they couldn't afford to keep the heat on at night, she'd sing along with the small hand-me-down radio by the side of her bed until she passed out from exhaustion. Through the inevitable and thoroughly petty high school dramas it had been the never-ending reel of Broadway show tunes memorized from singing the lead in the annual theater productions. And then through her first major and demoralizing heartbreak, she'd spent her hard-earned money on a five-disc CD set she'd found in a discount bin of her local Target of the most depressing love songs ever written so she could wallow in the music instead of in the sense of loss and sorrow that had threatened to take her under.

Emma began singing out loud the words to the earworm song that had been stuck in her head all day, something old by Creedence Clearwater Revival often played on the Sirius classic rock station she most frequently listened to. When she had Wi-Fi. She had to slow her pace as she walked, stepping high to avoid the sheep paddies hidden between tufts of grass. "Wellll, don't go round tonight, 'cause it's bound to take your liiiiife, there's a bad moose on the right . . ."

A loud groan came from behind her. "For the millionth time,

Emma," shrieked Kat, "those aren't the correct lyrics! It's 'bad moon on the rise.' I don't know what's worse, your inability to recall the right words of a song or your skill at voice texting. Either way, you're a total fail."

Emma swung around. "Well, at least I know how to dress so I don't look like I'm for sale. Word of advice—don't hang out for too long on any street corners. People will get the wrong idea."

"Girls!" cautioned Cassie, looking around the fortunately deserted pasture. "Keep it down. We're besties, remember? No need for name-calling. I think you should both apologize. A hug might even be in order."

Emma looked at Kat with matching horror reflected in the other woman's eyes. Kat began backing away, nearly losing her balance as she slipped on the edge of an impressive splat of sheep dung. "Actually," Kat said, "I was planning on heading back to the village to see if I can find Bruce and ask him nicely to let me into the Historical Society."

Cassie gave a little squeal of excitement. "That's a great idea, Kat! Why don't we all go together . . ."

"Sorry—can't," Emma interrupted. "I need to find Archie to see what else I can find out about Naughty Ned and the undocumented history of Kinloch Castle."

With an abrupt wave, she limped away from her two companions in the direction of the castle. If she were lucky—which hadn't been the case so far, but a girl could hope—maybe she could discover everything they needed to know so that they could leave sooner than expected. Despite all the uncertainties in her life, the one thing with which she was completely convinced was that her limit on faking being besties with two women she hardly knew and barely liked was fast approaching.

• • •

According to Morag's directions, Emma followed the path leading from the kitchen door around the back of the castle toward the Obelisk. Morag said the garden would be surrounded by a maze of hedges and situated between the two buildings and that's where Emma could find Archie tending to the bees. This last bit of information had surprised Emma. He didn't seem to be the type of person to consider beekeeping as part of his job description as estate manager. It seemed too . . . intimate. Too hands-on. Not that she knew anything about estate management. Or Archie for that matter. She made a mental note to add both subjects to her long list of things she needed to research.

Loren appeared between a gap in the hedge, her thick mane of white and gray fur wearing a halo of water droplets. A long fringe of hair hid her eyes, but the lolling pink tongue barely disguised what Emma was sure was a smile. She held out the back of her hand to the dog, who eagerly licked it in greeting and acceptance, something with which Emma was well-acquainted. Her family had always housed a menagerie of cast-off dogs, as if the unspoken agreement in their extended circle of family and neighbors was that the Endicott household was the repository of all things unwanted, too worn, or too old for anyone else.

She leaned over to scratch the dog behind each of its fluffy ears, a deep rumble of gratitude vibrating under her fingers. "I already like you better than anyone else here," she whispered. Which wasn't unusual. After college, she'd discovered that dogs were a lot more loyal and dependable than most people.

She stood then looked down at her new best friend. "Can you take me to Archie?"

Loren obediently turned back through the hedge opening and began walking, leading Emma along the perimeter path. The dog's lumbering gait reminded her of a bear, but its gray-and-white markings along with its thick and fluffy cankles looked a lot like the pictures of Cassie's Havanese, Sally. Except Loren was bigger. Much, much bigger. Emma had made the mistake of asking to see a photo, and Cassie had obliged with showing her an entire album of the small dog on her phone. Emma had hastily excused herself to use the ladies' room before Cassie could start on the photos of her six (six!) children.

She followed Loren's adorable backside with its wagging shaggy tail until they'd reached a small greenhouse, its glass walls and roof spotted with the incessant drizzle, hiding whatever grew within. At its side, the view unhindered by hedges, were rows of dormant trenches hiding their spring bounty. The structure was late Victorian, Emma decided, its wavy glass held intact by wrought-iron girders lending it historical authenticity. At least that was one authentic thing at Kinloch.

The garrrrrrden, as Morag had explained, supplied most of the vegetables, herbs, flowers, and honey to the castle, and she and Archie were the main caretakers. The old woman hadn't come right out and said it, but from the look in her rheumy eyes it was clear that if Emma so much as stepped on a single leaf, there would be consequences.

On the far edge of the garden sat a long row of oblong wooden bee boxes suspended above the ground on a legged platform. A slanted roof above them shielded the boxes from the elements, giving them the cozy look of a neighborhood street.

Archie was at one end of the row, stacking small plastic freezer containers with lids. Tucking a couple under each arm, he straightened, giving her a warm smile. "I hope I'm not disturbing you," she said, returning his smile. She felt at ease around him, something she never did around members of the opposite sex, and let her shoulders drop a bit. Maybe it was the mud-crusted wellies he wore, or the worn Barbour jacket that might even be older than her own. Or maybe it was the kind and intelligent green eyes that smiled with the rest of his face as he approached.

"Not at all," he said, stopping in front of her while Loren ran around them in circles as if they were two stray sheep needing to be herded. "I was just checking on my girls."

Emma's brows rose. "Your girls?"

"My honeybees. All the workers are female, you know."

"I didn't, but not surprising." She added honeybees to her long mental list of research topics.

His lips twitched. "Yes, well, the girls work hard all year long. They must shake and shiver around the queen throughout the winter to keep her warm. It's essential to the survival of the hive that she survive."

"And where are the males?"

"If they survive until winter, they become drains on the hive's food stores and are ejected from the hive."

"That's brutal. But understandable."

Archie's brow lifted, his eyes glinting with amusement. "You're not familiar with the intimate lives of bees, I gather?"

"I can't say that I am. I wish I'd brought my notepad so I could take notes."

"Oh, I don't think you'll be needing that. It's rather memorable." He shifted the containers under his arms then indicated that she follow him along the path toward the greenhouse. "The drones—the male bees—have one purpose and one purpose only. They don't have stingers so they can't protect the queen, and even though they're bigger than the workers, they don't do any pollinating."

"So, what's left? Hanging around the hive drinking beer all day and watching football?"

He raised that infernal eyebrow again. "I'm sure you can think of one more thing where they might be of use."

Her cheeks flamed and not just because she'd missed the obvious, but also because she was discussing sex—although that among apians—with an exceptionally attractive man. Who was gay, according to Kat. There was just something about his smile that made it very difficult to forget that little detail. And to not act like a twelve-year-old with a schoolgirl crush.

"The sole reason for drones to exist is to mate with the queen. They wait around for the day a newly hatched queen will leave the hive for her maiden flight where she will mate with as many as she can. And when the deed is done, the endophallus of each lucky drone falls off and the poor little man dies."

"Endophallus?"

"His, um, er, todger."

Despite her burning cheeks, Emma burst out laughing. "That's horrible. But also somehow . . . fitting. I mean, well, because, well, they . . ."

"Because they're not productive members of their society the way we humans perceive it to be?" Archie laughed. "'Bare Virtue can't make Nations live, In Splendor; they, that would revive' . . ."

"'A Golden Age, must be as free, for Acorns, as for Honesty,'" Emma finished.

Archie gave her an appreciative grin. "Impressive. So, you're familiar with Mandeville's *Fable of the Bees*?"

"Private girls' school education, I'm afraid." She didn't feel the need to add that she had been a scholarship girl, offered solely on merit—and because a long-dead Endicott had left the school a substantial endowment. "We're not all ignorant savages across the pond, you know."

With a mocking bow, he said, "I stand corrected."

Emma grinned. "Going back to Mandeville, if you agree with his theory, that would make Mr. Presley the island's benefactor, right?"

Archie's demeanor changed abruptly to one of businesslike seriousness. "So you really are one of his biggest fans, then."

She regretted having said that earlier and did her best to back-pedal. "I was just assuming that because Presley owned Kinloch he was responsible for all the improvements and upkeep of the island and the buildings."

"As I'm sure you're aware, Miss Private School Education, one should never assume. Mr. Presley is only leasing the land for ten years, in which time we are hoping to have made enough to fund the next phase of the castle's revitalization."

Emma's cheeks flamed as she recalled her sixth-grade teacher, Mrs. Anderson, snapping at every student who dared to use the dreaded word "assume"—because when one assumed, one made an ass out of "u" and "me."

Emma nodded as she willed her face to return to a normal color. "I see. I'll admit to being surprised because all the information about the castle and the writers' retreat more or less implied that Mr. Presley was the new laird. That he had purchased not just the land, but also the title."

"I agree that it's all very misleading. Presumably to make Mr. Presley appear more authentic and thus persuade interested parties to spend more money for the experience. It's apparently an effective marketing tool since you and your friends are here."

They had reached the greenhouse as Loren made one more lap around them before settling down on her haunches by the door. "If you don't mind," Archie said, indicating the handle. There was a key in the lock with a dangling ring of other, mismatched keys hanging from it. "I've already unlocked it—just open it if you would."

Emma did as instructed before moving aside. "Stay," he said as he went inside. She wasn't sure if he meant her or the dog, but they both waited obediently.

Undeterred, Emma asked, "If Mr. Presley isn't the laird, then who is?"

Archie had moved to the far side of the greenhouse where an ancient freezer sat next to a freestanding sink. He stuck one of the boxes inside the freezer before unceremoniously dumping the rest into the sink along with a healthy squirt of dish soap.

When he didn't respond, Emma rushed in to fill the silence. "I bet it's all buried in paperwork somewhere. I imagine it's some gallant philanthropist with a soft spot for decaying Scottish history. Or a Russian oligarch. They're buying up real estate everywhere it seems."

"That they are. Now, if you will just excuse me for a moment." He turned on the faucet, allowing it to run for a bit before shutting it off. "Sorry—Morag always scolds me for not cleaning the grease pattie boxes after feeding the bees."

"Grease patties?" Emma asked.

"Yes." Archie dried his hands on a towel wrapped around the freezer's door handle. "They help supply minerals to our bees over the winter in addition to keeping off those nasty mites. Doesn't sound appealing to us, but to bees it's quite a delicacy. Or so they've told me."

"You talk to the bees," Emma said, unable to keep the smile from her voice.

"One must to be a dutiful and humble beekeeper." He finally noticed that Emma was speaking to him through the doorway. "I didn't mean for you to stay outside—just Loren. Morag keeps her medicinal garden growing in here, and some of the plants are quite poisonous to animals. And to humans. It's why Loren isn't allowed in, and neither are the bees. Wouldn't do to have the bees pollinating the belladonna and producing poison honey, would it now?"

"Probably not a good idea." Emma stepped inside, taking in the rows of shelves and tables with pots of varying sizes, each containing indistinguishable plants growing in robust profusion in the protected environment of the greenhouse. "Wasn't Naughty Ned killed by a belladonna overdose?"

Archie leaned against one of the metal shelves, his arms crossed over his chest. "That's what they say."

"That doesn't mean that's what *actually* happened. My, um, friends and I are here to dig for the facts and tell the real story."

Archie straightened and began walking back toward the door. "Well, if it's information about the poison garden you're needing, you'll have to talk with Morag about that—she's quite the expert. As you have no doubt already discovered, some poisons can be rather beneficial in small doses, yet deadly in larger doses. Morag knows the difference."

"Good to know," Emma said with a nervous chuckle. "Hopefully she doesn't get confused when she's making our food."

Archie didn't return her smile as he pulled open the door before following her outside.

EMMA SAT AT the small table in the drawing room along with Cassie and Kat where their lunch of neeps and tatties (along with a "wee dram of whisky" poured by Calum) had been served. Cassie was saying something about castle floor plans that she'd been unable to locate, but Emma hardly heard. She had a full-blown blood blister on her toe from the torn lining in her boot and she could barely see straight from the pain of it. She'd had to swap into her loafers that were the same vintage as the boots sans any holes, but the damage to her feet had already been done.

"Are you feeling all right?" Cassie asked her, already digging into her ubiquitous quilted tote. "I've got Tylenol and Advil as well as an assortment of bandages in all sizes. And Neosporin. I've also got Tums, stool softener, gum, a bottle of Gatorade, and a roll of duct tape. There's more upstairs in my big bag if you need anything else."

"Okay, Mary Poppins," Kat said. "How about some more of that whisky? Kilt Man was a little stingy on the portion size."

Ignoring Kat, Emma said, "If I could have one of the larger Band-Aids I'd appreciate it." Emma tried not to cry as Cassie placed the entire box of bandages in her hand along with a single-wrapped piece of chocolate "for being so brave." There was something so motherly about Cassie's entire demeanor that made Emma almost forget that she didn't especially like Cassie. Or Kat. But her dislike for Kat was much more explainable.

"Anyway," Cassie continued, "I texted Chip to find the floor plans on my computer and email them over. Hopefully we'll be able to figure out where that secret tunnel is." Turning to Emma, Cassie asked, "Were you able to find out anything from Archie?"

Just thinking about her conversation with him made Emma smile. "I discovered that there's a poison garden adjacent to the regular garden and kept separate in a greenhouse so there's no risk of poison contamination in the honey produced here at the castle."

"A poison garden?" Kat asked. "How fascinating."

"Agreed," Emma said. "Morag is the expert there. Belladonna is one of the plants grown there."

"Belladonna!" Cassie exclaimed. "Wow—and that's how Naughty Ned died."

"Thank you, Captain Obvious," Kat said. "How could we ever solve this mystery without you?"

Emma sent Kat a withering look. "Pick on someone your own size, all right?"

"It's all right," Cassie said. "Even best friends snap at each other from time to time."

Emma wasn't sure if Cassie was delusional, or just the eternal Pollyanna. "Anyway, I thought it was interesting that it was Lady Ned who originally designed the poison garden—although I don't think that was the official name for it. But as the chatelaine of the castle, it would have been her responsibility to grow and tend to all the medicinal herbs for the castle's inhabitants, and belladonna was considered not only medicinal but cosmetic. In Renaissance Italy, women used it in eye drops to make their eyes bigger. Eye drops—can you imagine? And also . . ."

Kat was holding up her hands in a time-out position. "Can you ever let it rest, Emma? Nobody cares."

"Actually," Cassie interjected, "I do." She softened her words with a smile. "And not just because I'm interested in poisons, but because it really *is* interesting. I've discovered in my own research for my Haunted Farmers' Market series that atropine—that's the active agent in belladonna—is sometimes still used in eye drops. And then there are the 'home remedy' uses for depression and menstrual cramps. And, er, sexual malfunction in men."

"Finally. Something interesting to talk about," Kat said.

"Yes, well"—Emma cleared her throat—"as I was saying, I learned that Archie knows a lot about the sex lives of bees."

At the word "sex" Kat straightened. "Did he talk about melissophilia?

"What?" Cassie and Emma said in unison.

Kat assumed an air of authority, which, Emma knew, she was. "It's a specific kind of zoophilia, but with stinging insects. Like bees."

Cassie wrinkled her forehead. "You mean people fall in love with . . . bees?"

"No. They use the insects to sting them on their genitals."

Emma resisted the impulse to cross her legs.

Kat continued. "It increases swelling and hypersensitivity, which is said to enhance the intensity and length of their orgasm." Kat smiled wickedly while rubbing her index finger around the edge of her empty whisky glass. "In one study, the circumference of the man's penis increased from six and a half inches to nine and a half inches."

Cassie's eyes widened. "How do you *know* this?"

Kat licked the back of her fork before carefully replacing it on her plate. "Wouldn't you like to know?"

Emma sighed. "Because she literally has a degree in sex, Cassie. And I'm not interested in hearing about any of the hands-on research."

"Oh, but I think you should be, Emma. With a little bit of my 'hands-on' method, I was able to make friends with the sweet curator at the Historical Society in the village to get a private tour of their collection." She opened a manila envelope and spilled out more than a dozen photographs onto the middle of the table.

The three women quickly began flipping over the photos, turning them around to make sense of what they were looking at. "What exactly . . . ?" began Cassie.

"These are Edwardian sex toys," Kat said with satisfaction. "My new best friend and curator, Bruce, says there are many more, along with artwork, in the tower but that Mr. Kill It O'Clock over there doesn't allow anyone to view them yet. He's hoping to do a 'big reveal' celebration and open the museum, but nobody's allowed to see anything until he says so—and they'll have to pay a whopping great admission fee."

Emma picked up a photo and brought it closer. "Oh my gosh! Is this . . . ?"

"Edward VII's infamous sex chair? Yes, actually. It is. Or one of the authentic reproductions." Kat's face hardened. "Presley's having reproductions made so people can experience the, er, full experience. Consensually. Apparently."

"Ew," said Cassie. "It's just so . . ."

"Wrong," finished Kat. "The word you're looking for is wrong."

Emma stared at the photograph of the contraption that had been designed for the former monarch to hoist his considerable girth so that he wouldn't crush his lover during his frequent and lusty sexual trysts.

The eyes of all three women met above the table. After a long silence, Emma stood. "We have to get into that tower."

CHAPTER SIX

Kat

Excerpt from police interview with Ms. Katja de Noir,
10 December 2022

DCI: I was told that you were discovered lurking around the tower four days before the murder.

DE NOIR: Lurking is such a *loaded* word, Inspector. Look at these heels. [*deliberately crosses and uncrosses legs*] Do I look like I *lurk*?

DCI: I was told you were found *inspecting* the tower four days before the murder.

DE NOIR: Why wouldn't I be? I told you, we're writing a book about Naughty Neddie. His stone phallic symbol plays a large part in that, wouldn't you agree?

DCI: A large part? Er—I didn't mean—that will be quite enough, Miss de Noir.

DE NOIR: I'm guessing it was really quite small. No one needs a tower that large unless he has something for which he needs to compensate. Don't you agree?

DCI: Our informant tells us it was the occupant of the tower you appeared to be inspecting, not the tower itself.

DE NOIR: Speaking of small . . .

DCI: Do you speak from personal experience, Miss de Noir?

DE NOIR: No! I told you, it was his tower I was trying to get into, not his pants.

DCI: What did you intend to do once you were there?

DE NOIR: In his tower or his pants?

DCI: His tower, Miss de Noir. The structure made of stone known locally as the Obelisk. Do you need me to clarify further?

DE NOIR: We can discuss my needs another time.

WEDNESDAY, DECEMBER 7
Two days before the murder . . .

WHY, LOOK AT ewe."
Bruce, the Historical Society Guy, gazed up at Kat from the screen of her phone. By mutual agreement, all three women had retreated to their respective rooms after lunch to "pursue their own research," which meant that Emma was probably buried in dusty tomes and Cassie was compulsively trying to call her family. Kat had used her limited time and Wi-Fi to download Snoggr, the app that catered to the lonely hearts of the Inner and Outer Hebrides—including Kinloch and its horny historian. Bruce looked distinctly sheepish, and not just because of the woolly sweater that had "granny knit this for me" written all over it.

What? It was research. In its own way.

"Tempting as this is . . ." murmured Kat, and swiped left.

Darling Brucie had been attempting to woo her with photos of archaic sex implements, but she'd made it clear that the way into her leather leggings was a hard and stony one. No, not that kind of hard and stony. It was the plans to the castle she was after, specifically Neddie's little love tunnel from the castle to the tower.

It helped to think of him as Neddie. Because otherwise she'd remember that woodcut, that picture of a man caught between terror and ecstasy. Oh, Kat knew the real Ned had probably been your standard upper-class lout, more jowl than charm, with a port belly and unfortunate Edwardian facial hair, but there was another Ned, the Ned in her head, the one who'd taken possession of her imagination that first night at the castle.

Kat shivered at the memory. Or maybe just because she was wearing a black lace bustier in a Scottish castle in December. *Mind on your work*, she told herself sternly. She wasn't here to explore the erotic anguish of a man who existed only in her imagination.

Kat forced herself to focus on the screen of her phone. Swipe left. An unremarkable man in one of those ubiquitous caps. Swipe left again. Snoggr served the entirety of the Highlands, not just Kinloch. Kat had tried to narrow her search to men within fifty miles, but that still covered a number of other islands. This was an app for those who didn't mind their romantic interests a boat ride away. Possibly because the alternative was sheep.

Swipe, swipe, swipe.

And there he was. Mr. Kill It O'Clock. Sporting that weaselly Vandyke beard that made him look like an early 2000s dot-com wannabe.

He hadn't worn that beard at Yaddo.

He'd been deceptively clean-cut at Yaddo. He'd been going for a different aesthetic back then. Tweedy jackets with leather patches; big glasses that gave him a little-boy-lost look. The boy next door in your college dorm, the philosophy major with Big Ideas and Deep Thoughts, the guy who would steadfastly support you through your breakup with that bad boy you should never have dated in the first place, handing you tissues and making you instant oatmeal.

The one who peels off those glasses and you realize he was the hero all along.

Except when he wasn't.

Bile rose in Kat's throat. Breathe in . . . breathe out. Breathe in . . . breathe out. She'd failed out of therapy (*you shouldn't be thinking in terms of failure*, she could hear her therapist saying, as though that weren't just another way of telling her she'd failed yet again), but she'd kept the breathing exercises. In and out until her pulse stopped jumping and the sick feeling retreated down into the pit of her stomach and she could look, really look, at the picture on the screen without feeling like she was going to puke all over it.

Slowly, Kat swiped right on Brett Saffron Presley's picture.

Kat looked up, out her window, at the Obelisk. Over there, across the garden, Mr. Big Shot Author's phone would be buzzing. He'd click on it and see—not Kat, definitely not Kat, not Kat now, not Kat as she'd been back then—but a busty blonde named Kirsty.

She couldn't tell which room he was in. She couldn't tell whether he was getting her message or not. But Kat knew he was in there.

Kat felt a tingle of power at the notion. She could march over there—and what? Turn the tables? Make him feel the way he'd made her feel all those years ago?

No. Stick with the plan. And by plan, she meant Kirsty, the Imaginary Busty Blonde, the sort of woman who never existed except in a man's limited imagination.

Hey, handsome, Kat typed underneath the picture of Kirsty's prominent cleavage, and then quickly hit the delete key in a series of staccato movements, making the letters disappear one by one.

Did Scots say hey? Cassie had sent them all the DVDs of *Monarch of the Glen*, seasons 1–4, as well as a bunch of dog-eared paperbacks by an obscure '90s author named Alexandra Raife with titles like *Wild Highland Home*, but Kat had ignored that along with the plaid fanny pack and the cheat sheet on Clans of the Highlands and How Not to Offend Them.

Kat had eaten the shortbread Cassie had included in the package, though. It had sat in a sodden, buttery lump in her stomach, but that was nothing to the sick feeling she had now.

Hi, she typed. *Hi* had to be common to all the English-speaking peoples.

Hi . . . what. Hi, nothing. Kat jabbed the send button. Less is more, isn't that what her editors always said? Fine, so she had a tendency to overwrite. But not now. Just *hi*. The less said, the fewer mistakes she could make.

The less chance she had to back out.

Kat pressed her eyes closed, the phone clenched in her hand, fighting the urge to go back and delete it all, delete the Snoggr account, delete Kirsty, delete the whole dumb idea. If his picture made her feel queasy, how was she going to deal with the real man? She liked to think she'd changed, that the change went deeper than the new haircut and the stiletto heels and the belly button piercing that frankly hadn't been her best idea but had been part of her "screw you" to the world. She'd like to think she could tap a long fingernail to his chest and send him reeling with a touch, like the powerful mage-mistress in her books.

But who was she kidding?

Her phone buzzed in her hand. Kat flipped it over, fumbling it in her haste.

A messenger bubble glowed on the screen. *Hello, Katja, on page 94 of* Tender Is the Demon *you call Brand a spawn of Satan, but on page 124 you write "he remembered those days before his transformation, when his heart had still been human." How can he be spawn of Satan and also once have been human? Please reconcile.*

Kat's breath released with an audible whoosh. She didn't know whether to laugh hysterically or slam the phone against the table. Repeatedly. "How am I supposed to remember every freaking turn of phrase in a book I wrote ten years ago?"

Thank you for your email, she pecked out with one finger. *Brand IS a human turned demon—but aren't we all a little spawn of Satan?*

There. That should give—Kat squinted at the name—something to think about.

The phone buzzed again. If it was someone complaining about a typo, she was going to throw the freaking phone out the window, Snoggr or no Snoggr.

The name Bruce popped up. *I think I may have found what you're looking for.*

Kat banged her head against her hands. She hadn't swiped on Bruce by accident, had she? If she had catfished the wrong man . . .

Wait. That wasn't Snoggr. Stupid phone conversation bubbles. They all looked the same when they popped up; you couldn't tell whether it was text message or Messenger or Snoggr or your food delivery. Cautiously, Kat clicked the message open. This one was a direct text message. Kat remembered tapping her number into his phone with the tip of her dark purple nail, telling him to be in touch if he found anything.

He'd struck her as sweet but useless—unless you really genuinely wanted to know about the fishing industry in eighteenth-century Kinloch, which was apparently the subject of his dissertation in progress.

But there was nothing fishy about the pictures he'd texted her.

Bruce had sent the files as photos, one after another. The camera on his phone wasn't great, or maybe the images had been blurry to begin with. The plans were hand drawn, labeled in a spiky old-fashioned hand. They were clearly not the work of a professional architect. Kat could see the circular shape of the Obelisk, with its small protuberances on either side—seriously, could you get any more phallic?—and the bulk of the castle, which, when seen from above, had been constructed in the shape of a stylized letter *K*, with a long wing running across the front and two wings at diagonals branching off from the main wing. Cute. Also kind of obnoxious. Monogramming a backpack was bad enough, but a house? Towers had been set at all four ends of the *K*, making it even fancier, like a middle-school girl capping her name with hearts.

On one side was the dining room and on the other a formal drawing room. The billiard room, morning room, and music room stretched along one leg of the *K*. The kitchen, servants' hall, and coyly labeled "offices" along another. The space where the legs met was occupied by the Great Hall and the grand bulk of the staircase.

That was the ground floor. The second floor . . . the laird's bedroom, dressing room, and sitting room, the lady's bedroom, dressing room, and sitting room, unidentified other bedrooms and maids' cupboards and one lonely bathroom. This was the area that had undoubtedly changed the most. The rooms had been changed around, bits chopped up to create en suite bathrooms. Kat had been given the circular tower on the far end of the leg of a *K*, with a corner sliced off to create a bathroom.

The prime rooms were clearly the lord's and lady's, extravagant suites that stretched out in isolated grandeur along the front of the house. The laird's suite was on the same side as the Obelisk; the lady's on the kitchen garden side. Kat couldn't be positive, but she thought the space labeled "sitting room" on her ladyship's side was now the one with a brass plaque on the door advertising it as a library. She hadn't been in there yet, but she'd had a vague impression of dark woodwork and dusty books.

Kat squinted at the plans. It could just be bad drawing. It could be the pen trailing away. But two things caught her eye. One: the lady's sitting room, now the library, which was positioned next to the stairs on the second floor. There seemed to be an odd space next to it, where the legs of the *K* met, a little triangle shaded in on the plans. On the opposite side, the right side, there was a housemaid's cupboard. But on the left side, just that shading.

Two: the tower attached to the laird's suite. The anonymous author of the plans—Was the author of the plans really anonymous? She'd have to ask Bruce—had drawn a line looping around the tower, across the grounds, to the Obelisk.

A line from the laird's bedroom straight to his orgy tower.

The tunnel they had been looking for. A tunnel no one else knew about.

Kat's brain was buzzing like Archie's bees. So many possibilities. She could tell the others—she should tell the others.

But it was just a line. Possibly a slip of the pen.

Her face set, Kat carefully deleted Bruce's texts. Then she opened an existing text chain, one labeled "The Wonder Writers," which consisted mostly of agitated reminders from Cassie to remember their plaid and links to scholarly articles in obscure journals that none of them could get access to from Emma.

Ladies, texted Kat. *Meet me in the library.*

"You're sure Bruce said the library?"

Emma's ponytail swished as she frowned at the books lining the walls of the pleasant, square room.

"Well . . . He said the room that's now the library," Kat hedged.

This was the problem with dealing with real people rather than fictional characters. They asked questions. Inconvenient questions.

"But this Historical Society person didn't actually send you the plans?" Emma wouldn't let it go; she just kept worrying at the topic like Loren the sheepdog with a haggis-shaped chew toy. Kat was pretty sure she could smell sheepdog on Emma. Or maybe that was just wet socks. She had that healthy, pink-cheeked look, like she'd been out tramping the grounds.

Cassie, on the other hand, looked like she'd been curled up in bed, crying. Her cheeks still bore the crease marks of sheets and her eyes were suspiciously red.

"Bruce said the plans were too fragile to photograph—light exposure or something like that," Kat lied glibly. "But he was pretty sure there was an anomaly in the area around the library."

"That's so strange." Emma's brow furrowed, like she was contemplating a difficult shot at lacrosse. "I would have thought the library would have been the last place you'd put a secret passage— too public. Wouldn't it make more sense to have one leading off his bedroom?"

"Maybe that's exactly why he didn't. Like iocaine powder! You know that bit from *The Princess Bride*?" Putting a hand on Kat's arm, Cassie said, "Good work, Kat. Without you, we might have wasted time on the wrong room."

There was no reason to feel this guilty. It's not like they were really in this together the way they pretended.

Kat shrugged, dislodging Cassie's grip. "Oh, you know—it wasn't like he was tough to persuade."

"I still think it's weird that it's the library," said Emma.

"Look, I can ask him what the room was on the old plans, okay?" Turning away, Kat made a show of texting.

Thanks soooooo much for the intel! The room that's now the library—what was it in the bad old days?

She held up her phone so they could see it, then pressed send. It went off into the ether with a satisfying *whoosh* sound.

Emma winced. "Was it really necessary to add that many *o*'s?"

Kat looked at her from under her fake lashes. "Isn't it always?"

Emma looked blank.

Cassie looked worriedly at Kat's phone. She swallowed with some difficulty. "So your text—it's working?"

Kat's immediate impulse was to ask how she thought she'd received anything from Bruce in the first place, carrier pigeon? But there was something about the bruised expression on Cassie's face that made the words stop on her tongue.

"Nothing from your husband?" Kat asked brusquely.

"No." Cassie shook her head. Even her curls seemed to have lost some of their usual bounce. "I wonder if there's a problem with my phone. But your message got through okay. So I just don't know."

Over her bowed head, Kat's eyes met Emma's in a rare moment of mutual understanding.

"You know what technology is like," said Emma vaguely, putting a tentative hand on Cassie's shoulder. "Maybe your phone doesn't like the castle."

Okay, so much for sympathy. Kat grimaced at Emma. "You think her phone is sentient? I think you're in the wrong story."

Emma's ponytail gave an irritated swish. "You know what I mean. I lived in an apartment in college where I could only get service by holding my phone out the window. My"—her voice faltered for a moment—"my boyfriend's phone worked just fine. This stuff is weird. Maybe Cassie's phone just doesn't work here."

"Oh, sure, blame the woman," mocked Kat, keeping a careful eye on Cassie's ducked head. "Maybe it's his fault. Maybe his internet is down."

"Only you could make internet service sound suggestive," said Emma ruefully, but she was smiling, just a little.

"It's a talent," said Kat, and, just for a moment, they all smirked at one another in a weird sort of harmony—until Cassie's phone dinged. And not just a little ding. There was a full-on carillon going on there.

"Is it your husband?" asked Emma eagerly.

"Nooooo." Cassie's face crunched in on itself as she looked at the phone, like when Kat used to squish her Barbie's rubber head. "It's—it's a reader who wants to know why I'm wasting my time writing the Little Bake Shop series instead of m-more Hedge Witches."

"Hedge witches?" Emma looked like she had smelled something unpleasant or at least historically inaccurate.

Cassie didn't notice; she was too busy being upset. "You won't even know about it—*Kirkus* called it girl power *Cadfael*—they were medieval, the Hedge Witch mysteries, I mean, not *Kirkus*—but they didn't sell *at all*. But I still get these die-hard readers who are angry at me because the series cut off after three books. I mean, I *loved* them. I would have kept writing them if someone were willing to pay me for them, but diapers cost money, and Ellie wouldn't breastfeed; she needed supplemental formula—and it all just gets so expensive, and the Bake Shop books *sell*, you know?"

Cassie looked like she was about to cry. "Hey," said Kat. "Hey, it's not your fault. I've been writing deeply clichéd sexy demons for the past ten years because I have a very expensive Brooklyn studio to maintain."

She'd optimistically signed the lease after that first blockbuster book, when everything seemed destined to come up roses—black roses, of course—forever.

That was before Yaddo.

Kat forced herself to keep her voice light. "I still get readers emailing me being, like, why did you sell out? And it's, like, because I like to eat?"

A watery chuckle escaped Cassie.

"I got one just today about *The Unsinkable Prunella Schuyler*," Emma jumped in. "So, you know how the passengers on the *Cameronia* had to transfer to the *Lusitania* and the *Lusitania* had to delay sailing several hours, which may be why it wound up in the path of the fatal torpedo?"

"Um, no," said Kat. Cassie made a choking sound that was half a laugh.

"Well, anyway, this woman emailed me that she'd looked up the *Cameronia*—on Wikipedia—and it wasn't built until 1920, and clearly I'd gotten it wrong, and I'd destroyed her trust, and she was never going to read any of my books ever again and she was going to tell her whole book group not to read them either." Kat wasn't sure which upset Emma more, the lost sales or the insult to her historical integrity. "If this woman had only bothered to look at ANY reputable source about the *Lusitania*—or even just checked another Wikipedia article!—she would have known that there was an earlier *Cameronia* and it all happened *exactly as I said*."

"I have a special folder for those." Cassie's voice was rough, but she was making a valiant effort to pull herself together. "My WTH folder. You know, for What the Heck."

Good Lord, the woman really was that adorable. "Well, then," said Kat. "What are you waiting for? Send that reader email straight to heck."

There was a moment of silence, and then they all burst into laughter. Even Emma joined in with her high-pitched whinny. If there was a slightly hysterical edge to it, and if Cassie expelled somewhat more snot than was usually socially acceptable in the process, none of them commented.

Cassie yanked out a tartan tissue case. "We were meant to be looking for a tunnel, right?" she said thickly.

Kat found herself fighting a strange impulse to give the other woman a hug. She had no idea where it came from. She did not hug.

Kat took refuge in snark. "Isn't standard protocol to tug at, like, candles or books until something gives way?"

"You can't take *Young Frankenstein* as reference material," said Emma wearily. "That's not how secret passages work. We should be looking for bosses in the woodwork—"

Cassie charged right past her. "Oooh, look! Here's *Culpeper's Complete Herbal*! Oh my goodness, it looks like a really early copy—what do you think, Emma? Seventeenth century? I have a paperback repro edition at home—I used it in my Hedge Witch series. I mean, I know it's a couple of centuries too late, but folklore couldn't have changed that much, right?"

Cassie yanked on the giant calfbound tome.

A portion of the wall creaked open, revealing darkness beyond. And one very annoyed spider.

Kat struck a pose with a hand on one hip, looking pointedly at Emma. "You were saying."

"Well, since it's an inauthentic castle," said Emma stiffly, "I suppose it makes perfect sense that they'd have an inauthentic passage."

"This looks authentic enough to me!" Cassie rubbed hard at her nose, bravely putting her private worries behind her. "Secret passage selfie?"

"You're kidding, right?" Kat looked hard at Cassie, who was already fishing for her phone. "Right?"

Emma peered around Cassie. "That's not a passage. It looks like . . . a priest hole? Although that couldn't be right because the building is far too new to have one."

"A priest hole. Kinky," said Kat provocatively. The last thing she wanted Emma thinking about was why there wasn't a passage when they were meant to be looking for a passage. Fortunately, Emma was easily irritated.

It worked. Emma glared at her. "*Not* that kind of hole. We're talking oratories, not orifices. In the sixteenth century—"

Kat mimed banging her head against a shelf.

"Hey. You two." Cassie's eyes were shining, although part of that was down to the tears. "We found a secret room. An honest-to-goodness secret room! Are we really going to stand here bickering when we could be exploring?"

"I bet you read Nancy Drew as a girl," muttered Kat. "Yeah, yeah, you're right. It is pretty cool. Look, you can tell from the dust—no one's been here for . . . well. Emma can give us a date, I suppose."

They all hovered at the opening like the cover picture from a vintage Nancy Drew. (Yes, Kat had also read Nancy Drew, not that she'd admit it.) Kat wasn't sure whether their mutual reluctance to go in had more to do with the extremely pissed-off spider guarding his work or the heavy smell of centuries of dust.

"I've got a flashlight," said Cassie helpfully. "I mean, a *torch*."

She yanked one out of her inevitable tartan tote. Even the flashlight was plaid.

Three uneven steps led down to a small, triangular room, sparsely furnished with an old secretary desk and a tall cupboard filled with extremely dusty glass apothecary bottles. The writing surface of the desk was down, revealing a cobweb-covered ledger. Through the grimy glass of the cupboard's doors, Kat could make out books that looked even older than the ones in the library. Grimoires, her wayward imagination supplied. Ancient prophecies.

Or just someone's cookbook collection.

Kat wandered down the three uneven stone steps into the little hidey-hole, fascinated despite herself. If Disney had a Ye Olde Apothecarie section at Epcot, this would totally be what it would look like, she told herself, but she couldn't deny that there was something genuinely compelling about it. That woodcut flashed into her memory again, the girl brought to the sacrifice, who, in Kat's version, wouldn't be a sacrifice at all, but an equal and powerful combatant. She could imagine her having a room just such as this, a room crammed with bottles and potions and books with incantations in ancient and forgotten tongues.

The dust lay so thick on the old bottles that Kat could scarcely read the hand-lettered labels. She ran the pad of one finger across them, clearing a trail through the grime. The names stirred vague recollections deep in the recesses of her mind. "'Trefoil, Saint-John's-wort, vervain, dill; hinder witches of their will.'"

Emma's loafers clanked down the stairs. "How did *you* know that?"

"My books deal with the supernatural. Duh," Kat said loftily. Never mind that it was actually from an old Mary Stewart novel. Admitting to memorizing Mary Stewart novels didn't fit her image any more than reading Karyn Black.

What was it about this place? Kat felt like she was in sixth grade again, the girl who used to devour Mary Stewart and Karyn Black and Phyllis A. Whitney, anything to be anywhere other than where she was—or who she was. It made her feel strangely naked.

Cassie nestled in next to Kat, looking avidly at the bottles. "Trefoil was used to fortify the body against poison and pestilence—and the noisome vapors of the spleen. St.-John's-wort heals wounds and expels choler—and dill is good in soup."

Kat made a face at her. "How do *you* know all that?"

"My Hedge Witch series!" When the others looked blank, Cassie sighed deeply. "You know, my old medieval cozy series? The one I was just telling you about? About the orphan girl who has visions, so people think she's a witch. So she gets run out of the village, where she's taken in by an old hedge witch and—"

"Okay, we get the idea," said Kat.

Emma turned around from where she'd been inspecting the old desk. Looking pained, she scrubbed a dusty hand against her jeans. "That doesn't sound strictly historically accurate. The term hedge witch—"

"It has a talking cat," said Cassie.

"Oh," said Emma.

"You know, sort of like *Sabrina the Teenage Witch*, but late medieval. Gosh, I miss those books." Cassie turned her attention back to the bottles on the shelves, shining her light on each one in turn. "There's some serious stuff in here. Look, there's foxglove— that's digitalis, helpful in small doses, but fatal in large ones. And that—that's white hellebore. It's incredibly poisonous. They used to use it for abortions. Also tansy, this one over here. Although they used tansy both to cause abortions and to help conception, so that one could kind of go either way. And here . . ."

Her rambling pharmacopedia trailed off as she reached the end of the row, pausing in front of one last, dusty bottle.

Emma craned her neck to look around her. "What's that one?"

Cassie had a strange expression on her face. Although that might have just been the dust. Goodness only knew Kat's own nose was twitching like crazy. "That one is belladonna."

Their eyes met in the strange, wavering light of Cassie's flashlight. "Belladonna . . . the poison that killed Naughty Neddie," said Kat slowly.

Emma turned abruptly away from the shelves. She clasped her hands behind her back like she was a midshipman standing to attention on the deck of the H.M.S. *Pinafore*. "We have to find out whose room this was."

Kat could have made a good guess. This had been the lady's sitting room. Her secret hidey-hole. But if Kat admitted she knew that, she'd have to admit she'd seen those plans. Better to wait until Bruce texted her back with something he already knew she knew.

Besides, while Emma and Cassie were fizzing over this discovery, they weren't going to wonder what was going on with the passage they didn't know she'd already discovered. Or would discover. Without them.

A little historical research would be just the thing to keep them harmlessly occupied while Kat weighed her options.

"You're right," said Kat, keeping her face perfectly blank as she led the way up the three uneven steps, Cassie behind her, and Emma bringing up the rear. "We've got to find out who built this—and for whom?"

CHAPTER SEVEN

Cassie

Excerpt from police interview with Mrs. Cassandra Parsons Pringle, 10 December 2022

DCI: Just to be clear, then. You had or had *not* met the deceased previous to the—er, the events that resulted in his demise?

PRINGLE: Met? Met Brett Saffron *Presley*? [*laughter*] Goodness, no. Our paths never, ever crossed. Not—well, in a way—I guess that depends on your definition of *meet*—

DCI: I should think the meaning is clear, Mrs. Pringle. Have you encountered Mr. Presley? Had words with Mr. Presley? Would he have recollected the encounter?

PRINGLE: I think it's fair to say he would not have recollected the encounter.

DCI: So you *have* met him.

PRINGLE: I didn't say that.

DCI: You said—

PRINGLE: I used the conditional tense, Detective. He *would not have* recollected the encounter *if* he had met me.

DCI: Then you haven't answered my question.

PRINGLE: Didn't I?

DCI: [*sound of extended sigh*] Mrs. Pringle, I do have some experience questioning witnesses—

PRINGLE: *Witness?* I didn't *witness* anything. [*laughter*] What makes you think I witnessed something? Anything? To do with Mr. Presley? That's ridiculous. I'm a happily married woman. With six children. With my husband.

DCI: You never encountered Mr. Presley at any of the numerous conferences and retreats you attended together?

PRINGLE: We didn't attend them *together*, Detective. Those are *industry-wide* events. *Hundreds* of attendees. You don't understand, I write cozy mysteries. He's—well, he's Brett Saffron *Presley*. He wouldn't take any notice of little old me.

DCI: [*sound of Scottish noise roughly equivalent to* hmph]

PRINGLE: What does that mean? You'll have to be more articulate, Detective.

DCI: It means I'm perplexed, Mrs. Pringle.

PRINGLE: [*laughter*] Perplexed? My goodness! Why on earth? Haven't I been making myself clear?

DCI: I'm perplexed because you *say* you've never encountered Mr. Presley at any of the numerous events you've attended together—

PRINGLE: *Coincidentally*, Detective. *Not together.*

DCI: And yet, a routine Instagram search revealed this post, dated two years ago, in which the @crimeandcupcakes account— yours, I believe—was tagged. [*sound of shuffling papers*] Do you recognize the persons in this photograph, Mrs. Pringle?

PRINGLE: [*brief silence*] I—it's hard to say for certain—the lighting is so dark—

DCI: Can you say where it was taken?

PRINGLE: At a—at a bar?

DCI: It's the bar on the atrium level of the Marriott Marquis Hotel in Times Square, Mrs. Pringle, at the 2019 CrimeLovers Convention in New York City. The photograph was taken and posted by an account belonging to a writer named Deanna Raybourn, captioned "What happens after midnight at #Crimelovers2019 #oldfriendsnewfriends #authorsbehavingbadly #wellbehavedwomenseldommakehistory." On the left, Raybourn tagged herself and two others—fellow writers, I believe—named Wendy Walker and Deborah Goodrich Royce. On the right, you and Mr. Presley.

PRINGLE: Obviously she was mistaken.

DCI: Why *obviously*, Mrs. Pringle? And before you answer, I should note that your own Instagram post from that date, taken earlier in the evening, depicts you in a dress identical to the one worn by the woman in this photograph.

PRINGLE: But you can't see my—*her* face. Or that of Br—the other man.

DCI: And why is that, Mrs. Pringle?

PRINGLE: Well, because they're—that's why it couldn't be *me*, of course—because they're—well, they're—they appear to be—

DCI: Mrs. Pringle, I believe the technical term is *snogging*.

THURSDAY, DECEMBER 8
One day before the murder . . .

A T SIX A.M., Chip's voice rang out cheerfully from Cassie's phone. *Good morning, sunshine!*

Good morning, sunshine!

Good morning, sunshine!

Cassie turned off the alarm. At least he'd spoken to her *once* today, right? Even if it was just that snippet they'd recorded for fun when she first brought home the new phone, three years ago. Wasn't it funny how bringing home a new phone felt a little like bringing home a new baby? All its tricks and noises delighted you. How it looked different from its predecessors, yet the same. And Chip—*Here, let me set your alarm for you.*

Good morning, sunshine!

When he'd handed it back to her, he was grinning that mischievous grin that melted her, even after five babies—the human kind. *That's so my voice is always the first thing you hear in the morning, even when you're off on your adventures,* he'd said.

Cassie rolled on her back and stared at the alerts on the home screen. No messages, no missed calls. She'd tried to FaceTime Chip three times yesterday, and each time he'd declined the call.

Well, he was busy! He had his business to manage, houses to renovate. School drop-offs and pickups for the older kids, sports and music after school, dinner to make, lunches to pack. She'd left careful instructions but something always came up, some small disaster, some forgotten detail, like when she'd had to miss Marcus's first day of school and didn't tell Chip she'd left that all-important first-day-of-school homework out on Marcus's chest of drawers. Totally her fault. How was Chip supposed to know there was homework for the first day of school? What kind of power-drunk teacher assigned first-day homework for kinder-gartners?

Certainly it wasn't because of some stupid old photo on some stupid old social media post that a stupid friend had forwarded to him the week before she left. *I can explain*, she'd told him. *It was just conference hijinks*, she'd told him.

Sure, he'd said. *Of course. I get it.*

But his eyes, before he'd turned away. She'd never seen his eyes like that, so cold and hard. How was she supposed to tell him that this writing retreat was taking place at a castle that happened to be owned by the man in that photo?

Not when his eyes were that cold.

In her head she heard her mother's voice. *It's all very well to leave your husband to raise the kids if you have a* real *career, Cassie. A career that really* matters.

Her mother. Now general counsel at Third Fifth Bank in Charlotte. Her mother, who'd left Cassie's father back home in Davidson to raise Cassie and her brother in an old clapboard farmhouse, in between history lectures and faculty meetings. Mom, who lived in a sleek modern penthouse in downtown Charlotte and wore a strict uniform of beige with pops of black.

Mom's way was the only *right* way to do anything, wasn't it?

A cold draft hit the side of Cassie's face from the window she'd left cracked open, in the misguided hope that the bracing Scottish air would help her sleep. Well, so much for that. She lifted the covers and gasped at the chill. On the chair next to the bed, she'd slung her plaid sherpa-lined robe. She reached out her arm, snagged the robe, and belted it on. Shoved her feet into her plaid sherpa-lined slippers. Twisted her frizzing curls into a plaid scrunchie and shuffled to the window, where the approaching dawn had only just begun to tint the mist, and the Obelisk rose like a shadow from the smoky ground.

From the window near the top, a yellow light glowed.

Frick you, Cassie whispered.

DOWNSTAIRS, THE KITCHEN shook with the noise of an enthusiastic, rhythmic thumping, punctuated by satisfied grunts. Cassie stopped short on the threshold and peered inside, just as Morag whipped around from an enormous table at the center of the room and fixed her with a terrifying glare. The housekeeper's hands were caked with flour; a pile of dough rested on the marble surface behind her.

"And what business have ye got in the kitchens at this hour?" Morag demanded.

"I was just—I couldn't sleep—"

Morag made a noise that sounded roughly equivalent to *Hmph*. She cast her eyes down to Cassie's slippers and worked her way up the bulky plaid robe, belted at the waist, where she stopped and raised her eyebrows.

"And what in the name of bonny heaven have ye got clutched to yer bosom, madam?"

"Oh, this?" Cassie held out the metal tray for inspection. "It's a muffin pan. I packed it along with me, just in case."

"A *muffin* pan?"

"Muffins. You know, the American kind. Like cupcakes, only— well, larger. And no frosting, I guess."

Morag wrinkled her nose. "Cupcakes?"

"Don't you have cupcakes in Scotland?"

"Not as such," Morag said crisply. Then she frowned. "In case of what, pray?"

"I beg your pardon?"

"Whatever made ye think ye'd require to bake a dozen *American* muffins *in my kitchen*?"

"Well." Cassie blinked. "I mean, you never know, do you?"

Morag stared at her as if she were mad. A faint acrid smell whiffed the air.

"Ah, Mrs.—er, Morag? I think something's burning."

"Och! The brrrread!"

Morag snatched a towel and opened a door in the middle of the vast iron range that ran from one side of the kitchen to the other. "Blast," she muttered, drawing out a pair of loaves. She whipped around to drop them like stones on the table. "And what am I to do with these, pray?"

"I-I'm so sorry!"

"Sorry fer what?"

"For distracting you? Here, let me help. I think if we scrape away the burnt crust we can still salvage—"

"Never ye mind," said Morag resignedly. "We'll crumble them up for the pigs."

"Oh! Have you got your own pigs?"

"Of course we've got our own pigs. D'ye think we pluck the bacon from the trrrees?"

Cassie laughed. "Goodness, no. Would you like me to take a turn with the kneading? I'm considered a bit of a dab hand at these things."

"That won't be necessary."

Morag dusted her hands with flour and set back to work. Cassie laid the muffin pan carefully on the corner of the table and watched the woman's thick, strong fingers work the dough.

"What are you making?" she ventured.

Morag shot her a withering look. "Brrread."

"I mean, any particular kind of bread?"

Reluctantly, Morag muttered, "Caraway."

"Ooh, that sounds wonderful." Cassie cast her eyes around the room. Everything was built to an enormous scale—the marble-topped table, the vast range of black cast iron, the series of deep porcelain sinks, the array of bright copper pans hanging from the rack above the table—and reeked of history. Along one wall, the cupboards reached to the ceiling—china and crystal, probably. Two heavy wooden doors grew from the opposite wall. Emma would know where those led. Pantry or cold storage or silver.

For an instant, Cassie closed her eyes and imagined all the glorious meals that had been cooked here over the years—the sauces simmered in the copper pots atop the range, the cakes baked, the joints roasted.

"Coffee's in the cupboard, if ye'd like," Morag said gruffly, interrupting her thoughts.

Cassie followed the direction of the housekeeper's nod and opened the cupboard door to find a row of crystallized instant Nescafé in jars. After some searching, she located a mug and spoon and the kettle of water keeping hot on one of the stove lids.

Morag muttered something about cream and sugar on the tray.

"Do you do the cooking and baking all by yourself?" Cassie asked.

"Och, no. A local girl comes in to help with the washing and the peeling."

"You must have lots of interesting recipes."

"Some." Morag set the dough in a large bowl and covered it with a cheesecloth. "We keep the old ways alive here. I've Lady Ned's own recipes, passed down from herself to me nan, and me nan to me. A sacrrred trust."

Cautiously Cassie sipped the liquid in the mug. She wasn't quite prepared to call it coffee, per se, but it wasn't bad. And it was hot. And contained caffeine.

She felt her mood perk, just a little.

She wandered to an open shelf beneath a bank of windows that overlooked a damp stone courtyard. The old cloth bindings of the cookery books were so worn and well-used, she had to squint to make out the titles stamped on the spines.

"Ooh! *The Art of Cookery Made Plain and Easy. Dressed Game and Poultry. Savouries a la Mode.* Hmm, *Two Hundred Ways of Using Remnants.*" Cassie laughed. "Sounds pretty offal!"

From behind her came a sharp crack.

Cassie turned. Morag tossed an eggshell into the pile next to the mixing bowl and reached for another egg from the dish nearby.

"Did you catch that?" Cassie said. "Offal? Awful?"

Morag cracked the egg into the bowl and picked up a metal whisk. "I'll thank ye to keep yer mitts from me books."

Hastily Cassie stepped away from the shelf. "Speaking of offal. One item on my own personal bucket list—you've heard of the term *bucket list*, right?—things to do before you kick the bucket? Die, that is?"

Morag lifted the bowl into the crook of her elbow and began to whisk briskly.

"Well," Cassie went on, "my husband's family—*clan*, I guess you'd say—they emigrated from Scotland to what's now North Carolina after the Rising—thousands of Scotsmen did, they just filled the Appalachians right up—and I've been wanting to surprise him by making haggis."

"Haggis? Ye want to make haggis?"

"I'd love to try, if you'd show me. I'm sure you've got a wonderful authentic recipe."

"Weeell," said Morag, face thawing, "I might."

"Would you show me? I'd be so grateful. I do love to cook, and my husband, he's a Scotsman through and through—a little bit gruff but so clever with his hands, so resourceful, such a good, strong husband and father—of course, he loves a nice glass of whisky every so often—"

"Then he's a Scotsman, all right."

"I know he'd be thrilled. And so surprised."

"Well, of course the first thing is ye must have the proper ingredients. Just fresh, mind ye."

Cassie came to the kitchen table and set down her mug. "It must be so wonderful to have everything right here when you need it. Meat and vegetables and fruit right from the estate."

"That's so. These eggs were laid just this morning by me own chickens."

"We got our own chickens during the Covid lockdown. It's been terrific for the children." Cassie cleared her throat. "And an herb garden. I still get a little thrill from clipping my own rosemary."

"Och, we've got a fine herb garden here at the castle. Planted in by Lady Ned herself over a hundred years ago."

"Oh, is that what's in the greenhouse?" Cassie asked innocently. As innocently as she could manage, anyway. "I saw it when we were out for a walk the other day. Is it really a hundred years old?"

Morag nodded. "Lady Ned taught me own nan the way of it, and Nan passed it on to Mam, and now there's me to tend the plants. The good as well as the lethal," she added, with a gimlet eye.

Cassie clasped her hands together. "Poisons! I'm an expert on those. I write murder mysteries, you know, and poisons are my specialty. I've written a whole series—the Little Bake Shop? Poisons baked into delicious treats. Of course, you have to make sure the poisons are thermostable. Like the death cap mushroom, for example, although sadly there are few recipes for baked goods that call for mushrooms."

"That'll be true," said Morag, nodding.

"I prefer belladonna for that reason," Cassie went on. "Atropine, to use its chemical name. Perfectly lethal, and its potency is not reduced by baking." She forced her lips to make a bright, guileless smile. "I assume you have belladonna in your garden?"

Morag's mouth screwed into a tight, round hole. She glanced at her watch.

"Shouldn't ye be over at the spa with yer mates just now?"

"My mates? The *spa*?"

"It's in the itinerary, ye'll recall. Thursday morning, seven sharp. To firm and tone for the ceilidh tomorrow."

"Good gracious! *That's* where everybody's gone. I knocked and knocked on all the doors." Cassie ran to one of the large sinks with her coffee cup. "Oh my heavens. Half an hour late already. Are you sure it's seven? What about breakfast?"

Morag's voice floated behind her as she rushed out the door.

"We find the treatments are most efficacious when ye've fasted first!"

CASSIE'S PHONE STARTED buzzing as soon as she flew from the courtyard. She checked the screen while she ran. Fourteen messages, all from the Wonder Writers group chat.

KAT: spa time bitches

EMMA: Sorry on my way

KAT: where the hell is spa

EMMA: Old crappers hut next to the natural spring pool

EMMA: *crofters

EMMA: stupid autocorrect

KAT: need coffee!!

EMMA: Where's Cassie?

KAT: idk is there coffee at spa

EMMA: Cassie are you awake? Everything ok?

KAT: need coffee now!!!!!

EMMA: Cassie, going into treatment room now. Calum looks pissed.

KAT: calum always looks pissed

KAT: warning no coffee at spa

That was forty-one minutes ago.

"Gosh darn it," Cassie muttered. About fifteen yards away, the pathway made a fork. A small sign reading SPA pointed to the right. She turned right and broke into a jog. In the distance, a stream of thick white smoke rose from the thatched roof of a squat stone hut.

"Oh my goodness!" she gasped. She stretched out to a hard run. "Fire! *Fire!*"

As she drew near, the cloud of smoke enveloped her. Actually, it was more like . . . steam. She slowed to a trot. Steam that smelled of—of—

Cassie staggered to a stop just in time to avoid plunging into a spring that bubbled up from the dead winter heather. As she edged around it toward the hut at the far end, she sniffed the air.

Was that . . . *poop*?

The hut was small and plain, made of rough stone. The steam, she saw, poured from an exhaust pipe cut into the stone at the back of the building. SPA, read the signboard next to the wooden door. The place was as still as death.

Cassie pushed open the door. A faint noise of recorded bagpipes drifted across the threshold.

"Hello? Everybody okay?"

Kat's voice trailed out. "I think I'm stoned."

Emma's voice followed. "I can't feel my face."

Cassie plunged inside. Calum MacDougal stood in the middle of the room, wearing a white spa uniform and latex gloves while the bagpipe music swirled around him from some unseen speaker. On either side, Kat and Emma lay prone on towel-decked treatment beds, naked as newborns except for the thick yellow paste covering their faces and the layers of greenish-brown slime slicked over their bodies.

Before she averted her eyes, Cassie couldn't help noticing that Kat's breasts weren't nearly as large as they appeared in the vinyl bustier.

"You're late," Calum growled.

"I was—I was helping Morag in the kitchens," Cassie gasped.

He jerked his head to the bed next to the window. "Strip yer clothes and hop on top, then."

"Ooh, say that again," said Kat.

Cassie choked out, "Um . . . strip?"

"That's right. While the body wrap's still warm."

"Body wrap?"

"Our patented mixture of peat and fermented sheep's dung," Calum said, with a trace of pride. "Lady Ned's own recipe to maintain the skin's naturally supple texture and firmness."

"Dung?" Cassie said faintly.

"Not as bad as it sounds!" called Emma from her bed, sounding as if her lips were frozen shut. "Can't smell a thing!"

"The facial mask is hand mixed to Lady Ned's formulation of curdled sheep's milk and castle honey, combined with a secret blend of herbs from the castle gardens. The lactic enzymes melt away the top layer of the dermis, leaving the skin rejuvenated and renewed," said Calum. "Now shuck yer trews before I shuck them for ye."

"I think I just came," said Kat.

Cassie jumped back, knocking into a display of bottles and jars with homemade labels. She grabbed a couple before they toppled to the floor. One was labeled Lady Ned's Intimate Hemp Lubricating Oil; the other one Kinloch Genuine Lanolin Butter. A smaller inscription underneath read, in italics: *For external use only.*

"I—um—you know, I'm already late. I think I'll just have the face thingie," she said. "Do you have a robe or something I can change into?"

"Ye've got a robe on already," said Calum.

"It's just—I've never liked spas, to tell you the truth. So much indulgence." She spied a white plush robe hanging along the wall and scuttled to snatch it from the hanger. "I would really rather be working on one of my books."

"Copout," said Emma.

"Is this a changing room?" Cassie flung open a door.

"That'll be the fermentation chamber," growled Calum. "Fer God's sake, don't breathe in!"

By the time she'd whipped off her sherpa and pajamas and belted the spa robe around her waist, Cassie was feeling woozy. She staggered back into the treatment room and slumped on the empty bed.

"Roll over on yer back, then," Calum said, almost kindly.

Cassie rolled and closed her eyes. A pair of astonishingly gentle hands pulled her hair back into some kind of terrycloth wrap.

"Now hold still whilst I spackle on the paste," said Calum.

"But—"

Something heavy and cool spread across her cheeks and forehead, turning instantly warm. She tried to speak but her lips wouldn't move.

"Burns," she gasped.

"That'll be the enzymes," said Calum. "Ye might feel some temporary facial paralysis as well. Should be moving again by the start of the ceilidh tomorrow, odds are."

"Odds *are*?"

"The whole village'll be there, Mrs. Pringle. A right knees-up. Ye'll want to look yer best. Off with the robe, then."

"But—"

"Ye're paying for the body wrap, lass, so ye might as well have it."

Something buzzed against the skin of her hip.

"My phone!"

"I must ask ye to lie still—"

Cassie stuck her hand in the pocket of her robe and whipped out her phone. A message alert appeared on the screen, overlaid on a stylized image of a cupcake dripping blood.

Call me asap

"It's Chip!" she exclaimed, between her frozen lips.

She bolted off the bed and out the door.

CASSIE LURCHED FRANTICALLY around the edge of the spring, holding the phone in the air. Bars! She needed bars! She pressed the FaceTime button again and, after a few seconds of silence, heard a musical burr.

Please, she thought. *Please pick up.*

THEY'D MET WHEN she was nineteen, home for the summer from her first year of college. Dad was having the kitchen torn out at last—not because he'd felt the need to renovate, but because the refrigerator had died and when the replacement came in, they'd discovered the whole wall was compromised by water damage and black mold. Dad had hired a local builder named Chip Pringle on the recommendation of a fellow Davidson faculty member— a woman, as it happened—who raved about Chip's passion for historically sensitive renovations.

Cassie had arrived home from college to find a god in a toolbelt taking measurements of her kitchen.

Cassie could still hear Chip's voice as he'd explained the situation. So grave, so sympathetic. She couldn't remember what he'd said because she was staring at the cleft in his chin, several inches above hers.

"Sure," she'd said. "Whatever needs doing, right?"

Day after day he'd arrived at her house at seven sharp, wearing his jeans and work boots and worn, soft T-shirts, smelling of soap and fresh wood shavings. Day after day she'd come home from her job at the local bakery-café and sit under the tree outside the kitchen window, pretending to read a book while she caught febrile glimpses of his muscular arm, his square jaw, his thick shoulder. She'd closed her eyes and imagined him touching her chin with his finger, kissing her, whispering how he couldn't live without her.

Just fantasy, of course. Pure fantasy. She was a professor's daughter with frizzy hair and pale, freckled skin, geeking out on Agatha Christie and Dorothy Sayers and medieval cookbooks, while Chip was—well, he was a hunk. There was no other word for it. Splendid and skillful and out of her league.

Still, she'd made offerings. She'd squeezed fresh lemonade. She'd smuggled home the chocolate chip cookies she'd baked at work. She'd worn her contact lenses and gathered her hair back in what she hoped was an artfully messy bun that showed off her long neck, which she considered her best feature.

Once, she'd summoned the courage to ask about his nickname. "Chip. Is that because you're a carpenter?"

He'd looked at her as if she was an idiot. "Because of the potato chip."

"The potato chip?"

"You know. Pringles?"

"Ohhhh," she'd said. "Chip Pringle. I get it. Pretty funny."

"Yep. Real comedians, my buddies."

Then he'd turned away to finish screwing in the hinge of a cabinet door.

Cassie had stared at his triceps shifting adorably beneath his T-shirt and thought, *Well, so much for that fantasy.*

When at last the kitchen was finished, she'd handed Chip the cashier's check and a box of dark chocolate bourbon pecan brownies—one of her specialties—and he'd said, *I'm sorry, I can't take this.*

"What?" she'd gasped. "Why not?"

He'd looked at the ceiling, at the walls, at the beautiful cabinets he'd just installed.

Then he'd looked at her.

"Because I've fallen in love with you, Cassandra Parsons," he'd said.

He'd touched her chin with his finger.

He'd bent his splendid head to kiss her.

When at last he'd lifted his lips from hers and gathered her in his tremendous arms, he'd whispered that he couldn't live another minute without her.

Or her chocolate chip cookies.

Now CHIP's VOICE barked from the phone. "I can't hear you, Cass. Where are you?"

"I'm at the spa!"

"Spa? I thought you were working!"

"It's—it's research!"

"The screen's frozen again. What's going on?"

"I can't get enough bars! Can you hear me?"

The screen unstuck and Chip's face came into focus, thunderous, jaw distorted into a stone slab by the angle of the phone. "Why are you wearing a robe?" he demanded.

"Because I'm at the spa! What's the matter? Why are you asking me these—these ridiculous questions? And why"—a terrible thought was occurring to her, a swift calculation of hours and time zones that would have turned her cheeks hot, if she could still feel them—"why are you already up this early in the morning?"

"I'm not *already* up, Cass. I've been up all night."

Chip looked away from the phone, down and to the right, like he was attempting to swallow back some giant ball of emotion. Cassie tried to summon a word or two, a question, but she already knew the answer, didn't she? This sick feeling in her stomach— it wasn't just because of the soft reek of fermented sheep's dung clinging to the dank December air.

She just waited miserably for him to gather himself and continue.

"I've been up all night wondering why my wife didn't bother to tell me that the owner of the castle where she's having her so-called writers' retreat happens to be owned by the same man she's kissing in that photogr—"

The phone went silent.

"Chip?" Cassie shook the phone. "Chip? Are you there? Can you hear me? I've lost all my bars again, I don't know how, this stupid island—"

The blurred, frozen image of Chip turned black. *Beep beep beep,* said the phone.

A message popped up on the screen: Connection Failed.

"*Darn* it!" she yelled. "Darn it to *heck*! And *back again*!"

Cassie let her arm fall to her side. Tears welled behind her eyeballs.

Connection Failed.

CHAPTER EIGHT

Emma

EXCERPT FROM POLICE INTERVIEW WITH MISS EMERSON (EMMA)
ENDICOTT, 10 DECEMBER 2022

DCI: Mrs. MacDougal informed me that you were seen in the poison garden two days before the murder.

ENDICOTT: If you're referring to the greenhouse, then yes. I was. But I hadn't set out to be there. I didn't even know it existed before I ran into the estate manager.

DCI: Estate manager?

ENDICOTT: Yes—his name is Archie. Although technically, I ran into Loren, his sheepdog and she directed me to him. She's very large and fluffy and looks like a giant Havanese. I haven't done my research into sheepdogs yet so that's just a general term I'm using as I'm aware there are several different breeds that are used for herding and I'm most familiar with mutts and not purebreds. Please make sure that you've noted that in case I'm wrong. I'm a stickler for accuracy. Which is why I'm a little embarrassed to admit that I don't know Archie's last name, although I'm sure that with your expert detective abilities you should be able to ask around and find out.

DCI: [*sighs*] I've known Archie since we were wee lads. Go on, Ms. Endicott.

ENDICOTT: Yes, well, Archie was in the garden—the regular part—tending to the apiary. That's where bees are kept. For honey. I gathered that beekeeping is part of his job as estate manager.

DCI: [*coughs*] I see. And did Archie at that point in time tell you that belladonna was grown in the greenhouse?

ENDICOTT: He referred to it as Morag's medicinal garden. He told me that many of the plants were poisonous and that's why they were kept where the bees couldn't accidentally poison their honey. That's when he mentioned the belladonna. Please make a note that he volunteered that information and that I didn't ask him.

DCI: And that's the first time you learned that belladonna was grown there?

ENDICOTT: [*pause*] Yes.

DCI: Did he tell you anything else?

ENDICOTT: Not about the poison garden. He said I would need to ask Morag about the plants since it was her garden. But he did tell me a lot about bees, though. Did you know that after a drone mates with the queen, his endophallus falls off and he dies?

DCI: I probably shouldn't ask, but . . .

ENDICOTT: It's the drone's sexual organ. Don't worry, Archie had to explain it to me, too. But that's the best part about my job—learning new things that I can use later in my books.

DCI: I see. What else did you learn?

ENDICOTT: A lot about the sex lives of bees. But nothing that I feel comfortable repeating. You could ask Kat, but I wouldn't recommend it. There are some things you can't unhear.

THURSDAY, DECEMBER 8
One day before the murder . . .

EMMA STOOD ALONE in the massive entrance hall listening to . . . silence. Kat had slunk back to her den to write—or so she claimed—and Cassie had retreated to her bedroom in yet another attempt to reach Chip. Even the usual mutterings and pan banging from Morag in the kitchen were absent. It was as if everyone except her had a purpose. Or a place to be.

She moved her chin from side to side while lifting her brow, checking to see if the numbness from that morning's spa treatments had passed as Calum had assured her it would after a "wee bit of tingling." The wee bit had felt more like the stings of a dozen of Archie's honeybees, but even Emma had to admit that her pores had almost completely disappeared and her face glowed. Maybe there was more to sheep dung than anyone had ever imagined. She'd bought a bottle to take back home with her—assuming it was allowed by customs—and had plans to go back and grab one for their editor, Rachelle. It never hurt to butter up one's editor. Even if it was with sheep dung.

Her gaze fell on the poster of Presley. He was working on a book, undoubtedly the memoir he had announced that night at Bouchercon: the unvarnished, no-holds-barred account of the creating of a literary lion. The thought of his lies, all those lies, in print, as if they were true, as if they were fact, made Emma feel sick. If they wanted to know what had really gone into the creation of a literary lion, Emma could tell them. But who would listen to her? Who would listen to any of them?

Emma examined the face staring back at her, the overt smugness nearly obliterating the handsome features. Almost. She found herself starting to smile back until she read the words again.

Wake Up. It's Kill It O'Clock. Feeling bile rise from her stomach, she turned away.

An indistinct sound that might have been a sob came from upstairs, undoubtedly Cassie. Definitely not Kat, who'd probably never shed a tear that hadn't been deliberately orchestrated to provoke lust. Emma considered heading to Cassie's room to see if the other woman might need a consoling pat on the shoulder. Or just a pair of ears to listen. Listening was an underrated gift and one that Emma had in spades. She'd learned the art of encapsulating what a person was saying in a fraction of the time it took someone to say it, allowing her brain to wander freely onto other subjects that interested her. It made it easier to live with a mother who always had a ready litany of how things used to be versus how they were now, and how Emma should appreciate the hand-me-downs and the scholarships instead of complaining about taunts from her classmates.

Emma paused with her foot on the first step, hearing nothing. Even the constant prattle of rain against windows had stopped. Turning around, she almost ran to the front door and pulled it open. A pitiful sun struggled to rise above thick clouds, leaden weights fighting its attempts to burst forth and shine.

Despite the icy wind and sodden ground, Emma smiled. It was definitely going to snow. Having been raised in New England, she recognized the look and smell of a winter storm, relishing the only time of year when her family home could be disguised enough to resemble its regal neighbors. Never one to shy away from a bracing nor'easter, she sucked in a deep breath and stepped outside, shutting the heavy door firmly behind her. There was too much research still to be done and while Cassie might feel free to obsess over her Wi-Fi connection, and Kat her erotic prose, Emma felt the need to Get Things Done. Her *Mayflower* ancestors hadn't come to the New World to wallow, after all. Being productive was in her DNA.

Pulling up the collar of her coat, she headed in the direction of the village of Kinloch, bracing herself for the pain of her blister until she realized there wasn't any. Cassie had stitched up the hole in the boot lining (she apparently always carried a full-size sewing kit with her) and Kat had shown her how to securely bandage her foot. Kat had learned that particular expertise from all her strutting around in stilettos with pointy toes. This left Emma feeling uncharacteristically grateful for her two writing partners. At least that was one thing to like about them.

With no one around, she began singing out loud. "I can see clearly now, Lorraine is gone." Emma had no idea why a song about a woman named Lorraine always came to her when she walked outside after a good, soaking rain, but there it was, parked right there on the tip of her tongue. Every. Time.

The main street was nearly deserted, more than likely because it was teatime. She hoped that didn't mean that the small Historical Society that was supposed to be open today wouldn't be. If it wasn't, she could always dash into the pub for a "wee dram" and perhaps some local gossip to help with her research. Her mental clock ticked off the short time they still had in Scotland, each tick louder than the next.

The lights were on inside the building, and bells tinkled when she pushed open the door. It swung shut behind her, leaving her to take in the soft bagpipe music playing from an eighties-era boom box on a wall shelf and the intoxicating scent of musty fabrics, beeswax polish, and old books. Ambrosia for the historical biographer, and probably as much as a turn-on for her as a leather whip was to Kat. Or a Vera Bradley sale was to Cassie.

"Good afterrrnoon."

The heavily accented voice came from a tall, skinny young man, fully costumed in Highland regalia and standing next to a full-size wax Mel Gibson as Braveheart. The man carried a feather duster and finished with a swipe at Mel's face before approaching Emma.

"May I help ewe?"

Emma smiled. "I certainly hope so." She held out her hand. "I'm Emerson Endicott, and I'm one of the authors staying at the castle. And you might be . . . ?"

The man—really just an overgrown boy—switched the feather duster into his left hand to shake Emma's with a limp, sweaty palm. "I'm Brrruce MacHinist. The currrator here at the Historical Society." He smiled awkwardly, revealing slightly crooked teeth. But his smile was nice, and he had very fine green eyes; large with a thick fringe of russet lashes. "At your service. Especially if you've inquiries on the fishing industry in eighteenth-century Kinloch. I'm working on my dissertation right now so it's all fresh in me mind."

Bruce looked so hopeful that Emma hated to disappoint him. "Thank you. I'm sure it's fascinating and I promise to remember that for the next project. But right now I'm working on a book with two other authors about the history of the castle. I'd love to see anything you might have on that topic, especially a map of Kinloch Castle. Not as it is today, but perhaps the original plans from when it was built?"

His smile faded. "One of your friends was already here and I gave her a copy of the floor plans. Did she forget to tell you?"

"One of my friends?" It was hard to speak through her suddenly dry mouth.

Bruce's face deepened into a blotchy red that matched his hair and illuminated the smattering of pimples on his chin, telling Emma exactly which "friend" it had to have been. She couldn't imagine Cassie eliciting that kind of reaction.

"I see," she said. Even managed a smile. "She must have forgotten." Emma shoved her hands into the pockets of her jacket so Bruce couldn't see them curled into tight fists. Not that she'd ever even considered hitting anyone in her life—regardless of how deserving—it somehow felt empowering.

She took a deep breath. "If it's not too much trouble, would it be possible to ask for a copy of everything you gave my friend? She's very scatterbrained and this research is far too important to be left in her hands. I'm sure you understand the importance of historical accuracy—you're a museum curator!" Emma stepped closer and gave him her most ingratiating smile. "And I promise that you will get a signed first-edition copy of the book as soon as it's published."

His large Adam's apple bobbed in his throat. "Ew, I, um, weeeelll . . ."

"Great. I so appreciate it. And while you're gathering it all together, I'll take a look around. I am the literal queen of research and I can spot a well-curated collection of artifacts from a mile away. I can already tell that I won't be disappointed."

Despite his skin now resembling the deep red of a beet, Bruce's voice had recovered enough to say, "We have a wee gift shop in the back, too."

"Terrific! I'll check it out. I'll need some gifts to take back to the States."

With the resigned grimace of a kid who'd just been cheated of his lunch money, Bruce disappeared behind a curtained doorway beneath a wooden plaque, the word "OFFICE" printed in a Gaelic-type font.

Emma turned toward the large glass display cabinet by the door, which contained the obligatory muniments and bits and pieces of kitchen utensils found during the building of the new castle on top of the old one. A tiny stone cottage model labeled "Lady Ned's School for the Education and Improvement of the Girls and Women of Kinloch" sat next to a collection of handwriting samples and a textbook opened to a page about measurements.

Handmade dioramas with rudimentary clay figures depicting daily life in Kinloch from the Middle Ages to the present covered most of the shelf space. Emma looked for an attribution to a local primary school, but when she didn't find any, she had to assume that Bruce himself had made the dioramas during the long hours he probably spent alone among the exhibits.

She paused at a large hand-drawn poster next to the Mel Gibson mannequin, its title printed in large bold lettering: "FACT VS FICTION." Her eyes scanned the neatly numbered list, pausing at number three: The average height of a Scotsman is 170 cm (5 ft 7 in) and not 198 cm (6 ft 6 in). Her gaze wandered down the list, past things she already knew regarding clans and kilts and haggis, coming to a complete halt on the last: The average length of a Scotsman's erect penis is 13.12 cm (5.16 in) and 11.66 cm (4.59 in) in girth. Not 20.32 cm (8 in) long and 14 cm (5.51 in) as is depicted in popular fiction.

Emma took a covert picture of the poster with her phone, not wanting to subject poor Bruce to the questions she was dying to ask. She could probably google the most obvious and save the rest for some in-depth research. This last boosted her spirits a bit, although it did nothing to soften her anger toward Kat.

The sound of a copier machine whirred in the back office as Emma continued to peruse the various displays. A wooden table set at kids' height sat under a sign that said TOUCH ME! The tabletop contained various pelts of wool in different thicknesses with typed signage explaining how much time had elapsed between samples. A clay sheep (next to a DO NOT TOUCH!) with an improbable pink clay smile and large eyes with tiny clay eyelashes stood inside a shoebox pasture, a dangling sign informing viewers, I'M WOOLLY WOOLLY SOFT!

Emma snapped a picture, although she was fairly certain she'd never use it in her research. It was just that it was so, well, cute.

The museum had everything it seemed, except for any mention of Naughty Ned or his infamous sex toy collection. Not that she was surprised since it was clear that the man was not fondly remembered by the townsfolk. Or Archie.

Emma headed toward the back of the museum where another Gaelic-font printed sign identified the gift shop. She selected a few key chains and plaid hair scrunchies (Cassie would be thrilled) from the obligatory racks conveniently set near the register. Various clan paraphernalia hung from every wall and a thick rack of sweaters (wool, of course) lined an entire wall.

She headed toward a floor-to-ceiling bookshelf, hoping to find a selection of local history books. She hated to pay excess baggage fees, but she always made the exception for books. Mostly because she could expense them.

Except instead of the expected A to Zed of Kinloch history, she was met by a set of coordinated book spines with different titles all in the same gold-embossed flowery font. She recognized one from her own prized—yet hidden from her mother—book collection. A sign with a plaid background had been attached to the top shelf announcing AUTOGRAPHED BOOKS BY BESTSELLING AUTHOR KARYN BLACK.

With an embarrassingly shaky hand, Emma pulled out one of the books and read the title. *Sweet Savage Laird.* Cover model Fabio's familiar thick-maned head and bared chest was splashed across the cover and when she opened the book and saw the signature of her favorite author (not that she would ever admit that to *anybody* because she was a Serious Author and didn't read Those Kinds of Books) right there, she thought she might faint. And she was *definitely* not the fainting type.

Emma pressed the book against her chest. It was the first book in Black's The Lairds of Kinloch series. The same series that had gotten Emma through middle school and high school; the same series that had kept her warm on the long New England winter nights without heat. The same series that had taught her everything she knew about sex. In the past decade, Karyn Black had switched from writing historical romance to contemporary thrillers with kick-ass heroines. Emma loved those, too, and devoured each one as soon as they were available at the library, but her favorites would always be the romances of her lonely teenage years.

She scanned the titles, reading them out loud in a reverent whisper: *Laird of Ice; Laird of Fire; The Laird and the Lass; The Laird and the Lioness; Gentle Laird; A Laird in Winter; Laird, My Love; The Laird and the Lamb.* This last, seen with her adult eyes, carried with it an ick factor. She must have made a face because she was startled by Bruce interrupting her reverie with, "It's purrrrely metaphorrrical, Miss Endicott."

"Of course," she said. Turning back to the shelf, she quickly calculated how much the baggage fees would be if she bought the entire autographed series. "Do you ship?"

At his blank expression, she said, "Never mind." Reluctantly, she put the book back on the shelf. "Does Karyn Black come here often to sign her books?"

"Och, no. Not for a long time now. Her people send those so that we always have a good stock of 'em."

Emma noticed he was carrying a reusable tote bag with a graphic of the castle printed on it that bulged on the sides. "Were you able to make copies of everything?"

"Yes." He smiled but didn't hand her the tote even when she reached for it.

"That will be thirty-two pounds."

"Wait, what?"

"For the copier paper and the novelty tote bag."

She stared back at him, wondering if she should point out that she hadn't asked for a novelty tote bag. "Did you charge my friend, too?"

His face flamed a vibrant red, making her wish she hadn't said anything. "Never mind. I appreciate your help." She quickly added the key chains and scrunchies and handed him her credit card. She'd forgotten that the only race more frugal than New Englanders were the Scots.

Emma was still fuming as she trudged back to the castle, this time with the wind in her face and the bag acting like a hand pushing her backward. Her mood hadn't improved by the time the Obelisk came in sight, making her pause. The collection of Edwardian sex toys was inside, undoubtedly along with other valuable documents and items that Presley would want to keep to himself. That made her angrier, not to mention that there was an entire tower of secrets to be explored and she was the only one who apparently appreciated that fact. Otherwise, she wouldn't be standing there *alone*, would she? *Someone* had to find the hidden tunnel, and she was now in possession of the floor plan that just might show where it was.

If she had the time, she would wait for Cassie and Kat so they could explore together. But that was exactly it, wasn't it? They didn't have the luxury of time, and nobody seemed to care one little bit about the ticking clock except for her. Fine. She would just have to do what needed to be done.

With renewed purpose, Emma stomped toward the castle, stopping only when she'd reached the door and realized that she had no idea what to do next. She almost wished that her writing partners were there to confer. Kat would have some devious idea on how to explore without getting caught, and Cassie would probably have warm blueberry muffins in her quilted bag to give as a peace offering if they were found trespassing.

Emma let herself inside the castle and was once again met with an almost eerie silence, the absence of noise only compounding her sense of urgency. She ran up the stairs toward the library in the lady's tower where they'd found the hidden room, which Kat had said held the entrance to the hidden tunnel. Emma halted her ascent. But that would be assuming any words coming out of Kat's mouth could even be believed. Because Emma was about one hundred percent positive that nobody would ever put a hidden passage in a library. It was much too obvious. Not to mention the fact that the library was on the wrong side of the castle.

When she reached her room, she dumped out the contents of the tote bag and retrieved the sheaf of papers Bruce had given her. Sitting on the bed, she moistened her finger and began to efficiently scan each page until she found what she was looking for—a hand-drawn floor plan showing the basic layout of the castle. Emma sat up straighter, holding the page closer to make sure she wasn't imagining anything. Yes. There it was in faded yet plain ink. The laird's bedroom, sitting room, and dressing room. And a line skirting the castle's tower, then across the grounds. Definitely a tunnel, and a direct access leading from the laird's castle bedroom straight to the Obelisk.

Her excitement only barely eclipsed her anger at Kat. Kat knew about the tunnel—had *known* about it—when she'd put on the charade in the library with Emma and Cassie about how the entrance to the tunnel had to be there. Even when all of Emma's vast experience with these things told her that it wasn't possible.

With hands shaking in anger and anticipation, Emma jumped off the bed, shoving everything that Bruce had given her back into the tote bag, and marched down the hallway toward where the laird's bedroom door should be.

Emma stopped at the closed door, her enthusiasm quickly quenched by her inbred good manners. One didn't just show up at a stranger's bedroom door. She had no idea who might be staying in the laird's room, having not yet met anyone who claimed to be one. Quite possibly, BSP could have already taken up residence in what he considered his rightful accommodations and could be standing on the other side, ready to pounce. All right, maybe pounce wasn't the right word. But whatever movement or expression BSP might be preparing, Emma knew she didn't want to be unprepared for either one.

She took in a deep breath and exhaled slowly, willing her heartbeat to slow. She was no longer a gullible undergrad. She was a grown and accomplished woman, author of thirty highly regarded books with good reviews in all the right places. They might not have been bestsellers, but several prestigious university libraries had purchased a copy. And her aunt Wilhelmina, who lived on Beacon Hill in Boston, had hosted her at her book club of admitted literary snobs and Emma had been assured that her book had been well-liked. She wasn't a nobody, and she had as much right to knock on the door as anyone.

With renewed confidence, she raised her fist and pounded it against the door once, and then twice for good measure. Emma wanted BSP to be aware that she was there and she wasn't one to be cowered by charm anymore. She waited with righteous indignation for him to open the door, her speech already prepared to ask him in a nonconfrontational way to meet her downstairs so they could chat about the "good ol' days" at Bowdoin. She'd even plastered what she hoped was a provocative smile on her face. Not that she had any interest in discussing anything with him. She just needed him to leave the room for long enough so she could search for the entrance to the tunnel.

Except the door didn't open. Nor did she hear any movement from the other side. She waited a full minute—using the second hand on her ancient Timex—before raising her hand again and banging two more times. After another full minute, Emma pressed her ear against the wood, straining to hear any sort of sound or movement. But there was nothing.

She looked at the latch, wondering if it might be unlocked.

All she'd need to do would be to push it down with her thumb to find out. Her gaze traveled back to the imposing wooden door, as if willing it to open on its own so that she wouldn't be accused of trespassing. Although it wouldn't really be trespassing, would it? They were paying guests at the castle on a writers' retreat. Exploring the castle was part of the experience. Or at least it should be. It was probably in all the documentation that Cassie had sent when the retreat had been booked.

When the door failed to comply, she took a deep breath and before she could talk herself out of it, Emma grabbed the door handle and pushed down on the thumb latch. Something clicked and she froze, waiting for someone to appear and ask her what she was doing. With one glaring exception, Emma had always considered herself someone who moved boldly toward achieving her goals, never once having had to resort to breaking and entering. That was more Kat's MO. But the door was unlocked, she told herself. Which meant that wasn't breaking and entering. Technically. She was simply *exploring*.

She pushed on the door. It swung open, the heavy hinges giving out a prerequisite moan of protest, the sound most likely manufactured by their host in a misguided attempt at historic authenticity.

"Hello?" she called out.

Emboldened by the silence, Emma stepped into what appeared to be the sitting room portion of the laird's suite, her attention focused on a massive leather-topped Edwardian pedestal desk that stood tucked into an alcove formed by the curve of the tower. Emma knew what it was because an identical one had once sat in her father's study and had been in the family since 1903. Until it was sold to fund the new roof when a heavy snow had collapsed the old one into the back half of the house.

This particular desk sported an IBM laptop of a similar vintage as her own technological relic. A half-filled decanter with a lone double old-fashioned glass sat next to it. Emma recognized the now defunct Edinburgh Crystal thistle pattern, easily identified by the etched thistles on both the decanter's body and on the glass. The pattern was familiar to her because her grandparents had had a complete set, including the cordial decanter and eight glasses.

With a careful finger, Emma traced the fragile edges of the glass. She had always loved this pattern, the delicate etching of the pretty flower of Scotland, and the feel of the smooth crystal against her lips. Her grandmother had let her drink orange juice from them during her visits when she was small. Emma wasn't sure what happened to the crystal when her grandparents' house had been sold and they had been moved to a nursing home. Despite her grandmother's assurances that Emma would be left all the crystal, it had never materialized. Or it had and her parents had thought it more prudent to sell the glassware so they could use the money for practical things.

The only other item on the desktop was a framed, amber-tinted photo of Castle Kinloch as it must have been a century before. Instead of the modern outbuildings now surrounding the castle, the landscape was liberally dotted with grazing sheep and a large fluffy sheepdog replica of Loren sprinting toward a runaway lamb.

Nothing on the desk made her think of BSP. She would have expected an obnoxious vintage typewriter, a filtered water station, and a dozen photos of himself in various clichéd male author poses and wearing the same insufferable and self-satisfied smile he wore in the poster downstairs. But not these items that seemed to have been placed solely for their purpose and beauty for the person sitting at the desk, rather than to impress anyone.

With a tentative pull, Emma tugged on the center desk drawer handle, oddly relieved to find it locked. It was one thing to walk into an unoccupied room that may or may not be considered trespassing, but to go through someone's desk could only be defined as an invasion of privacy. And that was definitely not a line Emma was willing to cross. Yet. Unless it was the private papers of the dead.

Turning her back to the desk, she faced the opposite side of the sitting room where the entire space had been fitted with wall-to-wall bookshelves. She took a step forward, the bottom of her foot crunching over something on the stone floor. Gingerly lifting her heel, she bent to examine the shiny gold-and-black object. Pinching it between her two fingers, Emma held it close to her face, momentary confusion quickly replaced with disbelief followed by sheer, blind anger.

It was a piece of jewelry. An earring, to be specific. A gaudy spider earring with a fake diamond for its head and another slightly smaller one dangling like a, well, male appendage. An earring with which she was unfortunately familiar as she'd seen it dozens of times in the last few days. An earring usually attached to one of Kat's ears. Emma squeezed the offending item in her fist, feeling the pointed ends digging into her palm and feeding her anger.

But *of course* Kat had already been in the laird's suite. She'd had a full day's lead with the floor plans and would have come looking for the entrance to the tunnel just like Emma was doing. But why on earth would Kat be so secretive about the one thing they were all looking for? Did Kat believe she had a bigger right to it? Did she have any intention of sharing what she may have found with Cassie and Emma?

Emma took two deep, shuddering breaths to calm herself, then shoved the earring into her pocket. She'd have to confront Kat, but only after her anger had cooled. Otherwise, she wasn't completely sure that she wouldn't resort to violence with one of Kat's stilettos.

Before moving forward, Emma paused again, listening for any sound or movement outside in the hallway. Satisfied that she wasn't on the brink of discovery, she stepped closer to the rows of shelves, remembering how Cassie had discovered the secret room in the other tower by pulling on a book. So old-school, but whatever. She'd have to assume that Kat had already tugged on each book spine and prepared herself to do the same. Emma was nothing if not thorough. And the incentive of beating Kat at her own game was an invigorating motivator.

A handy ladder attached to a brightly polished brass rail traversed the entire width of the bookcase. The spines on many of the books appeared worn and cracked, making Emma begin to salivate at the thought of diving into them, perhaps organizing them chronologically or by subject matter before taking notes.

Resisting the urge to rub her hands together, she climbed the ladder and began perusing the titles still legible on the spines starting from the very top shelf. As she tugged on each spine, she read the titles: *On the Origins of Species*; *The Complete Works of William Shakespeare*; *The Republic*; *Critique of Pure Reason*; *A Vindication of the Rights of Women*; *The Wealth of Nations*; *The Meaning of Relativity*.

Emma continued across the length of the first shelf before moving onto the second as her bewilderment grew, and not just because she hadn't yet found a secret opening but because none of the books were ones she would have expected BSP to have on his bookshelves. *Writing for Dummies* and *The Kama Sutra*, yes, but not books like these that were meant to expand the mind and showed a keen intellect. After all, Emma had read all of them so she would know.

As she continued tugging on spines and reading titles, her confusion began turning to disbelief. Not only were these books definitely not the sorts of books that BSP would know about much less have in his personal library, but they were the exact same books Emma would have put on her own shelves if she could have afforded them instead of having only checked them out of libraries. These weren't just books she'd read, these were titles she'd loved and reread countless times. She wondered if these books were owned by the actual laird, whoever that might be.

Touching each spine was like revisiting old friends: *The Warrior Queens: Boadicea's Chariot*; *Cromwell, Our Chief of Men*; *The Weaker Vessel: Woman's Lot in Seventeenth-Century England*; *George Washington: Selected Writings*; *The House of Morgan*; *The Warburgs*. She nearly squealed when she came to the entire collection of Dick Francis novels, the set nearly overtaking the third shelf. Aside from Karyn Black, Dick Francis was her absolutely favorite genre fiction writer. She actually included this in her biography, wanting to appear more approachable to readers (something suggested by her editor) while also considering Dick Francis an acceptable choice since he had been the late queen's favorite, too.

Emma stepped off the ladder and began investigating the bottom shelves, forcing herself to go faster. It would be not only awkward to be caught snooping in the laird's suite, but also frustrating if she were caught before finding a tunnel or anything else that might be useful to their research—assuming Kat hadn't already succeeded. Emma doubted she'd get a second chance.

She gave the final book on the bottom shelf a firm tug, desperately hoping that this would be "the one." It wasn't. Emma turned around to resume her investigation. On the far side of the room, she noticed for the first time a small antique library table with slanted shelves beneath a flat writing space that sat against the wall dwarfed by the large desk beside it, which is probably why Emma hadn't seen it. A modern spiral notebook with a mechanical pencil rested on the flat top and a small collection of large ledger-size books protruded from the edges of the shelves.

Emma slid out one of the books, noting the cracked leather and various stains of unknown origin. Setting the tote bag on the floor, she sat down on the worn wool rug and carefully opened the book on her lap. She smiled to herself, surprised and delighted to find ruled ledger pages filled with columns of numbers showing debits and credits for what appeared to be household items—candles, flour, tea, wool, and whisky—as well as a list of names next to various amounts Emma assumed were wages.

Everything had been recorded in a neat, elegant hand. These were clearly the household accounts that would have been the responsibility of the lady of the house, perhaps Lady Ned herself. Emma flipped pages before realizing that she needed to take pictures so that she could give them a closer examination later.

She placed the book on the floor and took pictures of every page before snapping it shut, feeling more than a little annoyed that her requests sent to the Kinloch archivist for anything about Lady Ned while researching the Prunella book had gone unanswered.

Although, if she thought about it, the lack of attention to detail of the Kinloch staff might be the singular reason why she, Cassie, and Kat had been allowed into the castle at all. It was either a failure to communicate or the names of attendees were simply too insignificant for the illustrious Mr. Presley to want to know. And if Emma were a betting person—and she definitely wasn't—she would wager on the latter.

She was about to return the book to the shelf when she paused, opening up the ledger to look at it again, not at the content but at the handwriting. It was . . . familiar. Very familiar. Or maybe that was because all well-bred ladies of the Edwardian age had been taught by the same school of governesses. She tucked it inside the tote, wanting to examine it more closely under the desk light before replacing it on the shelf.

Moving faster now, she walked through the open doorway to where a massive four-poster bed, hung with draped Kinloch tartan plaid, dominated the equally massive room. The laird's bedroom, according to the floor plans. Emma walked toward the bed, taking in the unexpectedly light-filled room. Plaid curtains had been pulled back allowing unencumbered daylight to shine through tall windows. Dark fabrics and heavy furniture weren't usually on her list of favorites, but there was something about the sparsity of the room's contents that allowed the bed, an antique wardrobe, and a dark leather club chair and inlaid side table to stand out. There was even a casually placed book sitting on top of the table, another empty double old-fashioned thistle glass sitting next to it. It was decidedly a masculine room, but not *so* masculine as to be uncomfortable to anyone else. Even Emma could imagine lying down on those fluffy down pillows and snuggling under the plaid duvet. As long as BSP wasn't in it.

Through another doorway leading from the bedroom, she spotted a bathroom with floors made from the same stone as the castle along with a jetted tub decked out with brass fixtures. The deliberate ignorance of period appropriateness made her grit her teeth but didn't surprise her. She'd seen enough of the castle to expect particle board mantels and plastic chandelier medallions. And a Jacuzzi in the laird's suite. The tub was more BSP's style, but still. Despite the size of it, the absence of phallus-shaped candles, erotic art, and pictures of him made her again doubt that BSP had anything to do with the décor.

Entering the bedroom again, Emma studied the perimeter of the room's stone walls, searching for spots that might conceal a hidden door. Prepared to admit defeat, she turned back toward the sitting room just as her gaze fell on the table and chair, seeing again the book sitting on top, a piece of paper jutting out of the middle like a bookmark. The BSP she'd remembered had a disdain for other people's books, placing them face down and open-leafed, thus breaking the spine, or—worse—folding down pages to mark his place.

Listening for any sound from the hallway and noting a space behind one of the curtains as a potential hiding place, Emma retreated into the bedroom to get a closer look. With a giddy shriek she plucked the book from the table, taking in the familiar title: *The Unsinkable Prunella Schuyler* by Emerson Endicott. A postcard slipped from between the pages, and Emma found herself staring at the familiar face of Prunella Schuyler, survivor of the *Lusitania*, witness to history, and the woman who'd practically lived in Emma's head for the five years it took to write her biography. The postcard, being used as a bookmark, was from the National Archives, depicting a portrait hanging in the galleries of Prunella atop a large black stallion on a grouse hunt with the Prince of Wales in 1900. It had been taken right here, on the grounds of Kinloch.

The edge of an old photograph poked out from the back of the book. Emma carefully removed it. With a start, she recognized the faces of the two women standing next to each other in front of the stone fireplace in the keeping room of the castle. Prunella and Lady Ned. Emma felt another wave of irritation at the Kinloch archivist. This photograph would have been incredibly helpful, acting as confirmation to Prunella's claims through correspondence that she and Lady Ned were "dear dear" friends.

Emma closed her eyes and hugged the book to her chest, feeling vindicated. She wanted to snap a photo of the book and the room from where it had been found to prove to her agent that people *did* actually read biographies of obscure historical females and that Emma was quite possibly a pioneer in a brand-new genre.

She blinked, her smile quickly fading when she remembered where she was standing. And to whom the book actually belonged. Had BSP changed? Was he a different man than the one she'd known in her early twenties? Nothing, from the neatly tucked white bedsheets to the tasteful hunting prints on the walls to the utilitarian bench at the foot of the bed where a pair of wellies waited on the floor, reminded her of BSP.

"Are you a fan of Ms. Schuyler, then?"

Emma yelped in surprise, dropping the tote bag and scattering Bruce's photocopies. She jerked around and found herself looking into Archie's sparkling green eyes—although from amusement or anger wasn't clear.

"I, um . . ." She took a step back, her question of where he'd come from and why she hadn't heard the door open faded in her throat as she took in his equestrian garb: tall riding boots, snug pants, and a closely fit jacket outlining his muscled thighs and biceps. He held a riding crop, the sight of which brought beads of perspiration to her hairline. She may have swayed, causing Archie— what *was* his last name?—to reach out to steady her. Emma held out her hand. "I'm fine. You just caught me by surprise."

"Aye," Archie responded in the ambiguous one-syllable word that could have meant anything from, *Of course you are fine*, to *You're lying and we both know it*.

Attempting to regain her composure, Emma bent over to retrieve the tote and a handful of the papers, then slowly straightened to find Archie holding the postcard.

"Oh, thank you." Before she could free a hand, Archie plucked the Prunella book from her grasp and studied the cover before looking at her again.

"May I ask what you're doing in here?" he asked, his expression neutral.

Unable to meet his eyes, she focused on the signet ring he wore on his right hand. "Research," she said, although it came out sounding more like a question. Her words began to tumble out of her mouth in an attempt to speak so fast that he couldn't tell she was lying. "The door was unlocked, and when I spotted the books, I couldn't help myself." She offered what she hoped looked like an ingratiating smile. "I was hoping to find information about the history of the castle and maybe Naughty Ned himself. For our book." Which was all true. Up to a point. Still, she felt a lump of guilt in her throat. She hated lying, which meant she was terrible at it.

"So, then, you're a fan?"

"Of Ned?"

He held up the book and tapped the cover, the gold signet ring sparkling on his finger. "Of the Unsinkable Prunella."

Relieved that he seemed to have accepted her explanation, she said, "I wouldn't call myself a fan, but I will agree that she was an incredibly interesting subject to write about." She cleared her throat. "I'm the author." She couldn't hide the pride in her voice.

Archie studied the cover. "Ah, so you're Emerson Endicott. Your author photo doesn't do you justice." He flipped through the pages, stopping midway through, a smile crossing his face. "I loved this part about her chasing the Prince of Wales. Although we will need to discuss your assertion that his mistress, Lillie Langtree, saw Prunella as a serious rival and attempted to poison her."

"I found several primary sources stating that, including Prunella's memoirs and several letters that made that claim. I might have found more if the Kinloch archivist had ever bothered to respond to my requests for documents. But if you'll look at the footnotes that I very carefully . . ."

"Impressive," he said, cutting her off gently. "You did a brilliant job of citing your sources. I made an attempt to find many of them to read, but unfortunately, they were a little too obscure for a layman such as myself. You'll have to share your research methods with me some time."

Emma felt her chest expand. "I would be happy to. It's not often I meet another history aficionado. I'm afraid we're a rare breed. Especially those of us who are sticklers to the truth without any embellishments." She paused, looked up into his green eyes. "Does that mean you've read the book?"

"I have. It was my first of yours, and now I'm going through and reading your entire backlist. But I think I need to read this one again so I can picture your face as if you're telling me the story yourself. I imagine it would double my reading pleasure."

She flushed. "That's . . . very kind of you to say."

His smile faded as he noticed the spilled pile of photocopies still on the floor. "What are these?"

"Research. From Bruce MacHinist at the Historical Society. It's why I'm here, remember?"

He picked up the pages and began flipping through them. "And just what sort of research are you expecting to find in these?"

She straightened her shoulders, imagining her mother's finger pressed into her spine to make her stop slumping. "I don't know. Not really. That's the fun part of research—never knowing what I might find. It's always the obscure kernel that can make for the most interesting stories."

"Is it?"

There was something in his eyes that seemed almost like a challenge to see who would cross the electrified air between them first. "I'm sorry. I didn't mean . . ." Her words faded as she realized she didn't have anything to say.

Archie looked at her for a long moment without speaking. Finally, he handed the pages back to her. "You should probably go now."

He motioned her toward the door and she meekly obliged, but as she turned to go she spotted a missed piece of paper on the floor—the photocopy of the Edward VII sex chair. Archie picked it up, glancing at it with a raised eyebrow. "More research?"

"I, um, yes. As I mentioned, an avid historian never knows where she might find an important kernel of information. Or her next book idea."

His lips quirked and she was almost sure that was a twinkle in the green depths of his eyes. "Well, then. If I read about an Edwardian sex contraption in your next book, I'll know where you found the idea. Maybe I'll even picture your face while I'm reading."

Feeling faint from all the blood rushing to her head, Emma

shoved the book into her tote and headed toward the doorway wishing it were possible to just disappear instead of doing the walk of shame with his eyes boring into her back.

She'd reached the doorway but paused when he called her name.

"Miss Endicott?"

She turned, her reddened face hopefully enough of a punishment for him. She would literally expire if he made her leave the castle for trespassing. Her mother might never recover. "Yes?"

"What Sir Edward did still has a real resonance with the people of Kinloch and you and your friends should tread lightly. You seem the sort to appreciate the feelings and complexities of the historical people you write about so I would like to think that you can grasp that this is something that shouldn't be exploited or sensationalized." He took a step closer, allowing Emma to see the dark pupils at the center of his eyes. "There are some stories that are better not told. You'd best remember that."

With a quick nod, she hurried down the hallway, belatedly realizing that she still had the ledger book in the tote bag. She'd return it later, but not now. Definitely not now.

When Emma arrived back at her room, she fumbled for her key, her fingers suddenly turned to rubber and refusing to cooperate. After several failed attempts, the key fell to the floor with a soft clink.

Resigned, she pressed her forehead against the closed door, her thoughts rotating between her abject humiliation at having been caught trespassing, and the persistent question of where Archie had been before he'd appeared without having made a sound.

CHAPTER NINE

Kat

Excerpt from police interview with Ms. Katja de Noir, 10 December 2022

DCI [*holding up his phone*]: Do you recognize this woman, Ms. de Noir?

DE NOIR: Oooh, Snoggr. Do you Snog, Detective Chief Inspector?

DCI: Not during interviews. [*pause*] I take it that you are familiar with the app in question?

DE NOIR: Familiar sounds so . . . familiar. Let's just say I'm not unacquainted with it.

DCI: On Wednesday, the seventh of December, someone used your phone, Ms. de Noir, to register a profile as a Kirsty MacMackie. Did you create that profile?

DE NOIR: Research takes me strange places sometimes. . . .

DCI: Strange places—like the Obelisk last night?

DE NOIR: I didn't say that.

DCI: I would like to impress upon you the seriousness of your situation, Ms. de Noir. Last night, Brett Saffron Presley was found dead wearing clothing you purchased after he made an assignation with an imaginary woman you created. Is there anything you would like to tell me?

DE NOIR: Yes.

DCI: [*motions to PC to make sure to take notes*]

DE NOIR: Stay off Snoggr. It's really just not worth it.

DCI: I imagine Brett Saffron Presley might share that view . . . Kirsty.

Thursday, December 8
One day before the murder . . .

S HE'D LOST HER earring.

Not just any earring. Oh no, Kat wasn't talking about the subtle little pearl or diamond stud her half sisters or Emma might discreetly flaunt behind their shiny straight blond hair. Nope. Nothing that simple. These were enormous, spider-shaped faux Gothic extravaganzas Kat had found for three bucks at CVS in the post-Halloween sales. They were roughly two inches long and not only did the spider have a giant faux-diamond for a head, it also had a shiny faux-diamond dangle.

Crap. Kat put her hand to the empty hole in her ear where the earring should have hung. Crap, crap, crap.

It wasn't in her room. It wasn't anywhere along the corridor. Which meant . . . she'd lost it when she was crawling under furniture and sticking her head upside down to examine the woodwork in the old laird's chamber looking for the secret passage.

The secret passage she wasn't supposed to know about because she hadn't told the others.

Well, if she hadn't been able to find it, that was almost the same as not knowing about it, right? Kat told herself righteously as she hurried along the corridor to the laird's suite. But if anyone found that earring . . . She just had to find it first, that was all.

Kat was almost there, reaching for the giant Gothic room key she'd discovered opened pretty much every door in the castle— way to leave your guests vulnerable, Castle Kinloch; anyone could walk into any bedroom at any time—when the door swung open. And there, framed in the doorway, stood . . . Archie and Emma?

"Miss Endicott?"

Archie had his hand pressed against the doorframe in the classic *lean* move explained so well by Bill Pullman in *While You Were Sleeping*. Emma was looking up at him with her lips slightly parted and her cheeks flushed. Her bosom was heaving discreetly beneath her threadbare Brooks Brothers pullover.

Kat jerked behind a piece of statuary. What in the hell was Emma doing in the laird's chamber? What was Archie doing in the laird's chamber? Was Emma double-crossing them with Archie?

Or was their connection of a more . . . intimate kind?

No. It couldn't be. Kat's gaydar couldn't be that wrong—could it? The way yon braw laird was smoldering at Emma was enough to make her doubt her own instincts. It was this retreat, this castle; it all had her off-balance, overthinking everything.

From behind someone's large, stone head, Kat could just make out Emma beneath Archie's arm as he growled, "There are some stories that are better not told. You'd best remember that."

Kat crunched herself up behind the statue, wishing it were easier to crouch in stiletto boots—dammit, her thighs were killing her—as a bemused Emma reeled down the hallway. Kat couldn't blame her. That had been surprisingly sexy. Pure Karyn Black material.

Oh, Laird, my love . . .

Kat bit down on her lip hard, repressing the urge to laugh

maniacally. *Control yourself, de Noir.* Emma was busy fumbling with her room key, trying and failing to insert the key in the lock. And if that wasn't a metaphor . . .

Slowly, Kat straightened, inching down the hallway until she was at a place where she could plausibly be coming from the stairs. Changing her stride to a swagger, she called out, "Having a bit of trouble over there?"

Emma dropped her keys on the floor with a clatter.

Emma dove for the keys and came up distinctly red in the face, flipping her ponytail back like a mare swatting flies. "What are you doing here?"

"Looking for you, of course," lied Kat. She forced an insolent smirk. "So, what's the story, morning glory? Don't hold out on me. We're besties, remember?"

"You tell me—*bestie.*" Emma narrowed her eyes at Kat. "You're only wearing one earring."

Shit. Kat clapped a hand to her ear, wishing she'd thought to take out the telltale spider. "It's a look. And speaking of looks . . . *Someone* seems to be exhibiting *all* the classic hallmarks of sexual arousal. Flushed cheeks, flaring nostrils, heaving bosom . . ."

Emma went, if possible, even pinker. She retrieved her key from the floor and focused doggedly on fitting her key into her lock. "I had a peat wrap."

"So did I. I'm not palpitating like the heroine on the cover of a Karyn Black novel."

"Karyn Black." The door gave with somewhat more force than necessary. Emma stood in the doorway, blocking Kat's path. "You mean like the Karyn Black novels on display at the *Historical Society gift shop*?"

Emma had gone to the Historical Society? Kat had been so busy doing her own skulking, it had never occurred to her that Emma might double-check her sources. What had she been thinking? It was Emma. Of course, she had double-checked her sources. And if she'd gone to the Historical Society and seen Bruce . . .

Shit.

No wonder she'd been in the laird's chamber. The only question was . . . had she found the earring? Kat was amazed by how fervently she hoped Emma hadn't.

"I mean like the Karyn Black novels that were for sale in every supermarket and drugstore in the nineties." Kat breezed past Emma into Emma's room, draping herself seductively across a tartan settee. "Don't try to change the subject. You bumped into Archie, didn't you?"

"What if I did? He works here." Emma stomped into the room, dumping the keys and a tote bag with the Historical Society logo emblazoned on the front of it on her desk. Unlike Kat's room, Emma's barely showed any signs of habitation. Only a pair of navy blue pajamas with white piping, neatly mended and laid out carefully at the edge of the bed, betrayed any hint of the occupant. "I was doing research. He happened to come in."

"Oh, he came *in*, did he?" Sometimes it was almost too easy. Sometimes Kat hated herself a little. But she could feel herself relaxing slightly. Maybe she'd gotten lucky. Maybe Archie had seen Emma go into the laird's chamber and intercepted her before she could find anything. Like a tunnel. Or Kat's earring.

Emma's aristocratic nostrils flared. "Can you give it a rest, already? Must everything be tainted by cheap innuendo? He likes books," she burst out. "He's read my books. He appreciates good fiction."

Her lips pursed shut, like a Jane Austen character containing an excess of emotion lest an unseemly display of actual human feeling roil the tea. And this was why Kat wrote demon lovers instead of Regency drawing room comedies. She preferred to repress her repressions.

Kat propped herself up on one arm. "Oh, honey. *Good fiction* is all you're going to get with that one. Now, if you're looking for something more than good fiction, I'd say . . . go for the beefcake in the kilt. He may have a faint eau de dung, but beneath that lab coat, he was *ripped*."

"You can't just objectify them like that!"

"Why not? Men do it to us all the time. What do they say? Turn and turnabout is fair play. Not that I believe in playing fair. They can't screw us if we screw them first."

"Oh, that's your plan, isn't it—screw them all first?"

Kat rose to her feet. Kat's four-inch heels brought them just about eye to eye. "Isn't that my contribution to our little endeavor? You bring the archives, I bring the funk?"

Emma didn't look away. "I'm not the only one going after the archives, am I?"

It was something about the quiet dignity with which she said it that hurt so much. Like Emma minded. Like she thought they were really in it together.

"Do you have something you'd like to tell me, Kat?" asked Emma tightly.

It was on the tip of Kat's tongue to say something—apologize, even. But what was she apologizing for? They weren't besties, not really.

"I don't have any designs on your Archie, if that's what you're worried about," Kat said roughly.

Emma stared at her for a long moment. "It's not. If you—"

Just say it already, Kat thought, her heart racing under her push-up bra. *Just say it*. Then they could pull off the Band-Aid and have a knock-down, drag-out argument, but at least they wouldn't be pulsing with guilt and subtext.

"Yes?" Kat demanded. "If I . . ."

Emma turned abruptly away. "If you want to know what Calum has under his kilt, why don't you go after him yourself?"

"I didn't go after Calum because . . ." Because one night, when she'd still been a normal woman with normal appetites and normal dreams, Brett Saffron Presley had invited her back to his cabin at Yaddo on what she thought was meant to be a date. Kat pulled her stiff lips into a seductive pout. "Because I'm all work, work, work. Unlike some of us, I'm not wasting our precious time romancing the staff."

"Archie isn't staff. I mean, he is staff, but—never mind. You're right." Emma yanked another threadbare Brooks Brothers pullover off a neatly folded pile of threadbare cable-knit pullovers and tied it over her shoulders. She looked like an Abercrombie ad. "We came here to work, not to flirt. We have a job to do. Let's do it."

"Well, then," said Kat, not quite sure how to deal with this iron-spined Emma, the one who looked right through her. The one who knew she'd lied. "Let's go find the third of our merry little band."

"WHAT?" CASSIE FLUNG the door open, her hair standing out around her head like Medusa's snakes, her face mottled, a tartan makeup case in her hand.

Cassie's bed was a mad pile of patterns: Black Watch pants clashing with Royal Stewart pajamas, a Campbell pashmina sneering at a Gordon kilt.

"That's a lot of plaid," said Kat.

"I'm going home." Cassie took an armload of clothes and shoved them, without folding, into the Vera Bradley bag.

Kat could see Emma flinch, although whether it was at the sentiment or the lack of proper creases, she wasn't quite sure. "Now?" Emma asked faintly.

"Now! Tonight!" Cassie was shoving fabric in by main force, using two hands to push it down.

Emma gently reached around her, extracted a Lands' End Black Watch jersey dress, and began neatly folding it.

"It doesn't wrinkle," said Cassie distractedly. "That's why I packed it. Also because of the plaid. What was I thinking?"

"That plaid is the new black?" volunteered Kat. Just looking at all those tartans together was giving her a headache.

"Cassie." Emma put a hand on the smaller woman's shoulder. "Cassie, you can't mean to leave tonight."

"Why not?" Cassie jerked away, moving frantically to the desk to sweep up a laptop in a tartan case, a travel mouse pad—who still used a mouse?—and a mug featuring potbellied cartoon Highlanders holding blunderbusses with the legend "Haggis Hunting in Scotland." She dumped the lot on top of the mess of plaid. "Calum can drive me to the dock—"

"Whoa." For some reason, until then, Kat hadn't taken it all quite seriously. Sure, Cassie was piling her clothes on the bed. But Cassie always looked like she existed in the middle of a hurricane. Something to do with having six kids. But the mention of Calum and the dock made it all very real. "You can't leave tonight. It's too late."

"Why? We haven't done anything yet. We can still back out. I mean, we'd have to pay back the advance, but—I don't know, maybe we could still do the book, only long-distance. We could email each other chapters, or something." Cassie clutched a Stewart plaid robe against her chest, rocking back and forth. "I should never have come. I should have known it was a crazy idea. I can't do this anymore—"

"Cassie," said Emma, with incredible patience, "what Kat means is it's too late. The last ferry will have gone. And it's started to snow."

Kat hadn't noticed until Emma said, but sure enough, there it was, fat flakes drifting past the distorted glass of the casement windows, which had been broken and releaded to give the semblance of age. Some of the panes had been deliberately set so that the leading made a crooked letter *K*.

"It's just a flurry. There must be—I don't know—a seaplane or something. A helicopter—water skis!" Cassie hunched over, emitting a low, moaning noise. Kat had written about keening, but she'd never actually heard it before. It was a terrifying sound, like all the sorrows of the world come together in one throat.

"Hey." Kat patted her awkwardly on the arm. "We've got the ceilidh tomorrow, remember?"

"Who cares about the ceilidh? Chip w-w-won't return my calls. He knows. He knows. He knows Brett is here and he thinks—" Cassie's breath caught on the mother of all hiccups. Emma handed her a handkerchief with a faded monogram. "I've r-ruined my m-marriage and it's all for n-nothing."

"It's not all for nothing," Kat said fiercely. Never mind that a day ago she'd wanted nothing more than to be doing this on her own. Now the idea of not seeing this through together just felt . . . weird. Wrong. "We've got this."

"We?" Emma paused in folding a tartan tissue turtleneck. Her voice was etched with acid. "*We've* got this?"

Kat felt a sick feeling in the pit of her bustier. She folded her arms carefully across her chest. "That *is* the plan, right?"

"I don't know, Kat. Do you want to tell us about the plans?" Emma's blue eyes were like chips of ice. "I *know*, Kat. I saw Bruce today."

Always make it the other person's fault, that was something Kat had learned fast when visiting her mother's perfect second family. "Then why didn't you say so before? Why wait until now?"

Emma's hands with their sensible, unpainted nails tightened on the tartan turtleneck. "Because I don't like unpleasantness."

Cassie blinked damp lashes at them. "What does she mean, about the plans? Emma?"

Emma's back was very straight. "You tell her."

It had all made sense at the time, but here, now, in this snow globe of a room, Kat was finding it very hard to explain. "I may— I may not have been entirely truthful."

"Not entirely?" Emma drew herself up to her full height, looking the better sort of marble statue of Athena. All she needed was a helmet and a spear. "She got the original plans of the castle from Bruce at the Historical Society and *didn't tell us*."

"Not just the secret stillroom? All the plans?" Cassie stared at Kat, stricken.

Kat scuffed the toe of one of her stiletto heels against the plaid carpet. "I was going to tell you eventually. I—" She stuck, because the truth was, she wasn't sure she had intended to tell them. This had, in her mind, been her mission, not theirs. They were just inconvenient add-ons. She twisted a bulbous memento mori ring around and around her finger. "I—I wanted to talk to him first. To BSP."

Instead of making it better, she had made it worse. Much worse.

"We had a *plan*," Emma said frostily. "I couldn't afford this trip. I sold my grandmother's engagement ring to pay for the tickets. But I thought—finally—some sort of justice . . ." Her lips closed very tightly, which, in Emma-speak, meant she was very upset, indeed.

Cassie's face had gone stark white. "You had the plans. You had the plans all along."

"Not all along." Kat made an awkward move toward the bed- side table, where one of those ubiquitous plastic electric kettles had been set out. "Look, can I make you a cup of tea or some- thing? You're looking kind of—"

"I asked Chip to look for the plans—for nothing. If I'd never asked him—" Cassie moved jerkily forward, like an animated corpse from a low-budget horror movie. She poked one chipped nail at Kat's chest, hard. "When he looked for the plans he found out who the flipping owner was!"

"But why should that matter? You never told him about—"

"Someone sent him a photo," Cassie said brokenly. "Of me and Presley. Together. At that conference. And when Chip went looking for those plans . . ."

"He thinks you're here for sexytimes with Jerk Face?" Kat snorted at the ridiculousness of it all.

"Don't you dare make a joke out of it! It's all over. My marriage—my kids—If I hadn't sent him looking—*When did you get those plans?*"

Kat's lips felt stiff with horror. She'd never thought—"Yesterday. Yesterday afternoon."

"Cassie." Emma put a hand on Cassie's shoulder, gently drawing her away. "You emailed Chip about the plans two days ago. That was before—*she*—found them."

The level of disdain in that "she" would have made Kat hate herself if she didn't already. She tried to come up with a flippant response, but there weren't any. She had screwed up. Badly.

It was just—she'd never really thought of Emma or Cassie as people. Comic side characters. Minor annoyances. An inconvenience she had to deal with to get to Scotland and BSP.

But never people.

"I'm sorry," Kat said hoarsely.

Emma looked at her, narrow-eyed. Cassie had her hands on her knees and was making strangely organized panting noises.

Kat looked at Cassie's bent head, grateful for any distraction. "Is that Lamaze breathing?"

Cassie's curls jerked up and down in a nod. "I've done it so many times it just comes naturally. Chip and I—we have six kids together. If we're still together."

Guilt smote Kat like a demon's dagger. And she should know. She'd written a lot of demons and a lot of daggers, emotion couched in moonlight and metaphor, all at a safe remove. Not like this, just three women, three very different women, raw and hurting.

Dammit, where were the demons when you needed them? Kat was forced to face the unfortunate truth that in this situation: she *was* the demon.

"I shouldn't have kept the plans from you," Kat said gruffly. "It was stupid. And selfish."

Emma looked decidedly unconvinced. "Oh, great, so you apologize and we're just meant to *believe* you? How do we know you don't intend to lull us into a false sense of camaraderie and then go do your own thing?"

Kat wrinkled her nose at her. "When did I ever lull you into a false sense of camaraderie?"

Cassie blew her nose dramatically on Emma's handkerchief. "She has a point. She's never made any effort to be friendly."

"Jeez, drive the dagger a little deeper. You know, one of those little Scottish sock jobbies."

"A sgian dubh," said Emma stiffly.

Kat had known Emma would never be able to resist. "Right, that. Look. Cards on the table. I'm not lulling you. I couldn't do this on my own even if I wanted to." Kat took a deep breath and plunged into the worst of it. "I tried, but I can't. I couldn't get into that passage."

"So that's why you came back to us. I wondered." Emma held up something that sparkled in the light, a dime-store spider with impossible bling. "You dropped this. Go on. Put it on. Or would it spoil the *look*?"

There was something hypnotic about that spider. Kat felt utterly frozen, consumed by an unfamiliar sensation: shame.

"Would someone like to tell me what's going on?" demanded Cassie, her voice cracking.

Kat closed her hand around the spider, feeling the bite of its prongs against her palm. "This morning, after the peat wraps—"

That must, Kat realized, have been when Emma had gone to

the Historical Society, while Kat was using her hidden plans to find the tunnel on her own.

"This morning, after the peat wraps, I snuck into the old laird's suite. They've broken it up into three rooms now. One of them's the round tower bit on the end nearest the Obelisk. They've done it up as a tremendous en suite for honeymooners with a big Jacuzzi. According to the old plans, the secret passage is somewhere in the walls of that tower, but I couldn't figure out where the entrance was or how to get into it."

"Did you try looking at the bookshelves?" asked Cassie thickly.

"Of course. I'm not stupid. But I didn't have any idea what I was meant to be looking for." Kat looked at Emma. "I write about dark corners of the soul and sexually active demons. I don't know anything about pseudomedieval secret passageways. The only secret passageways in my books are—"

"Yes, yes, we get it," said Emma hastily.

"As much as we might hate it, we need one another. Look, this isn't easy for me to say, okay?" Kat looked from Cassie's blotchy face to Emma's horsey one. "I need you, both of you, all right? I'll be straight with you if you'll be straight with me."

Emma's face was carefully expressionless. "We have one day until the ceilidh."

Kat let out her breath, feeling like someone had just released the laces on a too-tight bustier and she could finally breathe again. That was as close to a yes as she was going to get. "All right. Let's sit down—together—and figure this out."

For a moment, no one moved. They were all watching one another, coming to their own private conclusions.

Then Emma broke the silence. "I have the plans of the castle. Bruce printed them out for me."

Kat set her phone down on the bed, open to a picture of a very busty blonde. "And I have the bait. God's Gift to Literature is under the impression that he's going to be having one *very* hot date on the night of the ceilidh. He's getting all his Edwardian sex toys ready."

They both looked at Cassie, who was staring at the pile of clothes on the bed, and the half-packed Vera Bradley bag.

"Cassie?" Emma asked gently. "Are you still in?"

Cassie lifted her head and wiped the tears off her cheeks. "Does everyone have enough plaid?"

CHAPTER TEN

Cassie

EXCERPT FROM POLICE INTERVIEW WITH MRS. CASSANDRA PARSONS PRINGLE, 10 DECEMBER 2022

DCI: Which brings us to yesterday evening and the murder itself—

PRINGLE: *Murder?* You've decided it was murder, then?

DCI: Mrs. Pringle, no doubt you're aware of the condition in which the body was found. Do you suggest that a man could render himself in such a state *by accident*?

PRINGLE: Men do the strangest things, don't they? [*laughs*] The most *peculiar* habits, some of them, and between us—no offense intended, of course—anyway, in my *experience*, most men don't tend to show a lot of common sense once they set their minds on something, have you noticed? [*laughs*] I mean, you'd be surprised how many suspicious deaths turn out to have been accidents. Have you heard of the Darwin Awards? No? Men—and it's almost always men, I'm afraid—killing themselves doing some stupid stunt. You wouldn't even believe some of them. [*laughs*] My husband does shifts on the local volunteer mountain rescue squad and he comes back with some crazy stories. Hikers going over the falls trying to get selfies, that kind of thing. Creative, though. I'll give them that. [*laughs*] Why, in the second book of my Moggies, Mocha, and Murder series—I don't want to give away any spoilers, of course, but the cat in question—his name is Hotspur, he's an orange tabby—*ginger*, as you say over here—

DCI: Mrs. Pringle, I must ask you again to return to the subject at hand.

[*long pause*]

PRINGLE: What was the question again?

DCI: I was *attempting* to direct your thoughts toward yesterday evening, just before the—the *incident*, if you insist. You and your friends attended the ceilidh in the village hall—

PRINGLE: Oh, that was such fun! So *Scottish*! Everybody was so welcoming, even though we wore the wrong kind of plaid, apparently. I can't imagine how I came to make such an obvious mistake! It must have been the L.L.Bean sale. I do go a little nuts when I see all that bargain plaid—

DCI: So you enjoyed yourself, did you? All three of you?

PRINGLE: Very much. The punch was delicious. I wonder if I might trouble somebody for the recipe—

DCI: And yet, a number of reliable witnesses claim that you and your friends left early and walked back to the castle together, despite the fact that a blizzard was raging outside.

PRINGLE: *Did* they? My goodness. What sharp eyes. Well, it's true. We did leave a wee minute before the festivities concluded, so to speak. To tell you the truth, we were all getting a little sleepy. Jet lag, you know.

DCI: But isn't British time ahead of American time?

PRINGLE: What difference does that make?

DCI: In the case of eastbound travel, shouldn't your natural circadian rhythm encourage you to stay up late, rather than turn in early?

[*long pause*]

PRINGLE: So I guess it must have been the punch?

Friday, December 9
A few hours before the murder . . .

A GIGANTIC SCOT in full regalia stood at the bottom of the staircase, adjusting the mouthpiece of his bagpipes. The sight was so dazzling, Cassie's anxiety flew right out of her head. She stopped on the landing, causing Kat and Emma to pile up behind her, swearing.

The Scotsman looked up. It was Calum, of course. A dark scowl settled on his features as he watched the three of them descend the stairs.

"Ye'll want to take off those scarves," he growled.

"Only if you promise to help," purred Kat.

Something snapped inside Cassie. "Don't be ridiculous," she said. "These are authentic Scottish tartans. I picked them all out from the clearance sale at L.L.Bean."

Emma lifted the corner of her scarf and examined the pattern. "Hold on a second. Is this dress Campbell?"

"I—well, I think so—"

"But didn't you *know*? The Campbells are mortal enemies of the Kinlochs!"

"Oh my God, she's right," said Kat. "I should have remembered that from *Laird, My Love*."

"Some people might mock Karyn Black," Emma said seriously, "but she did do her research."

"Surely no one will notice?" Cassie asked.

"Only if they're not stone drrrrunk by the time we arrive," said Calum. "So ye'd best hope the punch is potent."

THE SNOWFLAKES DOVE into the windshield of the Land Rover—*Follow me to Castle Kinloch!*—and filled the beams of the headlights. Beyond the whiz of furious snow, the thick black night had no end.

"It's like driving through outer space!" Cassie said, with forced cheer.

Next to her, Calum grunted. "Och, wrrriters," he muttered.

Cassie opened her mouth to make an indignant reply and checked herself. "I guess we must get on your nerves a little. We're a different breed, after all. Like sheep!" She made a small, nervous laugh. "Although we haven't even *seen* the most famous writer around here."

The Land Rover made a hard bounce. From the back seat came a pair of shrieks—Kat like a starlet filming a love scene, Emma like a debutante discovering a cockroach—and a faint bleat, which Cassie chose to ignore. The bump didn't slow the breakneck pace of the Land Rover over the ruts and bends. If anything, Cassie could have sworn Calum pressed the accelerator.

She looked at his giant hands on the steering wheel. The knobs of his knuckles reflected a faint glow from the headlights. In the darkness, the lurid shadow, she glimpsed a memory of Chip driving her down the highway in his pickup truck at midnight, laughing, singing along to some song on the radio.

She squeezed her eyes shut to clear the image and took in a deep breath. "Mr. Presley, I mean. Of course. I guess he lies pretty low around here?"

Calum shrugged one enormous shoulder.

"Not even the ceilidh tonight?" she said. "You'd think he'd want to join the fun. You know, take part in village life and everything."

Calum snorted. "Och, no. Not unless he's after a bit of skirt."

"Oh! So, all the time, then."

Cassie couldn't quite keep the edge from her voice. She felt Calum's start of surprise, his quarter turn in her direction.

"I mean, so I've heard," she added quickly. "Writer gossip and everything. Quite the Lothario, they say."

Calum turned back to the windshield, just in time to pivot the Land Rover around a hairpin turn.

"Ye shouldn't listen to gossip, Mrs. Pringle," he said gravely. "Only leads to trouble."

"I *don't—*" Just in time, she choked back the indignant cry.

"Don't what, Mrs. Pringle?"

From the back seat came Emma's voice. "Doesn't like to stay up late. So I hope this buggy can make it back to Kinloch before the road gets too bad."

Calum patted the steering wheel. "Och, there's no such thing as a road our Myrtle canna conquer."

"*Myrtle?*" muttered Kat. "Wow. Like *Beatrice* wasn't sexy enough."

The lights of the village hall burst through the blizzard and Calum skidded to an expert stop at the entrance. Cassie reached for the door handle, but by the time she'd opened the car door Calum was already there, holding her arm firmly so she wouldn't slip as she stepped into the swirling snow. *Just like Chip*, she thought, blinking away another tear. Emma popped out from the back seat, wearing a knee-length tartan pinafore dress that looked suspiciously like an old school uniform. On her feet were a pair of black patent leather penny loafers, somewhat scuffed and worn at the seams—*my dress Weejuns*, she'd called them, ideal for dancing reels in a medieval Scottish hall.

From the other side of the car, Kat staggered into view, leaning heavily on Calum's arm as she made her way across the gathering snow. Cassie had been so distracted by her own thoughts, she hadn't taken much notice of Kat's outfit—well, other than its customary skintight lines. Now she took in the scarlet leather bustier atop a pair of scarlet Royal Stewart tartan leggings that went on and on down Kat's legs until they—well, they *became* a pair of five-inch stiletto boots.

"*What*," she gasped, "are *those*?"

Kat released Calum's arm and glanced at her toes. "Panta-boots," she said, followed by an unspoken *Duh*.

"Panta . . . *boots*? But . . . *why*?"

Kat shrugged. "Lengthens the line."

"You look like a Tartan Slut Barbie," said Emma.

"That's the idea, honey."

A stream of profanity floated from the back of the Land Rover. At least, it presented like profanity, rendered in Gaelic. The three women looked at one another and hurried around the corner of the vehicle, where the back door stood open and Calum bent over the contents of the boot.

"What's the matter?" Cassie asked anxiously.

There was an indignant bleat. Beatrice hopped down from the tailgate to the snow and shook her black head. Calum lifted out his bagpipes and held the instrument gingerly at arm's length.

"Och, she's forgotten herself on me bladder," he said.

Emma bent to scratch the sheep between her ears. "I *thought* I heard something back there."

"I see you've brought your date," said Kat.

Calum made a dark Scottish noise from the bottom of his throat. "Ye've been reading too many Karyn Black novels, Miss de Noir." He bent to slap Beatrice on the rump. "Go on, then, love. Reckon the party can't start without ye."

Beatrice trotted toward the doors, from which light and music and laughter poured out into the night. Calum shook his head and lifted the bagpipes to his shoulder. "She'd only bleat outside for me, anyhoo," he muttered.

From the hall came a muffled cheer as Beatrice disappeared inside. Calum blew a long, melancholy note from the pipes, like a call to procession, and marched after her with measured steps.

Cassie stared through the open doors to the merriment on the other side of the threshold.

"What's the matter?" said Emma. "Come on, let's go."

"I was just thinking. Calum. He's everywhere. Wherever we go, there he is. You don't think he's . . . I don't know. Spying on us? Like he suspects something."

"Either that, or the castle can't afford more than one employee," said Emma.

Kat shrugged. "So we just make sure he's not watching when we blow this taco stand early tonight." She reached out and linked Cassie's elbow, then reached for Emma. "Ready, girls?"

THE HALL WAS packed with kilts and bright dresses, with shining faces and the sweet, rich scents of food and whisky. As they crossed the threshold to the noise of Calum's pipes, a roar rose from the crowd—almost as loud as the one that had greeted Beatrice. Tears stung Cassie's eyes. She blinked them back and turned to speak to Kat, but Kat's attention was already fixed on some object in the crowd of revelers.

"Rawr," she said.

Cassie followed Kat's gaze to a tall, dark-haired man in a snug black velvet jacket and Kinloch kilt. A leather sporran dangled from a silver chain at his waist. He must have sensed Kat's attention—well, who wouldn't?—because he turned his head in her direction. A familiar scowl settled on his features.

"Who's that?" Cassie whispered.

Emma leaned over. "Isn't he that man from the pub? The one who was leaving when we got there?"

"I think you're right!" said Cassie. "He certainly cleans up well, doesn't he?"

"Dibs," said Kat.

Calum's pipes finished with a flourish. In the next instant, a fiddle cut a few quick, merry notes through the air, joined by a second fiddle. A cry of excitement went through the crowd. Everyone scurried to the middle of the hall, where Calum had taken up a position near the fiddlers. His dark voice boomed out over the bustle.

"Form yer sets for the Laird of Kinloch!" he called.

"What the hell's that?" asked Kat.

"It's a dance, of course," said Emma. "That's what they do at ceilidhs. A Scottish set dance? In this case, lines of three couples each. Come on, let's go."

"Dance? To *that*? I don't even know the steps!"

"What, the Laird of Kinloch? It's one of the easiest dances in the book."

"There's a *book*?" said Cassie.

Emma sighed out the rest of her patience. "Look, all you do is follow along. Just do what everyone else is doing!"

"Yeah, well, I usually try to do the opposite," said Kat.

"Copout," said Emma.

"I am not a copout."

"Chicken."

"I am *not*—"

Emma made a beak with her hand and flapped it. "*Bawwwk bawk bawk.*"

"*Bawk* yourself, bitch."

"Oh, just come on." Emma grabbed Kat's hand. "I'll show you what to do. It'll be fun."

"Fun, she says. Right," Kat grumbled, as Emma dragged her

toward the lines of dancers. "And when we get back to the castle, I'll show you how to use a nipple clamp."

Cassie watched the two of them join the lines of dancers— Emma tugging Kat by the hand, Kat pretending to drag her pantaboot heels, which promised to impale any foot careless enough to dance near.

Neither seemed to notice they'd left Cassie behind, standing near the punch table.

Well, what did she expect? Married, mother of six, husband across the ocean. Naturally Cassie should be content to sit on the sidelines and watch the single ladies have their fun.

She stared at all the thick male shoulders in the crowd before her, the sturdy legs under their kilts. She thought of Chip and her chest ached, her eyes stung.

Put him away, she told herself. *Put the whole thing away in another part of your brain. Close the door and lock it tight until this is all over, until you can do something, until you can go back home and make everything right.*

If she could. Make everything right.

All she seemed to do anymore was to make everything worse.

The fiddles were warming up with little flourishes. Cassie saw Emma take her place across from Bruce MacHinist, the museum curator, gangly as ever in a kilt that looked like it might fall from his hips at any second. Kat had somehow maneuvered herself in front of Mr. Rawr from outside the pub.

"Aren't you joining the line, Mrs. Pringle?" said a grave voice to her left.

Cassie startled and spun. At her side stood Archie, resplendent in kilt and velvet jacket, frills of lace spilling from his collar and cuffs, the works. He looked at her gravely and offered an elbow.

"Do me the honor, Mrs. Pringle?" he said.

Cassie forced out a smile and looped her arm around his. "With pleasure."

They reached the lines just in time. Archie took his place at the end, next to Bruce; Cassie swung into position beside Emma. She heard Calum's voice boom above the bounce of the fiddles but she couldn't make out the words. Helplessly she looked to Archie for guidance, but he'd just sprung forward with hand outstretched to Emma. Emma sprang forward with a beautifully angled leg and pointed toe and met him. They clasped hands and whirled a circle together, then Emma leapt back into Archie's place in line, while Archie leapt into hers.

Cassie had just enough time to notice the startled expression on Emma's face before Bruce MacHinist grasped her hand and spun her in a circle before settling her back in his spot. She looked across at Archie, whose gaze was fixed on Emma, and turned her head back to her friend, whose face was now a ravishing shade of cranberry.

"What—" she began, but then Mr. Rawr sprang forward to take Kat by the hand, just as Archie reached for Cassie, and the whole line became one whirl of partners turning circles and lines forming and re-forming, and she forgot all about the flush on Emma's face. She forgot about Chip and the kids and the terrible dark stone that had sat on her heart for three years, squashing the life out of her. She forgot about the disastrous Thanksgiving dinner, when that stupid photo arrived on Chip's phone during the pumpkin pie. She forgot about everything but the music and the dance pattern and the whirl of colors and faces and sturdy Scottish palms grasping hers, and the laughter she didn't recognize until she realized, as she held Emma's hand and Kat's hand and crossed underneath the men's linked arms, that it came from some neglected corner of her own chest.

THEY DANCED TWO more reels before the fiddlers laid down their fiddles and bows—for a brrrief rrrespite, they said—and Cassie grabbed Emma's elbow.

"So what's up between you two?"

Emma pulled her arm away and started for the table at the end of the hall, where an enormous tureen sat on a tablecloth in the green Kinloch tartan, surrounded by cups of varying shapes. "Between me and whom, exactly?" she said innocently.

"You and Archie, of course! Every time you met in the line, you looked like you were about to pounce on each other."

"Did we?"

"Like Beatrice and Benedick," said Cassie. "And we all know how *that* turned out."

"Ha, nice try," said Emma. "Kat says he's gay, remember?"

Kat piped up from behind them. "Nice try, yourself. I saw that bosom of yours heaving away old-school in the doorway of the laird's chambers. Someone's got the hots for Mr. Unattainable."

"Wait, *what*?" said Cassie.

"I don't know what you're talking about," said Emma. "Either of you."

They reached the punch table. Cassie scooped up a pair of cups and handed them to Emma and Kat, then picked up one for herself. She raised the cup and met the others in a toast. Before they drank, she said quietly, "I thought we said no more secrets, right?"

Kat turned to Cassie. "It's no big secret. Our star student has a wee crush on a certain Scot whose name rhymes with Starchy, that's all."

Emma looked at Kat. "I told you, it was the peat wrap."

Cassie's head was starting to whirl, and it wasn't just the punch. "Emma? Is that true? *You* went inside the laird's chambers, too?" She looked at Kat. "And you saw her do it?"

Kat sighed and hooked Emma by the elbow. Together with Cassie they shuffled away from the punch table and the knots of merry Kinloch inhabitants. Kat turned to Cassie. "I went back to get my earring and saw the Preppy Princess here under the spell of the Kinloch estate manager."

"And you didn't *tell* me?"

Emma lifted the cup and drank her punch, all of it, eyes closed. When she finished, she opened them again and looked at them with her steady, serious gaze, the one that made you think you were catching a glimpse of the real Emma. "Look," she said, "that was before, all right? Before we had our talk last night. When I was mad at Kat for getting those plans."

"Oh, sure. Blame the slut," said Kat.

"But what happened? What did you find?" asked Cassie.

Emma cracked a tiny, wistful smile. "Actually, it was kind of neat. I saw my book there. You know—that one about the unsinkable Prunella Schuyler? With a postcard photograph inside. And a photograph of Lady Ned with Prunella herself!"

She looked hopefully from Kat's face to Cassie's, and Cassie tried to put on an expression of knowing intelligence, as if she'd actually read *The Unsinkable Prunella Schuyler*—well, she'd meant to! It was on top of her stack at home!—and remembered the whole book in vivid detail.

"My goodness," Cassie said. "How *neat*. To see your book right here at Kinloch, I mean."

"Well, I already knew Prunella had stayed here, of course, back when she was trying to hook the Prince of Wales. The same house party when Naughty Ned was murdered. But it was still—I don't know, kind of *magical* to see the proof, you know? Tucked in the bookshelves? Anyway. I also found these account books from Lady Ned's time, but I didn't have a chance to really look at them because Archie turned up."

"Oh, no," said Cassie.

"Oh, *crap*!" exclaimed Kat.

"Well, I tried to smooth it over, but—"

"No, I mean Calum's watching us. Don't *look*, for God's sake!"

Cassie swiveled her head and saw Calum standing against the opposite wall, arms crossed and face arranged in an expression of imminent thunder. For an instant, his gaze met hers. Then he uncrossed his arms and started off in the direction of Archie, who stood chatting at the punch table with a slender, attractive man Cassie recognized as Jamie, the veterinarian from the pub last week.

"Oh, crackers!" exclaimed Cassie. "What do we do now? What if he's saying something to Archie? We have to *do* something! A distraction!"

"I could flash my boobs," said Kat, reaching for her bustier.

"No, wait. Archie's coming over," said Emma. "What do we say?"

At the other end of the hall, the fiddles had started up again, gathering dancers to the middle of the floor—this time in pairs. Archie came to a stop before them. His expression was like stone, his face flushed. He cleared his throat and nodded to Cassie, then Kat. "Ladies," he said. His gaze shifted to Emma. He held out his hand. "Miss Endicott. Might I have the honor . . . the honor of your . . ."

Emma handed Kat her cup. "Hold my punch."

Amazed, Cassie watched the pair of them take their places in the dance.

"I hope she knows what she's doing," Cassie said.

Kat nudged her side and nodded to the wall, where a grim-faced Calum had lurched over to speak to the veterinarian Jamie, abandoned by Archie. "I'm more worried about what's going on over *there*."

"You think he's warning Jamie about us?"

Kat set the two cups on the ledge of the wainscoting behind them. "I don't know," she said, "but someone's got to keep that damn Scotsman out of trouble."

She marched to Calum and tapped his shoulder. He turned with a startled air. Kat seemed to ask him a question, to which he shook his head, gesturing to Jamie. The veterinarian grinned and

held up his hands, palms out, and Kat hooked Calum's elbow—
like a fish, Cassie imagined—and dragged him into the dance.

Cassie smiled into her punch cup and saw it was somehow
empty. *Well, that won't do*, she thought. She started forward to
the punch table. For some reason, she was feeling better now. She
couldn't imagine why. The air seemed softer, almost dreamlike.
The voices and music floated around her. She reached for the ladle
and missed. Tried again.

"Need a wee hand with that, do ye?" said a woman at her
shoulder.

"Yes, please," said Cassie.

The woman took the cup from her hand and ladled the punch
deftly inside. "Careful, now," she said. "That'll be a potent brew,
the Kinloch punch. Ye've got a strong head, I hope?"

"Oh, nashurally," said Cassie. "Cheers."

The woman raised her cup and clinked rims with Cassie. She
had blond hair and cheerful round cheeks and a sturdy, wholesome figure. Cassie snapped her fingers.

"Fiona!" she exclaimed. "From the pub!"

"Ah, so ye've got yer wits about ye, after all!"

"Of course I have," said Cassie. She gestured to the punch bowl.
"Alwaysh on the job, I see."

Fiona laughed. "Pour the drinks. Deliver the babies. Wee bit of
everything, really."

"You're a *midwife*, too?"

"Och, when I must. More a general practitioner, really. Only
doctor on the island. Me clinic's open afternoons. Mornings I
pitch in behind the bar. Me da's the publican, ye ken, but he's had
a puir spot of health of late, I'm afraid."

"I'm shorry to hear that," said Cassie. "You musht be awfully
busy."

Fiona shrugged. "Och, there's not so much, really. It's a small
island. Slap their bums when they come into the world, close

their puir eyes when they leave it. Not that we have so much of that anymore. Not like the auld days."

"Old days?"

"I'm sure ye'll have heard the stories about Naughty Ned. That Presley fellow's busied himself turning the sorry history of Kinloch into a fantasy for tourists—I reckon ye can't blame him altogether, with so many bills to pay—but the truth of those days is enough to make ye weep. A right muckle lot of girls who disappeared, a muckle lot of puir wee babes born with nae fathers to keep them. Why, look at dear auld Morag, over there. Holding proper court, like always."

Cassie tried to follow the direction of Fiona's nod, but she lost her way somewhere inside the blur of dancers.

"Morag's own grandmother was one of the foundlings. That's what we called them in those days, the wee Foundlings of Kinloch. Nae fathers who owned them, nae mothers either. Left on the doorstep of the kirk for the village to bring up as best it could. Why, will ye look at that!"

This time Cassie had no trouble finding the object of Fiona's attention. A hush was settling over the crowd. The dancers stopped dancing and backed away to the walls, revealing a couple in the center of the floor, executing an intricate series of steps that somehow echoed the duet of the two fiddles, weaving in and out, breaking apart and coming together again, eyes locked together as if communicating the movements to each other.

"Will ye look at that," repeated Fiona. "Our Archie. I've never seen him dance sae bonny."

"Why, that's Emma!" Cassie gasped. The woman danced so gracefully, so sinuously, that Cassie hadn't even recognized the vaguely schoolgirlish tartan dress she wore, the prim white blouse underneath with the piecrust collar, and she certainly hadn't recognized Emma herself, flushed and blooming, hair gleaming gold under the lights.

As for Archie—well, Fiona was right. He moved with the grace and strength of a ballet dancer. At one point he grasped Emma decorously around the waist and lifted her in a half twirl, set her down again, spun her in a circle, lifted her again. Cassie felt her skin tingle, her belly melt.

Like Chip, she thought. That time they went to the gala fundraiser for the historic preservation society and there was an orchestra playing, and Chip spun her into a waltz that was like making love, only dancing. *I didn't know you knew how to waltz!* she'd gasped, when the music lilted to a stop.

Chip had shrugged and grinned, like a man who'd found the perfect Christmas present at the Black Friday sale and kept it secret all December long. *First in my class at the Fred Astaire in Asheville*, he'd told her.

Cassie caught Emma's expression as Archie lifted her into another half twirl. There was something delirious about her eyes, something soft about her half-parted lips. Like Cassie felt in Chip's arms, like every woman who had ever fallen in love.

Or lust.

Either way, Emma was in trouble, Cassie thought.

Because by the time the sun rose, they'd have betrayed Archie and everyone on Kinloch.

"You see what I mean?" said Kat, who'd come to stand on Cassie's other side. "Look at him. Gay as Gay Paree."

The two fiddles joined together for a final flourish. For an instant, Archie and Emma held the last pose, hands joined, gazing into each other's eyes. Then Emma's face jolted awake. She backed away, flushing deeply, and fled for the open door. Archie started after her, but before he'd gone more than a few steps, Calum hurried up and muttered something in his ear.

"Well, well," said Fiona. "It looks like the laird of Kinloch has finally met his match."

Cassie spun toward her. "The *laird of Kinloch*?"

"Och, ye didnae know? It's our Archie that's leased the castle to that American writer. Trying to recover the Kinloch finances."

Before Cassie could reply, Kat yanked her arm.

"Come on," she said. "I think that's our cue to get out of here."

OUTSIDE, THE SNOW fell heavily. Cassie stared in amazement at the drifts around them. The Land Rover was buried, the street was piled a foot deep at least. She cast about for Emma and found her shivering against the wall, eyes closed, arms crossed over the bib of her pinafore dress.

Cassie's heart melted in her chest. She turned to Kat. "Could you fetch our coats from the Land Rover? And my handbag."

Kat opened her mouth to object and checked herself. She shrugged and picked her way through the snow to the door of the car.

Cassie went to Emma and wrapped the scarf around her shoulders. "I didn't know you were such an expert in Scottish dancing."

"I—I took a class for a book I was writing," Emma said, teeth chattering. "Research."

"Well, your thoroughness has really paid off. I think you've got Archie completely hoodwinked."

Emma straightened from the wall and wound the scarf around her neck. "Yeah, well, anything for the cause, right?"

Kat stalked up and handed them their coats. "I don't know, girls. It's pretty bad out there. There's no way I can make it through the snow in these." She shrugged into her red faux leather puffer coat and gestured to the five-inch heels on her pantaboots. "Maybe we should let Calum drive us home and wait until tomorrow."

Emma looked down at her patent leather Weejuns. "Crap. Maybe you're right."

"But our plans," said Kat.

"We might not have another chance," said Emma.

Everything seemed to balance in the air. The two of them looked at Cassie, as if she held all the answers, all the courage to do what needed to be done. She was the matron, after all. The mother of six. She was supposed to solve everyone's problems.

She peered out across the indigo night. The drifts of snow turned golden in the lights from the village hall before disappearing into the darkness. Somewhere beyond lay Kinloch Castle. Kinloch and its infamous Obelisk, where a certain man sat in his comfortable chair, enjoying his comfortable life, utterly careless of the lives he'd pillaged.

Fingers tap-tap-tapping away on the manuscript that could destroy them all.

His truth, he'd called it. The whole, unvarnished, no-holds-barred account of his life as the prince of literature.

It would be so easy to give up. So easy to head back into the hall for another round of punch, to put off the hard business for which they'd come.

Cassie squeezed her eyes shut. In her memory rose the images she'd tried over and over to banish—the bad movie that kept playing in her head, until she wanted to throw up.

The hotel. The bar. *That's Brett Saffron Presley,* someone whispers in her ear, full of awe. Then he turns to Cassie, as if he's heard the words. Walks over, grins, asks if she's having fun at the conference—as if the other woman isn't even there! Black leather jacket, single earring, a little dangerous. He signals to the bartender and leans to Cassie's ear, so close she can feel his breath in her hair. *I watched your panel on poisons,* he murmurs, in a low rough voice, bourbon on the rocks. *You know, I've always liked a woman with an edge.*

Cassie's eyes flew open. She looked down at her handbag and opened it.

"Don't worry. I took the precaution of bringing emergency footwear," she said, handing out the rubber objects from inside, one by one, checking each for size.

"What the hell are these?" Kat asked.

"Collapsible wellies from Lands' End. The handiest things! Just punch your foot through and they draw right up. Although in your case, Kat," Cassie said, fishing back inside the handbag, "we're going to need a pair of scissors."

"Scissors?"

"To cut off the boots from your pants, of course." Cassie snapped the scissors a couple of times and smiled. "Chop chop."

PART II

CHAPTER ELEVEN

Emma

The morning after the murder

A NOISE THAT sounded oddly like a siren stabbed a hole into the warm cocoon of a dream-filled sleep. It was a happy dream, filled with music and dancing. And . . .

The faint whirring sound intruded again, bringing with it an unwelcome thought. *Could* that be a siren? Here—at the castle? Doubtful. Probably just drunken revelers reluctant to end the ceilidh. Keeping her eyes firmly closed, Emma dove deeper beneath the downy mass of her duvet, wriggling her toes to the remembered rhythm of fiddles. She could still feel warm hands on her waist, and fingers entwined in hers. Smell the soft tang of cologne and perspiration as she'd been lifted and pulled close, then placed gently on the ground where her feet flawlessly pounded out the steps. Almost as if she'd been practicing her whole life.

She pulled the blankets over her head, eager to return to her dreams where she could relive the events from the previous night. She was drifting off again in a sea of plaid when her eyes shot open as she heard the wailing siren again, this time much closer.

Was that a door slamming? And definitely footsteps. Accompanied by male voices. She sat up, blinking sleep from her eyes. Was that a bleating sheep?

Emma fumbled on her nightstand for the bedside clock. Blinked a few times to see if the time might change, but the glaring red numbers were annoyingly consistent. Five-sixteen A.M. The sounds continued, propelling Emma out of her cozy bed and into the plaid flannel robe with matching slippers (both gifts from Cassie). It was the first time Emma had worn them, in deference to their newly professed solidarity. Before last night, she'd had every intention to return both gown and robe unused for a store credit, knowing that her current nightwear, although threadbare, still had years to go before being relegated to the ragbag.

As she belted the robe, she felt a momentary wave of pride at wearing the team colors. Of belonging. If she were Cassie, she'd probably call it Plaid Pride. But she wasn't so she wouldn't, but it made her smile just to think about it.

She pulled open her door, feeling a blast of cold air swirl around her, as if somewhere in the vastness of the castle someone had left a door to the outside open. Maybe she *had* heard a sheep's bleat. And that was *definitely* the deeper tone of men talking. Shouting, almost. In heavy Scottish burrs. Without hesitation, she knocked on both Cassie's and Kat's doors. Even though she knew she was more than capable of investigating the disturbance on her own, she was part of a team. And teams worked together.

Cassie emerged first, her bleary expression brightening when she caught sight of Emma in her plaid ensemble, a mirror image of Cassie herself. Kat's door swung open to reveal the third member of the team, except that her nightgown appeared to be absent beneath the plunging vee at the neck of the robe, and the stiletto-heeled slippers on her feet were certainly not part of the uniform.

"We are SO cute in our plaid!" Cassie squealed. "We need to take a selfie!"

Kat had already started walking in the direction of the noise downstairs but stopped. Pivoting on her heels, she faced Emma and Cassie, beckoning them to come closer before snapping a picture of the three of them. "There," she said, stuffing her phone into her cleavage. "If anyone's keeping track—I'm talking to you, Emma—give me two points for teamwork."

EMMA ROLLED HER eyes as she followed Kat down the stairs to the grand foyer with Cassie close behind. Because of her height she could see ahead to what awaited them and had the tempting thought to bolt back up the stairs. But that would mean trampling poor Cassie whose fingers were clutching the back of Emma's robe.

Mr. Rawr—the handsome dark-haired man in a kilt from the ceilidh—was standing next to Morag, who clutched a shawl close around her stark black dress, the white of her carefully coiffed hair glowing against the dark paneling.

Calum stood behind Mr. Rawr—really, she needed to get his actual name—his arms crossed over his chest like a hulking bodyguard. A rustle and a bleat brought Emma's attention to the woolly rear end of Beatrice, who was trying to nose underneath Mr. Rawr's dress kilt.

"Shove up, you're blocking the way," said Kat, and as the three of them half tumbled down the stairs, Mr. Rawr turned and frowned at them.

"What the devil are they doing here?" he snarled.

"These'll be the Amerrrrricans," said Calum resignedly. "The authors. Staying at the castle for the retreat."

"Is this like a booty call?" asked Kat, oozing around Emma, as if her Lands' End robe were a burlesque costume instead of sherpa-lined plaid. "You followed us back from the ceilidh?"

Mr. Rawr produced a flat case from the pocket of his velvet blazer. "Detective Chief Inspector Macintosh. Kinloch Police."

At least Emma had his actual name now so she wouldn't keep thinking of him as *Mr. Rawr*. But the revelation sent a shock of fear through her. This could not be good.

Could Presley have called the police?

But that had been part of the plan, hadn't it? That his calling anyone would have been out of the question. Because that would mean humiliation and exposing his true self to the world.

Then why were these people here?

Kat moved into the hall and faced the DCI. "*You're* the police?"

"Would you like to inspect my badge?" The inspector spoke with the merest hint of a burr. Perhaps he hadn't been raised in Scotland. Or had a parent who wasn't Scottish. Emma had done research for a project about the percentage chance of a child acquiring various accents due to upbringing and made a mental note to dig through her papers to find it. Later. After this man had stopped staring daggers at Kat.

"Well, now that you mention it," purred Kat.

DCI Macintosh stepped back as if to distance himself from Kat as Cassie and Emma flanked their writing partner. His gaze flickered over their matching plaid and it seemed to Emma that he was trying very hard not to roll his eyes.

Ignoring Kat, he continued. "I have been alerted by Morag MacDougal that the body of Brett Saffron Presley has been discovered in the Obelisk. . . ."

"A body?" Cassie's hand pressed against her chest. "As in a *dead* body?"

Kat turned her head sharply. "Is there any other kind?"

Cassie drew in her breath, visibly hurt. "Well, yes, but . . . are you saying that Brett is dead?"

A dark eyebrow rose. "Brett, is it?"

Emma felt Cassie's arm tremble where it linked with hers. "Yes," Emma blurted out, unwilling to be a witness to any kind of bullying. It reminded her too much of her own high school experience. "He's our host and although we've yet to meet him, we refer to him by his Christian name. Because we're writers. And writers are known for being friendly. Like us. Very friendly." The three of them bobbed their heads like dashboard dolls.

Kat pulled away. "*Are* you saying that he's dead?"

"Yes. That is precisely what I'm saying." The DCI studied each of their faces, his own expressionless. "From the looks of it, it appears that foul play may have been involved."

Calum coughed loudly as if attempting to disguise an outburst of incredulity. Or maybe laughter.

For a brief moment, Emma thought they might be the victims of a reality show and furtively looked around for hidden cameras and mics. But from the grim expression on the DCI's face, she had the sense that this scene was very, very real. "Are you saying he was . . . murdered?"

The DCI studied her carefully, making Emma squirm, which she was sure was his intent. The DCI continued without responding to her question. "With the three of you staying here at the castle in close proximity to where the body was found, I will need to interview each of you. Separately. I will also need to confiscate your phones and other electronic equipment. Calum will assist me and we would appreciate your cooperation."

Calum wrestled an empty flour sack from Beatrice before approaching the women with it, his face grim.

"But I need my phone to be able to reach my family. I have six kids and the littlest, Dash, is running a fever." Cassie's voice trembled as she spoke. Apparently not having access to her family was comparatively a far worse fate than being questioned about the supposed murder of their host.

Kat thrust out her chest, a challenging look on her face as she dug her phone from her cleavage before dropping it in the bag. "Will you need my vibrator, too? I'd be happy to go upstairs and get it. It might be a while, though, so you'll have to wait."

Mortified, Emma meekly dropped her phone into the out-stretched bag, silently apologizing for Kat.

Cassie linked arms again with Emma and Kat as they faced the two imposing Scotsmen. "You can't possibly think that we had anything to do with his death. We were all together at the ceilidh—anyone there can verify that."

"True," the DCI said with a curt nod. "Just as they can verify that you slipped out at 9:42. Together."

"You noticed?" Kat's voice sounded more like a purr meant to soften a barking dog. It was as if, Emma thought, Kat had a lengthy list of personas she could jump into when required.

It was as comforting as it was alarming.

"I did." The DCI finally met Kat's gaze. "You missed the haggis toss."

"There was a haggis toss?" Cassie asked.

"No," the inspector replied. "There wasn't."

Kat pulled her shoulders back, exposing more of her cleavage. "Wow. A Scotsman with a sense of humor. Do you always play with your suspects, DCI Macintosh?"

"What makes you think you're a suspect?"

Emma sucked in her breath, wondering at Kat's composure while she bantered with the inspector. There had been a *murder*, and the three of them appeared to be the main suspects, for Pete's sake. Yet Kat remained true to form, unfazed and oversexed. Emma refocused her attention from the DCI to Kat, an aware-ness blooming that Kat might know more than she'd shared with Emma and Cassie.

The main door opened, bringing with it a frigid blast of air along with Fiona from the bar. She carried a tool kit and was dressed in a white bunny suit covering her from head to toe and looking as if she'd just come from a nuclear reactor meltdown. Beatrice bleated in greeting.

Emma rushed to the door to help Fiona shut it against the raging wind, peering into the darkness as she wrestled with closing it. In the triangle of light from the open door, she noticed footprints in the snow on the front steps. Or, rather, the lack of them. Except for recent ones left by Fiona, and cloven hoofprints made by a sheep.

Emma studied the newcomer in confusion. "Aren't you the barmaid at the Laird and the Lamb?"

Cassie stood on her tiptoes to whisper in Emma's ear. "She's also the midwife and GP. Oh, and the medical examiner."

Emma turned to see if Cassie might be joking.

Cassie shrugged. "She told me when we were chatting at the ceilidh. It's a small island."

There was nothing normal about a barmaid being the island midwife and medical examiner as well as the local GP. But then, Emma thought, nothing seemed normal on Kinloch.

"Sorry to interrupt your chat," said the DCI, his tone clear that he was anything but. "I'm starting the interviews now while memories are sharp and before you've all had a chance to coordinate your stories."

Emma was offended, until she realized that was *exactly* what she'd hoped to do.

The DCI regarded the three of them again, his gaze moving down the line and stopping at Kat then moving back to Cassie. "You first. Follow me to the library."

With a panicked glance toward Emma and Kat, Cassie began climbing the stairs, the DCI close behind her.

"You two." It took Emma a moment to realize that Calum hadn't said "ewe two," and that the words had been directed at her and Kat. "Into the dining room."

Kat led the way, her chin and chest high, like Mary Queen of Scots on the way to scaffold, the very picture of innocence. But they all were. Weren't they? As Emma followed the tapping of Kat's stiletto heels, she couldn't completely quell the thought that if Brett Saffron Presley had been found dead, it wasn't out of the realm of possibility that one of them might have been responsible. One of them who wasn't Emma, of course. Or Cassie. Cassie, the most motherly and caring human being Emma had ever met, couldn't hurt a living creature. Emma had even seen her carefully move a spider onto a windowsill so that it wouldn't get stepped on. That left only . . .

"Take a seat, ladies," Calum said, indicating two chairs opposite each other near the head of the table. "We might be here a while." After seating themselves, Calum sat at the end before leaning back and crossing his muscled arms over his barrel chest. Lady Ned stared unblinkingly at them from her portrait over the sideboard.

"Why are you guarding us?" Emma asked, allowing her annoyance to come through. "You're a suspect, too. Or you should be. I saw sheep prints in the snow and we all know that where you go, your dutiful sheep closely follows."

"Hell hath no fury like a sheep scorned," Kat said before bursting out laughing, the sound a little higher pitched than usual and bordering on hysteria. She crossed and then uncrossed her legs, fidgeting like a schoolgirl waiting to be called into the principal's office.

Emma tried to catch her eye, to silently ask if there was something she should know before it was Emma's turn with the DCI. But Kat crossed and uncrossed her legs again, studiously avoiding Emma's gaze.

Emma leaned forward, hoping Calum would be swayed by her earnestness. It had always worked when asking for research interviews with unwilling subjects. "I don't understand. Why are *we* suspects? We don't have a motive. We don't even live here."

Calum's face remained impassive. "Save it for someone who needs to hear it. Like the police." The sound of bleating came from the other side of the door. With a low grumble, Calum rose from his chair to allow Beatrice into the room, giving her a hearty scratch behind each woolly little ear. "Shall I ring Morag for some tea, then? She'll be needing some herself seeing as how my nan's the one who's found the body."

"Morag found the body?" Emma's voice was tinged with hysteria. "But . . . when?"

"That's right—she's your grandmother!" Kat, of course, focused on the least important element. "Christ, you really *are* all related."

Calum's expression didn't change, making it clear that he wasn't going to answer. Embarrassed for Kat, Emma turned to Calum with a smile. "I would love some tea, please."

Kat crossed her legs yet again. Then recrossed them. "If you could ask your granny to put a wee dram of something stronger in it, that would be even better. On second thought, just bring the bottle and forget the tea."

As Calum approached the bell pull on the far end of the room, the main door opened and DCI Macintosh emerged along with a pale-faced Cassie, whose wan expression and plaid-clad body reminded Emma of Cindy Lou Who after discovering all the Christmas gifts had been stolen by the Grinch. Emma stood to give Cassie a hug but was stopped by Kat, who brushed past her to approach Cassie with a steady glare. "What have you done?" she asked, her voice barely louder than a whisper.

Cassie pushed back her shoulders and steadied her chin as she looked directly at Kat. "I told him the truth."

Emma's jaw dropped, her tongue even drier than before. Kat's carefully plucked eyebrows jerked up in a perfect birdwing angle. "The truth," Kat repeated slowly. "About . . ."

"About us. About how we're not even friends. That we can't stand one another."

Calum—or was that Beatrice?—emitted a loud snort. "Och, aye. I could've told ye that!"

DCI Macintosh turned to Kat, his eyes hard. "You're next." He pivoted on his heel and waited at the door before Kat decided that she'd best do as she was told and followed him into the hallway, the door shutting behind them with an ominous thud.

CHAPTER TWELVE

Kat

HE WAS DEAD. BSP was dead.

It was all Kat could think about as she stalked up the stairs in front of the inspector, doing her best to maintain her dignity in nothing but a Lands' End robe and a pair of stiletto-heeled slippers.

Dead, dead, dead. It should have been a relief; she should have been throwing confetti and organizing dancing munchkins to sing "Ding, Dong! The Witch Is Dead." But Kat didn't feel gleeful. She felt—angry. She'd wanted to crush him and leave him begging; she'd wanted to humiliate him and make him feel as weak and small as he'd made her.

It was like one of those fairy banquets that looked luscious until you bit into a peach and discovered it was ash and bark and you'd sold your soul for the bitter taste of it.

The inspector opened the door of the library and gestured Kat to precede him. It was a curiously courtly gesture, as though she were a guest and not a murder suspect, as though the armchairs set in front of the fireplace were there for a cozy chat and not an interrogation. Someone had even gone to the trouble to bring tea: not the plastic kettle and biscuits in plastic wrap, but a proper tea tray with a porcelain pot and delicately fluted cups and a dainty china plate laden with thick rounds of shortbread and scones pocked with currants.

Kat flicked a wrist at the tea table. "You might have told me we were having a tea party. Or is keeping your prisoners in a state of undress part of your interrogation technique?"

The inspector gestured Kat to one of the chairs in front of the fireplace. "Given what you were wearing last night, I'd say this is a state of dress for you."

Ha. He'd noticed. One point to her. Kat curled herself into the chair, twisting one leg over the other in a way that made the robe fall open. "Why, Inspector. I didn't know you cared."

"That's detective chief inspector," he said drily, waiting until she had finished her gyrations before taking the seat across from her. "And, yes, I care about anything that might be relevant to my investigation."

Investigation. BSP. Dead.

For a moment, just a moment, while she was taunting the inspector, she'd let herself forget.

Kat pulled the sides of her robe together. "What happened? How did he die?"

"Aren't I meant to be asking you the questions?" the inspector asked mildly.

Kat felt a surge of frustration. "I don't know. I've never been involved in a murder before. I don't write that kind of fiction."

"What kind of fiction do you write, Miss de Noir?

"*MS.* de Noir." Kat retorted. "Have you never heard of women's liberation out here in the boonies? I write speculative fiction. Dark literary erotica. Feminist magical realism."

Why in the hell were they talking about her books? How was this relevant to anything?

The inspector pulled a manila folder from beneath his arm. Kat could see her name scrawled across the front. A file. She had a file with the local police. Brilliant. "According to your publisher's website, you write . . . erotic romance novels with supernatural elements. Including . . . werebears?"

All the years of "Oh, you write *romance*?" rose like bile in her throat. Her mother asking when she was going to write a real book. Her half sisters making jokes about Karyn Black novels and ripped bodices and sweet savage love.

"You don't need to say *writing romance novels* like it's one step down from dumpster diving. I'll have you know my first book got starred reviews from *Publishers Weekly, Kirkus,* AND *Library Journal.*"

The inspector's face was carefully blank. "Oh?"

"Not that you'd know, but that doesn't exactly happen every day. Most people are lucky to get one starred review, much less three. I got a full-page write-up in the *New York Times.* De Noir transcends the genre, that's what they said. I was invited to *Yaddo.*"

Crap. Yaddo was the last thing she should have mentioned. But no. She had to shoot off her big mouth and prove how literary she was. Maybe he wouldn't notice. Maybe he wouldn't know. If he didn't know what a starred review was, he wouldn't know about Yaddo.

"You want murder," Kat said brusquely, "talk to Cassie. She's our mystery novelist."

"I know. She told me."

There was something very disconcerting about his steady gaze. Kat was used to a wide range of male reactions, all the way from lustful to extremely lustful. The inspector's gaze never strayed from her face. It made her feel vaguely panicky, as though her best weapons were blunted.

She wondered if they taught them this in inspector school. Was there inspector school? She was being as dithery as Cassie and as nitpicky as Emma.

"It's a known fact that mystery novelists solve more crimes than the police," Kat said roughly.

"Oh?"

If he said "oh" like that one more time, looking all smug and handsome and British, she was going to slug him. "Look at *Murder She Wrote*. Maybe Cassie can save you the hassle and solve the murder for you. If it was a murder."

Infuriatingly, he ignored the attempt to get his goat and went straight for the relevant bit. "What else are you suggesting it might be?"

Kat shrugged. "I don't know. At that level of success—who knows?"

"Are you saying Mr. Presley was staggering under the weight of three starred reviews?" The inspector's face was completely deadpan.

Oh, screw him. Just because she wanted to be taken seriously for once. "Mr. Presley was staggering under the weight of his own damn ego," Kat snarled, before remembering that anything she said could be used in evidence against her. Or could it? She knew she should have watched those *Midsomer Murders* episodes Cassie had put on the research list. "I don't know. I only knew him by reputation."

The detective chief inspector made a note. Kat resisted the urge to crane over and see what it said. "If you only knew him by reputation, what makes you think he did away with himself?"

"You never can tell with male authors. It's like pop stars. Sometimes they just can't take the pressure." Kat waved a dismissive hand, making sure he got a good view of her memento mori ring and long, purple fingernails. "I didn't know the man. I'm only just guessing. Maybe he committed suicide. Maybe he was spanking the monkey a little too vigorously and overtaxed himself."

"Spanking the—?"

"Oh, sorry. I believe you'd call it *wanking off*." Kat pronounced the words with an exaggerated British accent that was closer to *Ab Fab* than *Downton Abbey*. "Battling the purple-headed yogurt slinger. Engaging in a spot of onanism. Sowing his seed in the stony ground. Stroking the snake. Choking the chicken."

"Let's leave innocent poultry out of this," said the inspector. "Do you have knowledge of Mr. Presley's sexual habits?"

For a moment, Kat could see that room at Yaddo, tea lights set out in a parody of romance. She could see the silk scarf swinging lightly from Brett's hand. And then—last night—in the Obelisk— "I know men."

The detective's mouth quirked in a surprisingly engaging grin. "We're not all wankers." Before Kat could respond, there was a sharp knock on the door. "Yes?"

"Sir?" A uniformed police constable with her hair coiled neatly in braids beneath a smart hat stood on the other side. She was holding a piece of paper.

"One moment." The inspector nodded to Kat as he rose and crossed the room to the constable, bending his head to listen as she showed him something and murmured in his ear. Kat felt suddenly cold. Yes, it had been an interrogation, but bantering with the inspector had engaged all her wits and kept the demons at bay. But now, the cold reality of it all pressed down on her. That man with the engaging grin, his throat tan against his white collar, the laugh lines around his eyes, was an officer of the law.

And BSP was dead. Across the way. In the Obelisk.

The peat fire burned sullenly in the grate, snapping and crackling like the torches he had set out around the great room of the Obelisk last night. She'd felt like a virgin sacrifice, like that woman in the woodcut. . . .

Kat forced her face into blankness as the inspector returned. But he didn't sit. He stood there, looking at her. Looking down at her.

"Good view from that angle?" Kat asked tartly.

The inspector didn't rise to the bait. "Do you still maintain you had no personal knowledge of the deceased?"

Crap. The room shrank to the crackle of the fire and the pounding of Kat's pulse as she struggled to remember what evidence she might have left behind her. She swallowed hard, her mouth suddenly very dry. "No more than any other woman in the publishing industry. What does a girl have to do to get a cup of tea around here?"

Kat watched the muscles moving smoothly beneath his cheap suit jacket as the inspector bent to pour the tea from the fluted spout. The cup was patterned in flowers; Cassie would undoubtedly know exactly what they were. Probably something poisonous.

The inspector handed Kat the cup. "All right, Kathy Brown . . . tell me about Yaddo."

Tepid brown liquid sluiced across the floor. The cup shattered into a zillion bits of petal and stem as Kat jerked to her feet.

"I'm not Kathy Brown."

Kathy Brown was the girl with the mousy hair in lumpy braids and the clothes that said *my mother left me*. Kathy Brown was the girl who moved schools every year, the girl who sat by herself in the cafeteria, the girl whose perfect half siblings whispered about her behind her back.

The girl who, like that horrible Drew Barrymore movie, had made it through all of high school and most of college and never been kissed.

The inspector wasn't distracted by smashed Spode. He looked her in the eye. "Your birth certificate says otherwise."

Kat lifted her chin. She could hear china crunch beneath her heels as she took a step forward. "I had my name legally changed. It's Katja de Noir. *I'm* Katja de Noir."

"Noted." They were eye to eye, chest to chest, only a sliver of a teacup apart. Tension crackled between them like the peat on the hearth. The detective looked down at her. His eyes were a pale brown, like whisky. "In that case . . . Tell me about Yaddo, *Ms.* de Noir."

"What do you want to know?" Kat dropped back into her chair, trying desperately to maintain her air of cool. "It's the premier artists' retreat in the United States, didn't you know that? The food is bad and the company is worse."

"And by company . . . you mean Mr. Presley?"

Kat shrugged. Her robe slipped, revealing an expanse of pale shoulder and more than a hint of breast. "We may have been there at the same time. There were so many arrogant assholes, it was hard to tell them apart."

The inspector strolled over to the fireplace. Kat gulped in a brief breath before he turned, resting his arm on the mantel. "Is there anything you would like to tell me?"

The urge to just spill it all out, the whole sordid story, was ridiculously strong. But Kat knew better than that. She'd tried that at Yaddo. Look how that had turned out.

She should say something. Something sexy and challenging. Something like *I've got lots to tell you—are you ready to hear it?* But Kat's lips remained stubbornly closed.

The inspector sighed. "I know what happened at Yaddo."

Kat's paralysis broke. She rose to her feet. "No. You don't. You know what he said happened at Yaddo."

The inspector consulted the paper the constable had given him. "He says you attacked him. That you were obsessed with him. He says that you stalked him and attempted"—the detective chief inspector coughed politely—"to have your way with him."

Kat could feel her heart working overtime in her chest, drum, drum, drum like those old Energizer bunny ads. Any moment now, the panic attack would hit.

Her voice came out higher than usual. "If he says it, it must be true, right? If a woman wears short skirts, she must be an insatiable nymphomaniac. If I write about women enjoying their sexuality, clearly, it means I'm a desperate loser ready to fling myself at the first limp dick in a tweed coat who comes my way."

The inspector let her rant herself out and then asked, quietly, "What *did* happen at Yaddo?"

The click of the lock; the flickering of the tea lights; the swing of the scarf in his hand . . . The second man stepping out from behind the door, mouth open with excitement, his hands already on the zip of his pants. The wall behind her back.

Breathe, breathe. In. Out. Head up. Eyes fixed on the inspector. She wasn't Kathy Brown anymore. Scarlet lipstick. High heels. Black hair. She was Kat de Noir, and she wasn't going to let anyone break her.

Kat kept her head held high, bright color flaring in her pale cheeks. "Choose your own adventure. Maybe I was a desperate nymphomaniac. Maybe he made the whole damn thing up. It doesn't matter, does it? You'll believe whatever you want to believe."

She turned on her heel. Behind her, she could hear the inspector's voice, level, calm, BBC with just a hint of a burr. "It's not about belief. It's about getting to the truth—whatever that might be."

"Truth is what men say it is," Kat retorted, and yanked the door open.

"Ms. de Noir?" That quiet voice stopped her in her tracks. "PC McMorris will escort you back to the others. But first there's one more thing I'd like you to clarify for me."

"What?" Kat's voice crackled with tension as she swung around to face him.

The detective inspector's cool amber eyes met hers. "What's a werebear?"

"I'm going to be writing werebears from a Scottish prison." Kat chugged whisky from the tartan flask Cassie had handed her.

"What's a werebear?" Emma asked.

Kat scowled at Emma. "Not you, too."

They were all in Cassie's room, sitting on her bed in their matching robes, drinking neat whisky and scoffing down shortbread like some sort of demented sleepover. The sleepover of the damned. Now with more plaid.

"When will they give us back our phones?" Cassie was hugging her knees to her chest. In her tartan pajamas with her hair in a puffy ponytail, she looked like the cover of one of the original editions of the *Baby-Sitters Club.* "I need to know if Dash's temperature has come down."

Kat spoke without thinking. "It's not like you can do anything about it from here."

"Kat!" Emma glared at her.

"No." Cassie's voice was thick with tears. "She's right. I should've been home with him. . . . What if they never let me go home again?"

"If you're innocent, you have nothing to worry about," said Emma firmly. "I'm sure they'll get the right person."

She was looking straight at Kat. "What the hell? Why are you looking at me?"

Emma had her prissiest expression. The one that made Kat feel like a nineteenth-century scullery maid about to be told off for not cleaning the grate properly. "You were the one who went to the Obelisk last night."

It took Kat a minute to understand what Emma meant. "You both left me!" This was unbelievable. Kat folded her tartan-covered arms across her tartan-covered chest. "Oh, it's all sisterhood and teamwork until it gets down to it, and then what? You just run off and leave me holding the bag!"

"I didn't run off," said Emma, offended. "You told me to—"

"Distract Archie, I know." Kat was too angry and scared to be sensible. "But did you have to distract him that long? And as for you—"

"I'm sorry." Cassie scrubbed at her nose with a plaid handkerchief. "It was just that Chip was calling and—"

"Yeah, yeah, tiny Dash, blah, blah, blah." Once again, it was Kat left holding the bag. Cassie had her family; Emma had her archives. And Kat? Kat had the prospect of a Scottish prison. "Don't either of you dare give me any crap. I was the only one trying to make last night work."

"Yes, but did you have to kill him?" Cassie asked plaintively.

"Did I—what? You're joking, right?" Kat stared from one to the other. Cassie's eyes dropped. Emma looked politely away. "I didn't kill him!"

"Of course, you'd say that," said Emma.

Cassie fidgeted with the edge of the coverlet. "You did try to get into the Obelisk without us."

"And you were the one who suggested I head off Archie when we saw him moving toward the castle," Emma reminded her.

"Yes, because you have the hots for him!" Okay, Kat had always known they weren't exactly besties, but she couldn't believe either of them would think her capable of murder. What had happened to all that working together crap? "Wait. You think—you think I deliberately got rid of you both so I could go and kill the asshole?"

Neither of them said anything. They didn't have to say anything.

Kat scrambled off the bed. "Give me a little credit for self-preservation! You *knew* I was going there alone."

"Actually, I didn't," said Emma, always the stickler for details. "I thought you were with Cassie."

"*Fine.* Cassie knew I was alone. I went to carry out our plan. Just the plan. I had my phone on video. I was going to catch him wearing that ridiculous bustier and shame him into admitting what he did to me—and to both of you. Then I was going to make him feed the pages of his memoir into the fire, one by one. Justice. For all of us."

"So what went wrong?" asked Emma, clearly unconvinced.

"Aside from you two ditching me?"

"Once again," said Emma frostily, "I did *not*—"

Cassie silenced Emma by gently squeezing her arm. "What happened, Kat?"

"He was wearing the bustier," Kat said curtly. "That bit went right. But—"

He'd lit the torches on the walls. She'd thought—she'd thought he'd look absurd in that outfit she'd sent him, in the leather bustier and boots and leather mask. But in the torchlight, with the dusty tapestries glowering down around them and the lust and fear of generations echoing off the walls, the black leather had looked more sinister than laughable. He had a goblet in one hand, something metallic, studded with gemstones that glowed sullenly in the light—and a rope in the other.

Emma looked narrowly at her. "You're not telling us something. What are you not telling us?"

Did they really want to know? Did they want to know the filth he'd been spouting? The fear that had held her frozen until he was almost upon her?

They had left her. They had sent her in there alone, throwing her to the beast like some sort of virgin sacrifice in a bad '80s fantasy movie, and then they had the nerve to accuse her of murder, like she'd done something wrong, like she hadn't been holding the bag for all of them while they gallivanted off on their own whims.

"I don't know. What are *you* not telling *me*? Maybe you're both in on this together. Maybe you set me up. Maybe that was the plan all along." Kat froze, the flask halfway to her mouth. "Oh God. Why didn't I see it before? That's it, isn't it? You've set this up so that all the evidence leads back to me. The Snoggr account—that I opened. The dominatrix outfit—that I ordered. Then you send me in there. By myself. How in the hell do I know what you did after I left?"

"That's crazy. You're crazy." Emma was practically choking on her own spit in her righteous indignation. "Cassie wouldn't hurt a fly."

Kat lowered the flask. "Maybe not a fly—but what would she do if her family was in danger? And you—don't tell me you're not capable of it. I don't know where either of you was last night."

Emma's ears turned a guilty pink and her eyes slid sideways.

Cassie stared down at the coverlet, plucking out part of the helmet of the Kinloch crest, unraveling it one stitch after another.

"He was alive when I left him," Kat said fiercely. "He was completely out of his tiny mind on something. I don't know. Booze. Drugs. Whatever he's taking to get it up these days. He was raving. He kept trying to grab me."

Cassie's face was the picture of guilt. "If you killed him in self-defense . . . we'll get you a good defense lawyer. It's our fault, too. . . ."

"*I didn't kill him.*" What did it matter? No one would believe her. A whole lifetime of bitterness surged up in Kat's throat, all the people who had abandoned her, starting with her mother. Why in the hell did she always have to be the expendable one? "I wasn't meant to be alone in there. Not like that. You"—she pointed at Cassie—"you were meant to be behind me holding the camera. And you"—she pointed at Emma—"you were supposed to be burning the f-ing memoir while we kept him busy."

"I tried! But by the time I got there—" Cassie broke off, looking like a rabbit in the headlights as both women stared at her.

"You were there?" Kat felt like someone had rammed her with an electric prod; her whole body was humming with tension.

"Only—only for a minute. . . . Once I realized you weren't there . . ."

"What time was it?" Kat grabbed Cassie by the upper arms, giving her a little shake. "I was back in my room answering idiot emails by eleven P.M. If you saw him alive after that—Was he alive? Tell me he was alive."

Cassie shook her head dazedly. "I . . . don't know."

Kat dropped her arms. "What do you mean you don't know? Either he was alive or he wasn't! You don't need a medical degree from the University of Edinburgh!"

Cassie flapped her hands distractedly. "I only poked my head in for a minute! I just assumed—I mean, you don't *think* someone's been murdered, do you? Not usually. I thought he'd just passed out. The room reeked of mead. He was lying face down, and . . . Oh no. Oh no."

"Cassie?" Emma looked at her with concern.

Cassie's face had gone stark white. "I killed him. I didn't mean to—but when I saw him lying there in that puddle of mead—it never occurred to me—it doesn't take much, you know—just half an inch of liquid . . ."

"What in the *devil* are you talking about?" Kat demanded, pushed past endurance.

"The mead. What if he drowned in the spilled mead? I should have realized—I researched this for my Moggies, Mocha, and Murder series. There's a customer who's murdered and the medical examiner finds coffee in his lungs, and I don't want to give it away, but he was held down in a saucer of hazelnut latte, and that's all it took, just a saucer's worth. . . ."

"He didn't drown," Emma said stiffly. "I overheard the medical examiner talking."

Cassie blinked at her. "Fiona?"

"Yes, that one. The one who's also the barmaid. And GP."

"I don't care if she's Pope Francis," Kat snapped. "What did she say?"

"She said something about his having been . . . impaled."

"Impaled?" Cassie squeaked. "Like Vlad the Impaler?"

"Actually," said Emma, "if you look at the historical context . . ."

"*Don't.* Don't you dare start." Kat's brain was spinning like an old record on a broken turntable and all the songs were bad. "Shit. It's back on me again. If you read my first book—did either of you read my first book?"

Kat and Emma exchanged the sort of guilty looks you do at book parties when you haven't bothered to buy the book.

"I have it on the Kindle app on my phone," said Cassie. "I just haven't gotten to it yet."

"I'm sixteenth on the hold list at Pequot Library," said Emma.

"Great. Thanks. If you'd read it, you'd know that that's the big finale—my heroine has to impale the villain-hero-demon with a unicorn horn." Kat was back in her desk in that grad student apartment, lost in a swirling morass of good and evil and everything in between in a darkling world of her own devising.

"A unicorn horn?" said Emma, her flat voice breaking Kat's reverie.

"It was symbolic," Kat snapped. "He'd penetrated others against their will so he was penetrated against his. It worked in the book, okay?"

"Did Fiona say anything about what he was impaled with?" Cassie asked Emma.

Emma shuffled her feet in her bedtime Weejuns. "I heard something about horns. I assumed I'd misheard."

He'd been murdered. With a horn. When that hot detective inspector had asked her what she wrote . . . Maybe it hadn't been such a non sequitur after all.

"I'm a dead woman," said Kat flatly. She turned her flask upside down and shook it. "Anyone got any more of this?"

"I don't think they still hang people in England," said Cassie, taking Kat's flask and reaching for the whisky bottle.

"Scotland," interjected Emma. "It's a different country with its own legal system."

"Over here, they probably just stone you with sheep. Let him without sin throw the first sheep. Cheers." Kat took the once again full flask from Cassie and proceeded to make it a good deal emptier.

"We don't know that they'll make the connection," said Emma slowly, as Kat lowered the flask, gasping for breath.

Kat remembered that room, the detective's steady gaze, the questions that had seemed so casual, but weren't. She caught a stray drop of whisky with her tongue. Her throat burned and her lips felt numb. "The inspector isn't an idiot. We've practically left him a trail of breadcrumbs."

"Then we'll just have to clean up the breadcrumbs before he finds them." Emma was at her most starchy and New England. Both Emmas—Kat was starting to see double.

"Whaddya mean?"

"What do they have?" Emma began ticking points off on her fingers, one nail with clear polish after another. "Snoggr. Which means we need his phone. The bustier. We destroy any packaging."

"But won't they have secured those already?" The motion of the bed as Cassie leaned forward was enough to make the room spin. "In my books, that's one of the first things they'd do. But . . ."

"But?" Kat asked thickly.

"I have an even better idea. The best way to prove you didn't do it is . . ." Cassie looked expectantly at both of them.

When they didn't respond, she looked disappointed, but valiantly provided the answer herself.

"The best way to prove you didn't do it is to find out who did!"

The universe had a sick sense of humor. When Kat had taunted the inspector with mystery novelists solving crimes, she hadn't actually *meant* it.

"Christ," Kat groaned. "She's gone full Jessica Fletcher. This isn't Cabot Cove, Cassie!"

"Do you have a better idea?" Cassie's eyes shone and her ponytail bounced with excitement. "We let you down last night. We're not going to let you down again. Right, Emma?"

"Um . . ." It was not exactly a ringing endorsement. Kat would have echoed the sentiment if she hadn't been afraid that more than words would come out when she opened her mouth.

"Right!" Cassie took that as a yes. "Our first job is to inspect the crime scene."

It was all too much. BSP last night. The detective this morning. Unicorn horns. Cassie.

"Excuse me," Kat croaked. "I need to be sick first."

"I'll hold your hair," said Cassie.

CHAPTER THIRTEEN

Cassie

IT WAS CASSIE who'd discovered the entrance to the secret tunnel during their planning session two nights ago—a fact of which she was nearly as proud as giving birth to a nine-pound, fifteen-ounce baby without an epidural. (She had gone inconveniently into labor with Dash during the Super Bowl and Chip—who'd already seen five babies into the world—had insisted on watching the end of the game before driving her to the hospital, by which time she was already crowning. In his defense, the fourth quarter was a nail-biter.)

According to the plans, the secret passageway opened from the bottom of a staircase at the base of the castle tower that contained the laird's chambers. But the staircase itself was hidden behind the inner walls of the tower. Emma had tried all the cunning tricks she'd learned from her research into castle architecture; Kat had gone around pulling down books and pressing panels. It was Cassie who went back to the plans.

She'd always loved floor plans. They were like a window into other people's lives, like a window into some alternative life of your own. In the early, heady days of her romance with Chip, they'd sprawl for hours on the worn sheepskin rug in front of the fireplace, examining designs and building plans. Thanks to Chip,

Cassie knew how to read a set of blueprints—how to tease out the secrets of a house, how to turn the two flat dimensions into three living ones. While Emma and Kat had thumped and tapped and yanked, Cassie had stood guard near the door of the laird's chambers and bent over the floor plans with the tartan-handled magnifying glass she'd brought from home, and just as the others started making noises of exasperation, she'd looked up and said, *Did you know there's another access point at the base of the tower, through the wine cellar?*

Now Cassie hurried down the black, damp tunnel for the third time, following the bouncing finger of light from the plaid-handled flashlight in Kat's palm and fighting back the panic that rifled her gut at the smell of mildew, the reptilian air on her skin. Every time she blinked, the image flashed in front of her—a man in black leather, face down on the floor.

Why hadn't she checked to see if he was okay? Why hadn't she had the nerve?

You're a coward, that's what you are, she thought. A timid little ninny who makes up imaginary worlds where all crimes are solved like a jigsaw puzzle, all bad deeds punished, all bad people unmasked.

Not like the real world.

Even now, she lagged behind Kat and Emma as they approached the end of the passage. That first spark of courage had dissolved the instant her skin made contact with the dank tunnel air. The bob and pitch of the flashlight made her dizzy, just as it had last night.

Last night. When she'd followed Kat down the dark tunnel, each step closer to Brett Saffron Presley—face-to-face for the first time since she'd opened her eyes on the most horrible morning of her life. Dizzier and dizzier until they'd reached the steps that led up to the trapdoor and her phone, finding a signal at last, had buzzed with a curt text from Chip.

FYI Dash woke up running 102, giving him Tylenol

She'd felt the spike of familiar fear—the panic you always felt when a kid came down sick, even though you knew fevers were normal, kids got sick, no need to catastrophize, but still you catastrophized because you were a mom.

But she'd also felt a guilty relief.

Kat, I have to go back, she'd said. *Dash is spiking a fever. I have to call home and make sure he's okay.*

Fine, Kat had said. *No worries. I'll handle it.*

But in the glow of the iPhone flashlight, Cassie had seen the movement of Kat's eyes as she turned. The eye roll of unmistakable contempt.

Coward.

Kat had seen through her, all right. Dash was just the excuse. When the chips were down, when the game was finally afoot, what had Cassie done?

Cassie had bolted.

She'd fled back to her room and left two voicemails and three texts for Chip. Then she'd stood at the window and stared through the whirling snow at the nimbus of light from the octagon room in the Obelisk, where Kat was doing their dirty work. Brave, determined, capable Kat. Right this minute she was carrying out the plan—the dominatrix outfit, the photographs, the blackmail. Getting her hands on that manuscript at last. All by herself.

Cassie had looked at her phone—no reply from Chip. She'd made her way to the bed and lain there counting the minutes. Listening for Kat's returning footsteps in the hallway outside.

Hating herself.

The soft, faint click of a pair of high heels had drifted through the wood and stone. Cassie had shut her eyes. *Coward,* she'd told herself.

Just as sleep started to wash over her, she'd jolted awake with a terrible thought. What if something had gone wrong? What if Kat hadn't done everything they were supposed to do?

The manuscript. What if BSP still had the manuscript?

She'd stared at the ceiling, listening to the thump of her heart. The beat of truth in her head.

You have to make sure. That's the only way. If you want to rescue your marriage, your family, your kids, your soul, you have to walk out of this bedroom and do what needs to be done.

Three years ago, you made a terrible mistake. Now it's time to make things right.

Whatever it takes.

AHEAD OF HER, the flashlight went still, illuminating Kat's and Emma's faces turned up toward the trapdoor.

"Hold the flashlight while I get the latch," said Kat.

"Are you sure they can't see us?" whispered Emma. "What if someone's in there?"

"Nobody's in there," Kat said confidently. "I saw Calum and Beatrice standing guard outside."

"But they might see the flashlight," said Cassie.

Kat turned to her with the same hint of pitying scorn as the night before. "The curtains are closed. And they're thick velvet ones. Trust me, our boy didn't want anyone peeking on what was going on inside."

Cassie nodded meekly. Emma took the flashlight and pointed it toward the handle. Kat grasped the ring and pushed upward. One by one, they climbed the steps and emerged into the chilly black air of the Obelisk's octagon chamber.

"I can't see anything," Cassie whispered.

"That bloody detective, taking our phones." Kat brandished the small novelty flashlight, enameled in tartan. "This is like a Barbie torch."

"Did you just say *bloody detective*?" said Emma.

"What? No, I didn't."

"I think you did," said Cassie. "Also *torch* instead of flashlight."

Emma snorted. "Someone's got a crush on the detective chief inspector, methinks."

"I'm sorry, did you just say *methinks*?" Kat snarled.

"Oh, please—"

"Girls," said Cassie, "could we just, you know, focus? Look for the breadcrumbs? And the manuscript?"

"All right, all right." Kat ran the thin, shaky beam of the flashlight across the floor. Here and there, the numbered crime scene tags stuck to the flagstones. "Where did the rugs go? I remember some rugs."

Cassie was staring at the spot where Presley's body had lain. The smell of alcohol still clung to the air—the same smell that had assaulted her when she opened the trapdoor last night. She said numbly, "I'm sure the DCI had them removed for testing."

"Testing for what?"

"Oh, the usual. Blood. Hair. DNA."

"Mead," said Emma. She shook her head. "I remember how we used to go to Renaissance fairs together, back in college. He always ordered the mead. He got such a kick out of it. Who would have thought . . ."

"He would grow up and drown in it?" said Kat.

Emma made a noise like a dog attempting to laugh. "It *is* kind of funny, when you think about it. Dark humor, I mean."

"That's the best kind," said Kat. "The only kind, if you ask me. Look, there's no point poking around here. They've swept it clean. We need to look in his office. It's on the other side of the building somewhere. . . ." She rotated slowly to the left, passing the flashlight over the wall.

"To the right," said Cassie. "There should be one of those hidden doors in the paneling that opens to the staircase that leads up into the tower. The door to the study is on the opposite side of the stairwell."

The flashlight's beam swung around to hit her left cheek. She felt Kat's and Emma's gazes follow it, like question marks on her skin.

"What?" she said defensively. "It's on the floor plans."

PRESLEY'S OFFICE WAS smaller than she'd imagined, not that she'd really imagined it. She'd spent the last three years trying not to think about him at all. But if she *had* imagined his office, it would have been on a grander scale, with more trophies. This room was modest, overhung by low, beamed ceilings that made it feel even smaller. The stone floor was bare and rough, and the mantel above the small fireplace contained only a clock.

To be fair, it was a big clock.

But you didn't really notice the fireplace, or the clock, or the desk against the wall. What you noticed was the contraption in the middle of the floor that looked like a medieval torture device. A chill crept into Cassie's bones at the sight of it.

"What on earth . . . ?" muttered Emma, as Kat drew the flashlight over each rod and joint.

"If I'm not mistaken," said Kat, "*that* is the genuine replica of Edward VII's sex chair."

"It looks different in real life," said Cassie. "More . . . formidable."

"It's a *masterpiece*. A work of genius. Look, you can see how the angle of approach maximizes stimulation to the—"

"All right, all right. I get the idea," said Emma.

With a last shudder, Cassie averted her gaze from the contraption and made for the desk. It looked as if it had come with the castle furnishings. The wood was old and heavy, the legs carved to look like the paws of a lion. On the stained leather blotter rested an old-fashioned typewriter.

"Oh my God," said Emma. "*The* typewriter. It's the same one, I swear. The same one he had in college. He used to take it to Starbucks while everyone else worked on their laptops. He said it brought him closer to the text."

"It was in that photograph in the *Rolling Stone* profile," said Cassie. "The black-and-white one where he's gazing out the window with the inscrutable expression and the exposed brick wall behind him."

"'Can This Man Save Literature?'" said Emma. "That was the title."

"Douchebag," muttered Kat.

Cassie knelt to face the drawers on the right-hand side of the desk. She ran her fingers over the handle of the topmost and pulled.

The drawer wouldn't budge.

"I think it's locked," she said. She stuck her hand inside the pocket of her sherpa robe and fished around until she found a hairpin. "Give me a second."

"You can pick locks?" Kat sounded impressed.

"Of course I can pick locks. This nice detective showed me how, when I was first starting out. I had this idea I was going to write hard-boiled procedural-type mysteries, so I did all this research on picking locks and hot-wiring cars and tapping phones." Cassie stuck the hairpin in the lock and closed her eyes, feeling her way around the tumblers. "But then I started writing and my detective had all these cats and liked to bake and—well, she just kind of took control. Here we are."

The drawer slid open. Cassie removed the hairpin and slid it back inside the pocket of her robe. Behind her, Kat and Emma didn't say a word. She turned to look over her shoulder and saw their faces glowing faintly in the flashlight beam, a little shocked.

She smiled. "The good news: if it's locked, that means they haven't gotten around to searching it yet."

"Or it's a trap," said Kat.

But she stepped forward to rifle through the contents of the top drawer, while Cassie crouched under her to unlock the second one. Emma moved to the wall to hunt through the bookcase.

"Do you see anything?" Cassie asked, as the second drawer slid free.

"Just a bunch of crap," said Kat. "Chewing gum, cigarettes, a stack of receipts. Sharpies. Fine tip, probably his special book-signing Sharpies. One of those fancy gold lighters. With his initials on it, of course."

Emma's voice came from across the room. "Hey, don't knock monograms, okay?"

"Oooh, *these* are nice. Fancy chocolates. Jacques Torres. He must have had them shipped in from New York. Like the douchebag he is." Kat held up the box. "There's one left if anybody wants it."

"Ugh," said Cassie.

"He loves chocolate," said Emma. "He used to buy me these amazing artisan chocolates for Valentine's Day and then eat them all himself."

"What about the receipts?" said Cassie, as she rummaged through the papers in the second drawer. "Anything interesting?"

"Hard to tell without going through all of them."

"Then can I get a light down here? So I can see what's on these papers?"

"Well, well," said Kat. "What have we here?"

Cassie straightened and squinted at the object Kat held in her hand.

An old-fashioned pill bottle of brown glass.

"What are those?" Emma asked. "Some kind of medication? Or, like, party drugs?"

Kat pointed the flashlight at the small pills nestled inside. "I can't tell. Hold the flashlight for me, will you?"

Cassie took the flashlight and tried to hold the beam steady, though her fingers were shaking. Deftly Kat unscrewed the lid and spilled a couple of pills into her palm.

"Roofies," she said. "Douchebag."

Emma came over and peered at the pills. "Oh my God. Definitely roofies."

Cassie looked at Emma, then at Kat, then back at the pills.

"What's a roofie?" she whispered.

"Oh, come on. Seriously?" said Kat. "The High Priestess of Poisons doesn't know what a roofie is?"

"I mean, I've *heard* of them—"

"They're just pills that make you loopy," Emma said.

Kat dropped the pills back in the bottle and screwed on the lid. "Douchebags like Presley put them in your drink when you're not looking, then they take you upstairs and have their wicked way, and you can't remember a thing the next day. Oldest trick in the book, but it still works on the gullible."

Cassie's legs stopped working. She crumpled to her knees in one of those slow motion falls, like a tower toppling, and stared at the astonished, ghostlike faces of Kat and Emma—back and forth, back and forth, until she realized she might actually throw up. Or pass out.

"Are you okay?" asked Emma.

"Holy crap," said Kat. "The little bastard."

THE ARGUMENT ITSELF was so stupid, Cassie couldn't even remember what it had been about. Laundry, maybe. Or the cat litter box, or the dishwasher. It didn't matter. Chip could be a little stubborn and self-righteous when it came to misunderstandings about household chores, or the implication that he hadn't done them the right way, and sometimes Cassie let her feelings get a little too hurt. Either way, they should have made up before she left for the conference. Cassie should have apologized, but she was waiting for Chip to apologize first—never, ever tell a woman she's being too emotional—and somehow she ended up at the stupid hotel bar, feeling unloved. Unappreciated. Not . . . *cherished* enough.

Vulnerable.

Not that any of this was an excuse for what she'd done.

She could still hear the excited female whisper in her ear—*Oh my God, that's Brett Saffron Presley!* Like he was Mick Jagger or Brad Pitt or . . . well, she couldn't think of anyone younger; they all looked alike to her. Ryan Reynolds? Or Ryan Gosling? One of those Ryans. Anyway, the stallion had just pranced in, the stud of the herd, wearing leather and a smirk, just like his author photo. He'd pulled up the barstool next to Cassie— already a couple of drinks into her pity party—and shone his light on her.

And what did she do? Freeze him out? Pay her tab and walk away?

Nope and nope.

She'd basked in that light. Glowed in it. Or, more accurately, she'd reflected it back to him and his glorious ego in an infinite loop of self-regard.

So she had nobody to blame but herself.

She'd let him order her a drink, and another drink. Something fizzy and sweet, like candy. She remembered an elevator, she remembered hanging on his arm because she couldn't stop the spinning in her head. Feeling like a million bucks—an important writer, an important *person*, because Brett Saffron Presley *himself* wanted to see her latest manuscript.

Upstairs. In her room. Or his room. Or something.

That was all she remembered until she opened her eyes the next morning to a splitting headache and the terrifying sight of a hotel suite that was not her own, a head on the pillow next to hers that did not belong to her husband.

And the black weight of guilt that only became blacker and heavier when she realized a few weeks later that she hadn't had her period.

GULLIBLE. THE WORD banged against Cassie's skull. *Oldest trick in the book, but it still works on the gullible.*

She put her face in her palms. She wanted to curl in a ball on the flagstones. She wanted to drive a stake through his heart. Then she remembered he was already dead.

A hand fell on her shoulder.

"Cassie, honey. It wasn't your fault." Kat's voice, except it wasn't Kat's voice—low, gentle, almost kind. "Whatever you did— whatever he did to you, I mean—that's on him. He took advantage. He drugged you."

A sob shuddered out of her chest. "But I let him. Buy me. A drink."

"That's one tiny mistake, okay?"

"But I'm married!" Another sob. "To Chip!"

"So what? It was a conference. People buy you drinks. It's part of the game."

Another arm wrapped around her waist. "You didn't know. You didn't know what he was like. You're so sweet, Cassie, you probably never imagined someone would do that to you."

"Drugging women for sex is a crime, Cassie. It's rape."

At the word *rape*, Cassie made a noise somewhere between a roar and a moan.

"Oh my God." Emma's arms enveloped her. "Oh, honey. I'm so sorry. He really did, didn't he?"

"I—I don't know," Cassie said. "I don't remember."

"So that's why you're here," said Kat. "It wasn't just that stupid kiss at the bar."

"Now you know. Now you know what an idiot I was." Cassie let her head fall on someone's shoulder—Kat or Emma, she wasn't sure, because her eyes were shut tight. "Why I needed to get my hands on that stupid memoir of his and destroy it. Because if he wrote about what happened—if Chip realized—"

"Chip doesn't *know*?" said Emma.

"How could I tell him? I found out I was pregnant."

"Holy shit," said Kat.

Emma said slowly, "You mean . . . *Dash*?"

"It can't be!" wailed Cassie. "But maybe? *Probably* not. When I got back—Chip and I—well, I wanted to purge it all out, kind of redeem myself? So—you know—"

"So you went at it like rabbits?" said Kat.

"Well, yes. Chip, you know, he can be very *amorous*. Especially after I've been away. And the timing. But still. A tiny, *tiny* chance. I couldn't rule it out. I couldn't say for absolute *certain*. And that *bastard*. When he announced to the world he was writing that memoir—no holds barred, he said, unvarnished truth—I just knew he meant me, too. And it would destroy Chip. It would destroy everything."

"You could do a DNA test," said Kat, ever practical. "You just need a strand of Chip's hair or something."

"But you're too scared to find out for sure, right?" said Emma. "Because what if."

Cassie nodded against the shoulder that supported her head. It was Kat's shoulder, she realized. That silky material. The slim, strong bones underneath.

"Chip already knows about the kiss," she said. "Somebody messaged him with that old Instagram post. Right before I left for Scotland. Thanksgiving weekend. It was so awful. That's why

I was so upset, when he figured out about BSP and Kinloch. He thinks—he must think I'm here to have an *affair*—and I can't reach him, he won't respond—"

"Listen," said Kat, almost whispering. "Whatever happens, we've got you, okay? You're not alone here."

Emma's arm tightened around her waist. Something warm pressed against the crown of her head—surely not a kiss? Surely not a comforting, maternal kiss from the ice queen of New England?

"That's right," Emma said. "You've got the two of us now. For what it's worth."

Cassie felt the knob of Kat's shoulder under her cheek. The solid warmth of Emma's arm along her back.

Everything, she thought. *It's worth everything.*

"And for starters," said Kat, "we need to find that goddamn manuscript."

THE MANUSCRIPT WAS gone, if it had ever existed.

They searched every desk drawer, every shelf and corner of the bookcase. They searched under the rug and behind the curtains— BSP could be paranoid, Emma said. They even searched the Edwardian sex contraption.

No memoir.

"I guess it was a hollow hope," said Emma. "I mean, maybe he uses a laptop now. They stopped making ribbons for that stupid typewriter years ago."

"I bet the police took it," said Kat. "The laptop."

Cassie ran her gaze over the walls—so dark in the puny glow from the flashlight, she saw nothing but shadows. Every muscle ached, but her brain was painfully alert. "If it's on there . . ." she said. "You heard what he said at Bouchercon. And we all read the announcement in Publishers Lunch. *A graphic and no-holds-*

barred memoir of his life as the most innovative and controversial writer of his generation."

"In a major deal," muttered Emma.

"To Little, Black," said Kat. "My first publisher. Dropped me after the second book."

"So unless he's having the world's worst case of writer's block—"

"Was having," Kat interrupted. Her face was wan and exhausted, underlit by the flashlight. She looked at Cassie, then at Emma.

A hopeless stare, Cassie thought. The stare of capitulation.

"I have to know what's in that memoir. If Chip finds out . . ." Cassie let the words dangle in the cold air.

"Forget Chip," said Emma. "If that detective finds out . . ."

"Then I'm toast," said Kat. "We've struck out tonight. No packaging, no phone. The breadcrumbs were already cleaned up."

"And we haven't found anyone else's breadcrumbs, either," said Cassie. "We've wasted our time."

Kat shook her head. "No, we haven't. At least we know where we stand. We know what that bloodhound chief inspector knows. So we're one step ahead."

"But no closer to finding the real killer," said Emma.

Cassie shut her eyes. In her head, she heard Kat's voice—*You're not alone here.* And Emma—*You've got the two of us now.*

Did they mean it? Or were they just trying to calm her down? Keep her from going hysterical in the middle of BSP's office in the middle of the night?

If they knew the truth, would they feel the same way?

Cassie squeezed her hands together. The sweet one. Everyone always thought she was the sweet, good one. Nobody ever suspected the twisted thoughts in her head, the dark ideas, the fears, the rage. She poured it all into her books, like a confessional, so she could face the world all cleansed and—oh, what was the word? Pure. Innocent. Be the good girl everyone expected.

Even for Chip.

She took a deep breath.

"It was me!" she blurted out.

"*What?*" said Kat.

"*I* killed Brett Saffron Presley."

On the word *Presley*, Cassie opened her eyes to a pair of shocked faces.

Then the battery in Kat's flashlight made a last, flickering gasp and died, leaving the three of them standing in the middle of the room in absolute darkness.

CHAPTER FOURTEEN

Emma

EMMA WASN'T SURE which was more alarming—Cassie's insistence that she'd killed BSP or the fact that the three of them were stuck up in the pitch-dark tower and had to somehow find their way through the tunnel and back into their bedrooms before they were discovered.

"Great," Kat said, the word followed with something mumbled and definitely not G-rated. "Now what?"

No one answered. Only the sound of them breathing told Emma that they were still there.

Along with the echo of Cassie's story. What BSP had done to her was beyond unforgivable. It might even be a revenge worthy of murder. But not for Cassie, regardless of how justified she might be. Emma hadn't known her for long, but long enough to know that Cassie Pringle was about as wholesome as one could get. "What makes you think you killed him?" Emma asked, her face turned to where Cassie had been standing when the light flickered off.

"What Fiona said—about him having been impaled." Her voice skipped on the last word.

"Okay . . ." Kat said slowly. "Are you saying that when you came back after I left, you brought a horn and stabbed him with it?"

"No—that's not it at all. Remember the large stag's head over the door?"

"I do," Kat said. "But wait—"

Emma cut her off. "There's nothing there now."

"But you weren't here the night of the murder," Kat said.

"I know. But I'm here now, and I definitely didn't see a stag's head. I would know because I have a photographic memory."

"Of course you do," Kat muttered.

"Stop, you two," Cassie cried. "How are we going to solve anything if you two keep bickering?"

"Sorry," said Emma. "Go on, Cassie."

"That's just it. It's not there. Because when I left him sprawled on the floor and foaming at the mouth, I was so scared that I slammed the door behind me. That must have been what happened, don't you see? The stag's head toppled from above the door with such force that it fell on him and one of the antlers stabbed him to death. Which means I killed him."

Emma would be lying if she didn't find the mental image somewhat gratifying, but that didn't make it true. "No, you didn't. Trust me."

"How do you know for sure?" Cassie couldn't keep the thread of hope from her voice.

"I took a physics class for a book I was researching about a seventeenth-century scullery maid who'd been accused of murder. I know all about angles and trajectories, energy, speed, and mass. You can check my math, but I'm rather positive that the force required to penetrate a leather bustier by a slightly curved antler from a height of fourteen feet just isn't within the realm of possibility."

"See?" Kat said. "Einstein here says you couldn't have killed him so you need to stop thinking that you did, all right? That's why we're here. To find out who really did do the deed so we can all sleep at night. Preferably not in a Scottish prison."

Emma let the comment about Einstein pass. She'd been called much worse. Besides, Cassie wasn't the only one who needed to come clean.

"It's all my fault," she said quietly, the pitch blackness like a confessional offering a temporary anonymity. Not that she was Catholic, but she had once sat inside a confessional while doing research for a book. At least until she'd heard a soft cough from behind the screen facing her and had immediately exited.

"What do you mean?" Cassie asked.

"I knew Brett before he met either one of you. I could have stopped him. But I was too embarrassed by what I'd allowed him to do to me. So I kept my mouth shut."

"You might as well tell us," Kat said. "Assuming you already told the inspector during your interrogation this morning."

Emma felt Cassie's hand on her arm. "Come on, everyone. Crisscross applesauce on the floor so Emma can tell her story."

"We're not your kids," Kat said as she plopped down on the floor.

"No. But you're all I've got right now so you'll have to do."

There was more rustling as she and Cassie sat down on the floor. Then, after a deep breath, Emma began to speak.

"I already told you that he stole my manuscript." She swallowed, the sound loud in the darkness. "But what I didn't tell you was that we were living together at the time. Because we were a couple. Together. For a long time." Emma paused, waiting for the other two to show their disappointment in her for not coming clean earlier. For essentially lying to them. But they didn't.

Encouraged, she continued. "We were freshman English Lit majors at Bowdoin. He was friendly and charismatic, and I fell for him completely. My only excuse is that I was only eighteen and had never had a boyfriend before. I was flattered that he chose me."

She stared straight ahead in the darkness, seeing a younger

version of Brett. The version of him before he'd adopted the male author affect of Vandyke beard and nonsensical slogans that only held meanings for those desperate enough to believe them. To believe *him*.

Emma leaned forward and rested her head in her hands, glad for the darkness that hid her face, and their expressions of disgust. "We were each working on our own books. I was flattered that he showed so much interest in mine, asking me to email each chapter as I wrote it. He said it was to offer helpful criticism, but he never did. He said it was perfect."

She closed her eyes tightly, wishing she could erase the vivid picture of BSP in their apartment, reading her chapters on his laptop, telling her how much he loved what she was writing. "That stupid typewriter was just a prop for the struggling artiste he wanted everyone to believe he was. But now I know that he was just creating his own computer file with my book. All he did was alter the character names and change the setting from Connecticut to a futuristic dystopia."

"Is there a difference?" Kat asked.

Cassie choked back a laugh then brought her hand to rest on Emma's arm in apology.

"I gave him my virginity to show how much he meant to me. But our entire relationship had been a lie. I learned that when his first book—*my* book—had been published. And that's when he left me. Just . . . left. Without a word, or apology. Without even saying goodbye."

"Oh, sweetie," Cassie said, patting her arm. Even Kat had moved closer.

"It didn't even occur to me that I had been completely and thoroughly duped until I visited an old family lawyer friend for free advice and he told me that I had no case and my best course of action was to move on. By then BSP had long since ghosted me, refusing my phone calls and all attempts to speak with him. I had been used and discarded like an old rag, my career now firmly downgraded into the corner of historic bio-fics about un-known women." She wiped away a stupid tear, glad the others couldn't see. "It was the only way I could be sure that BSP and those like him would have no interest in stealing my ideas."

"Did you tell the inspector all this?" Kat asked.

Emma shook her head, then remembered that they couldn't see her. "No. I admitted to knowing BSP in college. The DCI probably already knew this little tidbit if he was any good at his job and I figured it would make me look more honest in his eyes. But I didn't tell him about the book. Not just because it was too humiliating to admit that I'd been so gullible, but because it made me look guilty. Having one's career aspirations crushed is a pretty compelling motive and not one with which I wanted to muddy the waters. Why add humiliation to the whole murder suspect thing?"

"Amen, sister," Kat said.

Emma had the impression that Kat was holding up her hand to high-five, but after three failed attempts to make contact, finally gave up.

"Until today, I've never told anybody what happened. Mostly because I'm too embarrassed. I'm supposed to be so smart. So strong. But in reality I'm just a stupid girl who fell for a guy because she believed in his 'poor little rich boy' sob story and wanted to make it better."

"Wait," said Kat. "He wasn't rich growing up. He grew up in foster care. Depended on scholarships for school."

Emma laughed, a hollow, aching sound. "Yeah, that's what he put in his bio. But the real truth as opposed to *his* truth is that he's actually the only child of a very wealthy socialite whose six marriages to various financial movers and shakers propelled her to the top social strata. I think I was the only one he ever told. Maybe because we were both so young and in love, we wanted to tell each other everything. And we did. I told him about how poor my family was, and how everything was such a struggle but that my writing was my refuge and the one thing I owned outright. The one thing besides my parents' relentless quest for saving money that made my parents pay attention to me."

Emma felt someone squeeze her shoulder and was surprised to realize it was Kat. She took a deep, shuddering breath before continuing. "His own writing aspirations were such a disappointment to his mother. He said he'd practice for hours in the mirror how to smile the right way, how to walk into a crowded room filled with strangers and win them over just to make her proud. It didn't work, of course. He was still a failure in his mother's eyes because he wanted to get an MFA from Iowa instead of an MBA from Harvard."

She pressed her lips together for a moment, preparing to say out loud the one thing she'd never dared acknowledge. Until now. With these two women who knew and understood better than anyone else in the world. "That's why he stole my book. He wanted immediate literary success to impress his mother and saw my book as a shortcut."

She leaned back against the stone wall, feeling the chill through her robe. "And it was—a literary success, anyway. Yet still, even through my own anger and hurt, I felt sorry for him. Because I knew his mother wouldn't even acknowledge it. I think that's what still drives him—his unrequited quest for his mother's approval. Even leasing this castle was a power play meant to impress her. Which I'm sure it didn't." She swallowed back a rising lump in her throat. "The stupid thing is that I would have helped him if he'd confided in me in the beginning. I would even have forgiven him." Her throat tightened. "But he didn't care about forgiveness.

That was never his thing. He wanted to be an icon in the literary world at any cost. And he succeeded, didn't he? We were just collateral damage."

Cassie leaned over to envelope Emma in a warm embrace. "You poor, poor thing. I'm so sorry you had to go through that."

Emma stared in her friend's direction. "Poor me? What I went through only pales in comparison with what he did to you. And if I'd had any guts at all, I would have spoken up and stopped him before he could do much, much worse things to other women. For that, I feel nothing but guilt."

"Don't," said Kat, surprising Emma. "Only one person is to blame. And he won't be hurting anyone else ever again." Kat put her arm around Emma and the three sat in a group hug for a long moment. "So," said Kat, "now that we've cleared the air and have finally decided that none of us is a murderer, what do we do? We're stuck here in the dark, and I really don't think that inspector will be bringing us coffee and a smile in the morning when he finds us here."

"Hang on," Cassie said. There was a rustling sound and then a small pinpoint of light appeared beneath Cassie's chin. "I'd forgotten I was wearing this. My oldest, Amelia, gave it to me for my birthday. It's a light-up ring that I think she found in a cereal box. I just hung it on my charm necklace and forgot about it. Until now." She smiled brightly, as if they hadn't just been sitting in the dark for over an hour.

"Seriously?" Kat said, hauling herself up in her heels to stand. "You've had this the whole time?"

"Sorry," Cassie said. "They say each child takes one-quarter of your brain so I'm working on a deficit here." She laughed then headed toward the secret passage, Emma and Kat tagging along behind her.

● ● ●

Later that morning

AFTER LOCKING THEIR bedroom doors, Emma, Cassie, and Kat descended the stairs together, Cassie and Emma each with a matching pair of plaid wellies and Kat in her questionable stiletto snow boots. PC McMorris, the uniformed constable with the shiny brown hair pulled up in a neat bun under her cap, watched them warily as they approached the main door, her eyebrows raising as she regarded their footwear.

Emma smiled politely. "We were wondering if we might head down to the pub."

The woman didn't smile back, her attention more focused on their footwear. "Aye, ye can visit the pub. No way off the island right now, is there? Just don't be daft and get yerselves lost in a snowdrift."

"Right," Kat said. "We'll do our best not to. It's a short walk but maybe we should leave breadcrumbs?"

"She's just joking," Cassie said, ushering the three of them to the door. "Have a nice day." Her smile was so warm and ingratiating that the constable actually smiled back.

Emma rolled her eyes as she shut the door behind them, sucking in a refreshing lungful of brisk air. It made her a little homesick, a tug on the heart she hadn't felt in a long time. Maybe that's what happened when the prospect of imprisonment in a foreign country threatened one's freedom. Not that Emma had anything to be worried about. She hadn't killed BSP and neither had Kat or Cassie. Not that it mattered. Wrongful convictions happened every day.

That frightening thought spurred her forward to catch up with the other two women who were slogging through the wet snow. "I have a thought."

Kat turned and Emma could almost hear Kat's brain working on a quick comeback. Except there wasn't one. Either Kat was too preoccupied with the whole murder-suspect thing to think of something, or maybe she, too, was feeling the new bonds of friendship.

Betting on the latter, Emma said, "We need to put our heads together and figure out who the real killer is." She winced at the O.J. Simpson cliché. Except was it a cliché if it was actually true? "We have to think out of the box, beyond the coincidental evidence the police are looking at. Because we have the advantage, don't we?"

"We do?" Cassie asked.

Emma didn't roll her eyes or any of the usual things she did when speaking with others who didn't grasp the obvious as quickly as she did. Cassie's story had given her a lifelong pass. "Yes, we do! Because we know that the three of us are innocent, which puts us way ahead of the investigation."

Kat stopped and turned to face Emma, Kat's labored breaths coming out in fat white puffs. "So, you've decided to let me off the hook?"

Emma met Kat's gaze. "Yes. I don't think you would have ordered the dominatrix outfit in your own name if you'd really planned to do more than humiliate him. And I know you're not stupid enough to have done it accidentally." She'd meant it as a compliment but realized after the words had left her mouth that it might not be interpreted in the same way.

Kat's eyes hardened. "Maybe I'm double bluffing."

Cassie stepped between them. "Stop it. Both of you. We're a team, remember? We need to work together and figure this out."

Kat turned around and resumed walking toward the pub. "So, tell us what you're thinking. I can practically hear the teakettle in your brain starting to whistle."

"I think that there might be a connection between BSP's murder and Naughty Ned. There's a lot of unsavory stuff here, and if BSP had dug up everything about Ned's history, Ned's descendants might not be thrilled with the prospect of it all being revealed to the world."

Cassie squeezed in between Kat and Emma, linking arms in a show of solidarity and friendship but also, Emma suspected, for added warmth. "His descendants as in the current laird?"

"Yes," Emma said. "Although he isn't the only descendant. Naughty Ned was a pretty lusty guy, propagating his genotype all over Kinloch."

"Do you mean sowing his seed?" Cassie asked.

"I have an entire book on euphemisms for the sex act if we need it," Kat said.

"I'll keep that in mind," Emma said, then slowed her pace as a realization struck her. "They were pretty alike, weren't they? Naughty Ned and BSP. They both abused their power and position with the same goal in mind. Ned preyed on the village girls, and BSP on his fans—and those poor, newbie female authors who took his scholarships. And they both got away with it."

"Until they didn't," Cassie said.

They continued trudging through the snow in silence until the sound of a loud bark brought them to a halt. A large snow-encrusted furball with a familiar round black nose and two matching eyes bounded toward them, stopping at Emma's feet before politely sitting and looking up at her with a lolling pink tongue. Unable to resist the adoration or the cute face, Emma bent over and began scratching behind Loren's ears, Emma's enthusiasm turning to expectation when she remembered that wherever Loren was, Archie couldn't be too far away. Or was it the other way around?

A sharp whistle brought Loren to attention and an immediate redirection toward the tall figure of a man approaching them. Archie wore a wool cap and a thick woven scarf, but Emma recognized Archie by the way he moved, and by the piercing green gaze currently directed at her. She began to smile at him but was stopped by the coldness in his eyes.

"Loren likes me," Emma said, trying to soften his gaze. "She came right to me."

Archie's face remained impassive. "Loren's our Kinloch crime dog and works with the DCI on investigations. I suppose I need to tell DCI Macintosh about our encounter right now. Perhaps she's sniffed out the murderer, hmm?"

Emma expected him to smile, or laugh, or anything to show that he was joking. But he didn't. "You can't honestly believe that we . . . that I . . ."

"Are capable of murder?" he finished for her. "Aye, perhaps."

Emma stumbled over her words to get them out. "I . . . excuse me?"

With a final glare in her direction, he touched the brim of his cap and called to Loren before stomping away in his boots without another word.

Emma blinked. Twice. Her eyes stung and her throat constricted, reminding her of a similar moment in her past involving another man who'd apparently used her for his own interests without thought or care for her pathetically vulnerable heart. She closed her eyes and took a deep breath, wondering if she had some sort of target on her chest visible only to male predators looking for a kill.

"Ouch," Kat said. "What was that all about? Maybe all that dancing together at the ceilidh made him mad that he's gay?"

Emma felt her face redden. "He's definitely *not* gay."

"Of *course* he's gay. He wears jewelry!"

"That's a signet ring." Emma continued to march forward. "Trust me. Archie is definitely not gay."

Kat took her by the shoulders and spun her around. "What? You played hide the haggis with the man? You had a visit from old one-eye? You shook the sheets? Had some horizontal congress?" She gave Emma a shake. "Tell us!"

"Oh, Emma," Cassie said. "Did you and Archie sleep together?"

Emma could only nod because she knew if she opened her mouth she'd start sobbing.

Kat's hands slipped from her shoulders. "You were just supposed to distract him."

Emma swallowed. "I know. It's just that at the ceilidh we . . . Archie and I . . . had a connection. A *real* connection. And when I saw him approaching the Obelisk and my job was to distract him, well, everything just sort of happened naturally." She clenched her eyes to stop the dreaded sting of tears.

"I bet," said Kat. "Riding the bony express is the most natural thing in the world."

"Kat," Cassie said with a warning tone she probably used on her children. "I don't think that's the reason why Emma may have slept with Archie. He's a very nice-looking man. Who apparently isn't gay. I think it's lovely that Emma has found someone. I could tell by the way they danced together that there was something there."

"Sorry, Emma," Kat said. "It's just that I find it odd that he should give you the cold shoulder when he's got more motive than the three of us together. Assuming your line of reasoning is correct."

"Excuse me?"

"The Naughty-Ned-descendants angle you mentioned. As the current laird, Archie has the most to lose if you dig up more than he wants you to."

"Wait—what?" Emma looked past Kat's shoulder to see Loren bouncing happily in the snow next to her master, Archie. The laird of Kinloch. Who was definitely *not* gay. It was like a bad Hallmark movie except this wasn't a movie. This was her life.

"Fiona told me at the ceilidh," Cassie explained. "That's when I told Kat. I'd planned on telling you, too, but things progressed so quickly last night . . ." Her voice faded as she looked closely into Emma's face. Snaking her arm through Emma's, she said, "Come on. Let's go get you some coffee. And maybe a 'wee dram' of something stronger to put in it." She tugged on Emma's arm until Kat took the other elbow and forced Emma to move, practically dragging Emma through the snow until they reached the pub.

"Hey, look," Kat said, pointing a gloved finger at a glass-covered sign hung next to the pub's door. "It's a ghost tour of Kinloch." She brushed off clinging snow before leaning closer to read the fine print. "It says it's part of the Kinloch Historical Society's programs. It meets here at the pub." Turning back to her companions, she said, "We should do that. It will give us something to do while we're stuck on this godforsaken island and we might learn something useful, too." Her nose scrunched as if tasting something bitter. "Maybe our friend Bruce leads it. Might give us a chance to apologize."

"Us?" Emma repeated.

"Well, me mostly, I guess. I'll do my best to make it up to him," Kat said as she raised a suggestive eyebrow.

"Actually," Cassie said as she pointed to the fine print at the bottom. "It says here that the tour guide is Calum MacDougal. That should make you happy, Kat."

Kat reached forward and pulled open the door, allowing the heated air from inside the pub to wash over them. "We can interrogate him about Archie since Emma's laird has now moved to the number one spot on our suspect list as the person with the most compelling motive."

Emma opened her mouth to tell Kat that she was wrong, that the Archie she knew couldn't possibly be capable of murder, but no words would form.

"Come on, Emma," Cassie said gently, pushing her through the doorway. "Let's get you something to drink."

CHAPTER FIFTEEN

Kat

E MMA ORDERED A scotch.

If the landlord had any opinions about Americans knocking back his best Oban at ten in the morning, he didn't express it, other than by the faintest flick of one gray brow. The expression reminded Kat of someone, but she couldn't quite place who.

Whoever it was, it irritated her sufficiently that she put in an order for vodka soda. Just because.

"And I'll have an Irish coffee," said Cassie bravely, although Kat could tell day drinking wasn't really her thing.

"It's Scotland, ye ken," said the tall woman who joined them at the counter. She'd dropped the bunny suit and was wearing professional-looking tweed trousers with a cream sweater beneath the requisite puffer coat.

"Fiona!" Cassie looked more flustered than the situation called for, like the popular girl had shown up at their table in the cafeteria. "*Is* there Scotch coffee?"

"There is, but it isn't what you think." Emma roused herself from her misery long enough to impart information. "It's a mix of water, milk, sugar, and burnt breadcrumbs meant to simulate the taste of coffee when coffee was unavailable or too expensive."

"Fortunately," said Fiona drily, "we haven't had to resort to that yet."

In illustration, the very expensive Italian coffee maker behind the bar made happy chugging noises, unleashing a wave of heavenly steam. The landlord filled a large thermos with strong coffee and handed that and a brown paper bag over the counter to Fiona.

"Ta," she said.

"Not behind the bar today?"

"It's surgery today," said Fiona briefly.

Cassie's eyes opened wide. "You're *operating*?"

"Ach, I forgot. You'd call it—office hours? I'm seeing patients in the surgery." Fiona took a long swig from her thermos. "Everything from warts to compound fractures."

"To murder," murmured Cassie. There was a faraway expression in her eyes that Kat was beginning to recognize.

As they waved goodbye to Fiona, Kat muttered, "Don't tell me you're thinking of another series."

"A quaint Scottish island . . . a doctor who's also the local midwife and barmaid . . . I mean, she must know everyone's secrets. . . ."

"All it needs is a talking cat," said Kat.

"Or a sheep," said Emma. The scotch had put a little color back into her cheeks.

"Yeah, what would a sheep have to say? 'What are you doing, standing in a field?'" Kat mocked, shamelessly ripping off *The Vicar of Dibley.*

"In this case, the sheep might be able to tell us who murdered BSP," pointed out Cassie. "Wasn't Beatrice on the scene?"

"Great, who here speaks sheep?" said Kat. "Beatrice can be the star witness at my murder trial."

Cassie bit her lip. "What makes you think it will be your murder trial?"

"You're not—" Kat began, and then broke off as the landlord pushed Cassie's coffee across the bar, a thing of beauty with frothing homemade whipped cream and a sprinkle of fresh ground cinnamon across the top. The man's expression was carefully neutral. Too neutral. There was something about him . . . What was it?

"You're not drinking that standing at the counter," Kat hastily improvised. "Let's sit down."

They found seats by one of the windows, upholstered in creaking maroon leather, the dark wood tables polished nearly black with years of use.

"We need to be more discreet," she hissed.

Emma looked at Kat's leopard print leggings. "Discreet?"

Kat slouched into her seat, across from the others on the banquette. "Look, maybe you don't notice the servants, but that guy was listening to every word we said. You think it's not going to get around?"

"Good," said Emma, lifting her head. There were two spots of color in her cheeks from the wind and the whisky and possibly just a bit of laird stubble burn from last night. "Let them know we're trying to prove our innocence. There can't be anything more innocent than trying to prove our innocence."

"Except Miss Guilt over here was about to blame herself again."

Cassie took a slurp of her whipped cream. "That's Mrs. Guilt—unless Chip divorces me."

Her face was beginning to crumble again. "Hey," Kat said hastily. She'd only just stopped Emma moping by insulting her; she couldn't have Cassie breaking down next. "That guy behind the bar. He reminds me of someone but I can't place it."

"Oh! Didn't I tell you?" Cassie blinked away what might have been about to become tears. "Mr. Macintosh is Fiona's dad. That's why she helps out behind the bar."

Kat choked on her vodka. "Macintosh? Like the detective chief inspector?"

Cassie licked off a bit of whipped cream from the top of her lip. "It's a pretty common name, isn't it? I mean, think of the apples. And the raincoat."

Kat's throat felt raw from swallowing raw spirits the wrong way. "There are like three people who live on this island!"

"Two hundred and twenty-seven, actually," said Emma. "But I agree with you. Look at the cheekbones."

They all looked at the publican's cheekbones. He looked blandly back at them.

"A mole," said Kat darkly. "That's what he is."

"He must have been pretty hot in his youth," said Cassie. "Like Karyn Black hot."

He wasn't Karyn Black hot. Calum was Karyn Black hot. The owner of the pub must have looked just like Detective Chief Inspector Macintosh once upon a time, all long lean lines and controlled strength and disturbing intelligence. . . .

"So this means that the detective is the medical examiner, GP, barmaid's brother?" said Emma, just as Kat was replaying her earlier interrogation with some interesting additions.

"It's straight out of *Spaceballs*," said Cassie.

"Actually," said Emma. "It's the opposite of *Spaceballs*. The point there was that the relationship was extremely attenuated, whereas here . . ."

"Would you stop with deconstructing Mel Brooks movies?" demanded Kat. All very well for them to banter; they weren't the one the hot detective inspector was focused on. And not in a good way. Here they were, the only strangers in a population of two hundred and twenty-seven on a storm-isolated Scottish island. . . . Even Morag and Calum were related. "I had a thought and now it's gotten away."

Cassie looked at her sympathetically. "Something about *Space-balls*?"

"Something about everyone being related. Everyone except us. And BSP." Kat rubbed her temples. Her fingers were so icy cold it felt like being caressed by a corpse. Like BSP, on the ground, cold and stiff. Kat shuddered. "I feel like we've walked into something here. Like this was all already set before we blundered in."

"I told you." Emma neatly polished off the rest of her scotch. "This goes back a hundred years to the original Ned."

"No, that's not what I meant. . . ." Kat wasn't quite sure what she meant. She shook her glass, making the one measly ice cube clink. What was it with the Brits and their vendetta against ice? It was freezing outside. It wasn't like there was any shortage. On the other hand, it did keep the drinks stronger, so there was that. "I don't know. I just keep thinking, everywhere that asshole went he left a trail of broken lives."

Emma sat up very straight. "Ned?"

"*No.* BSP. Seriously, can you keep your mind out of the nine-teenth century for five minutes? This is about BSP. It's always been about BSP. It was BSP who was murdered, not Ned."

"Well, actually . . ."

"I mean now. The murder we're suspected of, remember? That one?" Kat's voice was rising, and the landlord was wiping the bar with a little too much attention to detail. She dropped her voice, leaning her elbows onto the old oak table. "Why? Why was BSP murdered here, now? Why not in Brooklyn? Why not at Bouchercon? You can't really blame the inspector—the way it looks—three strangers appear on the island, and boom! Dead. But we know it wasn't us. So what happened before we wandered in like idiots? Who else on this island did he piss off?"

"You think it's local," said Emma, who always liked to restate the obvious. "You think this was set in motion before we got here, and we're just—the sacrificial lambs."

"Staked out for the slaughter," said Kat grimly. "So who is it? Who wanted to kill him and used us as cover?"

"Archie." Cassie looked apologetically at Emma. "I know he's got that whole Cary Elwes thing going, but we've got to face facts. If he's the real laird . . ."

"Then wouldn't he have wanted to keep his golden goose alive?" Emma's spine was ridiculously straight. Generations of debutantes would be proud. "There aren't that many wealthy Americans willing to bankroll remote Scottish castles. If you look at the statistics—"

"The statistics," Kat broke in. That. That was what she had been missing. Of course. She grabbed the edge of the table, knowing she'd finally got it, she'd caught hold of that missing thought. "Do you know what the statistics are for serial sexual abusers?"

"I was talking about the statistics for Scottish castles," said Emma.

"Never mind the castle. It was never about the castle. It's about the *women*."

They both looked at her like she was crazy. Kat didn't care. She knew she was right. "You think we're the only ones he took advantage of? You think he stopped with us?"

They clearly had never considered it, any more than she had. Cassie's eyes had gone as round as Little Orphan Annie's; Emma was a well-bred blank that Kat now knew meant she was dealing with a gut blow.

Kat couldn't believe she'd been so blind, that they'd all been so blind.

"*Think about it.* It's like with each of us, he refined his methods. He actually pretended to care about Emma. He dated her for years before he screwed her. He spent a week flirting and building up my trust before he . . . ambushed me. He roofied Cassie the night he met her."

A shudder ran through Cassie.

Kay pressed on, following her line of thought, unpleasant as it was. "What do you think happened with those women he chose for his conference scholarships? He handpicked them, that was part of the whole mystique of it. They were grateful—indebted to him—and I bet he showed them exactly how they could thank him. I wonder how many of them actually went on to publish after that?"

Emma's face had gone gray. "It's my fault. Cassie. You. Any . . . others. I never thought that there might—be others. If I had said something . . ."

"Don't you dare!" Maybe it was the vodka talking, but Kat lunged across the table and grabbed Emma's cold hand in her own equally cold hand and squeezed. "It's not your fault. Do you understand? It's. Not. Your. Fault."

Cassie's voice was very small. "She's right. It's not. None of it."

Kat released Emma's hand and gave a sharp nod. "We need to remember that. All of us. He's a serial abuser. And it's always women. You really think he's been here—how long?"

"Eighteen months, two weeks, and three days," said Emma tonelessly.

"You really think he's been here that long and he hasn't been up to his old tricks?"

Emma's eyes met hers. "You think there's another woman on the island—that he did something to."

For once—for the very first time—Kat felt like they were on the same page and it felt strangely good. Like she had an ally. "You know what they say, *cherchez la femme*. Where's the *femme*?"

Cassie tilted her glass coffee cup, trying to shake down the bit of curdled whipped cream that had collected at the bottom. "You mean Morag?" At the expression on Kat's and Emma's faces, Cassie abandoned her whipped cream quest, saying defensively, "Morag is the only woman at the castle, unless you count Beatrice, of course, and I really don't see Calum standing for—unless you think BSP went after Beatrice and *Calum*—What?"

"I don't think he was screwing Calum's sheep," said Kat bluntly.

There was a horrible rattling sound from the other side of the table. Emma was gasping, her mouth opening and closing, tears streaming from her eyes.

"Are you choking—Emma?" Cassie immediately positioned herself to do the Heimlich. "I can—"

"No—no." Emma fended her off with a weak gesture, gasping for breath. "I'm just—Oh God—Calum defending the honor of his ewe . . ."

Now that she knew Emma wasn't dying, Cassie could see the humor of it. "Like something out of a Karyn Black novel! All those bulgy thews . . ."

"We don't—know that—his thews are bulgy," panted out Emma, always a stickler for detail, even when she could barely speak. "Kat—was going—to check—that."

"Hey, I don't want to fight Beatrice for him."

Cassie giggled. "That would be a woolly bad idea."

"Says ewe," Kat retorted.

Something about the looks on their faces—the approval?—had her laughing, too; they were all laughing, losing it with laughter, midnight on exam week sort of laughter, snorting and gasping and burying their faces in their hands, laughing until Kat's chest felt hollow with it, but in a good way, which was pretty crazy given that she was probably facing a murder rap.

Cassie dabbed at her streaming eyes with a handkerchief embroidered with Scottish thistles. "It feels good to laugh." Reaching out, she took one of their hands in each of her own. "Thanks, ladies."

Cassie's hand felt impossibly small and soft in Kat's. And warm. Kat could feel the warmth of it straight through to her shriveled black heart.

Kat blinked hard enough to dislodge one of her fake eyelashes. "Yeah, the sheep jokes are great, but they're not going to be so funny when I'm in a Scottish prison. Can we get back to work here?"

"You're right." Cassie rooted in her jacket pocket and produced a tartan-covered notebook and matching minipen. "Let's do this logically—the way one of my detectives would do it. Let's figure out what we actually know."

Emma made a little coughing noise. "We know Archie was with me when the murder happened."

"Do we?" Cassie grimaced apologetically. "Precise timing of alibis is very important in a novel. If a character can make it look like he was elsewhere . . ."

Emma looked like she wanted to sink through the floor. "It would have been hard for him to be elsewhere."

Kat couldn't resist. "Very hard?"

"Yes," said Emma flatly. "Let's just say I would have noticed his absence."

"But how long can that bit have taken?" Cassie looked expectantly at Emma, her pen poised over the notepad.

The look on Emma's face was enough to make Kat snort the remains of her vodka soda. "Oh, honey. Are you asking specifically or in general?"

"I don't know! I didn't time him!" Emma had gone as crimson as Cassie's Royal Stewart wellies. "And it, er, wasn't just the one time. If you must know."

"It's for the investigation," said Kat, but she couldn't help grinning. "So the boy has stamina, has he?"

"It wasn't all—er. We talked! And snuggled. It was very . . . affectionate." Until it wasn't. All of them could remember the way Archie had been that morning; they could see it in the pain on Emma's face. Emma turned on Kat. "How is this relevant? You were the one who insisted we stay on point."

"Oh, sweetie," said Cassie softly. "He was just being a jerk today because he's a boy. I just mean sometimes they have trouble expressing their emotions. Like the time Chip—"

She broke off, looking as pained as Emma.

Shit. It was the broken hearts club. Kat deliberately kept her tone bracing. Someone needed to hold it together. "Okay, so your young laird is emotionally stunted but sexually gifted. How long were you together for?"

"All night," began Emma, then stopped herself. "Actually . . . Archie had to leave. His phone buzzed—an emergency in the stables."

Cassie's eyes met Kat's before she asked Emma, very gently, "When was that?"

"I don't know! I wasn't checking my watch. It was sometime before dawn, because it was still dark. The sky hadn't lightened yet. When I woke up, he was gone. And there was all that hullaballoo outside."

"So—he could have crawled from your bed and gone a-murdering by the light of the moon."

"Ye-es," Emma admitted reluctantly. "Depending on when the murder happened."

"Well, that we can figure out, can't we?" said Cassie, with the exaggerated cheer of someone about to deliver very bad news. "So Kat went into the tower at—what time was it, Kat?"

"It would have been a little past ten." The memory of it, the torches flaring, BSP reaching for her, the smell of booze and ash and incense that made Kat's mouth go dry. Hell. It had been her vision of hell. "You can check—what time did that text from your husband come in?"

Cassie gamely checked her flip phone, her voice faltering only slightly as she said, "10:02."

"And when did you follow me into the tower?"

Cassie didn't quite meet her eyes. "I spent a while trying to get through to Chip. . . . I kept hoping the reception would come back and I could reach him. . . . It was at least half an hour. No. Make that forty-five minutes. I didn't look at the clock. Isn't it amazing the way in books everyone knows exactly what time everything happened?"

No one was that perky without being guilty of something. But not murder. Kat was amazed by how fiercely she wanted Cassie not guilty of murder. Not even to save herself. Crap. When had she started to actually care?

"That would make it around eleven," broke in Emma. "Archie was definitely with me at that point. That rules him out."

"It might . . ." Cassie looked distinctly uncomfortable. "It might if we knew when BSP died."

"But we don't, do we?" Kat said in disgust. "We don't know when he died, and we don't know what killed him. We don't even know if he died late Friday night or early Saturday morning. We fail at being Jessica Fletcher."

"When Cassie got there—" Emma began defensively.

"He was on the floor, but I don't know if he was actually dead. I didn't stay to find out, although in retrospect that was really rather awful of me, because what if he was still alive but needed help?" Cassie took a deep breath. "And we can't rule out the possibility that I killed him by knocking the stag's head onto him. If he were passed out drunk, and I, well—"

"Accidentally impaled him?" Kat drawled.

"It's not as crazy as it sounds! So I had a character accidentally impaled in the third book of my Haunted Farmers' Market series. Chip's reaction was pretty much the same as yours—he was like, who gets impaled accidentally? But did you know that hundreds of Americans accidentally impale themselves every year? It's particularly a problem at Ren fairs. You know, those lances."

Kat crossed her legs. "Yeah, but how many of those impalements are actually accidental?"

"Let's not go there," said Emma primly. "What I heard the barmaid medical examiner say was that he had been impaled with a horn. That doesn't necessarily mean that he was impaled by the stag's head. What if he was stabbed with a horn knife?"

Cassie perked up. "You mean like an athame carved out of horn? In my Hedge Witch series . . ."

"It would go with the ceremonial aspect of Naughty Ned's orgies." Now that she was back to her pet theory, Emma looked happier again. "I found the Edwardian account books and inventories in the laird's chamber. I could check and see if there's any mention in them of a ceremonial horn knife. If there is . . ."

Kat held up a hand. "Before you go breaking into the laird's chambers to find a horn knife we don't know exists, maybe— I mean, let's not be wild and crazy, but I just want to throw this out there—maybe we should *find out how he actually died*."

"There's no need to sound like that about it," said Emma stiffly.

Kat drained the last of her vodka and set it down hard. "Yes. There is. You"—she pointed at Emma—"are so busy trying to exonerate your precious Archie that you're grasping at straws."

"Or horns," put in Cassie.

"And you"—Kat rounded on Cassie—"just want to make everything your own fault with your freak drownings and accidental impalements. So stop. Both of you. That horn knife—it doesn't exist. Or if it does, we don't actually know that. We don't know if he was stabbed or if he drowned in mead or if he freaking asphyxiated himself with his own kinky dog collar. We're all great at crafting fictions but it is not helping us here. At that rate, maybe he was killed by werebears. It makes as much sense as anything else we've come up with."

She could tell Emma wanted to argue. But, to her credit, she controlled herself. If there was one thing Emma was really good at, it was control. Kat was starting to admire that.

"The detective chief inspector would know how he actually died," said Emma stiffly.

"I'll just ask him, shall I?" said Kat sarcastically. "I'm sure he'll tell me everything."

Cassie cast a sideways look at the bar and dropped her voice. "What about Fiona? She'd know. She did the autopsy."

"Kat's right," said Emma reluctantly. "What applies to the detective chief inspector applies to your barmaid friend. She's not going to just hand over the report."

Cassie had that faraway look again. "She doesn't need to hand it over . . . we just need to *see* it. If we can just get a look at it . . ." Her voice changed. She said loudly, "You know, I think I'm coming out in a rash."

"It was probably that horrible peat wrap," said Emma wearily. "You should put some cream on it."

Cassie glared at her. "Or maybe it's the first stages of scarlet fever! My head feels hot. Don't you think my head feels hot? Maybe I picked up whatever the kids have before I left. I think I need to be checked over by a doctor."

She folded her arms across her rash-free chest, daring them to contradict her.

They'd all had drinks on an empty stomach. And now they were going to try to burgle a doctor's office. For confidential police records. That might not even be there. In the middle of the doctor's office hours.

Forget Jessica Fletcher, it was pure Nancy Drew. Entirely improbable.

But did Kat have a better idea? Nope.

"C'mon." Kat pushed back her seat, tottering just a bit on her stiletto snow boots. "Let's get you to the doctor before you go all Beth from *Little Women* on us."

CHAPTER SIXTEEN

Cassie

I THINK IT's scarlet fever." Cassie thought of Beth and coughed delicately into her fist. "Or consumption."

Fiona unwrapped the blood pressure cuff from her arm. "Och, dearie. Seems a bit of drama, no? Kinloch hasna seen a single case of scarlet fever since the time of Naughty Ned."

"But I feel terrible," said Cassie. "All . . . shaky and feverish. And itchy. Are you sure you don't see a rash?"

"Nae rash, nae fever. Temperature fair and lungs all clear. I reckon ye're under a wee strain, is all."

Cassie fixed Fiona with her most forlorn look. The office—surgery, as Fiona called it—was nothing more than the front room of a thatched cottage four doors down from the pub, warm and cozy, nothing like the sleek, sterile, white-and-stainless-steel rooms to which she took her children for their checkups. Cassie sat on an examining table that seemed to have been repurposed from a Victorian chaise longue, while Fiona sat on a wooden stool that rocked from one leg to another every time she shifted position. A bookshelf covered one wall, stuffed with textbooks and journals. Against the other wall, a giant iMac perched on an ancient desk, surrounded by photographs, papers, paperweights, and souvenir coffee mugs filled with pens and wooden tongue depressors. The air smelled of woodsmoke and camphor. Fiona waved a tongue depressor in front of her nose and Cassie obediently opened her mouth.

Fiona flicked on her penlight and peered at the back of Cassie's throat. "Pink and perfect," she announced. "Ye're certain it's sore?"

"Very, very sore." Cassie turned her head to cough into her shoulder. "My toddler's running a high fever right now. I must have picked it up from him."

"But that's been a week, at least?"

Cassie blinked pitifully. Fiona patted her hand and spoke in a kind voice.

"Och, now, dearie. I dinnae doubt ye're feeling poorly, with all the fash and bother the day. Nor sleeping well, neither—"

Something about the tone of her voice made the tears well up in Cassie's eyes. And they weren't fake, either. Not entirely. "I haven't been sleeping at all," she wailed.

"What, not a wink?"

"Of—of course not! Th-there's been a *murder*! What if the murderer returns and kills us in our beds?"

"Mrs. Pringle, I dinnae think—"

"It's terrifying, I tell you! I mean, I don't even know how the killer did it. At least you have some idea. In your official capacity, I mean."

Was it Cassie's imagination, or did Fiona glance swiftly toward her computer?

"I'm afraid I cannae discuss such matters," Fiona said primly.

"No, no. Of course not. I wouldn't dream of asking. It's just the strain, you know. The not knowing." Cassie drew in a deep, shuddering breath. "And Dash! My baby! He's terribly sick, and that detective took our phones and laptops! I haven't been able to read my messages or emails. My husband might be trying to reach me and I wouldn't know!"

"Now, Mrs. Pringle. I wouldna fash meself about that. Surely if there were an emergency, yer husband could ring the castle direct?"

"Would he? I don't know! That's the trouble! You know men, they don't always think of these things."

"I'm *certain* he would, dearie."

Cassie wiped her eyes and leaned forward. "Mrs.—I mean Miss—I mean Doctor—"

"Fiona will do."

"Fiona," Cassie said earnestly, "I'm sure you can imagine what it's like. All the way across the ocean, cut off from your family, knowing your baby is sick—*suffering*—with a high fever. I'm— I'm just *crazy* with worry."

Fiona reached out and patted her hand. "I'm certain ye are, Mrs. Pringle."

"I'm a wreck. Just look at me! If only you could speak with your brother—"

"Me brother?"

"DCI Macintosh. I'm sure you could convince him to let me have my phone, just for a minute, to check my messages." Cassie sat back and sighed. "If I could even get a signal inside that drafty old castle."

Fiona nibbled her bottom lip and glanced at the computer on her desk.

"Just one little message," Cassie said. "That's all I need. Just a—a single crumb of reassurance."

"Look ye," Fiona said. "Me brother can be a wee bit of a stickler, ye ken. I cannae see him returning those phones until he's good and ready. But I reckon—seeing as this is a medical matter— there's no reason we cannae check yer email from this computer. All official-like."

"Would you mind?"

Fiona stood up and moved to the chair before the desk. "Nae trouble at all. Come right here and stand by me. I'll just enter the password." Fiona's fingers clattered on the keys and the home screen popped open. She clicked on the browser icon and turned to Cassie, who had come to stand by her shoulder. "That'll be Gmail? Or sommmat else?"

"Um, Gmail," said Cassie. She spotted the Outlook app on the icon bar at the bottom of the screen and squinted at the red circle. Did Fiona really have 236 unread emails? "It's crimeandcupcakes."

"I beg yer pardon?"

"My Gmail account? Crimeandcupcakes at gmail dot com."

"Oh. Right. Crime . . . and . . . cupcakes . . . at . . . gmail . . . dot . . . com. Here we are. Password?"

"Um—do you mind?" Cassie stretched her hands toward the keyboard.

"Och, of course not. I forget, ye're nae Kinlocher. We're a bit lax about such things around here." Fiona leaned back in her chair to make room. "Well, most of us, anyhow. Go on, then."

"Um—I don't mean to be rude, but—if you wouldn't mind? You know, privacy?"

Fiona's voice took on a little frost. "Mrs. Pringle, I'll remind ye I'm a medical professional. Taken an oath of confidentiality."

"But it's—well, they're personal affairs—"

"I'll close me wee eyes."

Distraction, Cassie thought desperately. She needed a distraction. She glanced out the window toward the pub, where Emma and Kat waited for her, huddled over their coffee cups. Probably checking their watches.

"Mrs. Pringle?" said Fiona. "I'm afraid there's another appointment coming up."

"I—"

The door flew open from the hallway. In stomped a short, wide man with grizzled gray hair, accompanied by a wafting odor of stale whisky.

"And there he is," muttered Fiona.

"Fifi!" he roared.

Fiona rose from her chair and spoke in a thick Scottish burr. "Now, Mr. MacDougal, as I've told ye often enow—"

"Fifi Macintosh, I'll remind ye I striped yer bum when ye was nae more than a wee lass, and I'll not be kept waiting for me appointment—"

"Yer appointment's in five minutes, Mr. MacDougal."

"Och, lass, didna ye hear me on the telephone? I cannae wait! Me hemorrhoids be acting up fierce again!"

"Pardon me just a wee moment, Mrs. Pringle." Fiona moved around the corner of the desk and took the man gently by the elbow. "I must ask ye to sit yerself on the bench in the hallway until yer turn's arrived, Mr. MacDougal. As ye can see plain enough, I've got a patient here already."

"*Sit?* Do ye not ken, Fifi lass? Me bumhole's all aflame—"

"Mr. *MacDougal*!"

"—and I canna sit to save me soul!"

Cassie clicked on the Outlook icon. Up popped Fiona's email inbox. Eight unread emails at the top. Swiftly she skimmed the subject lines—request for appointment, pregnancy advice, Viagra prescription refill . . .

Re: Autopsy results.

Cassie glanced at Fiona, who was trying unsuccessfully to guide Mr. MacDougal out the door. Her own heart was pounding so hard, her fingers shook on the mouse.

She clicked on the email.

. . . primary cause of death not yet determined . . . considerable fluid in lungs . . . catastrophic puncture . . . pending toxicology report . . . no later than 17 December . . .

"Ye'll recall, MacDougal, I did warn ye to take those laxative pills each evening with a wee dram of whisky and soda—"

Cassie moved the cursor to the Message menu and clicked on Mark as Unread.

"And so I did, Fifi lass, and each bluidy morn I bound for the toilet like a puir wee rabbit chased by a fox—"

As Cassie moved the cursor to close the Outlook window, her nervous fingers clicked on Fiona's other email inbox. A gmail account, FifiMac82. Her personal email.

Virtuously, Cassie averted her eyes. But not before a name snagged her eyesight, down at the bottom of the column.

Brett Saffron Presley. Sent on 7 December.

She clicked.

Hey babe. Loved everything about dinner last night. And I mean *everything.*

"You're sure it was from BSP?" said Kat.

Cassie forced herself to speak through her chattering teeth. "Of c-course I'm sure! I might have been nervous, but I can still r-read. The sender was Brett Saffron Presley and the date was two nights before the m-murder."

It was almost eleven o'clock and the sun had climbed high in the southern sky, melting the snow into a heavy slush. Cassie felt a faint warmth penetrate the top of her woolen hat, but not enough to do more than thaw the top of her scalp. Kat was getting a real workout in those stiletto snow boots, not that she seemed to notice. Her face was a fierce mask of concentration.

"I think we've just *cherchez*ed our *femme*," she said.

"Oh, for goodness' sake," said Emma. "So they had dinner together. There's nothing in that email that suggests anything . . . *untoward* took place."

"Of course not. From *his* point of view, it went well. He loved everything about it, he said." She snapped her fingers. "I'll bet it was a Snoggr match. They both had profiles."

Emma turned to Cassie. "So how did Fiona reply?"

"I d-didn't see a reply," said Cassie. "Although I *was* in a hurry.

She looked over at me just as I was closing the window and—I don't know, frowned a little. I just panicked and closed the window."

"See? No reply," said Kat. "No reply means BSP was up to his old tricks. If she didn't reply, it means she was pissed off."

"Or busy," said Emma. "Or just looking for a no-strings hookup. Anyway, how could she possibly have planned a murder like that in two days? Plus, she's a doctor. She's sworn to do no harm."

Cassie ventured, "Actually, doctors commit proportionately more murders than almost any other profession. It's all related to the God complex. Plus plenty of means and opportunity. I mean, if you're a sociopath, medicine would be an attractive career option. Not that every doctor is a murderer. Or even most. Obviously."

"And it's the perfect cover," said Kat. "Not only is she the sister of the village DCI, she performs the autopsy herself."

"I don't know," said Cassie. "It does seem a little suspicious, but *murder*? She seems so . . . so . . . *happy*. Confident. Comfortable in her own skin."

"Not the kind of girl BSP likes to pounce on," said Emma, kicking a wad of half-melted snow.

"What's that supposed to mean?" snarled Kat. "Sexual trauma only happens to weak women?"

"Of course not! I just mean that he's a bully, right? *Was* a bully."

"And bullies prey on the vulnerable," Cassie said quietly. "They sniff it out. Like bloodhounds."

They came to a stop in the wet snow and stared at one another's boots. The damp air blew against Cassie's numb cheek, carrying a faint chorus of *baaa*s from some unseen flock a few fields away. She clenched her fist to ward off another full-body shiver.

"I'll bet Fiona was more vulnerable than we think," said Kat. "You never know what's inside of people. The ones who seem the most confident are sometimes the ones who . . ."

Her voice didn't so much trail away as choke off. Cassie reached out and squeezed her hand. For an instant, Kat returned the squeeze, before she pulled the hand back and resumed her march toward the castle. Pearls of slush flew from her boots. Cassie and Emma looked at each other, shrugged, and hurried to catch up.

"I don't know," said Emma. "Call me a Fiona skeptic. I just don't see her pulling off murder."

"Of course not. You still think it's something buried in the past," Kat said. "Naughty Ned again."

"The past repeats itself, doesn't it? Just in a different key. Naughty Ned, now BSP. Sexual predators have been doing their thing around here throughout history. We just have to figure out which of Ned's descendants holds the biggest grudge. Or the most murderous intentions."

"Well, Archie had the most to gain, didn't he?" said Cassie. "He's the laird of Kinloch. Now that he's pocketed BSP's money, it makes sense to bump off the leaseholder so he's got the place back to himself."

"Fiendishly clever," said Kat. "I like it."

"Archie's not a *fiend*," said Emma. "There's no way he'd murder anyone."

Kat made an exasperated noise. "You're spending too much time around Pollyanna here. You don't think Fiona could do it. You don't think Archie could do it. So who the hell *could*?"

At that instant, a long, familiar *baaa* reached their ears, much louder than the murmuring from the Kinloch flock. Cassie looked up and saw a tall, sturdy man tramping across the slushy field toward them, accompanied by a bounding sheep.

"Him," said Emma.

"Who, Calum?" said Kat. "But he's so . . . *hot*."

"Hot men commit murder, too, you know."

"She's got a point," said Cassie. "Emma did see sheep tracks in the snow the next morning. That had to have been Beatrice."

"And wherever Beatrice goes . . ." Emma allowed the rest of the sentence to fall unspoken.

As they stared across the white field, Calum turned toward his gamboling ewe and lifted his fingers to his lips to make a tender, coaxing whistle.

Kat shivered. "Great. Now I'm jealous of a sheep."

"But why?" said Cassie. "He had opportunity and means. So what's the motive?"

Calum must have sensed the three female stares fixed on his shoulders, because he turned his head toward them. Cassie couldn't see his face clearly, but she felt the force of his scowl drilling through her forehead.

"There's one way to find out," said Emma. "Who wants to join me on the ghost tour tonight?"

Kat stared blankly at her. "The ghost tour? Why?"

Cassie clapped her hands together. The thick tartan mittens made a dull thump against each other. "Duh! Calum leads the ghost tour, remember? The sign at the pub?"

"Oh, right," said Kat. "Because Calum does everything around here."

Cassie started forward toward the kitchen entrance. "Black Watch plaid would be perfect for a ghost tour, don't you think?"

CHAPTER SEVENTEEN

Emma

EMMA FOUND HERSELF humming a familiar tune as the three women trudged through the snow back to the pub that evening for the ghost tour. Despite the heaviness in her chest every time she thought of Archie, she found the cold night air invigorating. Cleansing, even. It gave her back a little of the confidence that had been taken from her. And although she couldn't recall all the words to the tune she was humming, she felt compelled to burst into song just as they came in sight of the pub.

"I ain't afraid of no goats. Doo doo doo doo. *Beat beat.* Frosting makes me feel gooood."

Kat stopped to face her. "What on *earth* are you singing? It sounds like the theme song from *Ghostbusters*, but those are definitely not the right lyrics."

Emma started to protest, wanting to let Kat and Cassie know that it had taken years after her disastrous relationship with BSP to even think about singing again. And not just because one of his last words to her had been to inform her that she couldn't carry a tune in a bucket. She'd known he'd just said that to be hurtful as she'd had a lifetime of people complimenting her voice, but still. It had hurt enough to shame her into silence.

But then she got a good look at what Kat was wearing and

burst out laughing. She'd seen her at the castle before they'd left, but Emma had been too eager to leave the castle and its memories of Archie to notice.

"What's so funny?" Cassie said as she moved in closer. She was definitely seeking out shelter from the icy wind behind her two companions. Unlike Emma, Cassie was a warm-blooded southerner and believed that anything below sixty-five degrees was freezing.

Emma pointed at the Black Watch plaid beanie, complete with white yarn pom-pom, bobbing on top of Kat's head. "She looks ridiculous!"

Cassie frowned. "I think she looks adorable. And so do you. I think our matching outfits will warm the attitudes of the locals, don't you think? Maybe make them feel like we're one of them."

Emma blinked at her several times but didn't have the heart to tell her that it would most likely have the opposite effect and might actually instigate a mob reaction involving pitchforks. When Cassie had handed out the matching Black Watch beanies, scarves, and capes, Emma had been too preoccupied with curiosity over how Cassie had managed to fit all of it into her Vera Bradley bag to think too much about how they would look to the locals. Until now.

As if reading her mind, Kat said, "It's too late to go back now. We'll just have to suck it up and pretend that looking like we're auditioning to be extras in *Outlander* was an accident." She shivered as a piercing wind blew through her pantaboots. Although, in deference to Cassie, they were plaid pantaboots.

"Well, then," Cassie said as she reached into her plaid backpack and pulled out a thermos and three tartan cups. "If you're too embarrassed to be seen with me, I suppose you don't want some of this hot fresh-brewed coffee." She unscrewed the top, allowing the enticing aroma to reach them.

"I didn't say that," Emma protested. "I will proudly stand next to you if you would share your coffee with me."

"Same," said Kat, taking one of the cups. She eyed Cassie suspiciously as the steaming black liquid was poured into their cups. "Where did this come from? Did you also pack a coffee maker?"

"Don't be silly. Who would pack a coffee maker? Let's just say that Morag and I have come to an understanding."

Emma put her lips against the cup, enjoying the smell and heat for a moment before taking a sip. "An understanding?"

Cassie nodded. "She's a fountain of knowledge about herbs and plants and home remedies. I've learned a lot from my book research and have started my own kitchen garden at home so I'm not as much of an expert as Morag, but let's just say that our shared knowledge has been beneficial to both of us."

"I'm sure," Kat said, gulping down the hot coffee as if it were water. Emma restrained herself from asking if Kat had any nerve endings left in her oral cavity. If they were to be friends, there were some things that shouldn't be asked.

The door to the pub opened, revealing a large, kilted figure standing in the doorway. He was backlit so Emma couldn't make out any of the man's features, but there was no mistaking the brawn of Calum MacDougal.

"If ye don't want to freeze yer bollocks off, I suggest stepping inside."

"I think he means us," Emma said as she handed her cup back to Cassie and bolted toward the door. Not because she was cold, but because she'd always been a rule follower.

As they clustered around Calum inside the pub, Emma looked around for other tourgoers. "Where's everyone else?"

Calum raised a ruddy eyebrow. "Who else d'ye think would be daft enough to do a tour in the snow? I was planning on getting meself blootered this evening, but now I suppose I can't." His eyes widened as he took in their clothing.

Fiona's dad, the publican, appeared with three shot glasses filled with something strong enough that Emma could smell it from arm's length. "A little something to keep ye lasses warm," he said with what looked like a warning in his eyes.

Emma's eyes watered from the fumes as she looked at her companions. Without preamble, they each lifted their glass and clinked them together. "Slàinte mhath," they said in unison before swigging back the whisky in one burning gulp. Emma eyed them proudly. She had spent an impressive amount of time teaching them the correct way to pronounce the Scottish translation of "cheers" and was glad to see it had been worth it judging from Calum's grudging grunt of admiration.

Kat sidled up to Calum, just like a, well, cat after a bowl of cream. "I feel very hot right now. But I'm not sure if it's from the whisky."

Emma looked away so that the alcohol wouldn't come back up. She imagined it burning twice as bad as it had on the way down. She could only hope that this was part of Kat's plan to soften up the big Scotsman so she could interrogate him without his noticing.

Except he looked more annoyed than interested as he stepped back to where four flashlights sat on a nearby table. "These torches are on loan from the Historical Society," Calum explained as he handed out one to each of them before claiming one for himself. "There's a two-pound convenience fee each. We'll just add it to yer ticket charge along with yer gratuity."

Emma examined her flashlight, noticing the Historical Society's logo printed along the side before handing it back to him. "Two pounds? That's ridiculous. I'd use my own phone if it hadn't been confiscated. Maybe I can borrow one?" She looked pointedly at Calum's phone on the table.

"Ye think? Some tourgoers have found that their phones lose power when out on the tour, leaving them in total darkness. But if ye've no qualms about walking the cliffs without a torch, I'll just have ye sign this waiver here. . . ." He began to rustle through a stack of papers on the table.

Cassie picked up the flashlight and handed it to Emma. "It's probably best that you take this. My treat," she said with an understanding smile.

Emma wanted to protest that she'd said no not because she couldn't afford it, but because it was simply an unnecessary expense that boiled her New England bones.

"Fine," she said, taking the flashlight. "But I can pay myself."

Kat and Cassie paid for their tickets with credit cards while Calum sighed impatiently as Emma counted out each pence. Twice. "Will Beatrice be joining us this evening?" Emma asked in an attempt to erase his scowl.

"Och, no. Don't be daft. It's too cold out for the little lamb. She'll be waiting for me by the fire like a good lass."

There were so many questions Emma wanted to ask about the whole Beatrice situation but didn't have the chance as Calum headed out the door to begin the ghost tour.

They turned right outside the pub, before crossing the street almost directly across from Fiona's surgery to a squat, stone house, its single window lit by flickering candlelight. After pulling from his sporran a large iron ring full of keys, Calum unlocked the front door to allow them inside.

The dark and dank interior was just as cold as outside, but at least the old stone walls blocked the biting wind, although it was doing its best to skate through the chimney and into the room through the empty fireplace, bringing with it the smell of damp and old ash. An ancient wooden bed sat in the corner next to a hopefully empty chamber pot. The only other furniture was a table with two chairs of similar vintage as the bed, the seats of the chairs rubbed nearly white with use.

"What is this place?" Cassie asked. From somewhere in the

depths of her backpack she'd produced a spiral-bound notebook and a pencil that was now clenched in her mitten-covered fingers.

"The old midwife's cottage," explained Calum. "All bairns in Kinloch for over a century were born within these four walls, ye ken. Some say on warm summer nights when the moon is full, ye can hear the screams of a woman." His eyes widened as he fell silent and the three of them listened as the wind whipped down the chimney.

"That sounds terrifying," Kat said, wrapping both hands around one of Calum's bulging biceps. "Were you born here?"

Calum stepped back, making Kat drop her hands. "Every bairn in the last forty years has been born in the doctor's surgery across the road, including meself. Although many of the old-timers say child birthing is best done at home." He shrugged his huge shoulders. "I no ken say fer certain, but I know from lambing season that nature knows best."

"So," said Kat, her hands now at her sides. "You must have a lot of medical knowledge with all your sheep handling. Did you study veterinary medicine at university?"

With a withering glare, Calum said, "No. But I'm on good terms with the local vet. He gives me what I need."

Kat studied him in silence as Cassie continued to scribble in her notebook. "Is there any particular ghost here that we should know about?"

Calum nodded sagely. "Aye. The old midwife. Her daughter was murrrderrrred, ye ken. Or so the legend goes. Some say it was suicide, but others call it murrrderrr just the same. Depends on who ye blame, but the story ends with the poor lass's untimely death."

The orb-shaped blobs from their flashlights added to the spooky atmosphere, as did Calum's scowl that was accentuated by the shadows caused by the direction of his flashlight from beneath his chin. It made him appear . . . sinister. Emma felt a small shiver of foreboding tiptoe down her spine, taking only a small bit of comfort from the knowledge that she had Kat and Cassie with her. For whatever that was worth.

"Do you know when this happened?" Cassie asked, her pencil poised over the notebook.

"Aye. And we'll be talking more aboot it when we're at the Langford Point cave. That's where the poor lass met her fate." His baritone voice deepened further as he spoke the last words.

"You must be so cold in your kilt," Kat said. "And I can't imagine what a strong wind does to your . . ."

Emma stepped between Kat and Calum to save Kat from further embarrassment. Whatever it was her friend was attempting wasn't working on Calum. "Well, then, I say we head to Langford Point. The name was changed from something unpronounceable in 1902, although I wasn't able to find out why in my research."

They all headed toward the door, Kat in the lead. "I've seen Langford Point on an aerial map. It has an interesting shape, doesn't it?"

Emma followed Calum dutifully out of the cottage, hoping Kat wouldn't say anything else because Emma had also seen it on an aerial map while at the history museum and knew exactly what she was about to say.

Apparently, Calum thought the same thing because he coughed and focused all his attention on locking the door.

"What do you mean?" Cassie asked, all innocent curiosity.

Before Emma could discreetly slam her hand over Kat's mouth, Kat said, "It's shaped like an enormous erect penis! Complete with two outcroppings on either side that look just like . . ."

"Stay close," Calum interrupted loudly, changing the subject. "And put a sprint in yer step, aye? No frostbite allowed on the tour!" He charged off down the road toward snow-covered fields, leaving them with no option than to follow.

Emma's long legs had no problem keeping up, but she could

hear Kat and Cassie struggling behind them. "Can you slow down a little?" she asked for their benefit.

With an aggrieved sigh, Calum slowed down just a notch. "It's no like we're hiking the Himalayas, aye? Tis a wee island. An auld man with a cane could manage the tour just fine." He sent a withering glance toward the panting Cassie and Kat.

"But it's cold and blustery out, not to mention a bit slippery. Not all of us are wired for the elements," she said, diplomatically including herself in the blanket statement. Because that's what members of a team did. "Maybe if you'd give us a rundown of the itinerary so we'd know what to expect, we can pace ourselves." At his deepening scowl, she quickly added, "We did look it up on the website, but it said that tour stops were subject to change." She smiled up at the large Scotsman, hoping to soften his expression. It didn't.

He may have rolled his eyes, but Emma couldn't be sure since her flashlight wasn't aimed at his face. "Keep walking while I talk. Won't do to freeze where yer standing and make me carry ye back." Calum began walking at a slightly slower pace while Emma linked arms with Kat and Cassie to help them keep up.

"After the midwife's cottage we're meant to see the blacksmith's workshop and the headless Highlander who haunts it, but Reggie goes to Spain in the offseason, so he's no here to give the tour. The Obelisk used to be next, but Mr. Presley put an end to that until he opens his museum. Not sure what will happen now. Lots of folks were none too happy about his 'Kinloch Experience,' to be sure." He offered a raised eyebrow. "I don't think the citizens of Kinloch will be grieving too much for the passing of Mr. Presley."

"Including you?" Kat asked.

"Aye," he spat out. "Including me."

"Why is that?" Kat persisted.

Without averting his gaze from his forward march, he said, "Best save your energy for walking and not talking." He picked up his pace again and Emma tugged on Cassie's and Kat's arms to keep up.

"So, what's left?" Emma asked.

"The caves where the puir lass met her untimely end. And finally, the cemetery," he added, dropping his voice.

"But what about the other spots mentioned on the history museum's website?" Cassie asked between pants. "Like the hunting lodge and the ruins of the whisky distillery? Will we be visiting them on the way back?"

He graced her with a cursory glance and even managed a brisk smile. She was obviously his favorite of the three. Which, Emma considered, wasn't saying much. "Och, no. Reggie manages those, too. It's the offseason, ye ken? Only a true bampot would be out on a ghost tour in this weather."

"Could you please spell 'bampot' for me, Mr. MacDougal? I want to remember it for my notes." Cassie smiled sweetly as he patiently spelled it out for her. Emma wanted to ask what it meant, but she was pretty sure she already knew.

"Is the Obelisk haunted?" Emma asked.

Calum slid her a glance as if weighing whether or not it was safe to answer. "Aye. Verrra. It was the site of most of Naughty Ned's debauchery. Many young maidens from the town were taken there for sport by Ned and his friends. It's been said that the um, er, historical toy collection was from that period and used on the poor lasses. They say some were never heeerd from again."

Emma glanced at the other two women, wondering if they, too, had heard the ominous tone in Calum's voice. But Kat and Cassie seemed focused on keeping warm with their heads lowered and their chins buried in their scarves as they continued walking in silence.

The sound of rough surf breaking over rocks alerted Emma that they were nearing Langford Point, which, according to the online map of the tour, meant they were also near the cemetery.

There'd once been an old church, she'd discovered upon further research, but it had been abandoned over a century before. Which meant it technically wasn't a cemetery but a graveyard. She'd have to let Calum know so they could change it on the website.

Emma pointed her flashlight away from the sound of the water in the direction of where the graveyard should be, the beam weakly showing a jagged line of uneven headstones and Celtic crosses. The graveyard was close enough to the cliffs that Emma imagined that mourners would have had to strain to hear the funeral rites over the crash of the waves. Emma turned toward Calum to ask him, but he had increased his pace, widening the distance between them.

They'd reached what appeared to be a clearing, a wide expanse of sparsely snow-coated rocks leading to the edge of the cliff. Anyone who wasn't paying attention or who happened to be without a guide as they traversed Kinloch at night was liable to keep walking until they fell over the edge like a lemming.

The wind was stronger here, and much colder as the water's spray coated them in a fine, icy mist. It was almost too much for her northeastern constitution and she was about to ask Calum if they could go back when he made a quick turn and disappeared.

"Stop!" Emma shouted, as much as to get Calum's attention as to prevent her companions from accidentally plummeting over the edge. But her words were snatched by the wind and tossed out over the cliffs.

Cassie and Kat looked up and stopped their mindless march to the sea, both registering surprise to discover where they were. "Where's Calum?" Kat asked.

"He must not realize that we're not right behind him," Emma said, hoping that she was telling the truth. "Follow me," she said as she headed in the direction where Calum had gone. Feeling grateful for the extra two pounds she'd splurged on the flashlight, she aimed it toward the last spot where she'd seen their guide, registering a dark groove in the rocks that she surmised must be a path leading down. Pretending a confidence she didn't feel, she carefully headed toward the path.

The stones beneath their feet were worn smooth, the misty spray making the path more than a little treacherous. But someone, maybe centuries before, had carved out shallow steps on the ground as well as small handholds along the side of the cliff preventing pedestrians from tumbling down to their deaths. Not for the first time since she had embarked on this journey of revenge with Cassie and Kat, Emma doubted her sanity. As she painstakingly climbed down each step her internal monologue went on a loop between curses for Calum for leaving them behind like a typical *man*, and a memory of her mother telling her long ago that when bent on revenge, it was best to dig two graves. Or, as in this case, four.

"Where'd ye go?" Calum's voice echoed from the bottom of the cliff, full of indignation. "I didn't take yeens for stoters, but going off on yer own like that isn't safe. Ye could have been killed."

Emma was tempted to tell him that the only one in danger of losing his life right then was him. Cassie and Kat had joined her at the bottom of the path, and Cassie put a restraining arm on Emma as they examined their surroundings. The ground here was silty and wet, the weeping water along the sides of the cliff reflecting the light from their torches. The pulse of waves echoed nearby, the sound growing more ominous as they followed Calum toward the entrance of a cave.

Cassie squealed, "Are we at the haunted cave? I read about this on the website!"

"Aye, it's very haunted." Calum paused for effect. "The midwife's daughter I told you about—her name has been lost to history, but not her storrry. Naughty Ned and his fellow villains had their way with the puir young woman on her wedding night. When she was heavy with child, her husband found out what had happened and he abandoned her. Even her mother rejected her, blaming her for what had happened."

Kat made a choking sound, but when Emma turned to ask if everything was all right, Kat looked away.

Cassie put her mittened hand over her mouth. "That's terrible. What sort of mother would do such a thing?"

Calum smiled tenderly at Cassie. "Aye. It's why her mother haunts the midwife's cottage, her shrieks of guilt and grief carried on the wind for all to hear." He began to walk inside the mouth of the cave, and Emma hurried to follow, not eager to be left behind again.

They didn't walk far, but still deep enough that the solid darkness of it made Emma shiver. Calum continued his tale, his voice deep, each word bouncing off the walls of the cave, the incessant slap of waves his almost cinematic accompaniment. "In her despair the lass came here to give birth, leaving the child inside while she walked into the tide to drown. They say that when the tide changes ye can hear the cries of a woman in childbirth mixed with a bairn's wails. I've even heard it a few times meself." His eyes seemed to glow in the reflection of his flashlight, making Emma turn away.

Cassie sniffed as she used a mittened finger to dab at her eyes. "At least she saved the baby."

"It was a miracle the wee babe survived. When the tides roll in, this cave is filled with the sea, drowning any foolish enough to be caught inside at the wrong time."

Cassie looked so distraught that Emma took her hand in hers and squeezed.

"But the wee bairn didn't die as his mother swaddled him warmly and left him on a high ledge so he was untouched by the water. Fortunately, Lady Ned was out on a walk and heard the cries and rescued the bairn."

"So, Lady Ned raised the child as her own?" asked Cassie, a

true believer in happy endings. It made Emma wonder why Cassie didn't write romance like Karyn Black instead of the murder and mayhem of her cozy mysteries.

"Och, no. But she brought the wee bairn back to Kinloch where the child was brought up strong and healthy."

"Oh, thank goodness," Cassie said, now openly weeping.

Emma's own eyes were misting so she looked behind where she was standing to see if the usually inscrutable Kat had been affected. Except Kat wasn't there.

CHAPTER EIGHTEEN

Kat

CALUM WOULD CALL her a stoter.

Kat didn't care. She didn't care if she was being an idiot going off on her own while the others were listening to Calum's tale of woe in the cave. If she stayed, she was going to scream. She was going to scream like that abandoned baby there on the ledge in the cave with the tide rising. Because that was what she was. That abandoned baby there on the ledge, the waters rising. Life, threatening to engulf her, and no one to hear her screaming.

Kat half scrambled, half stumbled up the path they'd inched down with such care, her flashlight barely making a dent in the darkness. She'd go back to the pub and wait for them there. *What?* she'd tell them. *I'm communing with the spirits.* And she'd hold up a drink in illustration.

Great plan. Pithy line. Except she was sliding and slipping and there was no sign of the pub, just gorse—was that gorse?—and snow and snow on gorse.

In Brooklyn, there'd be a bodega by now; there'd be streetlights turning the sidewalks the color of a winter afternoon in the dead of night; there'd be at least one giggling drunk girl.

Here, there was nothing, not even the distant lights of the

village pub, just the vague shimmer of the moon and the rush and roar of the water.

Shit. She'd gone the wrong way.

Story of her freaking life.

Kat's legs felt like ice in her plaid pleather pantaboots. Not exactly designed for warmth, her clothes. Not like that baby, wrapped up well. At least that mother had cared enough to bring a blanket.

I can't do this anymore—that's what her mother had said before she left. Kat had heard her parents, even though she was supposed to be in bed, creeping out to stand outside the living room door, clutching her favorite stuffed rabbit.

That was all. *I can't do this anymore.*

But they all knew what "this" was. This was Kat. She was leaving Kat.

She'd never come in to say goodnight or goodbye or any of that. She'd just been gone in the morning when Kat woke up and never came back.

There wasn't anything dramatic or tragic about it. It wasn't like Kat's mother had walked into the surf off Langford Point never to be seen again, or lost herself in drugs in Haight-Ashbury, or taken a vow of silence in an ashram in India. Instead, Kat's mother had booked herself a first-class flight and gone home and married the guy she'd been dating before she met Kat's father at a Kappa Kappa Gamma mixer with West Point.

Kat had been welcome for visits—if by welcome you meant put in the guest room and treated like something vaguely unclean, an embarrassing souvenir of an unfortunate escapade.

Stupid ghost tour. Stupid story. Stupid Kat for letting it get to her. She was feeling really quite alarmingly cold. Outdoorsman though she wasn't, she knew enough to know she should probably find some sort of shelter.

The outline of a building loomed in front of her, and Kat felt a momentary relief before realizing that an outline was all it was. Her flashlight beam skipped over the empty hole of a doorway and a ragged collection of crosses rising from the snow.

Not the pub. A church, built out of stone like the rest of the island, now short one roof. No one had worshipped here for a long time.

Except the dead. Inside the dubious shelter of the churchyard, weathered stones huddled together, some tilting drunkenly, some leaning against each other as though for comfort. The winds were harsh; the punishing salt had scoured away half the carving, leaving only the faintest ghostly lines on the stones.

Kat had always liked old cemeteries; they appealed to her sense of the macabre. Some writers wrote in coffee shops. When the spirit moved her, she would take her laptop and coffee and write among the mausoleums of Green-Wood, comfortable in the company of the dead. The dead didn't criticize her. They didn't tell her she should join a team or ask her why she didn't have a boyfriend. Instead, they shared their stories with her, bits of poetry, cryptic carvings, Masonic symbols, lambs, and pyramids, and the occasional pithy epitaph.

Kat trained her flashlight on the worn stones, trying to ignore her frozen toes, her frozen fingers, her frozen heart.

"In Loving Memory of George MacDougal, beloved husband of Mairie MacDougal . . ."

"Beloved mother . . ."

"Beloved son . . ."

"Beloved daughter . . ."

So many beloveds. Beloved beloved beloved. Whole families planted in the same ground together, generation after generation.

Kat's flashlight wobbled in her hand, casting an uneven light across the stones.

Even her mother rejected her, Calum had said.

Like that was unusual. Like mothers didn't usually walk away from their children.

Ice stung her cheek. Not ice. Tears. Stupid, stupid tears. Kat scrubbed at her cheeks with a cold fist, trying to rub them away before they froze her face and they found her iced over in the churchyard, just another monument.

Calum could make her part of the tour. The stoter who didn't listen to instructions and froze and no one missed her.

Out of the darkness, a hand settled on her shoulder. Kat made a horrible squawking noise, and tried to run, succeeding only in pitching face forward over the tombstone in front of her.

"Miss de Noir—Miss de Noir. It's DCI Macintosh."

Her flashlight had fallen, creating a pool of light on the ground. A man was on his knees beside her, helping her up where she'd fallen, saying her name.

Kat's knees stung with snow; she'd scraped her hands on something. Everything hurt. Also, she felt like an idiot.

"*Ms.* de Noir," she said acidly, and staggered to her feet, trying to ignore the pain of a skinned knee. "What in the hell are you doing creeping around graveyards in the middle of the night?"

"I was driving home and I saw your light." The inspector picked up her flashlight and handed it to her.

Either she'd been very lost in her own thoughts or he'd been driving without lights. "Right, I get it. You were shadowing your prime suspect. Afraid I'll strike again?"

She couldn't make out his face at all, just the shape of him in the dark, but she could sense his amusement. "There's no one here you can hurt."

Oh, yeah? Kat took a step up to him, too angry to feel the cold anymore. She ran a finger up along the buttons of his macintosh. "Maybe I'm a necrophiliac. Maybe I'm here to commune with the spirit of Naughty Ned. Sounds like the man could give me a few tips—or perhaps I could give him some."

The inspector's gloved hand closed over hers. "You don't have to do that. That . . . sultry act."

"What makes you think it's an act? I know a lot of men have a tough time with women who are up-front about their sexuality. I was hoping you weren't one of them."

This was where he was supposed to go on the defensive. It worked every time. Except, apparently, tonight. "You don't use your sexuality to attract. You use it to push people away."

Kat stiffened. "What's that supposed to mean?"

"Exactly what it says on the packet." He changed the subject before she could demand that he explain. "I noticed something interesting in your books."

"You've read my books?" Kat wasn't sure how to feel about that. She was never quite sure how to feel about anyone reading her books, and particularly about the inspector. Especially given the whole impaled-on-a-horn thing.

"I'm a tremendous fan," he said, deadpan.

"That's not funny."

"I'm not joking. You're a very talented writer."

Kat folded her arms across her chest. "Have you read all our books, or just mine?"

If he said yes to all, she'd know he was lying. Cassie alone had something like fifty books to her name. Emma had fewer, but they tended to be roughly the length of *War and Peace*, and that was before you counted the Author's Note.

"Only yours."

Kat batted her fake lashes at him. "I bet you say that to all the authors."

He refused to be distracted. "Tell me . . . Why is your first book so different from your later books?"

That first book. All those hopes and dreams. The raw magic of putting her fears and fantasies onto paper through the prism of a mythical world of good and evil that overlapped with the real world but spun out into realms unknown.

When that book had exploded and been the hit no one expected it to be, Kat had been asked about themes. Kat had come up with all sorts of glib responses, but never anything close to the truth, which was that the entire book was a meditation on the question that had dogged her whole life: How flawed was too flawed to find happiness?

Her heroine was a witch who became a vampire; her hero was a necromancer who became a demon. Both doomed. Both trying to reclaim their humanity, pitted against each other in a struggle for survival and redemption. And, possibly, love. If they didn't destroy each other first.

Kat shrugged. "My first book I didn't know what I was doing. I didn't know about genre conventions. I just wrote what I wrote."

"It seemed to work for you. Why change?"

"I have an expensive studio apartment in Brooklyn to support." After Yaddo, her publisher had dropped her. They'd been BSP's publisher, too. He hadn't just killed her sex drive; he'd killed her career. She'd been lucky another house was willing to pick her up—even if it meant writing what they told her to write. "Publishers like to sell what they know will sell. I wrote a vampire? I needed to write more vampires. Vampires are a category they understand."

"But your vampires aren't like other peoples' vampires," said the inspector. "You've turned the trope on its head. In your books, it's the predatory female vampire who goes after the men."

"As an avenger. For justice. Do you think she *wanted* to be a vampire?" Kat was so sick of this, so sick of all the hypocrites who mooned over the macho alpha male date rape heroes but treated an assertive woman as transgressive and taboo. If a man became a vampire, he got to be tormented, ooh, that poor man, nothing he did was his fault; if a woman was turned against her will, she was suddenly a vamp, in more ways than one, and unworthy of sympathy. "Why shouldn't she use her powers to fight for women who can't fight for themselves? And what do you know about literary tropes?"

"Policemen are allowed to read, you know—when not engaged in our employment."

"So you're telling me that when you're not engaged in your employment, your capacity for innocent enjoyment is just as great as any honest man's?" Kat bared her teeth at him. "Oh, great. I see what you did there. You flipped the trope. It's the pirates, not the policemen. Har, hardee har har."

"I wouldn't have pegged you as a Gilbert and Sullivan fan."

Kat put her shoulders back, sticking out her chest. "How *would* you peg me?"

"I wouldn't." It felt like a slap in the face, until he followed it up with, "You don't adhere well to pegs. The more obvious you try to be, the less obvious you are. Who are you really, Katja de Noir?"

Kat had a theory that it was mutual incomprehension that fueled attraction; once you figured out who the other person was—well, it didn't last long. It was why she was never herself. She was Cat Woman; she was Princess Leia in the brass bikini; she was every male fantasy made flesh, always just out of reach.

"Who do you want me to be?"

"Yourself," he said, as though it meant something, and, for a moment, Kat almost believed it, almost forgot that he was the detective and she was the suspect, and that this was an interrogation, not a date. "You tell me you're not Kathy Brown. But you're not Katja de Noir either. Who are you?"

Cold. That was what she was. Standing in a Scottish graveyard with a man who was only here because he thought she'd committed a murder.

"I'm no one," said Kat flatly. "I've always been no one. I was born no one. This? This is all there is to me. You strip all this away, there's nothing underneath."

"I don't believe that." The way he was looking at her was hot enough to make mist curl off the snow. "There's a lot going on under there."

"Yeah, a push-up bra." Kat backed up. "Don't let yourself be fooled. I'm less than the sum of my parts. And I didn't kill any-one."

"Not even as an avenger?" he asked softly. "For justice?"

Kat could feel the blinding rage rising, that he'd taken her words—her words about her book—and twisted them against her. It made her angrier that it was, in its own weird way, kind of a turn-on. "That's *fiction*, Detective. Don't confuse me with my characters."

If she was one of her own characters, she'd be naturally tall, with midnight black hair, not five foot five with mousy roots that started to show after three or four weeks.

"What would you do for justice?"

"Not what you're thinking," Kat snarled. The one man she'd been genuinely attracted to for years and he only wanted her for murder. "Don't think I don't know why you're looking at me."

There he was, smoldering quietly at her again. "Don't you?"

"Maybe it's because I'm an easy target. Maybe it's because there'll be no one to care if you throw me into a cell and throw away the key." Cassie had her sixteen children; Emma had a powerful family behind her. But Kat? She and her dad dutifully spoke on the phone once a month, awkward, stilted conversations where neither actually said anything at all. Kat hadn't seen her mother—or her half sisters—since just after her first book came out. "Makes it easy to pin it on me instead of where it really belongs."

The more Kat thought about it, the more obvious it seemed. Corrupt policeman saving his sister. And Kat, once again, expendable.

The inspector looked quizzically down at her. "Where it really belongs?"

"Is that something they teach you in inspector school? To just parrot back everything anyone says?" Kat didn't wait for him to answer. "You want to know what really happened to BSP? Talk to your sister."

He stared at her, his breath misting in white puffs in the cold air. "My *sister*?"

"You know, blond chick, works behind the bar and also delivers babies?"

"I know who my sister is!" The inspector wasn't being suave anymore; he sounded as frazzled as Kat felt. "What in the bloody hell does Fiona have to do with any of this?"

"Shit." Kat goggled at him. "You didn't know. You really didn't know."

"*Kat!*" The light of three flashlights—one decidedly larger than the others—lit up the churchyard. Cassie was waving hers madly around her head, scrambling and slipping down the path and shouting Kat's name.

"Yo," said Kat, and turned to her friends, but the detective tugged sharply on her arm.

"What the devil are you talking about? About Fiona?"

Kat looked at the inspector, his eyes dark holes in his face in the darkness. Like a tormented necromancer demon facing off with a witch vampire.

"Ask her about her date with Brett Saffron Presley." She tugged her arm free, turning neatly on one stiletto boot heel. "Now if you'll excuse me, Inspector, I've got some ghosts to hunt."

CHAPTER NINETEEN

Cassie

THE BEAM OF Cassie's flashlight zigzagged across the piles of wet slush and the dull gray tombstones. On the path ahead of them, a pair of dark figures separated.

"Kat!" she called out. "Kat!"

"She's fine," said Emma. "I'm sure she's fine."

"How do you *know* she's fine? *Kat!* Yoo-hoo! Is that you?"

Cassie grabbed Emma's hand to pull her along. Panic swelled inside her chest, crowding out her breath—the familiar old panic of motherhood. *In the middle of the night, Miss Clavel turned on the light and said, Something is not right.* That was motherhood, in a nutshell.

Panic—a side effect of love.

EMMA, ON THE other hand. The only thing that swelled inside Emma's chest was sarcasm. When Cassie had turned around, down among the rocks of Langford Point, and realized Kat had vanished, Emma had listened, unperturbed, to the list of awful things that might have happened to her.

"What if she fell off the cliffs?" Cassie had demanded, in between yells of *Kat! Kat!*

"If she'd fallen off the cliffs, we'd have heard her," Emma had said, in her practical voice. "Besides, Kat always lands on her feet, right? Get it? Kat? Lands on her feet?"

"How can you *joke* at a time like this?"

Emma's voice had softened. "Look, I'm sure she's okay. You know Kat. She wanders off when she's bored."

"In the middle of the night? Outdoors?" Cassie had raised her voice to call out to Calum, who strode on ahead, flashlight bouncing purposefully. "Yoo-hoo! Mr. MacDougal!"

Calum had stopped and turned so swiftly, Cassie skidded to avoid running into him.

"Aye?" he'd demanded, scowling quizzically downward in a way that made Cassie feel like a small, naughty child.

"I'm just concerned about our friend," she'd said meekly. "You don't see her footprints or anything, do you?"

Calum had spun back around and continued marching. "Nae," he'd said, over his shoulder, "but ye're not to worry."

"Why not?"

"She's the sort of lass that always lands on her feet," he'd called back.

"See?" Emma had said, in the brusque, no-nonsense voice she used to comfort you, which most people used to reprimand their dogs.

Cassie had ground her teeth and pushed her pace a little faster. Her breath came out in hard white puffs. Her fingers were no longer cold; in fact, she was sweating. That was one good thing about exercise, anyway. The only thing.

At each step, the castle grew larger, a giant hulk, dark as coal. The stones seemed to swallow up the feeble light from the windows.

"Where are we headed?" she'd called to Calum.

"The cemetery," he'd growled back.

"It's actually a graveyard," Emma had corrected. "Because it has a church? You'll need to change that on the website."

Calum had muttered something unintelligible.

"Why are we going to the graveyard?" Cassie had asked, struggling to keep up.

"'Tis the auld grrraveyard where the lairds and ladies of Kinloch were buried," Calum had told them. "I've a hunch yer friend's giving herself a tour."

And he was right.

ONE OF THE dark figures started moving toward them on a pair of spindly, awkward legs, like a baby horse. Cassie drew her flashlight upward along the tartan thighs to the sleek tartan puffer coat, to the pale, pointed chin. An arm threw itself over the eyes.

"Ouch! Put that away, you idiot!"

"Kat!"

Cassie ran down the path and threw her arms around Kat's thin shoulders. To her surprise, Kat didn't pull back. She even leaned her chin, just for an instant, on Cassie's faux fur coat collar. Cassie inhaled the feral scent of Kat's perfume. The pheromones tickled her sinuses. "What are you doing here?" she cried.

"Me? Oh, just got tired of waiting around for Calum's ghosts to turn up, so I went for a ramble in the cemetery."

"You vanished! I thought you'd been k-killed!"

"Not to be pedantic," murmured Emma, "but technically it's a graveyard. Even though the church is no longer in use."

Kat disentangled herself from Cassie's embrace, straightened her beanie, and looked quizzically at all the stiff faces. "Killed? Are you kidding me? Killed how? Stumbling over an old gravestone?"

"The c-cliffs?"

As she said the words, Cassie realized how lame they sounded. She turned to Emma, who sent her a sympathetic smile and looked at Calum. He had stopped next to a large memorial stone topped by a statue in the shape of a woman cradling an infant and stood there silently, arms crossed over his chest.

"Well, what next?" she said. "Aren't there any ghosts here?"

Calum cast the beam of his flashlight on the statue's face.

Cassie gasped. The graceful lines of cheek and forehead, the half-parted lips, the tender expression—she knew that face. Each morning at breakfast, each noon, each evening this woman had gazed down on them from the wall of the dining room.

"Lady Ned!" she exclaimed.

"Aye," said Calum. "'Twas her dying wish to be buried here, among them she loved sae well. There are some as say, on a quiet night, if ye listen close, ye can hear her sing a sweet lullaby to the innocent bairns of Kinloch."

Cassie strained her ears into the night air. Around her, Kat and Emma had gone utterly still. The wind whistled among the tombstones, smelling of salt and sorrow.

"I don't hear a thing," said Kat.

Calum snorted. "Och, well. Reckon ye're none sae innocent, come to think of it." He snapped the flashlight's beam to the right, toward the castle, where it disappeared into the sea of floodlights illuminating the walls. "We'll be moving on, then. The grrrand finale, as ye Americans say."

"But that's just the castle," said Emma. "We've already been there."

"Ye havena hearrrd the tale of the ghost cat in the cellar."

"Oooh, a ghost cat?" Cassie said eagerly.

"Who the hell cares about a ghost cat?" said Kat. "What about the Obelisk? It's the most *fearrrsome* building on Kinloch. I'm sure it's packed with ghosts."

Calum glared at her. "I've already told ye, the tour doesna stop there. Besides, 'tis a crime scene now."

"All the more—"

"Um, excuse me?" broke in Emma. "What's that?"

Cassie turned just in time to see a flicker of white appear between a pair of tombstones, then vanish again.

"What the hell," said Kat.

"Och, it's nothing. A trrrrrick of the eye."

"Of *all* our eyes? At the same time?"

Around the corner of the ruined church, the white flash appeared again. The figure of a woman, Cassie realized. A woman dressed in pale, floating robes, racing across the empty churchyard to disappear into the night. "Over there!" she exclaimed.

"Lady in White," Emma murmured. "Just like—"

Before she could finish, Kat darted forward after the ghostly figure, in the direction of the castle and the nearby tower. Cassie took a deep breath and scrambled after her, flashlight bouncing off the gravestones.

"Now hold on just a moment—" Calum called out from behind them.

But Cassie and Emma were too busy trying to keep up with Kat, who moved awfully fast for a woman wearing a pair of stiletto pantaboots. As Cassie dodged another slush puddle, she lost sight of the beam of Kat's flashlight and faltered. Emma bumped into her and swore.

"Where's Kat?" Cassie said. "I can't see her light!"

"It was moving toward the Obelisk. Let's go!"

Emma grabbed her arm and pulled her forward. Cassie scrambled along, panting with effort or excitement or fear or *something*, who knew. The slush flew from her shoes. The floodlit walls of the Obelisk grew brighter and larger. Kat came into view, bounding across the courtyard like a fawn in those stupid pantaboots.

"There she is!" Cassie gasped.

Emma charged after her, too fast for Cassie to keep up. She looked over her shoulder for Calum, but he had disappeared into the darkness somewhere. Ahead, Kat staggered around the curving base of the tower, followed by Emma. She passed the entrance to the Obelisk and dropped to an uncertain walk, then stopped. Just as Cassie caught up, the door flew open and caught her on the shoulder.

"Oomph!" she said.

An arm snagged her. "What the *devil*—"

"Archie!" Emma gasped. "What are you doing here?"

The laird of Kinloch—how on earth had they ever imagined he was the *estate manager*, Cassie marveled—stepped into the pile of slush outside the door and into the full glare of three flashlights. To his credit, he didn't flinch. "I might ask the same of you," he said icily.

"We're on the ghost tour!" Cassie said. "And we were at the old ruined church and saw a ghost in the cemetery—"

"Graveyard," said Emma.

"—so we followed her all the way up here to the Obelisk, where she seems to have . . ." Cassie looked at Kat.

"Disappeared," said Kat. "I don't suppose you've seen the ghostly figure of a woman in white hanging around the walls, have you?"

But Archie didn't answer. His attention was fixed on the paving stones before him. An object lay there, pale and fuzzy. He bent to pick it up and dangled it from his fingers, frowning. Four small limbs stuck from the bottom of a round lump of wool. A tiny tail fluttered from the back.

"That looks like a sheep," said Emma.

"A stuffed sheep," said Cassie.

"Except its head seems to be missing," Kat said.

She reached for the strange animal, but Archie pulled it from her grasp and stuck it into the pocket of his coat. "It's nothing. A child's toy, probably."

"There aren't any children around the castle," said Emma.

Archie looked at her coldly. "I thought I made it clear to Calum that these tours were to cease without further notice. That all of this . . . this . . ."—he made a gesture with his arm—"this *rubbish* is to cease."

"Rubbish?" said Emma, indignant. "This is *history*."

"No, Miss Endicott," said Archie. "This is not history. This is my family. *Our* history. All of this—the ghost tours, the memorabilia, the cynical exploitation of Kinloch's unhappy past—must stop. At once."

"But—well, you'll excuse me, but weren't you behind everything?" asked Cassie, a little timid. "Leasing the estate to Mr. Presley, to recover the family fortunes? I thought I heard—"

"What about the spa? The Edwardian sex toys?" Kat demanded.

Archie turned an angry glance toward her. "You can chuck all that erotica shite in the nearest loch, so far as I'm concerned. Now that this damned American has met his richly deserved end, we're not beholden to anyone."

To her left, Emma drew in a gasp. Cassie realized her jaw was hanging. She snapped her mouth shut, opened it again to say something, and realized that—for once—she couldn't think of a single word.

"Fascinating," Kat murmured.

Archie closed his eyes and drew a deep breath. Almost at once, they flashed back open. "Speak of the devil," he growled, "where *is* Calum?"

COMPARED TO THE chill, dank night air, even the chill, dank air inside the castle's main hall felt warm against Cassie's numb cheeks. Sort of. She slapped her hands against each other to thaw her fingers. Kat yanked off her plaid beanie and shook the mist from the pompom. Nearby, Emma stood and scowled at the staircase, where Archie climbed up the steps like a mountain goat, two at a time.

"That was . . . interesting," she said.

"Hardly," said Kat. "All those stupid stories about mothers howling for their lost babies. Or babies howling for their lost mothers. Whatever it was. Lady Ned the Lady Bountiful. So fake. I almost gagged."

"I don't think there's anything fake about Lady Ned," said Emma. "I think she's one of those women I like to write about. Erased from history."

"Here she goes," said Kat.

Cassie stared past Kat's shoulder. "Look! There he is."

"Who?"

"Calum."

Across the hall, the broad-shouldered Scotsman disappeared around the corner, toward the kitchen stairs, without so much as a glance toward the damp, shivering women in the doorway.

"Looks like he gave up on us and went back home," said Kat.

"You know," Cassie said, "I think I'd better go wash off these coffee cups before I forget."

"Could you bring me back an Irish coffee, while you're at it?" Kat called after her. "Or a Scottish. Or whatever. As long as there's whisky in it! Not picky!"

Cassie waved her hand as she turned the corner and peered down the corridor. She caught a glimpse of movement and called out Calum's name.

There was a resigned grunt. "Aye? What is it, Mrs. Pringle?"

"I was just—I was just wondering if you've had any messages. Here. At the castle. From my husband." She caught up to Calum and stopped awkwardly. The light was dim and the air was chill, and maybe her brain had gone numb because she couldn't think what to say. Her chatter seemed to have deserted her.

"Weeell now," Calum said, in a kind voice, crossing his unwieldy arms. "I reckon ye'll have to ask me nan about that. Me being outdoors with the three of ye this past hour."

"Oh. Right. Of course. I'll—I'll go find her."

"She'll be . . ." Calum's lips tightened. "She'll have gone to bed by now, I expect."

"Oh. Maybe in the morning, then."

"She'll be rising early, nae doubt. As usual. To ready the breakfast. Ye'll find her then."

"The thing is, though . . ." Cassie snapped her fingers. "That's right. I remember. I just—I was just thinking about this little thing Archie said. After you left. He was coming out of the Obelisk and he said something about putting a stop to the ghost tours. About . . . about not being beholden anymore. Now that poor Mr. Presley was dead."

Calum sighed. "Did he, now?"

"Something to that effect. We just thought—well, it was a strange thing to say. Don't you think? Under the circumstances. Not that we were thinking—I mean, of course we don't imagine for a *second* that he would—you know—"

"Now, Mrs. Pringle," said Calum soothingly. "Ye know I'm not the sort of lad to go about discussing other men's pairsonal affairs, like."

"No! No, of course not."

Calum looked past her shoulder, down the corridor, and then back over his own shoulder.

"All the same," he said softly, "I reckon I might as well straighten the record, here and there, so ye dinna go off thinking yer wee mad thoughts about puir Archie. He's a good man, Archie."

"Oh, of course he is! I certainly wasn't—I hope you weren't thinking I was accusing him of anything. Suspecting him of anything."

Calum took her upper arm and pulled her down the corridor, then around the corner to a small alcove below a tiny window. The light didn't reach them here, and Cassie couldn't see Calum's face—just a few shadows. She could feel the enormous heat of his body and smell the peculiar scent of him—whisky and outdoors, she supposed. *A bit like Chip*, she thought again. She crossed her arms over her stomach to muffle the pain. The tartan thermos banged against her hip through the canvas tote bag.

"Archie's a good man," said Calum, in the same low, confidential voice, "but he did a rare foolish thing, signing that lease with that Mr. Presley. A nefarrrrrious dog, that one."

"Is he? I wouldn't know."

Though she couldn't see Calum's expression, Cassie felt his sharp eyes assess her. She tried to keep her face straight. Innocent. Chip always said he could read even the tiniest of little white lies on her face the instant she'd told it. That's how he knew he could trust her.

"Weeeell, as ye might guess, Archie needed the money, what with the castle falling to ruin and the villagers leaving for work on the mainland. So he made his deal with the Devil, he did, and what's more, he never thought to read the fine prrrrint. He's a gentleman, ye ken." Calum tapped his temple sadly, as if being a gentleman were next to being the village idiot.

"And there were . . . terms?" Cassie tried not to sound too eager.

"Aye, there were terms. Namely that Mr. Presley planned to turn Kinloch Castle into—och, what's that fun park ye've got in America, bit like Blackpool except with mice?"

"Do you mean Disneyland?"

"That's the one. Turn Kinloch into Disneyland, except instead of mice ye've got sex toys."

"I beg your pardon?"

Calum threw out an arm. "He had the plans all drawn up. A Naughty Ned theme park, he called it—the Kinloch Experience, that was the name on the brochures—and there was naught puir Archie could do except go along with it. He'd signed this agreement to act as manager of the property, thinking all along that Mr. Presley only wanted to fashion a quiet retreat for daft writers such as—weel, such as yerselves. And Archie's a gentleman, ye ken, and always keeps his sworn word." Calum sighed. "No way out of it."

"Except if Mr. Presley met an unfortunate end, prior to the end of the lease."

"Aye, except that." Calum roused himself. "But Archie's a gentleman, as I've said. He'd never contemplate murrrrder."

"No, of course not! I wouldn't dream of suggesting it."

"See that ye don't." Calum started off out of the alcove, looking both ways, and then glanced over his shoulder back at Cassie, who stood like a statue, mind spinning. "And see that ye don't tell those interfering crones of yers about this, neither. They'd make mischief out of it, nae doubt of that. I've only told ye purely to clear the air, ye ken. And because I . . . well, because I trust ye, Mrs. Pringle."

Cassie gulped. "Of course."

"That's a good lass."

He continued down the corridor, leaving Cassie to stand there, clutching her tote bag.

Into the chill air, she whispered, "Because I have absolutely no idea how I'm going to break this to Emma."

CHAPTER TWENTY

Emma

Emma sat at the dining room table the following morning, despondently stirring her "parritch" as Morag had called it as she'd set it down on the wood surface with a heavy thunk. Emma half-heartedly considered googling the etymology of the word and its connection to what she knew as porridge. But even if she could find the enthusiasm to dive down the rabbit hole of research, she was still without her phone and laptop.

Of course, there were at least two libraries within the castle filled with all sorts of books into which she could disappear for hours, but the library she was most interested in was strictly off-limits. Just the thought of being near the laird's—Archie's—bedroom sent a confusing wave of longing mixed with dejection rippling through her.

The door to the dining room opened and Cassie entered with her trusty quilted bag, followed by Kat, who wore large sunglasses and walked carefully as if the sound of her heels tapping on the stone floors might be too loud.

"Good morning," Cassie said, a little too brightly. Even the smile she sent to Emma seemed inauthentic. Like the kind of smile Emma would use at a book signing when a random stranger would approach her to suggest a collaboration because he (always a man) had a great story to tell but not the time to write it.

"Why are you shouting?" Kat whispered. She sat across from Emma, being careful not to make any sudden, jarring movements.

"Was there a party last night that I missed?" Emma asked.

She could feel Kat's steady gaze from behind the dark glasses. "I wish. Since I can't access my OnlyFans site, I had to find other ways to entertain myself. Let's just say that a bottle of Glenfiddich isn't quite as much fun, but it gets the job done."

"Is that like TikTok?" Cassie asked as she sat down next to Emma.

Emma and Kat shared a look. "Not really," Emma said quickly before Kat had a chance to answer. "Like TikTok, it's geared for those with the mental maturity of a thirteen-year-old boy . . ."

"But with a lot less clothes," Kat finished, her grin quickly turning into a wince as Morag thunked down two more bowls of parritch.

Cassie began rummaging through her quilted bag before pulling out a bottle of Advil and placing it in front of Kat. "You can keep it. I've got more." Turning to Emma, she slid over a foil-wrapped piece of chocolate. "For you."

Emma examined the candy with suspicion before raising her eyes to Cassie and seeing that brittle smile. "If I had a dog, I'd think you were about to tell me that he died. But I'm between dogs right now, so my next guess is that I've been ordered to exchange wardrobes with Kat for a year as punishment for a crime I don't remember committing."

Neither Kat nor Cassie reacted, which made Emma drop the spoon into her bowl. "Did anyone else die that I don't know about?"

"No," Cassie said. "But I have some news that you might find difficult to take."

"Archie actually *is* gay?" Kat's muffled voice came out from under the cloth napkin she was using to steam her face over her bowl.

Emma sat up. "He is *definitely* not gay." Her cheeks flushed. "Trust me. Nobody could fake it that good." Somehow, knowing that didn't make Emma feel any better.

Cassie poured herself a full mug from the ceramic teapot in the shape of a castle that Morag had gently placed on the table in front of her. The old woman had even smiled. Cassie seemed to have that effect on everyone. "No, nothing like that. But, well . . ." She took a deep breath, but her lips remained firmly pressed together.

Kat pulled the napkin off her head. "I feel as if we're about to hear the first three verses of 'My Favorite Things.' Please don't. Because then Emma will have to start singing and the words will be wrong and my head will hurt more. Just tell us already. Please."

"Fine, then. I will. It's about Archie."

Morag entered the dining room with a platter of scones and clotted cream. She plunked it down on the table making Kat wince. "How that lad lives with himself after what his family has done," she muttered to herself as she placed cutlery and plates at each place. "It's a disgrace, rrrreally, what he's done. Getting in bed with the devil, I say." She slammed down a jar of honey in front of Emma, rattling the silverware before turning to leave. "He's a true Kinloch, all right. Ruled by lust and evil . . ." Her words faded away as she headed back to the kitchen.

Emma watched her go, then shared a confused glance with Kat and Cassie. "What was that all about?"

"The old hag's bunion is probably hurting," Kat said. "Or Archie told her she needed to start baking gluten-free. Either way, I wouldn't worry about it—she's harmless. Now go on—spit it out."

Cassie's face folded in on itself as if the words she was about to impart were causing her physical pain. "Archie killed BSP. I have proof."

Emma had started shaking her head before Cassie had finished speaking. "That's not possible. The Archie I know couldn't commit murder. He's too much of a gentleman."

Kat made a strangled sound in her throat. "Please don't make me laugh. Being a gentleman and being a murderer are not mutually exclusive. Actually, they sometimes go hand in hand. Have you never seen a James Bond film?"

Ignoring her, Cassie patted Emma's arm. "I'm so sorry, Emma. I truly am happy that you found someone. He seems like a wonderful man. Except for the murderer part, of course."

Emma stood, her chair legs scraping against the floor, making Kat grip her head with both hands. "No, that's not what I meant. I mean, he couldn't have committed the murder because he was with me that night, remember? In my bed. With me. Not sleeping." She felt her cheeks redden. She was a grown woman and yet her upbringing still made it difficult to talk about sex.

"Doing the rumpy-pumpy, as they say." Kat managed a tight smile. "I think that gives our laird a pretty good alibi."

"Exactly." Emma's head bobbed up and down in adamant agreement as she faced Cassie. "What sort of proof do you think you have? It's obviously wrong, but we should hear it."

"As Mrs. Fusselbottom from my Hedge Witch series would say, the evidence is soundly compelling because it gives our hero—Archie, in this case—a solid motive. You see, Mr. MacDougal—Calum—told me that BSP's death was the best thing that could have happened to the laird. To Kinloch, really, but especially to Archie. Calum said that Archie had admitted to him that Archie didn't read the fine print when he signed the lease agreement giving control of the castle, village, and island to BSP for a period of time in exchange for funds Archie desperately needed for improvements. He believed BSP only wanted to make Kinloch into a sort of writers' colony. Except, well, it was all a lie. He never intended for that to happen. He wanted to turn Kinloch into 'Naughty Ned's Playground.' The Kinloch Experience, he called it. Sort of like Disneyland but with a different kind of ride entirely, if you know what I mean."

Emma frowned. "I'm afraid I don't."

Kat slid off her sunglasses revealing bloodshot eyes. "Correct me if I'm wrong, Cassie, but I think it means turning Kinloch Castle into the Playboy Mansion on steroids. With lots of plaid. I can imagine the marketing now—'See what's under the kilt!' Even I think that's a bit over the top. Or should I say, 'under the skirt'?" She snorted, immediately followed by a wince.

Emma sat down again. "That's . . . horrible. Poor Archie. He cares so much for Kinloch and its heritage. He would have been devastated."

"He was," Cassie said gently. "But the lease agreement is all null and void now that BSP is dead, you see? Of everyone who wanted to see the man permanently out of the picture, Archie had the biggest reason of all."

"Yes, but . . ." Emma's eyes darted from Cassie to Kat and then back again, waiting for one of them to tell her that this was some horrible joke. Except they didn't. "But he has an alibi. I'm his alibi. And I'll even tell the DCI that he was with me when the murder was committed. I agree he has the biggest motive, but he wasn't there!"

Cassie went back to patting Emma on the arm as if Emma were an inconsolable child needing settling. "Honey," she said, "I would agree with you except . . ." She pressed her lips together. "Except that I happen to know a lot about poison. While researching my first—and last—book in my cycling series, *Gone with the Schwinn*, I learned that many poisons don't have to be administered in person. They can be put on something as a conduit to be injected or imbibed inadvertently at a later time. Which means . . ." She stopped speaking as Emma's face began to crumble.

"Which means that Archie could have planned everything—not just the murder, but his alibi," Kat finished, her words matter-of-fact but missing their usual pointed edges.

Kat and Cassie looked at Emma with sympathetic eyes that did nothing to soften the blow to her heart or relax the tightness in her throat. Both were familiar feelings, bringing back the horrible months after she'd discovered what BSP had done to her. She'd thought Archie was different, cut from a different cloth than BSP. Something warm and soft and comforting. Something plaid. But apparently, he wasn't.

"They're all the same, aren't they? Men, I mean," Emma said. The realization had stirred a spark of anger, a spark strong enough to dry up the—thankfully—unshed tears of humiliation and regret. She slapped her hands on the table and jerked back her chair as she stood. "I suppose I don't have a choice." She began marching toward the door.

"What are you going to do?" Cassie asked.

"I'm going to ask Archie. Right to his face." She jerked open the door.

"Wait!" Cassie began digging in her bag again before pulling out a pair of long knitting needles, a line of bright pink yarn trailing from one of them. "You'll need a weapon. To protect yourself."

Emma considered for a brief moment before giving a single, solid shake of her head. "No. I won't need a weapon. The laird is about to find out that hell hath no fury like what I'm about to unleash on him."

She could hear Kat clapping as the door shut behind her, encouraging Emma to sing out loud as she ran up the steps two at a time, "I am puma, hear me crawl, and I am too big to ignore . . ."

The clapping stopped. "Wrong lyrics, Emma!" Kat shouted from the dining room. "Helen Reddy is rolling over in her grave!"

Emma ignored her as she made it to the top of the staircase, breathing heavily as she approached the laird's suite. She stopped in front of the door to catch her breath while keeping hold of her anger and preparing what she was going to say. Instead, her thoughts were hijacked by memories of that night at the ceilidh, of how perfectly in sync she and Archie had been. Each knowing where to touch and step, moving to the same shared internal rhythm. It had been the same when they'd made it into Emma's bed; each move, each sigh as if choreographed by Cupid himself.

She clenched her eyes shut. She was starting to think like a Karyn Black romance novel. Not that there was anything wrong with that, of course. It was just that she needed to remember that she was a woman scorned and the object of her wrath was on the other side of the door. Before she could change her mind, she brought her fist up to the door and pounded on the wood.

Emma leaned closer to hear any sound through the thick door. If the builders of the castle had had any sort of restoration training, or any thoughts toward careful reconstruction, the answer would have been an easy no. Which meant her ear was pressed against the door when it was yanked open, causing her to fall forward into the arms of a surprised Archie.

His hands fell to her waist to steady her, and for a brief moment she was back again at the ceilidh, feeling for the first time in a very long while that she had found something special. *Someone* special. Someone she could trust. Someone who wasn't BSP.

Merely thinking his name made her jerk back. Archie's hands lingered for another moment before he stepped away, his eyes watching her carefully. "And to what do I owe the pleasure?" he asked, his British accent clipping his words and sounding so buttoned up and oh-so-polite. And completely different from the man who'd danced with her both in and out of the sheets.

She felt her cheeks flame at the memory and quickly distracted herself by mentally listing the first line of the Plantagenet family tree. "I need to ask you a question."

"Do you now?" He stepped back and opened the door wider. With an arm and hand flourish worthy of one of the Musketeers— all he needed was a feathered hat—Archie indicated the chair on the other side of his very messy desk. As Emma settled herself into the chair, she noted a laptop alongside piles of modern ledger books covering most of the desk's surface while what appeared to be invoices were sprinkled on top of the books like confetti.

Archie waited for Emma to sit before settling himself into the chair behind the desk. With studied casualness, he said, "And here I was thinking that I should be the one asking the questions. I'm afraid I'm at a bit of a loss because there are so many of them that I haven't had the time to put them in any particular order." He indicated the cluttered desktop. "The unexpected death of Mr. Presley has added to my workload. I've hardly had the time to wonder why you chose to lie to me and everyone else about being the best of friends with the other two women when clearly you're not. It's made me wonder what else you might be lying about."

"Oh, no you don't," Emma said from the edge of her seat. "You do not get to turn the tables on me. I might not have been completely forthcoming . . ."

Archie let out an inelegant scoff.

". . . but it wasn't to deceive *you*. I'll admit that there might have been a bit of . . . misleading, but it wasn't meant to keep anything from you, personally. Because we didn't know you. *I* didn't know you." Emma felt her cheeks flush again, but she pressed on. "By the time I realized that you weren't gay . . ."

He sat up. "Excuse me?"

Emma squirmed. "Kat was convinced that you were. She's an expert on sex, you know, so of course I believed her. But to be honest, I have no idea how I could have been so blind because you are definitely not gay. . . ." She stopped so her cheeks wouldn't burst into flames.

He sat back in his chair, wearing a look of amused confusion.

"Anyway," Emma continued, "by the time I realized you, well, weren't, it was too late to go back and start over. But however inexcusable what I did was, at least *I* didn't kill someone."

Archie's eyebrows raised. "That sounds more like an accusation than a profession of innocence."

"Maybe because it is. I know about Naughty Ned's theme park, and how you didn't know his plans until you'd signed everything and it was too late. He was going to destroy everything you've worked for. Disrespect your heritage. Your family." She leaned forward, her eyes seeking his. "It would make most people consider murder."

He jumped up from his chair, sliding half the clutter off the desk onto the floor with a loud crash. "Of course it would! All the work I've been putting into Kinloch, trying to make something good of this place. To make up for the sins of my forebearers. And then Mr. Presley walks in with his bag of promises that are too good to be true, and I jump at the chance to see my dreams of rebuilding Kinloch turn to ash because I was too naive to read the small print. Instead of creating something of redemption and value, he wanted to turn tragedy into a bloody theme park!"

Emma stood. "So did you? Did you kill him?"

He stared at her with incomprehension. "How can you ask me that—after what we shared?"

Emma felt the familiar nudge of insecurity that refused to disappear regardless of how many times she buried it. "I thought I might have been just a . . . a bit of après ceilidh."

He took a step toward her so that she could smell the familiar scent of his skin. Her bones shivered. "It wasn't just the ceilidh."

She managed to hold his gaze. They were standing so close, close enough to kiss. Archie stepped back, the air between them seeming to crack and sparkle. His voice was very soft when he spoke again. "I suppose it doesn't matter now."

With that, he turned on his heel and let himself out of the door, closing it softly behind him.

Emma blinked at the pile of books and papers on the floor, at the old Edwardian desk and the crystal decanter. She kept blinking so she wouldn't start crying because she wasn't sure she'd be able to stop. And she didn't cry. She never cried. It just wasn't *done* in her family. She wasn't sure how long she stood there, in the middle of the room and blinking, until the door handle turned and Archie reappeared.

She looked at him expectantly.

"Er, um, this is my office. I really need to see to these accounts."

"Oh, right. Yes. Of course. I'll just go now, shall I?" She dropped her gaze then skittered past him and through the doorway before running down the hall to her bedroom. After carefully folding back the duvet, she crawled back into bed and lay face down on the pillow so no one could hear her cry. Except that no matter how loud she sobbed, she couldn't drown out the niggling thought that Archie hadn't said no.

CHAPTER TWENTY-ONE

Kat

N o," said Morag.

The sun was shining brighter than the Scottish sun had any right to shine, even through Kat's giant shades. She had the kind of hangover that called for gentle mists and gloomy dawns. But, no. Today was the day the Inner Hebrides decided to go L.A.

Or maybe it just felt that way after spending the night downing most of a bottle of whisky. That was whisky with a "y," rich with peat and self-loathing.

Last night had been . . . weird. For someone whose books had been hailed by the notoriously cranky *Publishers Weekly* for their rich lyricism, Kat was having trouble mustering the vocabulary to process her feelings. Of course, she knew, the problem wasn't the vocabulary, but the feelings.

You don't like feelings, one of her many therapists had informed her, like this was a surprise.

In other news, water was wet.

So, for that matter, was melted snow, which was seeping through the pseudosuede material of her pantaboots, which had claimed to be waterproof, but, like so many of her nearest and dearest, had clearly lied to her.

Well . . . that wasn't entirely true. Her dad had never lied.

He loved her. Kat knew he did. He just didn't know what to do with her and never had. Her mom hadn't lied, either, not really. Kat remembered the slamming cupboards, the simmering resentment. She'd been the one who had tied her mom to her dad and a life her mom had hated. So, yeah, they'd all been pretty clear.

And BSP . . . he'd never actually told her he wanted—oh cringe—to date her. He'd just implied. Implied he was falling for her. Implied his intentions were, to use the archaic phrase, honorable. Or maybe that was all in Kat's head. She'd spun his straw to gold, and then been disappointed when it wasn't a diadem with which to crown her queen of his heart but plain old straw all along, braided into a switch with which to beat her. Literally.

They weren't the problem. Kat was the one with the problem. Expecting too much. Expecting affection. So just don't expect anything at all. That was the obvious solution. Particularly not from a shoe-legging combo she'd bought for $39.95 from some dodgy seller on Amazon.

But last night—they'd come looking for her. Cassie and Emma. They'd been thinking about her, worrying about her, concerned for her. Cassie had hugged her like she cared.

Cassie would hug a sheep, Kat told herself harshly. The woman's heart was so soft she made the Pillsbury Doughboy look like an Iron Man contender.

But Kat couldn't stop remembering that hug, all the same. And Inspector Macintosh, in the mist of the graveyard. And the baby, wrapped snugly on its ledge, as its mother walked into the sea. They were all mixed together in her head, pushing and shoving, making her feel things she didn't want to feel.

And that was when Kat turned a corner, not really paying attention to where she was going, and heard Morag's distinctive burr growling an emphatic "No."

Kat paused on the flagged path, hidden by one of the jutting wings of the castle. Two women were emerging from an elderly greenhouse. Morag was dressed in her usual Mrs. Danvers chic, a long, severely tailored black dress with a white collar and an equally austere black wool coat. The other woman was a few inches shorter, clad in a pair of form-fitting jeans and a sleek black puffer jacket, her dark blond hair pulled back in a tidy ponytail that highlighted her high cheekbones.

"You're certain sure no one's been in the garden?" Fiona Macintosh demanded. "No one's been messing about with your plants?"

"And wouldn't they be hearing from me if they did? There's nae muir than two keys to this garden, as well ye know. I wear mine tuckit aby my—" A word Kat didn't quite know, but took to mean that someone would have to do some real foraging to retrieve the key from Morag's person. "And t'other would be with yon young laird. He'd sense enough not to let that great glaikit-lookin' sod in the towerrrrr have the keeping o't. So if yer lookin' for some- one wi' the key to the poisons—look no furrrrrrtherrrr than yon Kinloch."

Fiona rubbed her temples as though she had a headache. "There's been nothing plucked?"

Morag gave a champion cackle. "Ye're as daft as ye are days old. Ye think I count every leaf and berry? I'd as soon number the hairs on a sheep as the berries on the bush."

Berries. What was it Cassie had seen on Fiona's computer? Something about a toxicology report. One didn't need to write murder mysteries to know that toxicology meant poison. Poison berries.

And then Morag added slyly, "Ye should ken. I've seen ye among my plants, plucking away."

"That's different—it was just the foxglove for Donnie MacTavish's heart—and you were with me holding the basket!"

Morag hefted an enormous key, made of the same dark material as the gate of the garden, and ornamented in the same style. "Aye, all wi'in yon walls can heal as well as harm—or what would be the purpose? But there's healin' and there's healin', as well ye know."

Whatever Morag was implying struck a nerve. Fiona turned sharply on her heel. "I'd best be doing some of that healing myself. I'll have patients waiting."

"Yer going the wrong way, lass." The words were fraught with meaning.

Fiona sent her a look over her shoulder. "I ken the way to the village. I've messages for Mrs. Pringle in the castle."

"Ye'll find her in my kitchen. Eh—that's a lass as knows her way around a stove." Morag flapped a hand at the bewildered Fiona. "There's nae call to stand their gawkin' like a bampot. Go on with ye—I havna the time to stand here haverin'. I've me own business to attend to. Kinloch business."

"Isn't it always," muttered Fiona, and stamped off toward the kitchen, her chin pulled down into her collar like a turtle.

Like someone with something to hide.

With poison berries to hide?

Kat didn't waste any time. She forced her frozen toes to move, slipping and sliding across the slush-covered flagstones to the poison garden.

As poison gardens went, this one was something of a letdown. If Kat had her own poison garden, she'd encase it in a wrought-iron pavilion of gothic whirls and curlicues, with one of those big Paris Metro signs that said POISON in art nouveau letters, something menacing and beautiful and horrible. If this were her garden, she would lounge between the belladonna and foxglove and write dark poetry like Baudelaire. Possibly in French.

Instead, this was a workaday sort of structure, a sharp pointed roof sloping down toward a basic rectangle, with a single white-painted door set in the middle of one of the short walls. They could at least have painted it black.

"Did you say something about berries?" Kat demanded, skidding to a stop next to Morag.

Kat tried to peer inside, but the old glass was wavy, creating a murky effect. Through it, Kat could just see long tables full of plants, but, not being Cassie, she had no idea what any of them were.

Morag hooked the giant key on the chain around her waist. A chatelaine, Kat realized, just like the one worn by Lady Ned in the portrait in the dining room, clanking with keys and miscellaneous chased silver accoutrements. "This be off-limits to guests."

"I'm not a guest anymore; I'm a suspect." Kat squinted through the blurred glass. "I'll bet it was the lab results, right? She got the lab results and came to ask you about what's missing from the poison garden."

Unless, of course, Fiona knew exactly what was missing from the poison garden. How hard would it be to abstract a few berries while Morag was bending over cutting the foxglove for her?

Morag grabbed Kat by the scruff of her collar and hauled her back. For such a stick thin woman, she was surprisingly strong. It must be all the pummeling dough. "I'll thank ye not to stick yer nose in the private business of other pairrrrrrsons."

The way she rolled her "r" practically constituted an offensive weapon. Kat wasn't that easily deterred.

"It was belladonna, wasn't it? It was belladonna that killed him." Not the spilled mead; not the stag's horn. Poison. One didn't need to be in the same room to administer poison.

"It may well ha' been. Or it may not." Morag moved to block Kat as Kat reached for the gate. "Ye're treading where ye oughtn't."

Kat glared at her. "I'm clearing my name."

"What's in a name? A man's a man for a' that. Some worse than others. And a woman should ha' better sense than to be pokin' around in that which doesna concairrrrrrn her. There's a reckoning a'comin', lass, and ye dinna want to be in the way of it."

Kat thought being accused of murder pretty darn well concerned her. "Who are you protecting? Is it Fiona?" No response. Not so much as a flicker of an eyelash. "A man's been murdered here!"

"There's some as need killin'. And there's some as shouldn't be blamed for taking it in their own hands." Morag looked pointedly at Kat. "However unsteady those hands might be."

Kat resisted the urge to stick her hands behind her back. They weren't that unsteady. The whisky was mostly out of her system. "You're looking at the wrong hands. I didn't do it."

Morag looked at her with something like pity. "Whit's fur ye'll no go by ye. Mercy's day is gane."

With that incomprehensible pronouncement, she turned her back on Kat and stalked toward her kitchen.

"Wait—what does that even mean? Yo, Morag! Wait!" Kat started to follow her, but she was pulled up short by her body going one way while her jumpsuit went another. Her heel was stuck in a crack. Kat desperately shook her foot, trying to loosen it. "Morag! Dammit. Stupid bloody pantaboots."

"Why do you wear these things?" asked a voice behind her, a pleasant tenor voice rich with amusement.

Of course. DCI Macintosh, wearing a macintosh.

Kat turned as far as she was able, which wasn't far, given that her heel appeared to be having a threesome with the stones on either side and wasn't interested in emerging any time soon.

"Well, I have to wear something," Kat said irritably. "I'm not a nudist. Look, are you going to stand there and mock, or are you going to help pry me out?"

The inspector inspected her. He inspected her from her stuck heel up to her neck, where the pressure from the pull on her boot was yanking down the material on her leg, which was pulling taut the leotardlike bodice of the jumpsuit, over which she hadn't bothered to button her coat because she'd been thinking of other things.

Not, clearly, the same things the inspector was thinking about as his eyes took in the whole straining leotard situation.

"Out of the cobbles, you pervert!"

The inspector held up his hands. "I didn't say a word."

"No, but you looked."

"That getup is designed to make me look," he said, but Kat was pretty sure his ears had gone red. He knelt down on the path beside her, getting his clean raincoat all slushy, making a show of checking out her wedged heel. "How deep does this go?"

"'Oh, what is higher nor the tree and what is deeper nor the sea?'" Kat quoted flippantly.

The detective looked up at her, the sun picking out the bronze in his brown hair. Softly, he replied, "'Oh, heaven is higher nor the tree, and love is deeper nor the sea—and so, fair maid, I'll marry with thee, as the dove flies over the mulberry tree.'"

His voice was velvet and honey: there was magic in that old poetry, written by goodness knew who goodness knew when. The words wove over and around them as the sun's rays shone down on them like a net of golden threads, binding them together, thee to thee, as the dove flew over the mulberry tree.

And then a bird cawed—Kat had no idea what kind of bird it was, but it sure as hell wasn't a dove—and the spell was broken, leaving her with a nasty, bitter taste in her mouth. "No doves here, dude. Just a raven. Anyway, it's four inches. The heel."

"Four inches?" The detective inspector seized on the change of subject, which, perversely, offended Kat.

Fine, so she wasn't anyone's idea of a fair maid—maid being code for "virginal and meek and therefore marriageable"—but he didn't have to look so alarmed. Besides, she wasn't the one who had been quoting bits about marrying with thee, even if she'd started the poem, and, oh, whatever.

"I wear four-inch heels because it's hard to loom impressively when you're only five foot four," she explained impatiently.

The inspector looked up, his hand on her ankle. "Do you feel you need to loom?"

It was a scene from a tapestry—or one of the more mawkish Pre-Raphaelite paintings—the hero kneeling at her feet. But Kat knew the pose of submission was just that, a pose. If he wanted to, he could slap her in handcuffs. And not the fun kind.

"I'm a woman," Kat said sharply. "We need every advantage we can get. Speaking of which . . . Have you spoken to your sister?"

"I speak to her all the time." The detective chief inspector sat back on his heels, not meeting Kat's eyes. He dug into his coat pocket and pulled out a Swiss Army knife, flipping out a short but businesslike blade.

Kat eyed the knife askance. She was pretty sure this counted as witness intimidation. "Are you planning to saw me out? Because I have to tell you, if that's the case, I'm not up for amputation."

"I'm loosening the dirt around your heel." The inspector plunged the blade into the crack between the stones. After a moment of venting his feelings on the dirt—and probably blunting his blade—he asked abruptly, "What does my sister have to do with what we were just talking about?"

"Women. Being taken advantage of. Seeking revenge." Kat gave her foot an exploratory wiggle. Whatever he was doing with his blade seemed to be loosening things up nicely. And, no, that wasn't a euphemism. "She was just here. In the poison garden. She appears to be very familiar with it. Chummy with Morag, too."

"We grew up here. Grew up with Morag. Except when we were—not here." A muscle danced in his jaw, just like a Karyn Black hero. "Morag was like a grandmother to us."

Morag, who was like a grandmother. Fiona, who used the poison garden. Archie, who had the only other key. All of them bound by shared history. Shared secrets.

Kat yanked her heel out of the loosened stones, tottering a bit before she caught her balance. She stepped down hard on solid stone. "It was poison, wasn't it? It was poison that killed Jerk Face over there."

The inspector rose slowly, flicking his Swiss Army knife shut and stowing it neatly back in his pocket. "I'm not at liberty to say."

Kat folded her arms across her chest. "Not at liberty. That's good. I'd like to remain at liberty, thank you very much."

The detective chief inspector took out a handkerchief and began wiping the mud off his hands. His eyes were as hard and cold as the stones at Kat's feet. "You Americans have a thing about liberty, haven't you?"

"Wouldn't you? Oh, it's fine for you to stand there in your raincoat and look all judgy, but you're not the one facing life in prison for something you didn't do!" Kat took a deep breath. "Let me rephrase that. For something *someone else did.* I think you know. And I think you don't want to know."

Oh, here was the face of the law all right, closed and cold, except for that muscle in the jaw again that told her she'd gotten him good. "Our only goal is to bring the murderer to justice."

"What's this 'our,' Inspector? You're the law around here." Kat flicked one of his macintosh buttons with one purple-nailed finger. "So what was going on between Mr. Presley and your sister?"

His lips pressed very tightly together.

Kat pressed her hand flat against his chest, a human lie detector test. "Did you talk to her? Or are you just hoping that if you don't say anything and you don't ask anything it will all go away? Maybe you're too close to this case, Inspector Macintosh. Maybe they need to call in someone who won't use his position to shield his family. Maybe . . . we need Scotland Yard."

"You've been watching too much BBC America," said the detective inspector coldly, but Kat could feel the tension underneath.

"What? Are you afraid if a disinterested party came in they might find things you don't want them finding?" He didn't need to say yes; she could tell by the way he was barely breathing. Kat dropped her hand, her stomach all twisted into knots by anger, desire, fear, and the sour remnants of last night's whisky. "You just all club together, don't you? You, Archie, Fiona . . . Morag. It doesn't matter who you sacrifice, so long as it's not one of your own. Just tie me to a rock and call me Andromeda."

"No one is tying you to a rock," the inspector said tightly.

"Oh, yeah?"

"They weren't dating."

Kat rose up on her toes so they were practically nose to nose. "I bet that's what she told you, isn't it? Just one dinner. Didn't mean anything, blah, blah, blah. With Brett Saffron Presley it was never just one dinner. He—" Crap. Kat cut herself off before she could tell him he'd roofied Cassie the first night he met her. "He was toxic. Like the plants over there. The plants your sister knew all about."

"My sister wouldn't have—" The muscles in his throat worked. "My sister knew better than to involve herself with a fly-by-night American writer with more ego than heart. She's not that much of a fool."

Kat felt like someone had just shoved cold snow down the back of her jumpsuit. Behind her, the raven cawed. She struck a pose as best she could, thigh out, knee bent, breasts forward. "Don't spare me, handsome. Tell me how you *really* feel."

He stared at her for a long moment, his eyes burning like ice. "Bloody frustrated." In a clipped, staccato voice, he added, "If you must know, we do have a suspect. And I'm here to bring her in for questioning."

CHAPTER TWENTY-TWO

Cassie

A DRAFT OF hot cinnamon rushed over Cassie's face. She closed her eyes and breathed deep. *One, two, three.*

Now breathe out—*one, two, three.*

(From behind, a pair of arms encircle her waist. A warm kiss on the side of her neck, a gentle nuzzle along her jaw. Chip's rumbling, teasing voice in her ear—*Stress baking again?*)

Cassie opened her eyes, took the dish towel in her hand—oven mitts were apparently Not the Thing in Scottish kitchens of the Edwardian era—and pulled the muffin tray out of the oven.

"Mrs. . . . Pringle?"

Cassie whipped around so quickly, the muffin tray nearly flew from her hand. She grabbed the hot metal with her other hand and yelped in pain.

"Mrs. Pringle! Are ye well?"

Cassie rushed to the sink, dropped the muffin tray on the wooden counter, and pumped cold water on her left hand. "Oh yes! Silly me! It's nothing!"

Fiona Macintosh came up next to her, smelling of damp, fresh air and disinfectant soap. "Just a flesh wound, aye? Let me take a wee look."

"Don't be silly. I only touched it for an instant."

Fiona dragged her hand from under the stream of cold water and examined the palm and fingertips. "Hmmph. Nae sign of blistering, so that's grand. Och, I'm that sorry. It's me own fault, sneaking up on ye like that."

"It's the coffee, that's all." Cassie forced herself to smile. "And I startle easily."

Fiona looked up. She was bundled in a black puffer coat and her cheeks were already flushed from the heat in the kitchen. When she frowned and shook her head, the blond ponytail sloshed back and forth. "Still, ye'll want some cream for this, to be safe. I've a tube of silver sulfadiazine in the surgery."

Cassie pulled back her hand. "That's not necessary. I burn myself all the time in the kitchen at home. Chip says I . . . my husband says I'm too busy thinking about other things. You know, while I bake." She forced out a smile. "Anyway, if you're looking for Morag, she should be here any minute. Preparing lunch. In fact, I'm surprised she's not here already. You know how seriously she takes mealtimes! Noon on the dot!"

Fiona dug into the tote bag that hung from her shoulder. "Matter of fact, I came looking fer yerself, Mrs. Pringle. I ken how worrit ye've been, without seeing yer messages, so I printed off everything that's come into yer account since yesterday."

"Oh my goodness!" Cassie took the papers, held together with a metal clip. "That's so kind of you!"

"Och, 'tis naught. I had a queer feeling ye hadn't got all ye needed when ye stopped by for that wee visit yesterday."

Cassie glanced up. Fiona's blue eyes locked with hers, the approximate color and temperature of a deep Scottish loch. In winter.

Exactly how Cassie's mother would look at her, when she'd caught Cassie lost in some tattered old Dorothy Sayers novel when she was supposed to be cleaning her room.

"I . . . well, I . . . well, your next patient was so eager for his examination—you know, the . . . er . . . the—"

"Hemorrhoids?"

"Yes. My father used to get them so I know what a pain in the . . . er . . . well, you know. What I mean is . . ."

Fiona folded her arms. Her eyes hardened into ice. "Aye, Mrs. Pringle?"

Cassie exhaled slowly and looked back down at the papers in her hand. At the top of the first page, her gaze caught on the subject header *Mispronounciation in the Cat who lost his Mittens (Turkish)*.

"I guess you could say I've been losing my head. My kids keep getting sick—I mean, I think we've gone through just about every virus in the book this autumn—and my husband and I hit a rough patch and now this awful murder." Cassie looked back up. "One worry after another, you know?"

The muscles of Fiona's face seemed to loosen, just a bit. "Aye, I ken what ye mean."

"You see, I made a terrible mistake a few years ago. An awful mistake with an awful man. And ever since, things haven't been the same. All through Covid and the lockdowns and everything. This terrible shadow over my head. I feel like my marriage is going to break up any second. I don't know what my husband is thinking or feeling anymore, and I know it's just making things worse, overthinking everything; I mean, whenever there's radio silence, like now, I start to—oh, what's the word, I saw it on Twitter a few months ago and I was, like, that's it, that's exactly what I do— catastrophize! That's it. I catastrophize! Which is kind of funny when you think about it—*cat*-astrophize, get it?"

Fiona raised her eyebrows helplessly.

"Cats. My mystery series. Moggies, Mocha, and Murder? *Cat*-astrophize? Anyway, that's what I do. I rush straight to the worst-case scenario, every time. Dash runs a little fever and right away I'm thinking meningitis, right? And then I start to worry that Chip won't recognize the signs of meningitis—you know, the handprint test and everything—and I want to remind him but I don't want to be *that* mom, right? So I worry and fret and drink coffee—"

"Aye, and how much coffee *have* ye drunk this morning, Mrs. Pringle?"

"A cup or two," Cassie said modestly. "And I bake. Cookies, pies, cakes, scones. And muffins, of course. Muffins are my specialty. This morning I went through Morag's larder for ideas and found some lovely crystallized ginger. So I shredded some carrot and added cloves and cinnamon and just a pinch of nutmeg and voilà! Ginger and carrot muffins. I haven't tasted them yet, but they sure smell delicious, don't they?"

Fiona cast a bemused gaze to the kitchen table, which was covered with muffins cooling on racks, crusted with coarse sugar and fragrant with ginger and spices. "I see," she murmured.

Cassie cleared her throat. "Care for a muffin?"

"Mrs. Pringle," said Fiona, "ye'll be aware that the island's detective chief inspector—well, the only detective inspector—happens to be me own brother, Euan."

"Oh, is that his name?" Cassie murmured. The burn on her finger was starting to hurt again. She stuck it in her mouth.

"So perhaps ye'll have some special insight into why he saw fit to interrogate me last night about me own love life. Such as it is. In particular, a dinner I happened to share with the unfortunate deceased on the evening before his . . . well, his decease."

"I . . . I guess it's possible I might have accidentally spotted an email on your computer—you know how it is, you can't *not* read something right in front of you—and I might have mentioned it to Emma and Kat. In passing. A little innocent gossip."

"Innocent, is it?"

Cassie balled up her apron between her hands and smoothed it out again. "Look, I don't judge you for it. Me of all people! I know how charming he can be. Believe me. I wish I didn't, but I do, and I don't blame you for—well, for anything you might have done to—because of anything he might have done—"

"Och, Mrs. Pringle. Dinna fash yerself. There was naught betwixt that bowfin gowk and me but a wee bite of supper and a dram o'whisky, and that I drank afterward." Cassie started to speak and Fiona held up her hand. "Mind ye, I wouldna ha' been opposed to a bit of male company, the island being sae lonely and me being blood to most of the lads here, if ye take my meaning."

"Oh. I didn't think of that. How awful!"

"Och, it's nae sa gloomy as that. But when a fresh profile pops up on Snoggr . . . weeel." Fiona shrugged. "Ye see how it is."

Cassie scurried to the cabinet and pulled out a mug, which she filled with the dregs of the coffee remaining in the ancient pot Morag had dug out of the pantry. She handed it to Fiona and selected a muffin from one of the racks. "Here, sweetie. Have a muffin."

"I really shouldna . . ."

"Yes, you should. They're delicious! Now sit down a moment." She shoved Fiona down on one of the chairs next to the kitchen table and plopped atop a neighboring chair. "What do you think?"

Fiona nibbled the sugary edge of one of the muffins. Her eyes widened and melted. "Och, that's pure barry, it is!"

"You see? You need to treat yourself sometimes. All you do is work, work, work. The pub, the surgery, the . . . er, the morgue."

"It's none sae bad, like I said. Only the lack of eligible male company."

"But that's ridiculous. Look at you. You don't *have* to live here, do you? You could be practicing medicine anywhere. Why stay on Kinloch?"

Fiona swallowed back a mouthful of muffin and sipped her

coffee. "Duty, I reckon. Euan and me stayed on to look after me da, since Ma bolted on him."

"Your mother left you?"

"She was American, ye ken. She stayed sae long as she could, until she couldna bear it nae longer. We were about thirteen or fourteen then, Euan and me."

"But why did she leave? Didn't she love your father?"

Fiona tore off a chunk of muffin and popped it in her mouth. "She loved him like mad, she did. Else she wouldna ha' stayed sae long as she did. But like most Americans, she found the reality of Scotland wasna quite what she'd pictured. She had a grand imagination. She was a writer, like yerselves."

"A writer! Would I know her?"

Fiona eyed her over the rim of the coffee mug and set it down carefully on the edge of the kitchen table. "Like as not," she said. "Ye've heard of Karyn Black?"

"Karyn *Black*?" Cassie clasped her hands together and winced. "Oh. My. *Gosh!*"

"Ye've read her books, I take it?"

"*Read* them? I *loved* them! *A Laird in Winter* is my favorite book of all time! I must have read it about twenty times at least. I used to pass it under the lab table to my best friend with the pages open to one of the hot scenes. The virginity scene was like, my *goodness*! It almost ruined my first time for me. I was expecting fireworks and rainbows and . . . well, anyway. I have the very first edition. You know, the one with the famous typo on page 225?"

Fiona rolled her eyes. "Where the printers changed the 'f' to 't' in *shifted*, on accident?"

"That's it! I still giggle a little when I say that sentence to myself."

"It's the wee pleasures."

Cassie sat back in her chair and stared rapturously at Fiona. "Oh my word! You're Karyn Black's *daughter*? Just wait until I tell Emma! And Kat!"

Fiona waved her hand dismissively. "It's none sae grand as ye think. Like Kinloch itself. The reality's hard to measure up to the imagination. But she was a fair good mother. She stuck with us until we were teenagers, at least. Never a dull moment, either."

"Did Presley know? Is that why he sought you out on Snoggr?"

"Och, no. He was after something else." Fiona tossed the last piece of muffin in her mouth and winked at Cassie. "Medical advice."

"Medical advice?" Cassie frowned. "What kind of medical advice? Was he sick?"

"Not as such. Ye might say it was a certain condition as troubled him." Fiona held up her finger, straight out, and let it slowly sink downward.

Cassie clapped her hand over her mouth. "No!"

"Aye. He was after looking for home remedies." Fiona rolled her eyes again, as if Karyn Black and BSP belonged in the same madhouse. "Something more natural than the wee blue pills."

"And did you give him any suggestions?"

"Och, there's any amount of remedies meant to recall a lad's tadger to its duty. Whether they work or nae, that's the question. But he was after trying them all."

"You're saying he was dosing himself with home remedies for . . . er, for erectile dysfunction?" Cassie leaned forward. "Could one of them have been belladonna, perhaps?"

Fiona startled. "And what makes ye say that? What do ye know about belladonna?"

"Oh, I know about all kinds of poisons! I'm a mystery writer, remember? I pretty much know everything about how to poison people. My Little Bake Shop series covers just about every lethal poison you can think of. The research is fascinating."

Fiona turned her head to the racks of muffins and swallowed hard. "Nae doubt it is."

"Don't worry!" Cassie laughed. "I don't test them out in real life or anything. At least, not for human consumption."

Fiona looked back to Cassie. She touched her lips with her forefinger and frowned. "But how did ye know . . ."

"How did I know Presley was poisoned? The symptoms, for a start. Foaming at the mouth, vomiting, hallucination—"

"Hallucinations?"

"That's what Kat . . ." Cassie stopped. Running off at the mouth again. When would she ever learn? She smiled at the furrow that had popped into place between Fiona's eyebrows. "That's what Kat told me, anyway. She probably heard it from DCI Macintosh—your brother, I mean. Thick as thieves, those two! And Kat has a way of—"

"Hallucinations? I've heard naught about those."

"Did I say hallucinations? Must have popped out."

Fiona gathered herself up. "In any case, Mrs. Pringle, there's nae proof 'twas belladonna that killed him. Not until the final toxicology report comes in. And besides, 'tisn't the season for the berries, and there's nae sign of the plants being harvested."

"You checked?"

"I might have looked them over, in passing."

Cassie stood up. Her heart was beating wildly, and it wasn't just the coffee. She felt as if some magic surprise awaited her, just around a corner. "But the garden's not the only source of belladonna, you know."

"It's not?"

Cassie held out her hand. "Follow me."

FIONA STOOD IN the middle of the room and turned around slowly, mouth hung open in amazement, taking in the shelves crammed with glass bottles and jars.

"I didna . . . I never . . ."

"There's no reason you'd know about it. We found it by accident, really. Well, almost." Cassie smiled at Fiona's astonishment. She knew that feeling—like when all the pieces of a mystery came together, and you sat down with your laptop and stayed up all night finishing the book, words pouring from your fingers, the rest of the world dark and still around you. Everything in perfect balance. Everything just right.

Fiona nodded, still wearing that expression of numb wonder. "I never imagined."

"Isn't it incredible? We think it might have been Lady Ned's secret apothecary, where she kept the medicines she used to treat all those poor girls. Or maybe it even goes back further than that."

Fiona's ponytail whipped as she turned back to Cassie. "Who else knows about this?"

"I wouldn't know, would I? But the dust is so thick, I think it's a good bet that nobody's known about it for years. Unless Presley had a good snoop?"

Fiona stepped closer to the wall and squinted her eyes across a row of dusty bottles, each labeled in careful, faded ink from another age. "Ye say there's belladonna here?"

"Yes. We saw the bottle. Let me see . . . over here somewhere . . ."

Cassie didn't bring a flashlight, and the light from the staircase was so faint, it was hard to read the labels. The smell of dust and medicine hung in the air. She leaned closer and dragged her finger along the shelf. "Oh! Here's the hellebore. So it must be this row . . . right at the end . . ."

Cassie froze, one finger on the wooden edge of the cabinet.

"What's the matter?" Fiona came up to her shoulder and peered at the shelf. "Did ye find summat else?"

Cassie turned to her. For a moment, she couldn't speak. Then the words came out in a whisper: "It's gone."

CHAPTER TWENTY-THREE

Emma

IT WAS GONE. Any doubt about the vial Emma held in her shaking hand was gone. She leaned closer to examine the faded black letters of the word on the yellowed label, each spidery leg more transparent than the previous one. The opacity just enough for her to compare the handwriting on the vial to that in the ledger she hadn't yet returned to the laird's library. Archie's library.

She carefully placed the vial into the pencil holder on the small desk in her room. The piece of furniture was another antique, but much plainer and less expensive than the Edwardian masterpiece in Archie's suite, yet appropriate for a writer's room at a writers' retreat. BSP had done his best to mislead Archie into thinking his plans for Kinloch were strictly honorable by outfitting the rooms with desks and pencil holders and even outlets near the desks for a computer just like one would expect from a legitimate writers' retreat. Emma gritted her teeth. BSP's duplicity had been outrageous and, yes, even worthy of the worst sort of revenge. Yet try as she might, she still couldn't imagine Archie killing anyone despite the niggling fact that he had yet to deny it.

She bent over the opened ledger book on the desk's polished surface. The ledger, along with the photocopies, had sat untouched inside the Kinloch Historical Society's tote bag since she'd dumped it on top of the desk. The events of the last few days had, for the first time in her remembered life, stolen any interest in digging into the past.

That was until she'd spotted Kat and Morag in the poison garden. Emma had gone out for a walk to ostensibly clear her head, although she wouldn't have been opposed to running into Archie again. Maybe being outside the castle walls would give them a chance to start over. To clear the air. To deny allegations of murder. She'd headed toward the bee houses where she'd run into him before, hoping to at least spot Loren, recalling that where the sheepdog was, Archie couldn't be too far away.

But all she'd spotted was a cluster of grazing sheep huddled like lumpy polka dots in their winter woolly coats in a snow-dusted paddock. Even Calum and Beatrice were nowhere to be seen as she'd circled the castle, an unnamed tune in her head keeping time with her footsteps. She was doing one last pass of the gardens on her way back to the castle when she'd overheard Kat speaking to Morag. *It was belladonna, wasn't it? It was belladonna that killed him.*

Emma stopped short, keeping herself out of sight behind the large hedge alongside the gate that enclosed the garden. She'd only had a fleeting glance of the two women, but she'd recognized Kat's voice. It had been the mention of belladonna that had sent her brain whirring and made her retrace her steps back to the castle and immediately up to Lady Ned's suite and the hidden room behind the bookshelves.

As she'd plucked the belladonna vial from the shelf and quietly closed the door behind her, she wanted to smack herself in the head. When she'd first seen the ledgers she'd *known* the handwriting looked familiar. But then there'd been so many distractions—first the ceilidh, then the after-ceilidh (she felt herself blushing just at the thought), and then the murder and the confiscation of her phone and laptop and she'd just . . . forgotten. Like she was a stupid teenager with her first crush and not the award-winning historian who was known for hunting down every last factoid about the most obscure historical characters.

Yet here she'd been sitting on the discovery of a century while her thoughts were instead focused on a man. Not just any man, of course, but still a man. And if her experience with BSP had taught her anything, it was that even the vaguest bit of unearthed fact would always be a lot more satisfying—and safer—than any relationship with a man.

But now here she was, in her element, her hands literally on the primary source of Lady Ned's household accounts with the woman's neat and elegant handwriting splayed out in front of her line by line. Emma wished she had the tartan-handled magnifying glass she'd spotted in Cassie's bag, but even to her naked eye it was clear that the handwriting on the poison vial was the exact match to that in the ledger.

She sat back in her chair, her fingers tapping on the edge of the desk. It helped her to think, especially during times like this when she'd just uncovered something big but hadn't quite yet determined how it fit with all the other pieces.

Emma leaned over the ledger again, flipped a page, and began scanning what appeared to be a list of grocery items, or perhaps a budget since a total monetary amount had been double underlined at the bottom of the page in the last column. Each row listed an array of supplies: *coffee; tea; lavender powder; paregoric; leeches; cigars.* Sitting back again, she pictured the noble and gracious Lady Ned as she appeared in the portrait in the dining hall, her squared shoulders and steady gaze. All that was missing was her halo and wings. The woman had diligently supplied her castle and its inhabitants and guests with all their needs. She saved babies from ledges and bought cigars for her debased husband and his cronies while managing the daily running of an entire castle. She was Superwoman before Superwoman was a thing.

She continued tapping her fingers on the desk, the chiming of the large grandfather clock in the downstairs hall marking the noon hour barely registering as Emma continued to think. She grabbed the Kinloch Castle history book she'd purchased from the Historical Society gift shop that she'd previously only glanced at while chatting with Bruce and began flipping through the pages until she found what she was looking for.

It was a two-page spread dedicated to Lady Ned's improvements to the castle and village, including, but not limited to, the installation of a midwife and the building of an apothecary. The page included photographs of the midwife's cottage from the ghost tour and the building she recognized as now being used as Fiona's surgery, both tributes to the grand and visionary lady. A fitting ancestor of the current laird whose hopes and dreams for a better Kinloch ran in tandem with hers. Hopes and dreams that were very nearly ended but for the timely death of the current leaseholder.

Emma swallowed, allowing her index finger to tap against the page as she continued to scan the text. But it was the pictures of the illustrious lady herself, both photographs of paintings—one being the portrait currently hanging in the dining room—that Emma focused on, while waiting for the proverbial click that would happen when she put two pieces together. It was almost like sixth sense to her now, this researcher's phenomenon. The certainty that there was something else, some connection, and that if she kept looking, she'd find it.

Her gaze took in the formal portrait, now hanging in the Scottish National Portrait Gallery in Edinburgh, before moving to the photograph of the portrait in the dining room, the noblewoman in a much more casual pose than the first, wearing a high-necked white lace pin-tucked blouse with a dark, narrow fitted skirt. Her hair was done in a simple style, and she clutched a bouquet of flowers in one hand.

Emma adjusted the well-placed desk lamp to see better, studying the piercing gaze of the intelligent eyes, the elegant lines of the woman's arms, the pale ivory of her fingers as they held the flowers. She shifted her attention to the tiny waist where the blouse had been tucked into the skirt, and to the glint of gold almost hidden behind her arm. The gold of a belt. A chatelaine's belt.

Emma squinted, trying to see what household tools might be dangling from the belt, wishing again for Cassie's magnifying glass. She held the book up to her face, tilting it so that the light—as dim as it was—brightened the page. She could now clearly see what tools Lady Ned carried with her. She spotted a pair of silver scissors, a thimble, a watch, a filigree vinaigrette, and a key ring from which dangled several keys including one that was noticeably larger than the others.

Emma stood so quickly that her chair rocked behind her, threatening to topple. For the second time that morning she wanted to smack herself in the head for being so completely obtuse. If there were a governing body for historical bio-fic authors, she was quite sure her credentials would be rescinded immediately. She had made the novice mistake of falling into the classic trap of stereotyping a historical woman in the Madonna/whore tradition, which had completely blindsided her to the fact that it very well could be much more complicated. And was. She was sure of it. She would bet all the plaid in the world on it.

Emma hurriedly gathered up the open ledger then ran out into the upper hallway. She'd made it to the stairs before running back to retrieve the vial of belladonna. She glanced at the grandfather clock as she ran past it, noticing the time as fifteen past noon. In her haste to open the dining room door without dropping the vial or book, she barely registered the lack of an enticing aroma of hot food, which usually announced mealtime, something for which Morag was sure to scold her.

She raced to the far end of the room where Lady Ned surveyed her domain from her portrait on the wall. Emma could now see the trace of a knowing smile lifting her lips. Just as she could see the unmistakable glint of a ring of metal keys on her chatelaine's belt. "That's it!"

A deep throat clearing behind made her whip around. Cassie, Kat, Fiona, DCI Macintosh, and Archie were all seated at the table adjacent to the sideboard with its noticeably empty chafing dishes and no Morag bustling about plunking down dishes and muttering. All eyes settled on Emma as she clutched the ledger against her chest and the belladonna vial in her raised hand.

Kat rose from her chair in a fluid feline motion and snatched the vial from Emma's hand. "Is there something you want to tell us, Emma?"

Emma blinked at her, not understanding why Kat was looking at her with narrowed eyes. Or why everyone else was looking at her the same way. She dropped her gaze to the vial in Kat's hand and then back to the group at the table, then blinked again as comprehension dawned on her. "Oh, wait. No. It's not what it looks like!" She took a gulp of air to steady her breath. "I *told* you it had to do with the past! The past *always* matters. Sooner or later the past will find you."

"You stole that from Beatriz Williams's website," Kat said dismissively.

The inspector slowly pulled back his chair and stood before approaching Kat. "May I have that, please? I believe that's evidence."

"Wait—I'm not done." Holding out the leather-bound book, Emma said, "This is one of Lady Ned's ledgers, filled with her handwriting. When I first saw it, I *knew* that I'd seen the handwriting somewhere, but it wasn't until this morning that I figured out where!" She pointed at the vial. "It's the same handwriting that's on all the vials in the secret room in the lady's tower. Meaning that Lady Ned made all the labels and knew what was in them. She was the lady of the castle and had all the keys, including to the poison garden."

Her eyes settled on Archie's just as comprehension settled in. "Lady Ned killed her husband by poisoning him with belladonna! Which is most likely the same way whoever killed BSP did it. Someone who had access to the garden."

Archie's eyes had grown cold. What had she expected? She was accusing his ancestor of murder. And just as likely someone close to him—or Archie himself—of killing BSP.

Emma cleared her throat and looked away but continued to feel the heat of his stare. With slightly less enthusiasm, she continued, "Like I said, there's always a connection with the past."

The odd expression on the inspector's face made her take a step back. "That's a very interesting theory, Miss Endicott. One might even accept it as the truth. Except for one small fact that tosses all other theories out of the window."

"And what small fact would that be?" Kat asked, sauntering over to stand next to Emma in a surprising show of solidarity.

"The small fact that Mr. Presley had an heir who has much to gain with his death. A widow, in fact, who is alive and standing in this very room."

The room began to spin as Emma gulped for air. It was as if she'd just been thrown out of a plane from a very high altitude. Almost like being smothered and strangled simultaneously, the thought of both more welcoming than the glares coming from the room's other occupants.

The DCI continued, "Miss Endicott forgot to mention that she was once married to Mr. Presley."

She felt Kat stiffen beside her as a strangled sound came from where Cassie was sitting, but Emma couldn't focus her eyes to be sure.

"And that there was a will prepared in the early days of their marriage where they gave all their earthly possessions to each other."

"But we . . . we were divorced," Emma choked out.

"Yes. I know," said the DCI. "And the will was apparently forgotten but not null and void simply because of divorce as I suspect you already know. Which means you are still his heir. As well as the one person in this room with the biggest motive to see him dead."

Archie's hard stare seemed to be boring a hole in the side of her head, but she couldn't look at him. "But I . . . I didn't know. And even if I did . . ."

She felt another presence beside her along with arms wrapping around her waist. Cassie and Kat. Joined together with a mutual hatred for a single man. And in plaid.

"She didn't do it," Cassie announced. "She doesn't know poisons like I do. As well as others in this room know." Her gaze glanced on Archie before returning to the inspector.

"That's right," Kat said. "Emma may be many things, but she's not a murderer. There is no way that she would have had enough time to analyze every angle of the ABCs of poisoning someone to have committed the murder."

"Thanks. I think," Emma said dryly.

The DCI moved closer. "You three need to stop playing Miss Marple."

Cassie shuddered with indignation. "I *am* a mystery novelist."

The inspector closed his eyes and gave a brief shake of his head. "That's not a professional qualification. A man's been murdered. He may have been a slimy toad, but he still deserves justice. And I can't bring the murderer to justice with you lot messing about and hiding evidence!"

"I wasn't hiding the evidence," Emma protested. "I was using it to prove a point."

Kat scoffed. "Well, Mr. Chief Inspector, pardon me from

having to point this out, but *you're* the one consorting with all the suspects."

The DCI stepped in front of Kat, his eyes blazing as he pointed a finger in her face. "You meddling Americans. This is a real murder and you're obstructing justice. Believe you me, I'm a hair away from drawing up warrants for your arrests for obstruction of a police investigation." He pulled out three phones from his pocket, each wrapped in a plastic evidence bag. Looking at Emma, he said, "Which one is yours?"

She pointed to the one with the cracked screen, an old iPhone that was one generation away from a flip phone. The DCI repocketed it. To Cassie and Kat, he said, "Take your mobiles. You've already done enough damage to the investigation. I can't imagine you could make it worse." To Emma, he said, "I'm going to keep yours for a bit longer. I'd like you to come to the station for further questioning."

Archie stood, his chair scraping against the floor as he made his way to Emma's side. "Euan—is that absolutely necessary?"

A warmth flooded Emma's chest. Archie had stood up for her. Despite whatever feelings he had. He'd stood up for her.

Fiona approached and stood next to her brother. "Euan, really. If yer thinking it was the belladonna, it's not likely the century-old specimen Emma found could do much of anything."

He looked from Fiona to Archie and let out an aggrieved sigh. "I still need to do my job, Fee." Directing his attention toward Emma, he said, "I've other business to attend right now, but ask Calum to bring you to the station at three o'clock. Unless you all stop lying to me, I'll have no choice but to arrest the obvious suspect."

The DCI exited the room, allowing the door to slam shut behind him. The four women and Archie exchanged glances in the ensuing awkward silence.

Cassie cleared her throat. "Would anyone like some freshly baked cookies?"

CHAPTER TWENTY-FOUR

Kat

WAIT."

Kat hurried after the detective chief inspector as he stormed out of the dining room, clumping after him through the echoing hall with its disapproving portraits and trophies of long slaughtered animals. One of her stilettos was giving a little too much whenever she stepped on it, making her gait uneven.

"Hey! Are you going to stop for a minute or are you going to make me lurch after you like Igor?"

He didn't stop. He gave her a look over his shoulder and disappeared behind a screen. Kat gave up and ran after him. Her heel suddenly snagged on the rich, red carpet, sending her sprawling in front of him.

Kat glared up at the inspector. "You tripped me."

"You compromised my investigation."

They stared at each other, locked in . . . something. Kat had written plenty of these scenes, but now that she was in one, she had no idea what was going on, other than that the room felt very close and very warm and she damned well wasn't going to be the first to look away.

The inspector held out a hand, too much of a gentleman to leave her lying on the floor like some sort of virgin sacrifice.

Kat put her palm in his. That was all. Just a hand. But that skin to skin, palm to palm—Kat yanked her hand away, feeling like an idiot. Or like a Jane Austen character going all fluttery because, oooh, he touched her with his ungloved hand.

"I can manage," Kat said, and painfully crawled from her knees to her feet, pressing one hand against the wall for balance.

They were in an anteroom rich with wood paneling, tucked away under the grand staircase. It had probably been designed for minions and menials to take up their trays on their way to the Great Hall. At some point, it had been converted to a fancy phone booth, with a red leather bench inset into the wall next to a shelf on which an old-fashioned rotary phone perched.

"I take it you wanted to see me," the inspector said, and managed to make his voice sound credibly dry, but under it Kat could hear the crackle of frustration, the remnants of that anger that had driven him from the dining room.

Kat pointed to the red leather bench. "Sit. I have something to tell you. If you can spare the time before you arrest Emma. *Who didn't do it.*"

The inspector folded his arms across his chest. He did not sit. "Give me one good reason I should listen to anything you want to tell me."

"Because it's your job?" Kat stamped the foot with the broken heel, which really wasn't a good idea, since she was off-balance enough as it was. "Damn it, do you have to make this hard? I'm here to confess."

The look he gave her was so stony it gave a bad name to granite. "If you're planning to fake a confession to save your friend, don't."

"Do I look like the sort who would sacrifice myself for anyone? Anyway, Emma's not my friend. But you know that already. You know the whole *we're besties* story is a lie. But it's not the whole lie. You want the whole lie? I'm here to tell it to you."

"The lie, the whole lie, and nothing but the lie?" His mouth twisted on one side. "I'd rather have the truth."

"The lie *is* the truth. I mean—never mind." This was getting far too metaphysical. Kat stared at him, willing him to listen. Because he was right, dammit. He was right and they'd screwed up and now she had to fix it. "You know they say the best lie is one that's based on the truth. So that's what we did. We based our lie on the truth."

The inspector leaned one shoulder against the wood-paneled wall. "All right. I'm listening."

It wasn't exactly a ringing endorsement, but Kat bludgeoned on ahead anyway. "The three of us did meet at Bouchercon. Just like we said. Brett—"

Kat's voice broke. She hadn't said his name, his actual name, in so long; she'd avoided it as if he were Voldemort.

The inspector raised a brow. "Brett?"

Kat sat down hard on the red bench. Her calf muscles hurt from balancing on one leg. All of her hurt. She'd been limping along for so long. "*Brett* was delivering the keynote address. He'd written some sort of deconstructed thriller. You know, one of the books that's meant to be so esoteric it's amazing but is really just one big cliché of stuff everyone's done before but you can get away with it when you're a male author—sorry. I'm getting off track."

Without fuss, the inspector seated himself on the red bench beside her. "You're all right. Go on."

Kat knew he just wanted the truth out of her, but the weight of him on the bench next to her, the warmth of him, the smell of his shaving soap, made her feel inexplicably comforted. And like she just wanted to curl up in a little ball against his chest and hide her face there.

Which was beyond silly. This was a man who was looking for

reasons to arrest her. Or one of her friends. And when had she curled up on anyone?

"You were saying?" he prompted.

"Right. Bouchercon." Kat forced herself to focus. "Everyone was sitting there, just lapping it all up. All the *I'm so brilliant and marvel at my process*, and if you wear douchey glasses you, too, can earn zillions a book and spend months crafting each precious sentence instead of trying to spit out a book a year and hope you can balance your writing time with your promo time. Anyway. Whatever. His audience was all into it. And I just couldn't take it anymore."

For a moment she was back there, in that bland ballroom that might have been any ballroom in any hotel in any city, with its beige walls and crystal chandeliers and carefully neutral carpet.

"I went out to the bar. It was one of those events where they make you pay for your own drinks—you get one measly little ticket and then you're on your own—and the bar is out in the hallway outside the ballroom so the booze hounds don't interrupt the pursuit of genius. I'd thought I'd be the only one—but I wasn't. Cassie was there in front of me, fumbling around for her ticket in her bag—she still had her ticket but she couldn't find it—and Emma stopped to help her look for it."

So weird looking back, thinking how little she'd known either of them. Cassie had just been some frizzy-haired cozy mystery author and Emma was a blond ice queen who reminded Kat of her half sisters wearing something hopelessly simple that made the rest of them look tacky and overblown. Kat had almost turned back when she'd seen them there, but it was brave the bar or go back to the ballroom, so she'd sauntered forward, shouldering past them, and ordered a bourbon.

"I can't remember entirely how it started—it was not my first drink—but one of us said something like, missing out on hearing the great man speak? And that was how it all started." Cassie had gotten whipped cream from her Irish coffee up her nose and had had to blow her nose on one of the bar napkins. Emma had done her best marble statue impression. And Kat had knocked back her drink and immediately ordered another, just to drown out that voice from the other room, and the sound of clapping, so much clapping. It made her feel so angry and so helpless. "There we were, the four of us, the only ones not worshipping at the altar of the great man. Because we knew what he was."

The inspector's spine straightened. "The four of you?"

Kat rubbed her temples with the heels of her hands. Her eye makeup was probably smudged to hell and back but she didn't really care anymore. "Oh, yeah, didn't I mention? Rachelle, our editor. She was there, too, knocking back the espresso martinis. I mean, she's pretty well caffeinated generally, but this was a whole new level, even for her. She was both sloshed and buzzed. Otherwise I don't think she would have said anything. Not to us. Not to anyone."

"Said what?"

"What he'd done to her." It was hard to remember now. Kat had been so drunk and so angry and so . . . scared. Really scared. And then suddenly there were Rachelle and Cassie and Emma, and Kat wasn't alone anymore. "I think she was the one who made that not listening to the great man comment. She was there, next to the bar. I think she'd been there with Cassie—she's been Cassie's editor for forever."

Kat could hear the red leather creak as the inspector shifted on the bench next to her. "What did he do to her—to your editor?"

"What he always did." Kat tucked her hands under her armpits, hunching her shoulders. "When she was a baby editor—like a really, really, really junior editor—they sent her over to his apartment with his copyedits. It's usually all on the computer, but Brett made a big fuss of liking things old-school, and the feel of a pencil in his hands, marking the virgin page, blah blah blah."

She remembered him at Yaddo, in those glasses and his tweed jacket, such a cliché it was almost trendy again, and that aw-shucks manner he had affected with her—in the beginning—talking about the purity of one's art, the meaning one got from working on paper instead of the debased glowing screen. And like an idiot she'd nodded and agreed, impressed by his dedication to his craft.

"So instead of sending him a computer file, he got the traditional sheaf of paper marked up with green pencil and sticky notes. And since he was such a big deal, rather than FedExing it, Rachelle went to deliver it personally. This would have been—oh, ten years ago? Something like that."

It wasn't her story, it was Rachelle's story, but Kat could feel her own anxiety building; she was dragging it out, trying to avoid getting to the point. There was a very, very bad watercolor on the wall, a view from the very top of the Obelisk, looking down at the castle, the gardens, and the tiny village beyond, all of Kinloch laid out in wobbly panorama, bordered by the sea. Kat stared blankly at the misshapen towers, but all she could see was the elevator doors opening onto a marble lobby, one of those private landings, Rachelle had said, in a very expensive building, the kind where you need a key card to go up.

"She was young and cute and wearing black boots—the black boots are important to the story—and apparently when she handed over the manuscript he complimented the boots and told her he wanted to see her wearing those boots and nothing else. Like, right away. So she tried to make a joke out of it, as one does."

"Does one?"

"What do you think?" Kat instinctively crossed her legs. The broken heel dangled limply off the bottom of her shoe. "When you get those sorts of comments—and, trust me, we do, we all do—you have two choices. You can throw a fit or try to laugh it off. He was one of their star authors. She had to try to make it a joke and hope he'd take the out."

"But he didn't." It wasn't a question.

"No, he didn't." Kat took a deep breath and plunged on. "It turned out, we all had history with Brett. He'd dated Emma and stole her book. You know, that first book, the international sensation that put him on the publishing map? That wasn't his. That was Emma's. He pretended he loved her and then stole her work and dumped her. When she figured it out, he went around telling people she was just a woman scorned, blah blah blah. Oh, and jealous of his talent. Scorned *and* jealous. Why do you think Emma fact-checks everything fifteen times before she can decide what to order for breakfast? She doesn't trust anything—much less her own judgment. She hasn't written anything she can't foot-note since then. As far as I can tell, she also hasn't dated anyone since then."

"And Mrs. Pringle?"

"He roofied her," Kat said bluntly. "Date rape drugs. In her drink. At a conference."

The look of complete and utter horror on the inspector's face was incredibly bracing. Sometimes, Kat forgot that in the normal world men didn't do these things. Her expectations had been so warped.

"So there we were," she said roughly. "The four people in the world who actually knew Mr. Marvelous for the rotting pile of slime he actually was."

The inspector's voice was soft, but his knuckles were very white against the edge of the bench. "You've told me what he did to them. But you haven't told me what he did to you."

Kat stared at her antique memento mori ring, the stark lines of white skull against the ebony background. She didn't want to talk about that. Not to him. Not to anyone. But particularly not to him. "You know about Yaddo."

"No," he said roughly, and something in his voice made Kat turn and look at him. "It seems I *don't* know about Yaddo."

Kat shrugged. "You would only know what *he* said happened at Yaddo. That's enough for most people."

"I'm not most people." He wasn't pretending to be calm anymore. "*What happened at Yaddo, Kat?*"

It was the first time he'd used her given name. Not Miss de Noir, not hey you. Kat stared at him, seizing on the small detail to avoid the big question. "You called me Kat."

"It's your name." In a gentler voice, he added, "What happened, Kat?"

Kat twisted her ring around her finger. "You may not believe it, but I used to be really shy. We moved around a lot when I was a kid, so I didn't get out much. I mostly lived in libraries—in books. When I met Brett, we'd each just had one big book out. We were both young. We were both critically acclaimed overnight successes. We'd both written books that used fantastical settings—dystopia for him, urban fantasy for me—to tackle larger issues. He seemed . . . he seemed like my kind of nerd. I thought he liked me."

It sounded so sophomoric. Like teenage girls giggling about whether he liked you or *liked* liked you. Kat wouldn't know. She'd never been one of those girls. Which was maybe why she'd fallen for Brett. She'd been such easy prey.

"He told me he'd read my book. He told me he was a huge fan. He told me there were elements of my work he wanted to explore together."

"When I said I admired your work, I meant it," the inspector said hoarsely.

"Yeah, well, you guys have different ideas of what constitutes literary criticism. His was more . . . hands-on." Kat stared at her hands, at her rings, her nails, grown into talons. For defense. Since Yaddo. "I thought he was asking me out. I thought it was a date. Romantic dinner in his room, sweet murmurings about tropes and metaphors, you know."

"No. I don't know." That muscle was working overtime in the inspector's jaw. "What happened?"

"He'd invited a friend. Some other guy. Not a fiction writer. I didn't know until the door closed." Kat's voice didn't seem to be working properly. The volume was all over the place. "He had— scarves. To tie me. I was—I was not okay with that. I told him I was not okay with that."

She could remember standing there, holding the bottle of wine she'd brought, wearing the wrap top and jeans she'd so carefully chosen for her romantic evening, smelling the sour grapefruit smell of her own fear as she'd backed up, not quite understanding, not believing, not wanting to believe, even as Brett laid it all out for her, detail by detail, everything he was going to do to her, everything they were going to do to her, like it was a treat, like she should be glad, like she wasn't sick with fear and telling him no, no, NO.

Kat hated herself for the sobs rising in her throat, the panic she couldn't control. "He told me I was frigid, that if I were any kind of real woman I would want to—want to—He said that since I wrote it—" She looked helplessly at the inspector, trying to make him understand, trying to make him understand the way Brett hadn't understood. "In the book, it's a ritual—to raise power—and it's her *choice*."

The inspector took her hands in his, squeezing them. She could feel both the comfort and the anger in the gesture. "You shouldn't have to explain yourself to anyone."

"He took my work and reduced it to—to mere titillation. I broke his nose."

"Good for you," the inspector said roughly.

Kat struggled to control her breathing. "You can see in the pictures—his nose is slightly crooked. He told everyone it was a skiing accident, but it wasn't. It was from when he tried to hold me down so his friend could rape me."

"Did you tell anyone?" the inspector demanded fiercely. He was still holding her hands, Kat realized. "At the time?"

Kat yanked her hands away. "You mean after I finished scouring myself and all the things you're not supposed to do?"

She could remember crouching in the shower, still wearing her tattered clothes, her high heels against the tile floor. She remembered locking the door, double-checking the windows, terrified, terrified he was going to come and try again. She'd spent a day in a state of siege, crying and shivering, afraid to leave the room, afraid to call anyone. And who would she call anyway?

"He got there first with his side of the story. He got me banned from Yaddo. My publisher dropped me. He told everyone I'd assaulted him—that I was a man-crazed nymphomaniac. I thought—if everyone thought I was this raving sexpot, fine, I'd be a raving sexpot. But on *my* terms, not his. I dress like this for *me*. And so no one will ever do to me what he tried to do to me."

There was a moment of silence. And then the inspector said, in a voice that was quiet but still seemed to resonate off the wood-paneled walls, "If he weren't already dead, I would kill him myself."

It was pure hero stuff. In that moment, Kat had no doubt that if Brett Saffron Presley were here in this room, Inspector Macintosh would slap him in the face with his glove and then run him through with his sword.

And she couldn't quite cope with what that meant.

"And get your sister—the medical examiner—to cover it up? Convenient."

Well, that killed the moment. The inspector looked like he'd had ice dumped over his head. "I would never—"

"I know. You didn't mean it." Only he had. And he hadn't. This wasn't a Karyn Black novel. People couldn't dash around like

Errol Flynn skewering villains. This was the real world. Not some pseudomedieval fantasy. "And neither did we! Not to kill him, I mean. We just wanted to—humiliate him. Make the world see him for what he was."

Kat wasn't quite sure how it had happened, but her hands were on his chest, on the very soft wool of his sweater. It wasn't cashmere, but it had clearly come from a very contented sheep.

"You've got to understand, we all agreed that dying was too good for him. We wanted him alive and suffering."

"Aye." It took a long time for that syllable to come out. "I can understand that."

"So here. Here's the whole story." Kat took a deep breath. "Rachelle—our editor—was in on it with us. She came up with the idea of our writing a book together. She'd seen an article about the writing retreats and Naughty Ned and decided it made a great cover story. Three authors writing one book! Besties from different genres!"

"So it was your editor's plan."

"She was the one who came up with the initial idea but we all pitched in. Emma did the background research. Cassie bought a lot of plaid. I set up that Snoggr account. And I sent him the S&M gear. We all played to our strengths." Kat tried a wobbly smile but the inspector wasn't smiling back. "The plan was to get him into a compromising situation and then film him. Make him confess. Emma wanted him to admit to stealing her book. I wanted him to tell the truth about Yaddo."

"And Mrs. Pringle?"

Kat hesitated. "There's a chance that Dash—one of Cassie's kids—is his. From the night he roofied her. He was harassing her. Demanding a DNA test. He was writing a memoir and apparently there's a whole bit on discovering he might be a father and wanting to be part of the boy's life, blah, blah, blah. Cassie was terrified. Her family is everything to her."

"I can see that." They were back to the old reserve. It was enough to make Kat wonder if she'd imagined the intensity of his reaction before, the feel of his hands holding hers. "So you and Miss Endicott wanted him to tell and Mrs. Pringle wanted him *not* to tell."

"Yeah, pretty much." Kat could feel the exhaustion seeping in. "We were going to get him on camera confessing to stealing Emma's book and assaulting me and then we were going to destroy all files with his memoir. Don't look at me like that! I know it was a stupid plan. But it seemed like a good idea at the time. We were all—a little wound up."

"You wanted revenge."

"Justice," Kat corrected him. Biting her lip, she looked away. "No. Not even that. We didn't want him doing it again, to someone else. You've got to understand what it was like that night, at Bouchercon. All those people, clapping for him. All those potential victims. He wasn't going to stop. Not until someone stopped him."

"You say the plan was merely to humiliate him," said the inspector impersonally. "How do you know that one of your co-conspirators didn't take it a step further?"

"They didn't. For one thing, Emma was busy bonking the Monarch of the Glen over there."

The inspector looked at her sideways. "The Monarch of the Glen isn't a man; he's a stag. A male deer."

"Whatever. You know what they say about stags. Rutting like a . . . Never mind." Her editor would probably love a werestag. Kat pushed that unfortunate image from her mind. "Emma didn't want him dead. She wanted him shamed. We both wanted him shamed."

"You wanted him shamed. Mrs. Pringle wanted him silenced."

"Have you *met* Cassie? The only way she's killing anyone is with high cholesterol. And then she'd probably bake you bran muffins to counteract it."

"She knows about poisons."

"The way I know about werebears. It's not a personal acquaintance. Besides, the plants outside were in the wrong season—apparently—and you heard your sister. That belladonna in the bottle was too old to be effective."

"I gather there are other ways to get atropine. Antidiarrheals. Eye drops."

"Someone's been doing his research." Kat shrugged. "I don't know where it came from, but I think it was in the mead. When I came in, he was raving. Totally drugged out. He was holding a goblet in one hand and sloshing it everywhere. The room reeked of spilled mead."

"When you came in?" The inspector stood up, looking down at her where she still sat on the bench. "You never mentioned that you were in there. That night."

Kat glared up at him. "I hadn't gotten to that yet!" She stood up, too, since apparently they were standing now. "It was part of the plan. Confront him. Embarrass him. Film him. We were all meant to be there together, but then Emma and Archie . . . and Cassie got a call from her husband. . . ."

"So you went alone."

"Yes. I went alone. Go ahead. Tell me I'm an idiot."

"I think you're very brave," he said quietly.

Kat shook her head. "I was scared out of my freaking wits. I—I ran. I just ran. He was reaching for me and I—I ran. All that planning—the whole stupid trip—and I couldn't see it through. I didn't even get a picture."

"If you had," said the inspector drily, and Kat knew now, she knew that he spoke that way when he was trying to hide some other emotion, "we would have found it on your phone."

"Yeah, good for me, right? But also not good for me because I can't prove he was alive and raving when I left him."

A thought struck the detective. "You say you were in there—but we didn't find your footprints outside the Tower."

"We took the secret passage. I mean—I took the secret passage. Oh, crap. You might as well know. Cassie was there, too. She came after I left. But she also didn't kill him. She said he was face down passed out when she came in. She was worried he'd drowned in the spilled mead and it was her fault for not calling 911."

"Nine nine nine. He didn't drown. It was one of the few ways he wasn't killed." The inspector looked at her thoughtfully, and then seemed to make up his mind about something. "Your Brett was killed two ways—like someone wanted to be sure of him. There was atropine—belladonna—in his system. And then someone stabbed him in the back with a broken antler."

"A broken *antler*? Emma heard something about a horn but we had this idea that it might be a ceremonial athame or something like that. What? We're writers. Cassie had this crazy idea it might have been the stag's head, but Emma swore the trajectory was wrong."

"It *was* the stag's head."

"Wait, but—you're seriously saying that it fell and impaled him?" So much for Emma's physics. Cassie was not going to cope well with this.

"No." The inspector rubbed the back of his neck. "When I said stabbed I meant stabbed. The stag's head must have fallen down in the struggle. One of the antlers broke off. Someone stabbed Mr. Presley with it. In the back."

Kat wasn't surprised he looked exhausted. This was pure Agatha Christie. Or possibly Scooby-Doo. "So . . . the poison could have been administered at any time, but the person stabbed him to be sure?"

"Perhaps."

"Fingerprints?" Kat asked, testing her luck.

To her surprise, he answered seriously. "Only Morag's. She was the one who found him when she went in to clean."

Kat narrowed her eyes at him. "Are you telling me this to win my confidence?"

"I thought I already had that." He looked steadily at her, his eyes a clear, pale brown. "Or are you saying you haven't told me everything?"

Of course, she hadn't. She hadn't told him how much she liked the smell of his soap, or the wool of his sweater, or how much she wanted him to look at her again the way he had when he told her how brave she'd been, or how much, how ridiculously much, she wanted to wind her arms around his neck and kiss him, right here, right now, corpses be damned.

Kat waved one hand. "Uh, I've told you pretty much everything. Unless you want to know my bra size."

The inspector smiled reluctantly at her, like he couldn't quite help himself. "Is that relevant to this investigation?"

They were back on firmer territory now. Kat fluttered her fake lashes at him. "It is if you'd like it to be."

"Your shoe size would be more to the point—only we haven't any footprints. Except for Beatrice the sheep."

"Wait, but didn't Morag discover the body? Shouldn't her footprints be there?"

"She used the passage," the inspector said shortly. "Did you think you were the only ones who knew about it? Morag's worked here her whole life, since she was a girl. There's nothing about the castle she doesn't know."

Morag, who knew everything about the castle.

Morag, who had been like a grandmother to the inspector.

He was going to hate her. But it had to be said.

"So," said Kat. "You've got Morag with the body. You've got Morag's fingerprints on the horn. And you've got Morag with the keys to the poison garden."

CHAPTER TWENTY-FIVE

Cassie

VOICEMAIL. AGAIN.

Cassie set her phone on the kitchen table and buried her face in her palms.

What was that word again? Ghosted. When she'd first heard the term, she was intrigued. How evocative! How perfectly expressive of how you felt when somebody pretended you didn't exist. Cassie's brain had started tingling, the way your brain tingles when the seed of some new, terrific idea takes root and germinates. She'd called up her agent. *I have this new, terrific idea! A book about a woman who's been ghosted by her best friend and goes on this journey to find out why, and I don't know why yet but it's something terrible, some buried secret or something.*

To which her agent replied wearily, *Oh, sweetie. Psychological thrillers are not your thing, okay? It's not your brand. Bring me another cat mystery, okay? Your readers want cats and coffee. And cupcakes.*

Now her own husband had ghosted her. The irony! Except her brain wasn't tingling at all. Her brain—as she stared at the dark screen of her phone, this phone she'd wanted back so desperately, the unseen messages from Chip that would put her out of her misery, the unseen messages that turned out not to exist—just felt empty. Ghostlike.

Well, what had she expected? That the old Chip, in the space of a few magical days, would return? That all his suspicions, all the mistrust and the awkward, stilted atmosphere of something-is-not-right, would wash away in a flood of tenderness and proclamations of his forever love?

Or at least some assurance that the kids were all right?

"Your marriage is over," she said to the screen.

He's come to his senses. Realized he could do better than stay trapped in endless domestic hell with a frizzy-haired mouse of a midlist mystery writer who—by the way, a fact he was sure to find out sooner rather than later, if he didn't suspect already—had slept with somebody else. Had broken her marriage vows. Had possibly brought a child into their family who wasn't his.

Dash. Her chubby, cheeky Dashiel. She brushed away a tear that had somehow gathered on her lower eyelid.

And now she was embroiled in a murder investigation. There must have been news about it back home. He must have heard. No wonder Chip wanted nothing more to do with her.

She picked up the phone and the wallpaper image appeared— all six kids rolling down the grassy hill that sloped away from the garden to the field behind their house. A familiar ache gathered in her chest. She'd taken it on the last day before school started. She could almost hear the laughter, she could taste on her tongue that feeling you sometimes had, in the middle of all the day-to-day drama and tedium of raising kids, of *stop time now!* Just freeze this moment so you can savor their youth forever. Savor this family forever.

And now it was gone. Broken. She'd tried so hard to be a good wife, a good mother, a good writer, a good everything. To juggle all the plates, to make everyone happy. And she'd failed.

Presley was dead. Her marriage was dead. Her life—her children's lives—would never be the same. All her fault.

The smell of burning dough wafted past her nose.

Cassie grabbed a dishcloth and dashed to the enormous Edwardian range. The last batch of cookies shriveled on the metal tray, burned around the edges and undoubtedly on their bottoms. Darn it to heck! She'd even ruined the cookies.

She scraped the cookies into the dustbin and scrubbed off the tray in the sink. When everything was cleaned and dried and her hands were empty, she picked up her phone and checked her reader email. Maybe someone had sent one of those lovely notes that popped up from time to time—*Thank you so much for writing* The Bundt of All Fears! *I laughed, I cried, I lived inside every lyric sentence! You are truly my favorite author of all time!*

Those always made her feel better. Made her feel like there was *one* thing she could do right, at least. One part of her that wasn't a complete screwup.

At the top of the stack of unread emails, a subject line jumped at her: *Stupidest book I have ever read.*

BAKE. SHE HAD to bake something.

She'd done muffins, cakes, brownies, cookies. What else? Morag had promised to teach her how to make scones—proper Scottish ones, she'd sniffed, not the Sassenach kind or (worse yet) the American scone, which wasn't recognizable as a scone at all.

Where *was* Morag, anyway? She was always so punctual about mealtimes. So territorial about her kitchen. Was something wrong? Had Cassie driven her out with all her manic baking and her chatter? Poor Morag. She was getting on in years, after all.

Cassie headed to the shelf of cookbooks. Morag kept her own scrapbook of recipes here somewhere. Just the other day she'd taken out a sheet of yellowed paper on which was scribbled the instructions for haggis—*Mind ye*, she'd told Cassie, waggling the paper in front of her, *this is only for butchery days when we do the culling, the meat must be fresh*—and Cassie had glimpsed the scone recipe underneath it.

I add currants to mine, but ye can use what garnish ye like, Morag had said magnanimously.

Cassie scanned the shelves. There it was! Tucked between an ancient herbal and a dog-eared paperback of *Sweet Savage Laird*.

Cassie ran her finger down the creased spine and smiled, remembering how she and her best friend Mandy had pooled their babysitting money to buy a copy when the book came out. They'd flipped a coin to decide who got to read it first. Cassie had won, but she'd felt so guilty at Mandy's crestfallen face, she'd let her have it anyway. Goodness, that was ages ago. Mandy had stayed up all night reading and gave the book back the next day, so what was the difference? And Mandy'd had that tough situation at home and all.

She yanked out the scrapbook with both hands and carried it to the table.

Morag's kitchen might have been a model of tidiness, but her scrapbook was chaos. Recipe cards stuck between Picassoesque sketches of a half-man, half-sheep, and a baby with enormous trapezoid eyes, crying triangle tears. A page torn out from what seemed to be some kind of expensive society magazine, on which a thick red *X* was slashed atop one of the faces in the photograph. Floor plans—Cassie made a noise of satisfaction. Old newspaper articles about Naughty Ned. Recipes that read like witches' spells, sprinkling herbs and boiling toad livers and incantations—*and ye cock falleth off on the sixthe daye.*

Dear me, she thought.

Under one page she felt a large lump, which proved to be a kind of voodoo doll of pale muslin stuffed with—she sniffed.

Cloves? It wore a tiny Barbour jacket and miniature wellies and there was a toothpick stuck through right where the peepee came from. (Well, where it *would* have come from, if the doll were a real person.)

Cassie frowned at the doll's face. The snarling features were drawn in red ink and a line came down from the corner of its mouth, as if it were drooling blood.

A chill shivered down her spine.

She set down the doll and flipped back through the pages until she came to the photograph from the society magazine. She held the image closer and examined the group of well-dressed young people, smiles turned toward the camera, except for one girl who pursed her lips like she wanted to kiss the lens. They were at a party of some kind—formal, if the tuxedos and gowns were any clue. The *X* obscured the face of one of the men. He had thick hair that flopped over to one side and the trim, athletic build of a tennis player.

Underneath the red *X*, the features were familiar.

Cassie looked back at the doll.

"Emma!" she shrieked. "Kat!"

She tossed the doll back between the pages, closed the book, and hefted it off the table. "Emma! Kat! I need you!" she yelled. She staggered out the kitchen door and into the hallway, just as Emma came running around the corner.

"*Oof,*" said Emma.

"Careful!" said Cassie, just as Kat lurched smack into Emma's back.

"What the hell is going on?" Kat snarled, rubbing her nose.

Cassie waved the scrapbook. "Look at this! Emma, hold it for me."

She transferred the book into Emma's hands and turned the pages.

"Holy crap," said Kat.

"Where did you get this? *Spell for the shriveling of a man's boaby.*" Emma looked up. "What's a boaby?"

"Guess," said Kat.

Emma held up the magazine clipping. "Oh my God. That's—"

"I know! And look at this voodoo doll!"

Kat snatched it from her fingers. "Let me see that."

Emma looked at Cassie. "*Who* did you say this belonged to?"

"Whom," said Cassie. "It belongs to Morag."

"Morag?" said Kat. "Did you say *Morag*?"

Emma took the doll from Kat and looked back down at the photograph. Her face hardened into a deep frown. "Well," she said grimly, "it sure looks as if our Morag has it out for Archie."

"Speaking of which, where *is* Archie?" asked Kat. "I haven't seen him since lunchtime."

Cassie's stomach went cold. "Or Morag," she whispered.

"Crap," said Kat.

"What's the matter?"

"What's the *matter*, you half-wits, is that I came in here *looking* for Morag. DCI Macintosh is looking for her, too, out in the poison garden. I have a question or two for her, kind of a lightbulb moment, and—"

"Shh!" Emma held up her hand. "Did you hear that?"

Cassie tilted her head. The corridor was cool and damp, as if the Scottish winter had crept in between the flagstones. In fact, if she strained her ears, she could hear the faint howl of the wind coming in from the sea.

Wait a minute. That wasn't the wind.

She looked at Emma, who looked at Kat.

"The boot room," said Emma.

They pounded down the corridor to the boot room that came in from the garden. Kat flung open the door to reveal Loren the sheepdog, damp and shaggy, hunched miserably over a pair of rubber shoes. She looked up at them and whined.

"Oh, dear," said Cassie. "I think she's forgotten herself on Morag's garden clogs."

"Never mind the damned *clogs*," said Emma. "If Loren's in *here* . . . then where the hell is Archie?"

CHAPTER TWENTY-SIX

Emma

*W*HERE THE HELL *is Archie?* Emma's own words echoed inside her head as she met Loren's eyes, wondering if her own looked as stricken even though only one of them had seen the hideous flaxen-haired doll with the tiny wellies and mini Barbour coat. They stared at one another as the smell of dog pee and wet woolen socks assaulted their noses, although Loren seemed not to mind.

It was a good thing that there hadn't been any lunch to eat as Emma was very, very sure that her stomach contents would also now be sloshing inside Morag's clogs. And not just because of the smell. Abject fear made her stomach clench. Archie was missing. *Archie was missing!* Despite the urgency of the words in her head, Emma couldn't move. She imagined the unsinkable Prunella Schuyler sneering at her, comparing Emma's inability to act in the face of fear with her own heroics as a survivor of the *Lusitania*.

Icy realization slipped down Emma's neck. "This is why Morag didn't have our lunch prepared. She was planning something. Something to do with Archie. And whatever that is, she's had a long head start."

"I'll go get help," Kat announced.

"From whom?" Cassie asked. She reeked of burnt cookies, the added smell almost enough to send Emma over the edge.

"DCI Macintosh," Kat answered with the sort of solid confidence one might use when saying *Superman*.

Emma could only nod. Archie—*her* Archie—was missing. And so was the old woman who'd made a voodoo doll in his image.

Kat ran from the boot room as Emma reached past Cassie and pulled a familiar Kinloch plaid scarf from a wall peg.

"Where are you going?" Cassie asked. "You've got your appointment with the inspector at three!"

"I can't worry about that now. Archie's missing," she said, the words skirting around the lump in her throat. Leaning down to be eye level with the sheepdog, she let the animal sniff at the scarf. Then she held the door ajar and pointed toward the outside where the biting wind nipped through the opening. "Find him for me, girl!"

The dog raced past her in a blur of gray-and-white fur, almost toppling Emma over. Cassie steadied her before Emma bolted out the door in hot pursuit of the fleeing canine.

"Wait up—I'm coming, too," Cassie shouted from close behind, surprising Emma. Then again, chasing six children around all day was probably enough to stay physically fit. Which was a good thing because Emma had no intention of slowing down as she raced around the castle following Loren, who had a lot of speed despite her bulk.

Cassie's pace had begun to flag as they reached the Obelisk. "Shouldn't . . . we search . . . in here . . . first?" she panted.

"No!" Emma said, then pointed at the ball of fur now racing in the direction of the cliffs, not wanting to waste her breath on explanation. Her rising panic as she watched Loren head for the caves was already stealing most of it.

They ran past the graveyard, the standing stones like spectators at a race, and with a sick feeling, Emma knew where they were headed. Just as they reached the rocky soil of Langford Point, Loren mercifully stopped and began pawing at something on the ground, then circling whatever it was and emitting a high-pitched whine.

"Thank . . . goodness," Cassie panted as she caught up, stopping just short of Emma before leaning over with her hands on her thighs, struggling to catch her breath.

Emma focused on the small, shiny object on the ground that Loren had discovered and thought it important enough to stop and whine. "What is it, girl? What have you found?"

Loren sat back on her haunches, allowing Emma to retrieve the object, her rapidly beating heart seeming to crawl into the back of her throat as she recognized what it was.

"Is that . . . ?" Cassie asked.

"Archie's signet ring. He always wore it. I don't think I ever saw him without it on his finger."

"Even when—"

"Yes." Emma cut her off. "Even then." A stiff salt-drenched gust of wind blew at them, bringing with it the faint wail of a woman. Or maybe that was the keening she'd only read about but never actually heard. The kind of sound that carved out one's heart and soul and replaced them with clods of dark earth.

Cassie clutched Emma's arm, her eyes flaring. "It's the midwife's ghost, crying for her daughter!"

Emma shook her head, her gaze unable to look away from the darkening sky or ignore the incessant slap of the encroaching waves below. "No. That's no ghost. That's the sound of a woman who's lost touch with reality."

Loren leapt up and began racing toward the cliff, making a sharp turn toward the stone steps they'd climbed down before with Calum. Emma took off at a fast run, not giving herself time to think about what might be waiting at the bottom of the steps.

"Emma," Cassie called from behind. "Shouldn't we wait for Kat and the inspector? I think this might be too dangerous . . ."

Cassie's words were swept away by the wind and the sound of the sea pounding against the shore below as the tide turned and the land surrendered itself bit by bit to the ocean. Emma shook her head as she ran, knowing what Cassie—a cautious mother of six—might have said.

Emma paused to turn around and shout, "Stay here and wait for them so you can tell them I've gone down to the caves to look for him!" She had a brief glance of Cassie's terrified eyes as her friend nodded, then Emma took off in the direction where Loren had disappeared.

She forced herself to stop at the top of the cliff steps so she wouldn't end up in a broken heap at the bottom and unable to help Archie. And she *knew* he needed her. She felt it all the way through her wool sweater and plaid turtleneck to her very heart. If she weren't so completely petrified at the thought of being too late, she might have smiled at how very closely the enfolding scene was to a Karyn Black novel. There was even a laird! Before her mind could start crafting appropriate titles, her foot found the first step and she began the steep descent.

The wind was stronger than it had been on the night of the ghost tour, the skies emitting a peculiar glow. When she'd gained her footing on the silty sand at the bottom of the steps, she looked up to see what she recognized as a nacreous cloud. She knew others called them "mother-of-pearl" clouds because of their iridescence, but Emma wasn't one to call anything by its popular name if her research had taught her otherwise. She didn't remember anything else about them, except that they were usually seen in Canada and Scandinavia, not Scotland. Staring at the shimmering cloud, she reminded herself that she didn't believe in anything that couldn't be documented in a footnote, like the existence of voodoo magic. But right at that moment she needed to believe that the rare celestial light from above was a good omen. If she didn't believe in them before, she would now.

Loren barked and Emma turned to find the sheepdog sitting on a quickly diminishing sandbar looking into the darkened entrance of the cave. Emma sloshed through the ankle-deep frigid water, wistfully thinking of her wellies, to stand next to the dog and stared into the black abyss. "Archie! Are you in there? It's Emma!"

Another eerie wail drifted from the yawning mouth of the cave, the sound emerging from the dark like a specter. The hair at the nape of Emma's neck stood on end and she had to clench her teeth to keep them from chattering. She reached down and grasped Loren's collar, threading her fingers through the coarse fur, telling herself it was so the dog wouldn't run inside, but she knew it was really because she was scared out of her wits of what she might find in the cave and terrified of the rising water that was now up to her calves. Dog fur was the next best thing to a human hand. And oftentimes even better.

"Archie?" she managed to shout again, her voice high-pitched and wobbling like an untrained vibrato. "I'm coming in." She looked down at Loren whose gaze remained fixated on the cave. Emma glanced around for a ledge to place the dog to keep her safe, while at the same time knowing she'd never be able to lift the dog, nor would there be any guarantee that Loren would stay once there.

Cassie's voice came from behind Emma. "I'll take the dog back up to the cliff to wait for the police so I can tell them where you are."

Of course Cassie had followed. She was that kind of friend. The best kind. The kind who ignored danger to help a friend. Emma wished it hadn't taken her so long to figure that out.

Cassie looked down at the now-vanished sandbar and then at the shallow waves brushing over the bottom step. "I know you're going to do what you feel you have to, but I really wish you would wait with me for help to arrive. Calum said you need to make sure not to be in the cave when the tide comes in, and the tide has already turned."

"We don't have time. Archie's in there, and he might be hurt. He might not be able to make it out on his own." Her voice hitched on the last word.

"All right." Cassie nodded with a confidence Emma hadn't seen before. "Don't worry about Loren. I've got this."

Emma was about to ask Cassie how she was going to convince the dog to come with her when Cassie let out a shrill whistle using two fingers and Loren obediently went to her side and looked up at Cassie for further instructions.

"How . . . ?"

"I'm a mother. There's not much difference between corralling dogs and corralling children."

Emma's mouth lifted in a feeble attempt at a smile. Then she took the first step toward the cave, sucking in her breath as the icy water crept farther up her leg.

"How do you know he's even in there?" Cassie couldn't hide the worry in her voice.

Emma paused and took one last look at her friend. "Like you and Chip, I think. When you know, you know." Facing the cave once more, she hurried forward with the wind pushing at her back until the darkness swallowed her.

CHAPTER TWENTY-SEVEN

Kat

THE DINING ROOM was dark and cold. No food in the chafing dishes. No inspector by the coffee urn.

"Inspector Macintosh!" Crap, she didn't even know his first name.

He knew hers; he'd called her Kat. No, no, no time for that, push down the memory, no going all weird and gooey.

Kat careened through all the public spaces, through the Great Hall, through a dusty music room, through a billiard room where the felt of the table had begun to go a gentle gray with age. No inspector. No Archie. No Morag. Not in the poison garden, not in the servants' quarters, not in the solarium, not in the library, not in the dining room.

Kat's phone, with its snazzy blinged-out case, was still lying on the table where the inspector had tossed it before he stalked out, with Kat in hot pursuit.

Always chasing, never reaching.

Not everything had to be a metaphor, dammit.

Kat grabbed her phone, punching in—What had the inspector said? Oh, right—999.

"Kinloch Constabulary, how may I help you?" said a perky female voice.

"It's Katja de Noir from the castle," said Kat tersely. "Is the inspector there? Inspector Macintosh?"

"No—we've a bit of a to-do at the dock," said the voice, all chatty, as though a deranged housekeeper weren't stalking the halls of Kinloch. "You'll have heard about the ferry being kept in dock on the mainland—choppy waters, ye ken, and it's not that it canna get here, but they dinna think they could get it back again, not with the forrrrrecast being what it is—and we've some tourists from the States raising a bit of a din. . . ."

Kat was about to raise more than a bit of a din. "He's at the *dock*?"

"Isna that what I've just been after telling ye?"

Kat felt like her head was about to explode. What in the hell was he doing placating tourists when there was a killer at the castle? *I'll speak to Morag,* he'd said, and then his phone had buzzed, and off he strode, and she'd assumed, like any logical person would, that it was something to do with, oh, the fact there was a murderer on the premises, but no, he'd gone jaunting off to the docks to deal with Americans. Other Americans.

What the hell?

"Look, if he calls in, can you tell him—" *We now know that everyone's favorite local crone is a deranged murderer who might have made off with Emma's lovebug Archie?* "Can you just give me his mobile number?"

"I dinna—"

"We have a killer up here at the castle! If you don't give it to me, I'll get it from his sister."

"I s'pose there's no harrrrrm." The woman reeled off a series of numbers.

"Thanks." Kat jabbed the off button, mumbling the numbers back to herself on repeat, because, of course, she had nothing to write them down with.

She punched in the numbers, desperately hoping it wasn't Kinloch pizza delivery.

"You've reached Detective Chief Inspector Macintosh of the Kinloch Police—"

Kat waited out the voicemail message with feelings of rising hysteria. "Inspector. It's me. Kat. *Call me.* I mean, not like that. We think we've found the killer. Just call me, okay?"

Silence. All around her the castle was silent. Dead. Empty. Like they'd never been; like this was all one of those short stories where someone woke up in a pile of ruins to discover she'd dreamed the whole thing and the castle never was, this plot never was, none of this ever was.

Kat hit redial. "Inspector? It's me. Kat. Look, we think Morag may have kidnapped Archie. You're the police! You're supposed to answer your phone!"

Kat clutched her phone, helplessness making her feel as small as one of those cutesy little Disney mice helping Cinderella. *I'll call the inspector,* she'd said, like that was the answer to their problems, like the law would come rushing in and that would solve everything. Not like those idiot heroines who never bothered to inform the authorities. But what happened when the authorities didn't freaking answer their phones?

So here she was, with this useless piece of plastic in her hand, all alone in the deserted castle, while Emma and Cassie were out goodness only knew where chasing a killer, and Archie was goodness knew where, and where in the bloody hell was bloody Detective Chief Inspector Macintosh?

True, Morag was a mere slip of a woman and Archie was—well, not actually a World Wide Wrestling champion, but a reasonably fit man. A very fit man, if Emma was to be believed. But Morag had an advantage. He'd known her forever. Housekeeper at the castle for generations; like a grandmother the inspector had said.

If she'd handed Archie a cup of tea, he'd drink it, and probably be too polite to comment if it tasted funny.

Let's just go for a walk, she might say, and obediently, he'd stagger out behind her, wondering why the world was a little fuzzy around the edges, and, oh, look, there's a cliff—bye!

Kat hit redial again. "Where—the hell—are you?" she snarled into the phone.

No answer.

From the dining room wall, Lady Ned gazed coolly down at her. Lady Ned wouldn't stand here panicking and not doing anything. Lady Ned had been a badass in her Edwardian way, keeping an eye out on her husband, on the village—

An eye. On the village. That horrible painting she'd stared at and stared at while not looking at the inspector. The view over everything.

Kat was moving before the idea had fully crystalized, her legs getting the message before her brain did, sprinting out of the castle, across the sweep of gravel, down the flagstone path, toward the Obelisk, the highest point on Kinloch, a panoramic view of absolutely everything on the island.

Kat wrenched the door open, tugging aside crime scene tape. She lurched past Naughty Ned's orgy pit, only vaguely noting that someone had cleaned it since they'd last been there. The sickening smell of spilled mead had been replaced by lemon polish and beeswax.

Morag. Always Morag, and they'd been too damn dumb to see it.

Ageist, that's what they were. Ageist and sexist. Oh, what a cute old crone, they'd said. Straight out of central casting. But crones were creatures of power, and Kat, of all people, should damn well know that. Not to be dismissed lightly. All the best villains were crones. The maiden and the mother, they had their vulnerabilities—but the crone? She ruled.

The steps spiraled up and up and up, stone worn by generations that went far past the Kinlochs. Kat burst through an oak door onto the parapet, which was, as Morag had warned them, not in good repair. A wave of vertigo seized her; she pressed her back to the hard oak, the one solid thing for miles around. One false move and she'd be a pantaboot splotch on the flagstones below.

The roar of the sea seemed closer here. White knuckled, feeling like she was on the deck of a ship, everything wobbly, Kat minced toward the parapet, trying to get her bearings. That way was the village, looking like one of those Christmas villages, all tiny ceramic houses: tiny pub, tiny doctor's surgery, tiny grocery. Nothing to see there.

Kat sidled sideways, to the next point on the compass. The castle. Clearly shaped like a *K* from this angle. Calum's Land Rover, empty, parked next to one of the outbuildings.

Where in the hell was everyone?

Another careful shuffle, dead opposite the village now, looking out past the old graveyard, past Calum's spa, toward the rocky eastern shore. Dollhouse figures. Tiny dollhouse figures. Kat could just see them, down by—Was that Langford Point? That was Emma—she could tell because of the ponytail flapping behind her—running for all she was worth, with Cassie sprinting behind and Loren going mad next to them. Then Emma was down the cliff steps and sprinting across the land bridge but the tide was coming in, washing around her legs as she sloshed across, and Cassie was hesitating, turning—

What was on the other side, in that cave?

Kat was watching a tragedy unfold and she had no way to stop it, no way to get there. They'd all been so stupid. Kat wished she could just fling herself off the tower, spread her arms like wings, and float to them. The island seemed small until you had to get somewhere. Like, now.

Kat wrenched her phone out of her pocket and phoned 999 again.

"It's me, Kat, from the castle," she shouted over the roaring of the wind and the sea. The wind was so strong it seemed to want to pluck her up and send her straight to Oz. "Send everyone you've got to Langford Point—you know, that cave. The one with the baby. What? Not a baby now—you know. Just get there!"

What in the hell was going on? The roaring felt like it was going to consume her; the vibrations were so strong Kat could feel the rocks of the old tower shivering. What ancient powers had Ned awoken? What ancient powers had Morag called upon? Kat struggled to stand upright, tears streaming from her wind-whipped eyes, ready to face down dragons or demons or—

A helicopter.

It was a helicopter.

Kat didn't care where it came from or who it was carrying. All she knew was that this was something that could carry her through the air to Langford Point and it damn well would.

Kat scrambled down the stairs, clinging to the rope that served as banister, half sliding, half falling, hitting the ground running, bursting out of the Obelisk without bothering to close the door behind her, leaving it banging in the wind, letting the sea air blast away all those ancient secrets as she sprinted on the balls of her feet toward the helicopter that was just settling itself on to an open patch of lawn in front of the castle.

Kat waved her arms madly over her head in the universal symbol of *Hey you!* as she flung herself at the occupants of the aircraft.

"I need your helicopter," she panted.

There were two people inside: the pilot, who had an early '80s hot guy thing going, with slightly too long curly brown hair and one of those all-American faces, and a woman who was a dead ringer for Jackie Collins, with hair so shellacked that even the wind hadn't been able to touch it, vigorously sculpted cheekbones, exuberant eyeshadow, and enormous hoop earrings.

They were both staring at Kat.

"I—uh—I need to commandeer your helicopter—for a rescue mission," Kat said desperately. "We're looking for two novelists, a missing laird, a crazed murderer, and DCI Macintosh."

The woman's hoop earrings swung toward her. "DCI Macintosh?"

"Like the apple," said Kat. "Look, I know it sounds weird, but . . ."

"Novelists?" The hot guy swiveled in his seat. His voice was just what Kat had thought it would be: southern, like syrup on grits with a side of biscuits. "You've got novelists missing?"

"And a crazed murderer," said Kat impatiently. "Can you fly this thing for me? We have to get to them before something bad happens. I'm sorry to shove you out," she said to the Jackie Collins look-alike, "but you can hang out in the castle until . . . until we sort this all out."

"Honey, I wouldn't miss this for the world." The woman's giant hoop earrings swung as she moved over, freeing up a seat for Kat. "Climb on in! And by the way, I just loooooove those pants—and those boots! Are they pants or are they boots?"

"They're called pantaboots," said Kat, as she heaved herself up into the seat. The vacated chair smelled strongly of one of those perfumes that used to saturate women's magazines in the '80s. "Amazon, $39.99. Can we get going, please?"

"Buckle up," said the pilot grimly, and he did something to the controls that made the rotors spin madly. Kat's stomach lurched as the craft swung upward.

"They're at Langford Point!" Kat shouted.

"What's Langford Point?"

"It's a point! Like a large—never mind." Where in the bloody hell were the police? Kat waved frantically in what she hoped was the right general direction. "It's—that wayish!"

The helicopter swooshed left. Kat gripped the sides of her seat with both hands.

Next to Kat, the older woman, entirely unperturbed, had a giant phone out and was clicking busily. "Oh, look! They come in leopard print. Sold!"

"You just bought pantaboots?"

"It's a pant and a boot, how could I resist?" Her voice had the rasp of a lounge singer or a longtime chain-smoker. She turned her heavily outlined amber eyes on Kat. "Now, honey. Tell me why we're out chasing novelists. And DCI Macintosh."

"It's—it's an insane story." The crazy wind generated by the rotors took Kat's words and tossed them out into the abyss.

"Insane stories are what I live for!" the other woman shouted back cheerfully.

"My two friends and I—" Damn it, they were, weren't they? They were really her friends. Kat would deal with that later. "My two friends and I came here to work on a book—only not really. It's complicated."

The other woman pulled back as far as the harness would allow, raising her manicured brows as far as her Botoxed forehead would let her. "Wait a minute. I know you. You're that de Noir girl."

Anyone else and Kat would have retorted *woman*. But it was so clearly not meant as a slur. It was more of a Dowager Countess of Grantham vibe, if the Dowager Countess had worn stilettos and leopard print.

"I read *The Night Garden*," the other woman burbled happily, her voice nearly lost in the whir of the helicopter. "Masterful! I think your editor sent it to me for a blurb. And I really should have blurbed it, but I was on deadline, and *you* know how that goes. . . ."

She beamed a self-deprecating smile at Kat in a way that made Kat feel like they were members of the same club. Probably with a secret handshake.

"I don't usually read urban fantasy, but my editor said, *Karyn, sweetie, this has kind of a Highlander vibe, and we all know how you feel about Highlanders.* And, of course, she was right. She's always right. I adored it. I didn't adore it in time to blurb it, but I still adored it. You've got the gift, honey."

The woman was obviously waiting for Kat to say something, to acknowledge the compliment, but Kat found herself, for once, entirely without words. Karyn. Highlanders. Books hidden in her backpack, smuggled under the desk in science class. Dog-eared copies carried from temporary home to temporary home. *Sweet Savage Laird. The Laird and the Lamb. Laird of Ice.* A world more real than the real world. Brave warriors, plucky heroines, a single streak of white in her raven hair, bulging thews, villains who sneered and heroines who fought back.

Those old author photos had all had that late '80s glamour shot thing going, tastefully blurred and enormous clouds of hair, but if you peeled away about three facelifts and added some giant curled bangs, the resemblance was unmistakable.

"Are you—Karyn Black?"

"That's the name I write under." Karyn Black chuckled throatily, a whisky and peat fire sort of chuckle, an I-wrote-the-books-you-lived-for-in-high-school chuckle. "I chose it for my first book. Thought it made me sound mysterious. And it put me at the front of the alphabet. Take that, Woodiwiss!"

"You're Karyn Black," Kat repeated.

"That's just for my writing life," Karyn Black said, with a dismissive gesture, like her writing life hadn't comprised multiple number one bestsellers and made-for-TV movies starring Jane Seymour and Richard Chamberlain. Like she hadn't been the prop and mainstay of Kat's unhappy teenage years. "Here on the island, most of the old-timers still just call me Mrs. Macintosh."

"Mrs.—" Those cheekbones. Those eyes. Something clicked into place with a sickening lurch. Or maybe the lurch was the helicopter and entirely unconnected to the click. Kat stared at the woman next to her, with her Botox-smooth skin and seen-it-all eyes. "Are you the detective chief inspector's mother?"

358 Beatriz Williams, Lauren Willig, and Karen White

"Guilty as charged." Those thin, lipsticked lips quirked into a smile, but there was something sad beneath it. Karyn Black jabbed a lacquered finger out the far side of the helicopter, shouting so the pilot could hear her. "Ooooh, look, there's someone having a fit down there!"

It was Cassie, waving a plaid scarf for all she was worth.

"She's not having a fit. She's signaling. Hold on!" barked the hot guy at the controls, and the helicopter swooped to the side and down.

Cassie dropped her scarf and began pointing madly, trying to direct their attention to the land bridge—or what should have been the land bridge. The tide had sloshed over, cutting the cave off from the mainland. Over the sound of the rotors, Kat thought she could hear someone scream.

"Quick, quick," said Kat, pointlessly, as if he weren't already going as quick as the laws of physics and air resistance and the manufacturer's warranty would allow. "That's Cassie down there!"

"Who's Cassie?" asked Karyn Black, leaning forward as far as her harness would allow.

"Cassie Parsons Pringle—one of the missing novelists," said Kat.

"She's my wife," said the pilot.

CHAPTER TWENTY-EIGHT

Cassie

T HE WIND AND rain buffeted the helicopter as it swayed to earth. *Like a scene from a movie,* Cassie thought wildly, except this was real. The spray whipped off the rotors to sting her cheeks. The draft blew her hair into a giant frizzball. The plaid scarf tangled around her arms. At her side, Loren let loose a series of furious, soundless barks. Cassie cupped her numb hands around her mouth and tried to scream, but the gale ripped the words away and she couldn't even hear her own voice.

Instead, the desperate words echoed in her head.

The cave! Emma and Archie!

Morag!

Morag. Why hadn't they seen it before? Why hadn't she even suspected?

Because you were so eager for her to like you, Cassie told herself. *As usual. She was gruff and grumpy, so you wanted to win her over. You never stopped to think.*

She should have known. Should have sensed what was in Morag's heart. Cassie was a mystery novelist, for Pete's sake! She wrote about murderers all the time!

This was all her fault.

The skids touched the ground and a woman popped nimbly

from the open hatch to land in the wet grass on a pair of stilettos. The wind tangled her dark hair.

"Kat!" screamed Cassie. "Tell the pilot to—"

But Kat ran straight past her to the edge of the cliff. A surge of rain smacked against Cassie's macintosh. She ran toward the helicopter, ducking instinctively as the rotors swished to a stop overhead. Before she could approach the cockpit, a leopard-clad woman stepped gingerly out of the passenger cabin on a pair of stilettos equally as high as Kat's, though not actually connected to her sleek black leather leggings. Her gold hoops careered in the wind, although her enormous dark hair remained strangely motionless.

"You must be Cassie!" she called out, in a gravelly American accent. "I absolutely *adore* your bakery mysteries! Just perfect for a cozy night in with a glass of bourbon! Or two."

Cassie's plaid scarf, caught by a gust of wind, whipped up to cover her face. She pulled it back down again and gasped, "Thank you! Thank you so much! But I need your helicopter!"

"So I surmise. I'm afraid you'll have to sweet-talk this hunky pilot of mine, however."

Cassie turned back to the cockpit. A tall, thick-haired man leapt to the ground, yanking off his headset as he strode toward her. The rain and wind blurred his face. She started forward and opened her mouth to let loose a stream of incoherent pleading, but the robust, familiar rhythm of his stride—the jacket of beaten-up brown leather over his broad shoulders, the grim expression carved on his face—killed the words in her throat.

"*Chip?*" she choked out.

His hands gripped her shoulders. His gaze bored into hers. Like he knew everything, she thought in despair. Knew her every secret.

"I can explain—" she began.

"Never mind," Chip said. "I'm here now. Just tell me what you need me to do."

Someone screamed her name from the edge of the cliff. Cassie whipped around.

"I see them!" shouted Kat. "Right there at the cliff mouth! Emma and Archie!"

Cassie ran to join her. Loren bounded after her and skidded to a stop at the top of the stairs, barking wildly. Below them, two figures stood at the entrance to the cave—or rather, one determined female figure in a macintosh and loafers, supporting a man who slumped against her shoulders. Emma and Archie! The waves sloshed against the rocks at the base of the cave mouth and hurled upward in long, foamy tendrils to soak them both.

Emma lifted her head and spotted Cassie and Kat. She lifted one arm and waved frantically. At her side, Archie stirred and moved his head.

"He's bleeding!" Cassie exclaimed.

"There's no way he can climb the stairs," said Kat. "And look at the water! They'd have to swim!"

In the few minutes since Cassie had climbed back up the stairs, the sea had risen at least a couple of feet. There was nowhere for the helicopter to land, no way to get to Emma and Archie. She straightened back around to find Chip and bumped her nose on his shoulder. He was peering downward by her side, wearing the same deep, studious frown she remembered from his shifts on the volunteer mountain rescue squad.

"I'll have to winch down," he said. "Can anyone here fly a helicopter?"

Cassie looked at Kat. Kat stared back, appalled.

"I think I can," said Cassie, more bravely than she felt, "if you tell me what to do?"

"Nonsense," said a brisk female voice behind her. "I'll fly the damned helicopter."

The three of them spun around. Cassie had almost forgotten about the woman who'd climbed out of the helicopter—the woman who'd apparently flown to Kinloch in Chip's company. She knelt next to Loren, calming the dog with gentle strokes of her long, lacquered fingers. Her dark hair put up an impenetrable architecture against the storm, and the expression on her face might have been cut from steel. She rose to her feet and dusted off her hands.

"Don't look so shocked," she said. "I learned to operate helicopters while researching my book about fire jumpers. *The Flame and the Flyer*?"

Cassie stared after the woman as she strode back to the helicopter, leopard coat snapping in the gale. Chip followed her at a trot, all business.

"Who *is* that?" she asked Kat.

"That," said Kat, equally awed, "is Karyn Black."

In a matter of seconds, Karyn had climbed into the pilot's seat, arranged the headset carefully over her coiffure, and started the rotors whirling again. Chip swung into the cabin.

"Be careful!" Cassie yelled after him, but the draft snatched her words away. A sick feeling entered her stomach, the same worry that overwhelmed her whenever her husband rushed off in his truck, answering some call about a hiker who'd fallen down a cliff while taking a selfie above the falls or gotten caught in a late-season blizzard. All those times he'd hurried away to save some stranger, leaving her alone with the kids, worrying to death, and she'd raged in her head at the way he could just *flee* like that. The way he'd carelessly offer up his own body, his own life for someone else, as if she and the children didn't have a greater claim. That the safety of an idiot hiker meant more to him than his own family.

Now she was the one who needed rescuing. *Her* friend, her marvelous, irreplaceable Emma. And the sight of Chip inside the helicopter, buckling the harness around his massive chest—that chest she'd relied on for the past eighteen years, *her* chest, *her* heart inside that chest—girding himself to rescue Emma, just because she needed him to, made the tears spring from her eyes.

Or maybe that was the rain.

Another thought struck her. She ran toward the helicopter, waving her scarf. Chip's head poked from the cabin window.

"What about the kids?" she screamed.

"With my mother!" He stuck out his hand. "Come on! I'm going to need your help!"

"*Me?*"

Chip grasped her hand and hauled her on board, the way Cassie might lift a sack of groceries from the back of the Yukon. "If you need to puke," he said, "do it over the side, okay? I'll hold your hair."

"Ready?" called Karyn, over her shoulder.

Chip stuck up his thumb.

The helicopter lurched upward, dropped, rose again. Cassie seized Chip's shoulders and tried to scream.

"Whoopsie-daisy!" Karyn sang out cheerfully. "Been a while! Up we go, old girl."

"Whoopsie-*daisy*?" Cassie screeched.

Chip plucked her hands from his chest and set her on one of the passenger seats. "Stay here until I tell you, all right? Got to get hooked up to the hoist cable now."

Cassie nodded and glanced out the window just as the helicopter banked left. The ground fell away beneath them. Kat waved frantically from the edge of the cliff. Cassie clenched the seat with both hands and closed her eyes. She hated flying. Always took her motion sickness medicine, along with a glass or two of wine, and even *then* she had to close her eyes and sing "We All Live in a Yellow Submarine" during takeoff and landing. (In her head, of course.) The helicopter swung beneath her. She felt like she was falling. Or drunk.

Emma, she thought. *Emma needs me.*

She opened her eyes and looked out the window. Kat stood at the top of the stairs, Loren jumping by her side. On the other side, she saw the dark, wet rocks of Langford Point. Emma and Archie, clinging to the edge of the cave mouth. The helicopter swayed into place above the cave and Emma's sodden blond head disappeared under the edge of the helicopter deck.

Chip took Cassie by the shoulder and pulled her gently to the hoist control. The wind buffeted them both. "Listen to me, honey," he yelled, over the noise of the engine and the rotors and the weather, buckling the safety line around her. "I'm going down. I'm going to need you to operate the hoist, okay? Let it go until I'm down, then lock. I'll give it a couple of jerks when I'm ready to go back up. You'll have to tell Karyn what to do, okay? Can you do all that?"

Cassie looked into Chip's steady eyes. The whites, the calm blue surrounding the black pupil.

In a flash, she was back in North Carolina. The Blue Ridge Mountains, years ago. Hiking along that trail. He was her boyfriend then, her hunky boyfriend who always smelled of fresh wood and fresh air. The suspension bridge over the falls. *I'm afraid of heights*, Cassie had said, clutching the rope sides for dear life. *I can't do this.*

Chip had turned around and looked at her, just like this. Calm blue eyes.

You can *do this, Cassie Parsons*, he'd told her, with the certainty of a vow. *You can do anything.*

"Yes," she said now.

Chip leaned forward and kissed her hard on the mouth. "I just want you to know, I came here to fight for you. To fight for our marriage. I'm going to make things right between us, Cassie. Whatever it takes."

Before she could reply, he straightened, turned, and slipped out the window.

The drum spun wildly, unspooling the cable. Cassie reached for the drum lock and peered over the edge. Her heart dropped. The sea below was churning foam; Chip swung over the rolling, chopping meringue, suspended in his harness. No stretcher, no rescue bucket. He was going to have to carry each of them up, she realized.

The tail swung back and forth, buffeted by the wind, held on its mark by the constant corrections of the pilot. The quick, relentless thud of the rotors deafened Cassie. Chip had reached the cave mouth now. She yanked the lock back. Chip glanced up at her and stuck up his thumb, then called out something to Emma. Emma shook her head and yelled something back. Archie lifted his head and seemed to be saying something. Chip swung on his cable, not quite close enough to reach. He looked back up to Cassie and made some signal with his hand.

Cassie leaned to the cockpit. "Closer!" she yelled, gesturing her arm. "A few more yards thataway!"

Karyn nodded and looked out the window. She moved the control stick and the helicopter swung closer to the cave.

"I can't go any closer!" Karyn yelled. "He'll swing right into the rocks!"

Cassie returned to the open cabin hatch and looked down. With a final swing, Chip caught hold of Archie. Emma boosted him upward; Archie grabbed Chip around the shoulders. With one arm Chip heaved Archie into place, straddling his hips. He looked up and jerked twice on the cable.

Now, Cassie thought.

She looked up at the winch and panicked. There was a lever there somewhere. You pulled the lever and the drum rolled in reverse, hauling the cable back.

But what if she turned it the wrong way?

The helicopter swayed. There was some lettering that swam before her eyes. *Focus. Think!*

MAX WEIGHT 200 KILOS. DO NOT EXCEED.

Oh, poop, she thought. How many pounds in a kilo? What did Chip weigh? Two fifteen, two twenty? What was that in kilos? And how much did Archie weigh?

Screw it.

She found the lever and pulled it toward UP. The drum spun. The cable began to spool.

Slowly, Chip and Archie rose toward her. The rain spat on her face. The cable swung back and forth as the gusts of wind struck the two men, stuck together like a pair of bugs. Archie's face spun into view and Cassie gasped. Blood ran down the side of his face and matted his hair. He looked up at her blearily, like he didn't recognize her.

Then they were up. "Quick!" shouted Chip. "Not much time!"

Together they lifted Archie away and onto the passenger seat. Cassie buckled the seat belt around him and yelled, "What happened? Where are you hurt?

He shook his head. "Emma! Get Emma!"

Cassie turned back to Chip, who'd already turned the lever on the hoist and was dropping back down to the cave mouth. The waves tossed even higher now, and the sea itself sloshed up to the top of Emma's calves, though she clung to the highest rock. The spray kicked up by the helicopter obscured them both. Cassie glanced at Karyn Black. Her forehead was perfectly smooth, but Cassie could see from the way her lips had almost disappeared into her mouth that she was pouring every ounce of concentration into holding the helicopter steady over Emma.

Down below, Chip was nearly at the rocks. Emma stretched out a hand. A gust caught Chip and sent the cable swinging right into the rock wall. He put out his leg to absorb the impact. Cassie felt the scream in her throat, but it made no sound at all in the middle of all the noise. Was Chip okay? He swung back and toward Emma, reaching out his arm. Emma reached too. At the last second, she jumped.

But it was too late. She missed his grip and plunged into the water.

Cassie put her fist in her mouth. Fifty feet below, Chip let out some slack and dangled above Emma. The waves crashed over his legs. Emma flailed to keep her head above water.

With a last, desperate burst of strength, she threw up her hand. Chip reached down and grabbed it.

With a roar of effort Cassie could only imagine, Chip hauled Emma up until he could take hold of her waist with his other arm and drag her onto his lap, washed with the sea.

This time Cassie didn't need the signal. She pulled the lever hard and up they drew, Chip and Emma, twisting in the wind. Emma was so exhausted she couldn't lift her head, but Chip cocked his wet, reddened face toward Cassie and grinned.

THE HELICOPTER TOUCHED its skids to the ground just as a pair of police cars slammed to a halt on the grass nearby. From the first car popped DCI Macintosh and Calum MacDougal. The detective chief inspector strode up, shielding his forehead against the spray of water from the rotors.

"What the devil's going on here?" he yelled.

Kat ducked past him and ran to the open cabin door, where Chip helped a bloodied and unsteady Archie from the deck to the grass.

"Quite all right, quite all right," Archie said, though his voice was as wobbly as his legs. "Just a little nick to the head."

"What about Morag?" Kat demanded.

Archie looked at Emma; Emma shook her head.

"She wouldn't come," she said.

In the cockpit, Karyn Black removed the headset and swung her stilettoed feet to the grass.

DCI Macintosh stopped short. "*Mummy?*" he said. "Where the devil did you learn to fly a helicopter?"

She patted his cheek with her long, crimson-tipped finger-nails. "Euan, darling. If you can direct me to the nearest bottle of whisky, I'll tell you all about it."

CHAPTER TWENTY-NINE

Emma

A FIRE ROARED in the giant stone fireplace of the keeping room, the Kinloch coat of arms prominently displayed over the mantel. If Emma hadn't been so cold and exhausted from the adrenaline rush caused by the day's events, she might have felt the need to explain to the assembled group that the tartan background and badge depicting the head of a sheep and the clan motto were nothing more than Victorian-era romanticism. She wondered if anyone had even bothered to translate the nonsensical motto *Nolite Tangere Oves*. Even with her rusty high school Latin, she was pretty sure it meant *Touch Not the Sheep*.

But none of that mattered to her at the moment. All that did matter was the warmth of Archie's side pressed against her on the sofa, and his fingers entangled with hers beneath the wool blanket that Fiona had gently tucked over them after she'd tended to Archie's head wound. He now wore a white bandage over the gash in his forehead, making him appear even more debonair and handsome than ever. Like a young Peter O'Toole in *Lawrence of Arabia*.

"Will you be needing something for the pain, Archie?" Fiona asked as she rummaged through her medical bag. She'd been waiting at the castle when they'd arrived, and after a warm hug from her mother, Karyn Black (whose hair continued to defy both weather conditions and bear hugs), Fiona had quickly assumed her position as GP and set about tending to the various scrapes and contusions sustained during the helicopter rescue. Emma had no doubt that the scene would appear in the next Karyn Black contemporary thriller and felt a bit proud that she had been a part of it.

Fiona tsked as she peered closely into Archie's eyes. "No concussion, thank heavens. That rock Morag shoved you into managed to do a bit of damage to your puir haid, aye?"

Archie shook his head, then winced. "I'm fine." He squeezed Emma's fingers. "Which is more than I can say for poor Calum."

Calum sat at the diminutive secretaire with his head in his hands, his bulk nearly overwhelming the spindly chair, and Morag's notebook on the desk in front of him. Emma had stood next to Archie, looking over Calum's shoulder as he'd flipped through pages containing odd sketches of people and plants alongside gradually degrading handwriting that only hinted at the shadows in the old woman's head.

With a groan, Calum dropped his hands and straightened. "Me own nanna and I didna know how verra disturrrbed she was. I mean, I knew she was verra angry when Archie returned from England after being away fer so long and became laird of the castle. I thought she would be grateful that he took over the burden of running the estate, ye ken? But then everything changed for the worse when that Presley fellow arrrrived. Nanna acted as if Archie had made a pact with the devil himself. And I knew something was wrong with her then, but I didna know how to stop her. So I did nothing."

DCI Macintosh cleared his throat. "Don't be so hard on yourself, man. I've known Morag my whole life and I should have seen it, too. I'm a detective! Of all people, I should have noticed and done something."

Calum scowled at Cassie, Emma, and Kat. "Don't fash yerself, Euan. Maybe we would have if we weren't so busy focusing on the Americans! I've neverrrr seen such a busybody grrroup as ewe all. It's a miracle I wasn't sent over the edge as well!"

Archie let go of Emma's hand and stood, carefully tucking in the loose edges of the blanket around her. He moved to stand in front of the fireplace and stared into the flames as if searching there for the correct words. "But that's what started it, don't you see? Morag had been treated as an undisputed mistress of the castle all these years while I was away, and when I returned she was relegated to a servant's status, regardless of how I continued to show her the affection I'd always afforded her."

"But why would she hate Archie so much that she'd want to kill not just BSP but Archie, too?" Kat asked. "Obviously, some sort of psychosis was involved, but there had to be something else."

The room fell silent except for the crackling of the logs in the fireplace and Loren's soft snoring at Emma's feet. Slowly, Archie turned to face Calum. Their eyes met as Archie spoke. "Because she discovered that she was of Kinloch blood. And I'm not."

There was a collective gasp, although Emma suspected the most dramatic one came from Karyn Black, who had been watching them all with interest. Almost as if she were taking notes. Emma stared at Archie, wishing he'd look at her. But his gaze was focused on Calum. "You know the truth, don't you?

Calum stood, then nodded. "Aye. Morag told me. It's what made her mad, I think. She'd been rrraised on the old stories of what Naughty Ned did to her grrrandmother, and then this arrrrogant Amerrrican comes from nowhere—invited by Archie, no less—whose intent is to turn her family trrragedy into an amusement park. For a long time, when Archie was away, and it was just her and her grandson alone in the castle, she could prrretend that all wrrrongs had been put right. But then that bastarrrd . . ."

He looked up, his expression apologetic. "I mean bahookie Presley came along and it muddled her puir haid."

"What truth?" DCI Macintosh spoke from where he stood by Kat, not touching but close enough that he could.

Calum looked down at his feet. He struggled for a moment trying to grind out a word before stopping and shaking his head. "Och." He met Archie's eyes with a pleading look.

Archie nodded. "I started digging through the Kinloch records after Presley told me about the fine print I'd missed on that bloody contract. I was desperate, searching for anything that might give me a way out. And I did find it, but not where I'd expected. I was trying to find a way to tell you what I'd discovered when, well, I got distracted."

He sent a meaningful glance toward Emma. "It was in one of Lady Ned's diaries. She wrote about the grouse hunt and house party at Kinloch in 1900 attended by Prunella Schuyler and the Prince of Wales. The same hunt and house party where Ned was murdered. Apparently, they were hunting for more than just birds." He lifted his eyebrows before continuing. "One of the other guests was an Oxford classmate of Ned's, an Englishman by the name of Peter Langford."

"Langford?" Emma interrupted. "As in *Langford* Point? I knew the Point had been renamed at the turn of the last century, but I couldn't discover why in my research. No one ever responded to my queries sent to the Kinloch archivist." She sucked in a breath as she answered her own question. "Because you're the archivist. And you didn't want me to know."

Archie gave her the courtesy of not dropping his gaze. "All I knew then was about the affair. I didn't find out until recently that there had been . . . consequences."

Emma sat up straighter, feeling the odd humming vibrations she only felt when disparate pieces of information came together in an unexpected way. Like now. "Oh my gosh! How could I have missed that? In Prunella's own letters she made mention of her 'great friend' Lady Ned, and how the great lady had bestowed upon her the honor of keeping a secret. I assumed it was just Prunella being, well, Prunella. Are you saying that there was some truth to her boasting?"

Archie grimaced. "Apparently so. Lady Ned's only child, my great-great-grandfather, wasn't Ned's son."

"That wouldn't matter," said the DCI. "Inheritance laws don't care about blood—only legitimacy. And since Lady Ned was married to Naughty Ned when she gave birth, that son—your ancestor—was the rightful heir."

Archie nodded. "Legally, yes. But not morally. Lady Ned also wrote about the woman of legend giving birth in the cave before drowning herself." He paused. "That baby was Morag's grandmother. Your great-great-grandmother, Calum. The baby had been fathered by Ned himself, which makes you his blood descendant. And in my eyes and Morag's, too, you're the rightful heir and laird. Not me."

Calum was already shaking his head before Archie finished speaking. "Legally I suppose you have a point. But as I told me nanna, I dinna ask for it and I dinna want it. Ewe have done a grrreat job, Archie, and I'm happy to let things be and to support you in all of yer future endeavors. I just want . . ."

A commotion sounded from the hall and then the door to the great room was thrown open. The talkative young man Emma remembered from the pub burst into the room, his eyes searching each face until he found the one he sought.

"Calum!" he cried. He crossed the room in three long strides, the distinctive scent of wet hay and horse wafting behind him. He threw his arms around Calum in a bear hug before kissing him right on the lips. "Is everything all right? Fiona rang to let me know there'd been a scuffle and that you were all right and I was so worried. But Mr. Campbell's mare was having a difficult birth and I couldn't get away. It's not easy being the only vet on the island."

Calum's face lit up as he looked down into the man's eyes. "Aye, Jamie. All's well. I was just about to say that I'm no interested in being the laird of Kinloch. That was Morag's dream—not mine. I wouldna take on the responsibilities for all the sheep in Scotland. I just want a quiet life with my husband and my sheep."

A thick silence descended as everyone exchanged furtive glances.

"Not at the same time," Jamie quickly amended.

Emma was sure her breath of relief wasn't the only one.

"Here," Cassie said, breaking the tension in the room. She held up a tray of freshly made scones. "This will make everyone feel better. There was some clotted cream and jam in the refrigerator in the kitchen, but since that was Morag's domain, I thought it would be better to be safe than sorry. Chip says the scones are perfect on their own." She beamed up at Archie.

A reluctant smile crossed Archie's face as he selected two and took them back to Emma on the sofa. Everyone bit into their scones as conversations ceased and thoughts turned inward. Even for Emma, who lived on the adrenaline of uncovering obscure facts and the surprising secrets of the past, her mind was overwhelmed with what she'd experienced and learned in the last twenty-four hours. For what might have been the first time in her life, her thoughts went silent.

Emma swallowed her last bite, then curled up against Archie and closed her eyes.

"What tune is that you're humming?" Archie's voice was very close to her ear, his warm breath sending a delightful shiver over her skin.

"Sorry. I sing when I'm nervous. Or worried. Or happy." She gave him a wobbly smile to let him know it was the latter. "It's the main theme from *Lawrence of Arabia*."

"I thought so. It's one of my favorite films of all time."

"Really?" Her heart swelled in her chest. "Mine, too."

"May I ask why you're humming that particular tune?"

She glanced at the white bandage on his head, confirming her original opinion about Peter O'Toole, and felt her cheeks redden. "Because I don't know the words."

"Something for which we can all be grateful," said Kat as she stopped in front of them, her warm smile taking any sting from her words. "Since you would screw them up somehow and make a parody of what is actually a beautiful piece of music."

Kat handed Archie and Emma each a mug of hot chocolate. At some point since their return to the castle from the rescue at Langford Point, Cassie had retrieved her portable kettle and supply of chocolate and marshmallows from the depths of her Vera Bradley bag and was now making hot chocolate for everyone. Chip had barely left her side, and Cassie couldn't seem to stop touching him as if to assure herself that she wasn't imagining his presence.

Kat reached down and gave a gentle fist bump to Emma's shoulder. "But I'd be lying if I said I wouldn't miss your singing if you had . . ." Kat's voice hitched as she pulled away, her eyes suspiciously moist. She cleared her throat. "Yes, well. That doesn't mean I don't think you should learn the intended lyrics to your repertoire of songs."

Kat attempted to give one of her flippant looks, but she couldn't seem to stop the wide, genuine grin that had settled on her face since the rescue. Her former expression of perpetual ennui and general disdain for everyone seemed to have vanished in the ocean mist. It made Kat even more beautiful, Emma thought. Apparently, the DCI thought so, too, since he didn't appear to be able to take his gaze away from her.

Archie stared down into his untouched mug of hot chocolate. "I'm afraid I'm going to need something a bit stronger. Will you excuse me?"

He didn't wait for an answer before he stood and strode from the room. He'd barely disappeared through the doorway before Emma flung off the blanket and followed him. She paused briefly in the hall, listening before moving toward the sound of his booted heels in the dining room.

He stood at the sideboard over which Lady Ned presided, pouring an amber liquid from a crystal decanter into a glass. It seemed to Emma now that the lady's eyes held a hint of mischief in them she hadn't seen before, the spark of a secret kept. If Emma were to use Lady Ned as the subject of a future biography, she'd be hard-pressed to call her a murderess. She was so many other things—*good* things—and she didn't want them to be overshadowed. Not that she condoned murder in any form, but maybe . . . Emma squinted at the portrait and wondered if her exhaustion was making her imagine that Lady Ned was looking right *at* her. It was almost as if, Emma thought, there was another secret behind that enigmatic face. A secret waiting to be told.

She and Archie stood together, studying the portrait in silence before Archie spoke. "You're very brave, Emma. You saved my life. Thank you seems so very inadequate, but thank you."

Something brushed her hand. She looked down to see Archie handing her a glass, the smell of Scotch whisky burning her nostrils. Emma could hear the smile in Archie's voice. "I'm quite sure that Lady Ned would also be an admirer."

"Slàinte mhath," they said in unison as they faced each other and clinked glasses before throwing back the contents.

Emma grimaced as the liquid heat slid down her throat. "That's why you didn't want me in your library, isn't it? You were afraid I'd find something in the archives and force you to play your hand before you were ready."

Archie's green eyes twinkled. Just like the ones in the portrait above them. "Precisely. As much as I disliked removing you from my bedroom, I couldn't allow you to dig into my archives unsupervised. There is all sorts of correspondence tucked into some of the books, I couldn't risk it. It's where I found an unsent letter, actually. From Lady Ned to Peter Langford."

Emma felt the blood flow faster through her veins. "You did? What did it say?"

"What you've probably guessed. That she was expecting a child, and the child was Peter Langford's, who was, apparently, the love of her life. He'd asked her to leave here and follow him to England. You might wonder why she didn't."

"It's perfectly obvious why she didn't." Emma looked up with wonder at the woman's face in the portrait, recognizing what she saw in her eyes. She remembered the monument in the graveyard, the mother sheltering her children. "Because she loved Kinloch and its people. And her son was the heir. She knew that her responsibilities here had to be her priority. Even if it meant giving up the man she loved and a future with him." She sighed, the germ of a new book already beginning to wind its way around her brain.

He plucked her empty glass from her hand and placed it next to his own on the sideboard. "What do you say to you and I starting again from the beginning?"

He had placed his hands on her waist, pulling her closer.

"What are you suggesting?"

He brought his face closer to Emma's. "Would you like to see my archives?"

CHAPTER THIRTY

Kat

EMMA HAD KEPT insisting that the answer was in the archives. It was clear Emma's answer was in the archives and his name was Archie. Archie: it even began with the same first four letters as archive. Clearly, a match meant to be. Archie and Emma kept staring at each other in an inhibited overbred boarding school sort of way that was strangely moving. Like Emma Thompson and Hugh Grant in *Sense and Sensibility*, all quivering repressed emotion. Who needed a clinch when you could have awkward eye contact that said everything?

It made Kat weepy, in a crying at the movies sort of way.

Kat never cried at the movies. She had no idea what was going on with her. It was as if the tortoise shell of derision she'd built around herself had slowly softened until it was roughly the texture of one of those cashmere and alpaca blend coats, easily belted, but hopeless at keeping out the elements.

The detective inspector had blazed off to do whatever detective inspectors do when possible murderers are lost at sea.

Paperwork, presumably.

Either way, Detective Chief Inspector Macintosh was gone with the wind—or gone with the whatever—and Kat felt strangely let down. Wasn't he supposed to assemble them in a drawing room like Poirot? Another example of how life never lived up to fiction. And men never lived up to anything. Not like there was anything to be anything. She'd never been anything to him but a suspect, and she wasn't even that anymore.

To make matters worse, Cassie and Chip were canoodling like a pair of newlyweds. Or possibly like a pair of puppies; they both had that golden retriever thing going, all glossy fur and tail wagging.

She was, Kat realized, the odd one out. The spinster at the feast. Calum, still blank with shock, sat with his husband, Jamie, making them a party of seven for dinner. Three couples. And Kat.

With Morag lost at sea, Cassie did the honors in the kitchen, going overboard in her attempt to honor the deceased.

"From Morag's own cookbook," Cassie informed them proudly, as Chip carried in enormous platter after enormous platter to the dining room. "I've made rumbledethumps and cock-a-leekie soup and stovies—but not haggis. Morag said you only make haggis when you can get the bits fresh from the butcher."

Cassie's face crumpled and Chip immediately abandoned his platter on the sideboard to envelop her in one of his patented bear hugs. Kat could just see him covered with assorted children; he was definitely the kind of dad made to be climbed on and wrestled with. And, hey, he flew a helicopter, too.

The helicopter was currently parked on the lawn, pending its return to the mainland. When that return would be, no one was quite saying. Archie and Emma—it was definitely Archie and Emma now—had extended the hospitality of the castle to all for as long as was needed.

Someone—Kat suspected it was Archie—had quietly removed all the Kill It O'Clock photos. The only remaining sign of Brett Saffron Presley was a sad bit of limp crime scene tape flapping against the door of the tower.

If that wasn't a fitting memorial for the man, Kat didn't know what was.

Seated at the foot of the table, Emma delicately tapped her silver spoon against her cut crystal water goblet.

Her cheeks were flushed and the Kinloch plaid scarf she wore with her plain black dress suited her right down to the ground. She was, Kat thought, with a strange ache, going to make an excellent lady of the manor.

Emma looked down the table at Archie, and said, almost shyly, "Given that Morag's body may never be recovered, Archie and I thought it might be fitting to hold a memorial service for Morag here at the castle. You're all invited to stay for it."

"You're all invited to stay for as long as you like," Archie added. "I feel Kinloch owes it to you for the time you've had."

"If I'd said something—" said Calum hollowly.

"Don't," said Jamie, patting his hand. "You can't blame yourself."

"The fault wasn't Morag's," declaimed Archie, nobly, if not entirely accurately. He would have made a marvelous Robin Hood as played by Errol Flynn, Kat mused crossly, but Emma was lapping it up, starry-eyed. "The fault lies with the lairds of Kinloch. It's a wrong that goes deep in the past, but one we hope, with time and care, that we can make right. I can't make it up to Morag, not now—but I hope you'll be a full partner with me, Calum, as we make this estate what it ought to be."

"And now that Emma has BSP's money," put in Kat, "you don't have to worry about how you're going to fund it. What? You know it's true."

They were all looking at her like she'd dropped a pile of cockroaches into the soup.

"It's really Emma's money anyway," said Cassie quickly. "Since it was from her book. So it's all come right in the end. Just like a book! Eat up, everyone! Your cock-a-leekie is getting cold!"

"*Cock*-a-leekie?" Kat cocked a brow at Cassie.

"It's a chicken, leeks, and prune soup," explained Emma primly.

Archie beamed with pride.

Kat would have made gagging noises, but Cassie might have taken that as a verdict on her soup.

"I've been thinking . . ." said Cassie. "Someone ought to write up Morag's recipes. That cookbook of hers is really something—I mean, once you ignore all the murder-y bits about Archie."

She grimaced apologetically at Archie, who smiled back to indicate that a little bit of murder was nothing among friends.

Good Lord, could anyone be any nicer? Kat wanted to scream and scream and keep screaming. Lady Ned gazed coolly at her from the wall. Kat found her strangely steadying. *Good for you, Lady Ned.* She'd exacted her own justice—and she'd chosen the work and the people she loved over a man. She could have thrown it all over and gone off with what's-his-name, but she hadn't. She'd stayed right here, raising her child, running Kinloch, tending her garden, and righting wrongs.

Of course, it wasn't like Kat was staying here. That was Emma. Emma was staying here. Kat was back off to Brooklyn and her empty studio apartment. And werebears.

Dammit, she wasn't going to cry. Kat dropped her spoon in her bowl and took a bracing swig of whatever wine Archie and Emma had unearthed from the cellar.

"So what are you thinking? The Little Poison Garden mystery series?"

"Maybe," said Cassie seriously. "I'd love to do a series set on an island like Kinloch. Maybe with a heroine who's the local GP and midwife and also an herbalist . . . but I also was thinking it might be fun to do something a little different. Like Morag's cookbook. I could layer the recipes with bits of local lore and pictures and Morag's wise sayings."

Wise? Or bonkers? This time Kat kept her mouth shut. Besides, in her experience the line between wisdom and insanity was a wobbly one.

"That would be a kind tribute," said Calum. His handsome face looked puffy, his eyes red-rimmed. "But what she did—what she meant to do—"

"She wasn't in her right mind," said Emma firmly, already assuming her responsibility of comforting the peasantry.

"And we don't know that she meant to *murder* Archie," chimed in Cassie. "She might just have wanted to take him to the scene of that ancient crime and make him face his family's sins—you know, like we wanted to do with BSP."

That fell like a pile of prunes.

"I mean," said Cassie, digging herself deeper, "it's not like any of us ever wanted him *dead*."

"Didn't you?" said a dry voice, and, lo and behold, pat on his cue, there was none other than Detective Chief Inspector Euan Macintosh, closely followed by his sister, soon to be the heroine of a cozy mystery series, apparently, and his mother, the legendary Karyn Black, writer of bodice rippers and flier of helicopters.

Kat put her glass down with a hand that had gone just a little shaky.

"Oh. Inspector Macintosh," Cassie said brightly. "You're just in time for dinner. Would you like some cock-a-leekie?"

"I've just stopped by to deliver some news." Inspector Macinctosh looked exhausted.

Euan, his mother had called him. It suited him. It suited the soft stubble on his chin and the salt spray in his hair. He looked like a Euan, and not a chief inspector right now. Kat wanted to rest her hand against the stubble on his chin and smell the salt in his hair.

"News?" Archie sat up a little straighter in his chair.

It was Fiona who spoke. "We've had the lab report back. There was no belladonna in the mead."

"Wait, but then how . . ." Kat was back there, in that room, the goblet in his hand, the ceremonial chalice, infused with potions unknown.

Or just mead, apparently.

"What we did find," said Euan Macintosh, "was a number of searches on Mr. Presley's computer regarding the efficacy of belladonna in cases of erectile dysfunction."

"You mean his purple-headed tumescent manroot wasn't throbbing?" said Karyn Black, straight-faced.

Emma choked on her cock-a-leekie.

Kat raised her glass. "I could not adore you more."

"Mum!" Euan recovered himself. "Apparently not. To correct the problem of, er, insufficiently throbbing manroot"—from the other end of the table, Kat could hear Cassie's stifled giggle—"your Mr. Presley was apparently attempting to dose himself with belladonna. We don't know yet where he might have acquired it, but it's entirely possible that he prepared his own decoction from the plants in the garden and saved it to use at an auspicious time."

He looked straight at Kat.

"You mean," said Kat numbly, "when he thought he had a hot date."

With Kirsty, the busty blonde who didn't exist. The busty blonde Kat had invented. For whom BSP had overdosed himself on belladonna.

Calum lifted his head, his handsome face blurry. "So ye're saying Nanna didna do it."

"No," said the chief inspector. "By the time she stabbed him, he was already dead."

"Like *Orient Express*, where everyone did it!" exclaimed Cassie delightedly.

"You mean not at all like *Orient Express*, because NO ONE did it," retorted Kat.

Except Kat had. Sort of. She'd lured him to his death whether she'd meant to or not.

Kat stood, pushing her chair back from the table. The prunes in her cock-a-leekie bobbed reproachfully at her.

"Does that mean we're free to go, Inspector? Or are you planning to interrogate us a little longer just for old time's sake?"

"It was a suspicious death," said Euan quietly. "It was my duty to investigate."

By any means necessary. It was all right. Kat got it. "Sorry it was so onerous for you."

"I never said it was onerous."

"They need to get a room," muttered Chip. "Ouch! That was my foot."

"I expect it was just a muscle cramp—from all that helicopter flying!" Cassie leapt from her chair and tugged at Chip like a determined squirrel. "You probably just need to walk it off. I know! We'll go for a turn around the garden! Like a Jane Austen novel! Only with more plaid."

"It's dark out. And it's snowing," said Kat.

"There's nothing like walking in a winter wonderland! Oh, and there's cranachan for dessert, but it's cold, so it will keep. We can all have dessert—later. After a bracing walk! Chip, are you coming?"

"We'll join you," said Emma, engaging in alarming eyebrow gyrations at the oblivious laird at the other end of the table.

"Oh, yes," said Archie, belatedly getting the hint. "Er, Chip, I did want to trouble you for your opinion on some improvements for the estate. Emma and I were discussing the addition of an adventure center . . . for corporate retreats and whatnot."

"Ooops, books to write!" Karyn pressed a kiss to her son's cheek. Her leopard print coat flapped around her. "Don't screw this up, honey. I like this one. Come on, Fiona. Let's go make your dad give us free drinks in the pub and you can tell me what a terrible mother I was."

"Mum," said Fiona wearily.

With a last narrow look over her shoulder at Kat, she followed her mother out of the dining room, leaving Kat and the detective inspector alone with Lady Ned and a giant tureen of cock-a-leekie soup.

Kat swallowed hard. "Would you like some soup? Cassie made it."

"What I really want," Euan said bluntly, "is a hot cup of tea and to sleep for a week." Shrugging out of his macintosh, he dropped it over the back of a chair.

"Wow, wild." Kat wasn't quite sure what to say to him, not now. She wasn't his suspect anymore. Which meant she wasn't his anything. "After all this, you came away empty-handed."

"Did I?" He moved very softly. It must be that inspector training.

Kat could feel the back of her chair pressing against her spine. "I guess you got a solution. Isn't that what they call it? The solve rate. Death by misadventure. All the rest is—whatever."

"Whatever?" Euan rested a hand against the back of the chair next to hers.

He was doing it again. Echoing her own words back at her.

"He took that belladonna because of me. You can't convict me for it, but that doesn't mean I'm not guilty," said Kat flatly.

Euan let out a breath, somewhere between a sigh and a tsk. One of those indeterminate Scottish noises. "Yes," he said. "It does mean you're not guilty. Of that."

"Oh, yeah? What am I guilty of?"

"Distracting the police." His lips were a whisper away from hers; she could smell saltwater and some sort of very masculine soap. "Interfering with my investigation." He leaned in and kissed her, a slow deep kiss. "Disturbing a crime scene." Another kiss;

bent backward over his arm like the clinch on the cover of an old novel. "Making my mother purchase something called a panta-boot."

Kat pulled back, coming to her senses. "You never mentioned that your mother is Karyn Black."

That certainly killed the mood. He took a step back. "There's a lot you don't know about me."

"Yeah, well, there's a lot you don't know about me, either."

"Is there?"

"There are some things that don't come up in a background search," said Kat tightly. She resisted the urge to touch her lips, to feel where he had kissed her. "The whole point of your mother's books is that there's someone for everyone. The wolf has his dove. The laird has his lamb. But what if there *isn't* someone for every-one? What if some people are just too deep down unlovable?"

"I don't understand." For a bright man, he could be pretty dim. "What do you mean?"

"I mean *me*, you dimwit." Kat lightly shoved against his chest. "What if, once you got past the pantaboots and the push-up bra and the attitude, you decided there wasn't anything there? Not anything worth having, I mean. Not anyone worth knowing. I'm not any of the things I pretend to be. I'm just a girl whose mother didn't want her."

"My mother went to California when I was thirteen years old and never came back." Euan's lips hardened into a grim line. "They were doing a made-for-telly film of one of her books. She was supposed to be gone for three weeks. But then it became three months. And six months. And by the time it was a year, it was pretty bloody clear she was never coming home again. That this wasn't home to her and never had been."

"She just left you?" Karyn Black's heroines—they were loyal for life. Kat couldn't reconcile the books she'd lived for—the woman she'd met in the helicopter—with someone who'd abandon her children the way her mother had abandoned her. Out the door. No looking back.

"She offered us the option of coming to live with her in Los Angeles." The name had a bitter tang to it. "I lasted three months and then bought tickets on her credit card. Back to Kinloch. After that, we spent summers with Mum and the rest of the year with Dad."

"Did she—"

"No. They never divorced. They never remarried. My mother insists my father is the love of her life—the laird to her lamb. They just can't live in the same place. And maybe that was all right for them. But it was hell for us." A polite mask came down over his face. "You'll be going back to the States, I imagine."

"I have a Brooklyn studio apartment waiting for me."

This was where the story ended. This was where she pretended life was wonderful and she was going back to it and she didn't need him, she didn't need anyone. Pride salvaged. Head held high.

In a very low voice, Kat said, "I had this image of the life I was going to have. I was going to be that New York writer who knows her local bodega guy, who goes to Literary Lions things at the library, who shows up in the New York Social Diary at fancy fundraisers in designer gowns. My bodega guy has no clue who I am. I've been buying Ben & Jerry's there for years and he still has no clue who I am."

"And the gowns?"

"No gowns, designer or otherwise. I've been living there eight years and I've never once been invited to speak at the New York Public Library. Not even at their outdoor things in Bryant Park. Apparently my books are too lowbrow."

"I think your books are brilliant."

"I hate living in New York. I hate pretending to be the person I thought I'd be but I'm not. But I don't have anyone else to be." Kat looked at him, knowing how pathetic she sounded. So much for Katja de Noir. She was Kat de Nobody. "If I had a hometown to go to, I would go back to it. But I've never had one of those. I've never had a place where anybody knows my name or is glad I came. . . ."

Very, very gently, he brushed a finger across her lower lip. "I would be. Glad you came."

Kat could feel her face go bright red. Like the ingénue she pretended not to be. The flush wasn't just localized to her face. She could feel the surge of blood throughout her body.

"Um, yeah. About that." Kat ducked her head, staring at the buttons of his shirt. There was no way to say it but to say it. "I've never actually. Slept with anyone."

"What, never?"

"Well, hardly ever. I mean, I've made out with people." God, she sounded like a fifteen-year-old. Only she was thirty-five. "I've rounded all the other bases. I'm sure there are fundamentalist sects that would consider my virginity a pure technicality. Purist unicorns would refuse to appear for me."

"Purist unicorns?"

"You know, the old thing about how unicorns only appear for virgins."

"I'm confused," said Euan, and she knew he wasn't talking about unicorns.

There was only so long she could talk around the topic. "Look. I was a one-night stand that led to a ten-year train wreck. When I slept with someone—I wanted it to *matter*. So I had a rule. No sex until I knew it was serious. I wanted someone to want me because I was me, and not just because I'm a body and I'm there."

"And you've never found that?"

Kat forced herself to look him in the eye and say it straight out. "No. Most of them didn't last past the second date—when they found out I wasn't going to put out."

And then there had been BSP. But she didn't want to think about that. Not now. Not with Euan looking at her the way he was.

"Kat." He cupped his hands around her face, so she couldn't look away. "Those men were idiots."

"Is that your official assessment?" she asked breathlessly.

"It's my personal one," he said huskily, as his hands slid down the slippery fabric covering her back until they came to rest just above her waist. "Very personal."

Things were getting very personal, indeed, until Kat's bottom bumped a bowl of cock-a-leekie—somehow she had wound up sitting on the dining room table with her legs wrapped around the detective inspector and would have been quite happy to continue in that direction if it hadn't been for Cassie's blasted soup. And the fact that Euan couldn't find the fastenings on her pantaboots.

And Lady Ned looking down at them was sort of a deterrent.

Kat began to lend serious consideration to Chip's suggestion that they get a room.

As they were mopping up the soup, Euan asked, with deceptive casualness, "If you don't like it where you were—if there's nothing to tie you there—did you ever think of making a life someplace else?"

"On a small Scottish island, perhaps?" Kat asked sarcastically.

But even as she said it, she could picture sitting snug in the pub with her laptop, dinners at the castle with Emma and Archie, nature walks with Calum, girls' nights with Fiona.

Fiona might be a bit prickly, but Fiona's prickles were something Kat understood. They reminded her of her own.

"There are rooms to let over the pub," Euan said, putting down his soup-sodden napkin. "It's not a Brooklyn flat but you'd have a view of the sea. And coffee whenever you wanted."

"I could get a Nespresso machine for that. But the view over the sea—that would be something. My view right now is some guy across the way who watches a lot of sports on TV. In his underwear."

"It gets quiet here in winter. And cold. Not many people make it back and forth from the mainland. I can't promise you much."

"I never asked you to."

Kat wasn't quite sure when or how it had happened, but he was holding both her hands, holding them as though she was something infinitely precious and he never wanted to let go.

Kat looked up at him, at those clear brown eyes, with the big purple circles under them. He was right; there was a lot she didn't know about him. But she wanted to be around to find out.

"There was something your mother wrote in an article that I've never forgotten. It was in *The Writer* magazine, back in the nineties. She said she didn't write happily ever afters. She wrote happy under the circumstances."

He understood without her having to explain. "Do you think you could be happy under these circumstances? In Kinloch?"

"I think—I think I'd like to give it a try. I have an idea for a book," Kat blurted out.

The corners of his eyes crinkled. "Not werebears?"

"No, but points for paying attention." He looked so adorable, she just had to kiss him again. Just like that. As if he were hers and she could.

How was this her? Kat didn't know and she didn't feel like she deserved it, but she wanted to hold on to it with both hands, whatever it was.

"Your book?" he prompted.

Kat gave her head a shake. "I was thinking—something like Ian McDonald's *King of Morning, Queen of Day*, that same sort of multiple time periods and messing with the line between the real and the supernatural, but not with fairies."

She remembered that woodcut, the raw power of it, the way she'd felt looking at it, the stories swirling around her, just waiting to be gathered up and spun out again.

She never talked about her ideas to anyone. But this was different. This was Euan. "What if you have a young man who messes with powers he doesn't understand? What if his virgin sacrifice turns out to have hereditary powers of her own? What if the forces they unleash reverberate down the generations? I don't know why, but I feel like there's something there. I feel like this is the book I'm meant to write."

"Then you must," he said gravely. "And I'll be the first to read it. Even if there's a sad lack of werebears."

Epilogue

HOTEL VALLEY HO
SCOTTSDALE, ARIZONA
Two years later

N OBODY HAD WARNED the bartender about all the writers. He was having trouble keeping up with demand.

A book launch party, the manager said. Some book called *Fifty Shades of Plaid*, written by three madwomen. *Madwomen, I tell you*, the manager repeated to the bartender, shaking her head. *Like,* demented. *Real comedians, too, at least in their own minds. And they want a theme drink. A Scotch 75. Can you come up with something?*

The bartender had come up with something. Scotch, prosecco, lots of lemon to cover up the peculiar combination of flavor. Nobody seemed to care. "Oooh, these are *delish*," said the one in the knee-length plaid shirtdress that looked as if it came from Brooks Brothers. She sent the third glass down the hatch and held the empty in the air, like it was a bachelorette party or something. "So fun to get away from the babies, amiright?"

The one wearing the skintight catsuit of plaid vegan leather and the matching plaid stiletto boots . . . hold on a second, the boots *were* the pants. Or the other way around. One continuous pair of boots that climbed all the way to her crotch, merged into a leo-tard, and finished the journey as a kind of bustier-cum-swimsuit reminiscent of . . . of . . . well, anyway. That one. She picked up a copy of a thick hardcover book, whirled it above her head, and climbed with the agility of a mountain goat onto the barstool and then the bar itself.

"Everyone! Everyone!" she yelled, to no effect. She sighed, put two fingers—lacquered with nail polish the color of dried blood—to her scarlet lips, and let loose a whistle that probably punctured eardrums in Sedona.

The crowd fell silent and turned to Catsuit.

"Dearly beloveds," she said, "we are gathered here tonight to celebrate the final stop on the Best Book Tour of All Time—"

"Hear, hear!" squealed Brooks Brothers, grabbing a drink from the tray.

"The best book tour *ever*!" shrieked a frizzy-haired woman in a long-sleeved plaid Nap Dress that somehow became her. The bartender only remembered serving Nap Dress one drink, but it had clearly hit her hard. "In the history of the *world*!" she added, for good measure.

"So we invited all you readers over to the fabulous retro vibes of the Valley Ho—my personal favorite book tour hotel, hands down—from our sold-out event at the Poisoned Pen down the street—the *legendary* Poisoned Pen, I should say—"

The silver fox sitting on the stool to the bartender's right leaned forward and tapped his arm. "That's my bookstore," she said.

The bartender looked at her. The woman's short grond hair gleamed under the Valley Ho's stylish lighting. Her eyes gleamed, too. In front of her, on the counter, sat a copy of the same book Catsuit had waved above her head. Something clicked into place inside the bartender's frazzled brain. "Wait, you're Barbara Peters?" he said. "*The* Barbara Peters?"

She shrugged, smiling.

Right on cue, Catsuit boomed out, "—like to thank, like, a million billion times, the amazing Barbara Peters, *owner* of the legendary Poisoned Pen, who could not have been more supportive of our little book—everyone, big hip hip hooray for Barbara!"

Some drunken, uncoordinated whoops ricocheted around the crowd. Barbara waved them off.

The bartender leaned back to her. "So are these women really as crazy as they seem?"

"Oh, they're harmless," said Barbara. "And the book is really quite good, if you take out all the gratuitous sheep humor. Which, frankly . . ." She shook her head, as if the rest of the sentence were somehow too obvious for words.

"Everyone loves a little sheep humor," said the bartender.

Barbara fixed him with a look that suggested one person, at least, abstained. She tapped the cover of the book with one finger. "Of course, it didn't hurt that they got the world's best blurb from none other than Karyn Black."

The bartender felt his jaw swing open. "Karyn Black? *The* Karyn Black?"

Barbara lifted the book and read from the cover. "'*Fifty Shades of Plaid* is, hands down, the best book I have ever read, including my own.'"

"Oh my God! I *love* Karyn Black! Those fire jumper books! And *this right here* is the best book she's ever read? *Fifty Shades of Plaid*?" The bartender looked back at Catsuit on top of the bar with new appreciation.

"Well, sort of," Barbara said. "You might say blurbs work a little like social media. Also, there's a family connection."

Catsuit was continuing with her speech. "—and of course, it goes without saying—"

"Hold on a second," interrupted Brooks Brothers. "My turn."

"Geezus *H*, Emma. These lovely readers do not need another

damn *history lesson* about the development of the Kinloch *wool trade*, no matter how inexplicably loyal they are—careful—"

Laboriously, Brooks Brothers tried to climb on the bar, failed, and just sat there instead, worn black patent leather pumps dangling from her toes. (Patent leather pumps? In Arizona? The bartender shook his head.) She held up one finger in the air—*aha!*—and turned to the bartender. Sighing, the bartender handed her the Scotch 75 he'd just mixed together. "Tapadh leat," she said. "That's Gaelic for thank you, by the way."

"S e do bheatha," said the bartender.

"Och aye, so you'll be knowing the Gaelic, too, then?" said Brooks Brothers, in an atrocious Scottish accent.

"I had a Scottish boyfriend once."

"Ooh, was his name Calum?" asked Nap Dress. "We know a gay Calum!"

"Cassie, honey, you know how you told us to tell you when you strayed off topic?"

"Sorry," said Nap Dress. She looked at the bartender and mouthed, *We'll talk later.*

"But this brings me to my point," said Brooks Brothers.

Catsuit snorted. "Sorry, you have a point?"

"I do! I have a very, very important point. The point is this." Brooks Brothers took a sip of her Scotch 75. She blinked her eyes. "I love you two."

She pronounced the *you* with a curious swing to the 'y,' like *ewe*.

"Love ewe, too, Emma!" blubbered Nap Dress, wiping her eyes.

"No, I really mean it. I know we didn't exactly start out as besties, whatever we might have posted on social media—"

"I *knew* it!" yelled someone in the crowd. "Social media is a *lie*!"

"Yes, social media is a lie," said Brooks Brothers. "But this is *not* a lie. This book, my husband, my whole *life*—"

"Your castle," said Catsuit. "I mean, let's not forget the *real* love of your life."

"—not to mention our adorable baby, Nedda—"

"And that," said Catsuit, "is your cue, Cassie."

"My cue?"

"The FaceTime! Remember?"

"Oh my goodness!" Nap Dress set down her half-finished drink and ran to the flat-screen monitor that hung from the wall. "Wait, how do I do this again?"

Catsuit sighed and jumped down from the bar.

"While we are getting the technology working, folks," she said, "Emma will entertain you with a brief overview of our planned reader weekend at Kinloch Castle next autumn."

A cheer went up from the crowd.

"As soon as renovations are complete," said Brooks Brothers. "Mind you, it's a very sympathetic, careful restoration. Cassie's husband, Chip, has been working closely with my husband, the laird of Kinloch, to—oh! Oh! Look! There he is!"

The screen flashed to life on a scene of total domestic chaos. The bartender counted five men—one balancing a toddler atop a life-size stuffed sheep, one burping an infant in a daisy-patterned onesie, one crawling after a pair of naked babies. A few small sheep-dog puppies gamboled across the screen from left to right, chased by their harried gray-and-white mother. In the center of it all, two men sat on a sofa. One was nursing a baby from what appeared to be a large prosthetic breast strapped to his meaty shoulder.

"Och! We're on at last, clotheids!" he bellowed.

"Hi, honey!" yelled Nap Dress. "How are the twins?"

The crawling man snagged one wriggling baby and kissed the top of its head. "Karyn just cut a new tooth," he said. He snagged the other one. "And Calum here won't keep his diaper on."

"As you can see," said Catsuit, "things are rather busy back at the castle. Hi, Euan!"

The man burping the baby lifted his hand to wave, just as an arc of sour milk flew from the mouth of the baby onto his tweed shoulder. To his right, the stuffed sheep—well, apparently alive, after all—let out a melancholy *baaa* and started across the rug, much to the delight of the toddler aboard.

"Bit of a baby boom, you might say." Brooks Brothers waggled her fingers at the screen, where a handsome Jude Law look-alike—*rawr*, thought the bartender—waved back. "Calum! Jamie! How's little Fiona? Named after her surrogate mom," she added, for the benefit of the audience.

"A bonny wee lass!" called out the handsome man who sat next to the fellow with the plastic boob.

A message appeared at the top of the screen. INCOMING CALL: RACHELLE

"What the heckity heck," said Nap Dress, picking up her phone. "She knows we're in the middle of the party. Kat, honey, where do I hit decline on this thing?"

"NOOOO!" shrieked Catsuit.

"What? We can call her back later."

"But it's WEDNESDAY!" shrieked Brooks Brothers. "Wednesday at four P.M. New York time!"

"So?"

Catsuit snatched the phone from Nap Dress's hand and swiped a frantic finger. "Hello? Rachelle?"

The domestic chaos disappeared in a blink, replaced by a gigantic, sculpted female face. "Hello, everyone!" she said. "And how are my *NEW YORK TIMES* BESTSELLING AUTHORS this afternoon?"

"*What?*" shrieked Nap Dress.

"Oh my God," said Brooks Brothers. "Oh my God, oh my God, oh my—"

"What number?" demanded Catsuit.

Rachelle leaned forward and peered at her computer screen.

"Hello? Did I say *NEW YORK TIMES* BESTSELLING AUTHORS? I'm sorry. So sorry. My mistake."

"I knew it," said Nap Dress. "It's all right, girls. Next time we'll—"

"Excuse me!"

Everyone snapped to the hostess desk, where a woman in a brown UPS uniform held up an enormous box of chocolates, wrapped with tartan ribbon tied into an extravagant bow. "Can someone sign for this, please?"

Catsuit skittered over. "Jacques Torres chocolates! Rachelle! You shouldn't have!"

Nap Dress sniffed. "It's a lovely thought to console us. Not making the *Times* list and everything. I know you had *hopes*."

"Those presale numbers were so strong," said Brooks Brothers. "I don't get it."

The woman on the flat screen cleared her throat. "Girls, it was the least I could do . . ."

Everyone swung back at the television monitor.

The woman smiled, like she'd just stolen a saucer of cream from an especially fat cat.

". . . for my NUMBER ONE *NEW YORK TIMES* BEST-SELLING AUTHORS!"

Pandemonium.

FROM HER DESK high above the hurly-burly of Manhattan, Rachelle Cohen reached for her keyboard and tapped shift-command-3 to take a screenshot of the FaceTime screen. Her three authors hugging one another in a tangled plaid circle of love, brown-and-orange Jacques Torres box held aloft in the middle—what could be cuter?

She'd post on her Insta before bedtime.

For now, it was time to celebrate.

From her desk drawer she pulled a bottle of single malt

Kinloch scotch she'd been saving for just such an occasion. A hunch, you might say. She poured a generous slug into the teacup she kept in the place of honor on her desk—an elegant Wedgwood piece commemorating the wedding of Harry and Meghan—and toasted the plaid figures frozen on her screen.

Down the hatch.

Rachelle licked the rim with her tongue—mustn't waste!— and set the cup back down in its commemorative saucer. She opened her desk drawer again, pulling out a bottle of eye drops and a box of chocolates from Jacques Torres, her favorite local chocolatier. (You were nobody in New York if you didn't have a favorite local chocolatier to go along with your favorite local coffee roaster.)

She waggled the bottle to make sure it was empty and dropped it in the recycling bin.

"RIP, BSP," she said.

Then she selected a dark chocolate with a black currant center, popped it in her mouth, and leaned back in her chair to set her feet on the desk.

One stiletto heel over the other.

AUTHORS' NOTE

WHEN THE THREE of us first sat down together in the hotel bar at a writers' conference and decided we should write a book together (true story!) we had no ambitions except to successfully persuade some gullible publisher to underwrite a joint book tour—that is to say, a girls' trip—and possibly even our bar bill. Our first idea was for a historical romance anthology set in Scotland, to be called *Fifty Shades of Plaid*. Mercifully for the reading public, we ditched this concept once we'd sobered up the next day.

But as we came together in Newport, Rhode Island, a few years ago, wrapping up the draft of our fifth collaborative novel, we started playfully brainstorming a sketch based on this origin story, and the common misconception among readers that the three of us were somehow put together by our publisher, like the Spice Girls. We were having so much fun, we kept going and going, until somehow a whole book had outlined itself. (We were going to call it *Fifty Shades of Plaid*, but cooler heads at HarperCollins prevailed.)

The Author's Guide to Murder is a satire of many things— a bonfire, some might say—so before we start the ritual thanks to everyone who's ever touched our writing careers, we'd like to take the time to apologize. To the publishing industry; to the heroic writers of back-in-the-day, no-holds-barred historical romance that made our teenage years tolerable; and most of all to the

Scottish people, who have already put up with so much from Americans, and now *this*—well, we're sorry. The excruciating jokes, the atrocious Scottish accents, the tropes, the puns, the murder of nefarious male authors? It's all written with a wink and a nudge and a great deal of love, and maybe a teeny grain of truth. (As for what's truth and what's satire, we'll leave that for you to ponder.)

As always, we could not have created this novel without the assistance and the patience of a long-suffering cast of characters, starting with our editor, Rachel Kahan. (No resemblance whatsoever to Rachelle Cohen, of course.) She might not have put the band together, but she keeps feeding us book contracts and tour schedules and the occasional round of French 75s when we've behaved ourselves, so we're eternally grateful.

To our literary agents, Alexandra Machinist of CAA (Beatriz and Lauren) and Amy Berkower of Writers House (Karen), we can't thank you enough for your faith in our collaboration and your understanding of our friendship and its vital force for our writing careers, both together and individually. (Also, your skill and persistence in keeping those publishing contracts coming.)

ABOUT THE AUTHORS

Beatriz Williams, Lauren Willig, and Karen White are the co-authors of the beloved *New York Times* bestselling novels *The Forgotten Room*, *The Glass Ocean*, *All the Ways We Said Goodbye*, and *The Lost Summers of Newport*.

Beatriz Williams is the *New York Times* bestselling author of more than a dozen novels, including *A Hundred Summers*, *The Secret Life of Violet Grant*, and *The Summer Wives*. A native of Seattle, she graduated from Stanford University and earned an MBA in finance from Columbia University, then spent several years in New York and London as a corporate strategy consultant before pursuing her passion for historical fiction. She lives with her husband and four children near the Connecticut shore, where she divides her time between writing and laundry.

Lauren Willig is the *New York Times* and *USA Today* bestselling author of more than twenty novels, including *Band of Sisters*, *The English Wife*, and *The Ashford Affair*, as well as the RITA Award–winning Pink Carnation series. An alumna of Yale University, she has a graduate degree in history from Harvard and a JD from Harvard Law School. She lives in New York City with her husband, two young children, and vast quantities of coffee.

Karen White is the *New York Times* and *USA Today* bestselling author of thirty-five novels, including *The Last Night in London*, *Dreams of Falling*, and the Royal Street series. She currently writes what she refers to as "grit lit"—southern women's fiction. After spending seven years in London, England, and attending the American School in London, she obtained a BS in management from Tulane University. She has two grown children and currently lives in Atlanta, Georgia, with her husband and a spoiled Havanese dog and spends most of her time writing and avoiding cooking.